D0245960

A Woman of Integrity

A Woman of Integrity

J David Simons

**FREIGHT
BOOKS**

First published 2017

Freight Books
49–53 Virginia Street
Glasgow, G1 1TS
www.freightbooks.co.uk

J David Simons acknowledges support from Creative Scotland
towards the writing of this book

ISBN 978-1-911332-17-6
eISBN 978-1-911332-18-3

the publisher acknowledges investment from
Creative Scotland toward the publication of this book

Typeset by Freight in Plantin
Printed and bound by Bell and Bain, Glasgow

'Integrity is what we hope will emerge when our authenticity is put under pressure.'

Georgina Hepburn

Chapter One

Dumped!

Laura felt a horrible lurch in her stomach as she tried to absorb the news. 'You're dumping me?' she countered. 'After all these years?'

'You put it too cruelly,' Edy said, her New York drawl spanning the transatlantic telephone connection like some mammoth Brooklyn Bridge.

Laura could imagine Edy sunk down in her swivel chair, staring out across the Hudson to New Jersey. Her short black boots, tight black leather trousers, matching polo neck, all speckled with cigarette ash. 'How the hell am I supposed to put it?' she snapped back. 'Are you asking me to be grateful?'

'What can I say? I have no choice, I gotta prune my list. Orders from on high. I no longer get absolute choice over my own clients. You can't blame me, Laura. Everything's faceless and corporate these days. And global.'

Laura needed fresh air. She moved out of the bedroom, through the French windows and barefoot into the garden of her ground-floor flat. An area shaded by high walls and tall trees, only the glimpse of sun. But it gave her all the greenery and privacy she needed. Such a luxury for a London property. How was she going to afford all of this? She eased herself down into one of the wrought-iron chairs, heard Edy suck hard on a cigarette. 'What are you saying? It's not just New York. London as well?'

'LA, Sydney, Hong Kong. The whole fucking shebang.'

'Jesus, Edy. You're wiping me off the map.' Her voice was coming out all whiny now but she couldn't help herself. 'I've been with you since the beginning. Why me?'

'It's not just you.'

'Who else?'

'Who do you think?'

'Diane? Surely not Diane. Don't tell me you've axed Diane as well?'

'Top of the list.'

'She's won a bloody Oscar, for God's sake.'

'Only for supporting.'

'It wasn't even that long ago.'

'It was last century, Laura. That's another millennium already.'

'And Kate?'

'Kate had to go anyway. Have you seen the state she's in?'

Laura had seen. Doused in alcohol like some pickled relic. Just the other night on TV, sliding off her chair until the presenter almost had to peel her off the floor. 'In any other walk of life, there would be a law against this.'

'What law?'

'I don't know. Ageism. Discrimination. I'm sure there's something.'

'Come on, Laura. You've always known what a fucked-up business we're in. But it's not just that. The parts aren't there anymore. And when they are, Meryl and all your fancy *shmanzy* dames suck them up.'

'Why can't I suck them up too?'

'You're not royalty, darling. High class, maybe. But not royalty.'

Laura rubbed her palm against her forehead, felt the skin flaky and dry at her hairline. 'What am I going to do, Edy? What am I going to do?'

'I'm not the only show in town.'

'You know it doesn't work like that. I might as well hang a sign around my neck. Edy Weinberg's stock clearance sale. Past sell-by date.' She heard a New York police car wailing in the background. Then she heard Edy sigh, a rasping breath, it was hard to believe the woman was still alive. Or managing without an oxygen tank by her side. Sixty cigarettes a day ever since she was old enough to light a match. Every gasp of air into her rattling lungs threatened to be her last. It was torture to watch her laugh.

'Are you all right?' Laura was forced to ask after what could have been a deadly silence.

'Of course, I'm all right. And you should be too.'

'I'm definitely not all right.'

'Financially, I mean.'

'You mean if I forget about the mortgage and my tax bill.'

'What about *The Bentleys*?'

Laura could at least thank Edy for the repeat fees on that. An English nanny to two spoiled kids in a rich Afro-American family. *The Cosby Show* meets *Mary Poppins*. Two series. An Emmy under her belt. Sold to 52 countries worldwide. She was a big hit in Vietnam. Maybe she could move there.

'Those have just about dried up. And then what?'

'There's the Disney thing,' Edy added.

It was Laura's turn to sigh. The Disney thing. The voice-over for a crab. For Christ's sake, one minute she was hoisting a statuette in the air, the next she was an English accent for a love-struck crustacean. 'Yeah, the Disney thing.'

'See. That's your problem right there. You shouldn't be all sniffy about those kind of jobs. Most people love doing the cartoon stuff. It's like a paid vacation to them.'

Laura had to admit it had been fun. But it wasn't exactly where she envisaged her place in the acting world to be the wrong side of fifty. 'If I wanted a vacation I'd go to Hawaii...'

'...It opened real well too. The weekend box-office was over forty mil already. That's *Shrek* territory.'

'It was a salary job, Edy. It's not as if you got me a back-end deal.'

'There might be a sequel with that kind of opening.'

Laura stood up, walked over to the small pond. The water was covered in a green slime but a couple of orange-bodied carp still slinked below the surface. How they survived in there she never knew. She never fed them or cleaned the water. She lifted her bare foot to the stone edge of the pool, let her toes dip into the cool water. Her neck cocked to cradle the phone against her shoulder, Edy's voice still croaking away:

'...a chance to pick up all those projects you were always too busy for. I know it sounds clichéd, but this could be a fresh start for you.'

'You're right, Edy. My life is falling apart... and you do sound fucking clichéd.' Laura held her breath. Edy might dish out the 'fuck' word like she handed out cigarettes but she didn't like hearing it back at her. She waited. The wail of another siren.

'Well, if it's the truth you want,' Edy said eventually. 'I'll give it to you straight.' A pause. Edy always had a penchant for the dramatic, no doubt picked up from her clients. 'You wanna hear?'

'I'm all ears.'

'There comes a point when the world ain't interested in you anymore. Simple as that. It don't matter if you're Laura Scott, Julia fucking Roberts, a rock star or a hooker. You can either move on from that. Or you can sit at home in the dark, knock back a bottle of gin, watch re-runs of your best bits. Just like our friend Kate.'

Laura knelt down, trailed her hand in the pond slime. 'I'm going to go now,' she said quietly, letting the algae slide softly between her fingers.

'Yeah. I gotta go too. I gotta call Naomi next. Love ya.'

Laura lifted her neck, watched as the handset slipped from her shoulder, bounced off the stone wall and into the water.

Chapter Two

Extract from an unpublished memoir by Georgina Hepburn

Born in 1900, I am as old as the century itself, an only child who grew up in the tiny village of Five Elms Down in Sussex where nothing very much ever happened. Contrary to the stereotype of an infant raised without siblings, I was not spoiled nor did I have any imaginary friends. But did I turn out to be selfish and narcissistic? Well, I shall leave the answer to that question for others to decide.

I often wondered what a different turn my life might have taken if my English teacher, Mr Bemrose, had not selected me to play the role of the Indian princess Pocahontas in the school pageant to celebrate the Festival of Empire. Up until that point I had not displayed any talent or desire for amateur dramatics. I doubt even that Mr Bemrose's choice was based on any latent acting ability he might have perceived in me. Rather my dark hair and slightly olive complexion (my mother boasted some minor Italian aristocrat in her distant heritage) might have swayed my teacher's selection above those of my female classmates who generally were as fair as an English rose. I didn't have a choice in the matter anyway as the casting was his superior male prerogative, a privilege I was to confront later in my life with devastating consequences.

I still possess the newspaper account from that glorious day on 12th May 1911, cut out from the front page of the *Sussex Herald*. Even now as I write this, I can recall the sensation of my childish fingers struggling with the rings of the scissors, the heat of excitement searing my young body as I carefully trimmed the edges of the article containing the details of my acting debut. According to the paper, several hundred people had lined the streets to cheer a series of bedecked floats drawn through our village by finely dressed horses from the West Dene stables, each float representing a famous scene in celebration of our great Empire. One was of Captain Cook's landing in Botany Bay, another depicted Dr David Livingston's discovery of the Victoria Falls.

I saw none of this, too busy was I in preparation for my starring part in the pageant portraying the reception of Pocahontas and her husband, the colonist John Rolfe, at the court of King James. Eddie Shaw played the king with a certain lack of discipline that even then offended my thespian aspirations. Freddy Cranfield took the role of my husband Rolfe with slightly more seriousness while my other classmates played the parts of members of the royal court with varying degrees of competence. While Mr Bemrose recited the narrative describing Pocahontas's visit to England, I closed my eyes and tried to imagine what it must have been like for this young woman (she would only have been twenty-one at the time) to be presented before royalty. Even in my immature mind, I seemed to understand the demands, the complexity of the situation imposed on my nascent acting ability. Being the daughter of a great tribal chieftain, Pocahontas would have possessed a certain dignity and inner sense of her own importance. Yet at the same time she was being treated as some kind of noble savage to be paraded before the leader of this great nation. I believe that through my bearing and the manner in which I answered the king's questions regarding my impressions of the English way of life, I managed to capture these conflicting emotions. Certainly the audience seemed to think so given their enthusiastic applause as I made my bows. As did my mother who congratulated me with her usual restrained enthusiasm. I don't remember my father being present at all. I still have the new sixpence I received as a mark of my participation in the event.

It was the absolute joy I experienced from this brief acting role that persuaded me this was the vocation for me. I also happened to be fortunate that my ambition should coincide with one of the most significant advances of my century – the advent of cinema. Until then, only a life on stage – and particularly in musical theatre – would have been available to an aspiring actress. Now I could dream of the silver and silent screen.

If Mr Bemrose had looked over my shoulder as I was writing my class essay and said: 'That is an exceptionally coherent and complex sentence,' would I have decided to become a writer? If he had swung by the art room where I was painting a still life of fruit in a bowl and commented: 'I like the way you have captured the light on the skin of those apples', would I have run off to Paris to become a painter? There are some of us whose immediate talent shines through almost from the moment they exit the womb. But for those mere mortals like myself who lie in wait for an encouraging word, that encouraging word can take them places they never could have imagined. All for the sake of having one's self-worth appreciated.

In my later years, I happened to become friends with an American gentleman, Kipling Jones his name was, a well-known astrologer to the stars of Hollywood as well as of the stars of the firmament. Not for Kip the generalised predictions of the daily newspapers. He dealt with precise times and places of birth, major and minor aspects, this house opposite that house, eclipses and orbits in retrograde, equinoctial points and the return of Saturn. He would produce elaborate and beautiful charts along with eloquent texts explaining his subject's personality and proclivities – all for a substantial fee. I never really gave any serious thought to Kip's profession, if I can even call it that. However, there was one comment he made to me that has often given me cause for consideration. After I had confided to him my musings as to how my life might have been different if Mr Bemrose had not chosen me to play the part of Pocahontas, Kip laughed that hearty laugh of his, slapped his knee and said in a Southern drawl as smooth and sweet as syrup:

'Oh, Georgie. It would have made no damn difference at all. You think these turning points are important in your life but they are not worth a dime in the grand scheme of things. Destiny is destiny. You'd have ended up in exactly the same place as you've ended up now. Whether Mister Bemrose chose you to play that part or not.'

Chapter Three

Over the Primrose Hill

It was one of those wonderful London summer afternoons. Not too hot, not too humid, Laura in her summer dress, loving the feel of the breeze and sun on her naked legs as she hastened past the pavement cafes. She didn't think Primrose Hill was the same since the Russian tea rooms had closed but Victoria still insisted they meet there.

She was late. With all the traffic, she had paid off the taxi driver at the top of Regent's Park Road, was walking the rest of the way. She would have liked to have upped her pace a little but her heels, her upbringing and her reputation restrained her. If it had been anyone else but Victoria she would have cancelled, stayed at home, cried into her pillow. But Victoria was the best person to see in these moments of crisis, an angel perched on her shoulder giving her the best advice. Although she didn't always take it. For on her other shoulder, she had a whole epaulette of demons begging her to do the opposite.

'Where have you been?' Victoria asked, looking up from her phone. She was wearing an off-white peasant blouse, a floral skirt and very little make-up. Victoria hadn't changed her look since her hippy days thirty years ago, although thankfully she no longer exuded the constant scent of patchouli.

'There's been a crisis.'

'I tried texting you.'

Laura sat down. She would have preferred to have been inside but the place was packed. 'Mobile's not working.'

'There certainly has been a crisis then,' Victoria said as she slipped her own phone into her bag. 'A cappuccino's coming. I ordered when I saw you trying not to run up the street. Now will you take off those stupid sunglasses. You look like a giant ladybug.'

'I'm keeping them on.'

'No need to act the diva with me.'

Laura tipped her head down so Victoria could see over the rim of her glasses.

'Oh dear, tell me what happened.'

Laura related the conversation with Edy. Contrary to common wisdom, the telling didn't make her feel better. 'I suppose I've seen this coming. I was getting fewer scripts, smaller parts. The last thing I did was that Disney crab thing. All voice and no face. All the really juicy parts for actresses of my vintage are being aged-down for the youngsters. Soon, you'll have a teenager playing Lady Macbeth. Or a thirty-year-old playing Hamlet's mother. So basically, I've been fired.'

'There are lots of other agents out there.'

'Edy was one of the best. To be dropped by her is to be scarred for life.'

'Someone with your profile will always be in demand.'

'Not at my age.' Laura leaned back in her chair to allow the waiter to place her coffee. The cream had been patterned with a smiley face which she immediately obliterated with her spoon. She handed Victoria a sheet of paper.

'What's this?'

'Just read it.'

'It's a list.'

'From the top. Out loud.'

'Geena Davis.'

'Go on.'

'Holly Hunter, Elisabeth Shue, Mary McDonell. Debra Winger. I once worked on a movie with her.' Victoria had been a set designer before she had turned her skills to creating *feng shui* inspired interiors for the homes of the wealthy. 'What's your point?'

'All Oscar contenders in the 1990s.'

'And?'

'Where are they now?'

'No idea.'

'Exactly.' Laura snatched back the paper. 'Well, actually

some of them are doing TV. Quite successfully. But all these beautiful women in their fifties. No longer movie stars.'

'There's nothing wrong with doing TV these days.'

'It always feels like a step down for me.'

'What about your nanny in *The Bentleys*? That was a huge success.'

'I was just dropping in. A cameo. Full-time TV for me would be like... it would be like menopause.'

'At least it wouldn't be a money pause.'

Laura sipped on her coffee, waited until Victoria had finished chuckling away at her own joke before she said: 'Being a film actress is what defines me. Without that, life has no meaning.'

'Oh, stop being so bloody dramatic.'

Before Laura could reply, she was distracted by a young Japanese woman who had approached their table with a deep bow.

'Excuse me, I am so sorry to interrupt. But can I ask you... please?'

Laura looked down to see an autograph book and pen thrust in front of her. Not an envelope or a napkin, but an actual autograph book.

'Who shall I make it out to?' The young woman held her head away from her so she could only see a dark curtain of hair.

'Tomoko,' came the hidden voice.

Laura signed the book with a flourish. On the opposite page, she noted the other signature. Jude Law.

'See,' Victoria said, once Tomoko had left them. 'Still in demand. Even by a young, global audience.'

'Smugness doesn't suit you. Now what was I saying?'

'You were telling me about the meaningless of your existence.'

'I'm serious. Look at you. You've produced two adorable children. At the very least, when you look back on your life, you can say you fulfilled your biological function.'

'I do believe I've done more than that.'

'You know what I mean. Our whole existence as human

beings is defined around procreation. You have contributed to the continuation of the human race. Even if you end up failing at everything else, at least Tom and Pru give your life meaning.'

'I'm not sure whether you are complimenting me or criticising me.'

'I'm just stating a fact.'

'Where does that leave you then?'

'I, Laura Scott, having chosen not to have children, am therefore obliged to provide meaning for my life in other ways. My unused womb must not indicate an unfulfilled life. I have to prove to both myself and to the rest of the world that my sacrifice was worth it. Now my means of doing that have been taken away from me. Forever.'

'I think you're being a little too dramatic here...'

'...and when Tom and Pru grow up they will be there to look after you in your old age. While I will be left alone and penniless to survive on the generosity of the Actors' Benevolent fund.'

Victoria leaned forward with that earnest gaze of hers. Laura always thought that Victoria had old eyes. Wise, ancient eyes that could be traced back centuries, eyes that had somehow been passed down through the sages to this interior designer now living in Notting Hill. Or they could just be stoned eyes, for Victoria still liked the occasional joint, especially on a sunny afternoon with her children off doing whatever teenagers did these days. 'Oh for Christ's sake,' Victoria said, patting her hand. 'Let's order a bottle of wine.'

Chapter Four

The Hepburn Archives

Extract from an unpublished memoir

As the months, then years, went by after my appearance as Pocahontas, my ambition to become an actress did not wane. My parents never took my aspiration very seriously although my father was perhaps the more receptive of the two. He had trained as a mechanical engineer, such an underrated profession, I believe. As a society we laud those who can create beautiful things with words and colour and voice but tend to ignore those who design and build exquisitely intricate machines that impact greatly on the way we live our lives. Electric generators, heat exchangers, gas turbines, refrigerators and, of course, the internal combustion engine. He eventually became fascinated with the fledgling discipline of aeronautics which in turn led him to become one of the first human beings on this entire planet to learn to fly, earning an Aviator's Certificate from the Royal Aero Club in March 1914. When the Great War broke out four months later, he was immediately commissioned as a lieutenant into No. 5 Squadron, Royal Flying Corps.

It is hard to imagine Papa as a fighter pilot, as a violent assailant of the skies, for I remember him as a gentle man who always had his nose in a book. Mostly engineering manuals but he loved literature and philosophy as well. It was almost as if his career in the Royal Flying Corps was some kind of secret identity he changed into when my mother and I weren't looking.

I am grateful to my father for imbuing me with his sense of curiosity, the willingness to try new things, to be open to a different way of seeing the world. It was that sense of curiosity that led him to investigate Eastern religions and philosophies, an interest that irked my devout Church of England mother who often called him a heathen when, instead of attending church on Sundays, he would prefer to go for a walk across the South Downs.

'I'm not a heathen,' I remember my father protesting. 'I am merely an agnostic.'

'What's an agnostic?' I asked.

My father bent down to my level bringing with him from on high the smell of pipe tobacco and citrus shaving soap. 'It means I only believe in that which is known.'

'Does that mean you don't believe in God?'

'That's a very good question,' he said, with a smile and a quick glance to my mother. 'And the answer is that if God makes Himself known to me, then I will believe in Him.'

'So what do you believe in now, Papa?'

'I believe in universal truths. Universal truths that can be known and experienced.'

'What's a universal truth?'

'One day, I will take you up in an airplane and show you.'

I often wondered what attracted my mother to my father for she possessed hardly any curiosity at all. She rarely wandered from our village, content with a life that centred on her tiny family, her church and her garden. She had little more ambition for me than she did for herself. She taught me deportment and etiquette, how to bake, to make jam and to sew. To this day, whenever I pick up a needle, I can picture her winding thread around a loose button, biting off the extra length with her teeth and pronouncing the word 'There' to her completed task as if this was all that was needed in life to bring her satisfaction. While Papa was off flying missions over France, she contributed to the war effort by helping with the milking on a neighbouring dairy farm.

It was my Aunt Ginny who was more sympathetic to my cause. The two sisters could not have been more different. My Aunt Ginny was nine years younger for a start, poised in age exactly between myself and my mother. She was wealthier than my mother too, having married my Uncle Richard with his substantial farmhouse and its many hundreds of acres in East Sussex. While my mother possessed a straight back, tilted-chin aloofness and pinned up tresses, Aunt Ginny was all openness, wide-mouthed smiles and the first person I knew to have her hair cut in a bob. She drank gin and even smoked the occasional cigarette, none of which my mother did.

When I became old enough to be militarily useful, it was my Aunt Ginny who suggested I join a small theatre company up in London providing entertainment for the wounded men returned from the battlefields of northern Europe. My father was never home to care about what I did and my mother was too worn down by the war to protest. And so it was that Aunt Ginny arranged for me to stay in digs run by a Mrs Ridley just south of Tower Bridge while our troupe toured the military hospitals under the London Command District.

It was a pitiful task really, witnessing the desperate and the dying on a daily basis, trying hard to buoy up my own spirits so as to bring a bit of pleasure to those poor souls. We put on short plays mainly, interspersed with a song or a comic turn. Our cast consisted mostly of women with a couple of young men drafted in after they too had been wounded and were unable to return to the Front. Billy Morrison was one of them, his knee shattered by a bullet over in the trenches, giving him a serious limp that actually added great dramatic effect to the parts he played.

There weren't so many young men to choose from in those days. Billy wasn't particularly good-looking. Neither did he sparkle with intelligence, talent or wit, I guess I just felt sorry for him. I sneaked him into the room I shared with two of the other girls, it was late afternoon between performances, it was raining I remember that, and Billy had brought with him a couple of bottles of stout. We started kissing and I didn't think I would be going that far with him but the beer must have gone straight to my head. I remember thinking that I just wanted this to be over with, to pass through the threshold of pain, to know what it was like to be a woman. I had only heard sketchy information from the other girls in our troupe, my mother had told me nothing, it was amazing really to think how little we knew about sex back then. I certainly didn't know anything about contraception, I am just grateful now that Billy had the sense to pull out when he did. After it was over, Billy was having a cigarette while I was sitting there with this ache between my legs, utterly mortified to see all the blood and spilled semen staining Mrs Ridley's sheets. What with all that evidence of sex, tobacco and alcohol in the room, I nearly jumped out of my skin when there was a loud knocking at the door from Mrs Ridley, calling out to me by name. Billy scampered underneath the bed with the beer bottles, I pushed up the window and sorted the sheets in a matter of seconds, half-opened the door in a pretence of being woken from fevered sleep. Mrs Ridley said nothing as she passed me through the pale yellow envelope. The Post Office telegram read:

Father killed in action. Please come home. Mama.

Chapter Five

An Honest Appraisal

The telephone was ringing. Laura's actual telephone. Her landline that connected her to millions of other myriad souls on this planet through physical wires and cables. That was a concept she could understand. Rather than her mobile and all those invisible radio waves passing through the air and solid objects and everything else. Except the water in the pond in her garden. She glanced at the bedside clock. 5.53 PM. She had been out for the count for almost an hour. Not surprising given the two large glasses of wine she had consumed in Primrose Hill. She was still fully dressed, hadn't even taken off her shoes. She stretched out her hand, fumbled over her bottles of pills, her house keys, her sunglasses until she could gather up the receiver, bring it to her ear.

'Yes?'

Victoria's voice. 'Just checking.'

'Checking? That I'm alive?'

'That you're still going to Caroline's. Or should I say *Lady* Caroline these days.'

'Yes, yes, the dinner party.'

'Are you all right?'

'I just fell asleep, that's all. Wine in the afternoon. Not good for me.'

'Is that "wine" with or without an "h"?'

'Very funny.'

'So?'

'So what?'

'Are you still going?'

'I'm thinking about it.'

'It's important to get on with your life.'

'You said that after Jack and I went our separate ways. And nothing's happened since.'

'My orders to you are: Go to the party. Have a few drinks. Forget about your agent.'

'My ex-agent.'

'You never know who you'll meet.'

'I'm going to have a bath.'

'I'll call back in an hour.' Victoria clicked off.

As she replaced the receiver, she noticed the message sign flashing. She pressed down on the button.

'Hey, Laura. How are ya?' Edy again, this time full of forced cheerfulness. 'I tried you on your cell but no answer. I hope you're not ignoring me. Perhaps I was a bit too harsh earlier. I just wanted to say that despite our formal... how can I put it?... our formal disengagement, I'll still be looking out for you. If the perfect part for Laura Scott lands on my desk, fuck Meryl and all your fancy *shmanzy* dames, I'll give you a call. And next time you're in the Big Apple, let's do lunch. Yeah, let's do that. I mean it... not just saying it. Love ya.'

It was good to soak. She bathed in the Japanese way. She had a shower first, then when she was cleaned off, still warm and wet, she lay down in the tub, let the water fill and flow over her. No sense in lying in one's own filth. What was the point of that?

She stretched out one leg, let her toes play with the water spout. She had loved Japan. And Japan had loved her. Of course, the whole experience had been filtered through love-struck eyes. For that was where she had met Jack. One glorious month together there while they were filming the Tokyo scenes. And that month happened to be April too when the cherry trees were in full blossom, the flowers tinting their affair with a glorious soft-focus pink glow. Sipping sake in tiny late-night jazz bars in Shinjuku, a dawn visit to the fish market then sushi for breakfast, a rickety train ride through Kamakura to see the Big Buddha. Falling in love with your co-star. It was so hackneyed, so trite, such a Hollywood cliché. Yet, it made perfect sense really. In love on the screen, so why not in love in real life? Method acting is what Jack laughingly called their relationship. The movie had bombed at the box office. Perhaps he was right. Perhaps he had been acting all along.

She sank deeper into the water, held her breath, pinched her nose, slid right down so that her face was covered. This was what it must feel like to be in the womb. Breathless, warm, liquid and silent. What a gift that would be, the ability to start one's life over again. She eased herself back to the surface again, sucked in air. She thought of her earlier conversation with Victoria. She knew she hadn't been entirely honest. Acting didn't just give her life meaning. It gave her one other heady ingredient. Fame. Fame fed her ego. She loved that. To be treated kindly and with respect. To be noticed. She didn't want that to fade away. To go back to the end of the queue, for the invitations to dry up, to be ignored, to be like everyone else. Victoria would never understand that. For Victoria didn't need fame. Victoria didn't crave the kindness, adulation and respect of others. Victoria with her happy childhood could never truly appreciate the value of fame. The compensation it provided for a lack of parental love.

She rose from the bath, dried herself off, wrapped herself in her Japanese robe (a present from Jack), sat down in front of the dressing table. She set up the three mirrors. She was so used to playing other parts, it was easy to forget who she really was. She closed her eyes, thought to herself – *I am going to have an honest appraisal of myself* – opened them again, stared at the facing mirror, then glanced to each of her profiles. Her hair was still thick, dyed to its original dark colour. Brown eyes, slightly too large, smudges of tiredness underneath, lines of age and experience at the corners. Nothing exceptional there. Her main disappointment was that she lacked strong cheekbones, there was always a certain puppy-fat roundness to her jawline, her mouth not as generous as she would have liked. More Judi Dench, less Helen Mirren. She could still put on that look though, she did it now, the dipping of her gaze, a slightly sardonic smile that somehow captured the audience's attention, men and women alike. A sexual knowingness was how it had been described early on and she had perfected it. That look, that coquettishness, coupled with the softness of her features meant she had never been able to play the strong female roles but there was a charming authenticity about her. She should have been born French or a couple of decades earlier. She would have been ideal for *Breathless, Blow Up, Billy Liar* or one of Alfie's girlfriends. Perhaps even a Bond girl.

The phone started to ring again. Right on time. There was no way she was going to answer it. 'Yes, yes, Victoria,' she shouted as her outgoing message clicked on. 'I am going to Caroline's bloody party.'

Chapter Six

Extract from an unpublished memoir

My father, Captain Frank Hepburn, was killed on 1st July 1918, his plane shot down somewhere near Lens in France. One year previously he had been awarded the DSO for distinguished conduct under enemy fire during an aerial engagement over Arras. He was one of the oldest fighter pilots in the Royal Flying Corps with fifteen claimed victories. If he could have stayed out of trouble for just four more months, the war would have ended, and my father could have come home. Instead, his body was never recovered and only his name is commemorated on a memorial wall in the Faubourg-d'Amiens cemetery in Arras in northern France. I once visited the site when I was a middle-aged woman, touched my fingers to his name among the almost 35,000 other names inscribed there. The sense of the ghosts of wasted lives emanating from that place was overwhelming.

My mother became a widow at the age of thirty-six. I don't think she ever recovered from my father's death. Instead she sought solace by intensifying the things which gave her comfort in her life – her church, her garden, village life – but sadly not me. My father's death had somehow driven us apart rather than closer together. I had not only lost my father but my mother as well. I was an orphan at the age of eighteen.

When I look back at that time, I am ashamed at how little consideration I gave Mama in the aftermath of my father's death. I assumed there was some kind of War Pension due to her but I really had no idea about our income and expenditure or what her worries were concerning the maintenance of the cottage, putting food on the table and paying the bills. She had left all these matters up to Papa and now he was gone. How was she coping with the death of her husband? Why was she cutting herself off from me? What did I care? I was wrapped up in the hardness of my own selfish ambition. Perhaps it was my own way of dealing with my grief. But all I wanted to do was to get away from the village of Five Elms Down as quickly as possible. And my mother was in no fit state to stop me.

My best friend in those days was Polly McKenzie. Same village, same age, same class at school. Pretty Polly. Yes, that was what everyone called her. Fair hair and freckles, blue eyes, tiny retroussé nose, and a Cupid's Bow of an upper lip. She certainly used to shoot off a lot of arrows with that bow of hers, scored a lot of bulls-eyes too. While Polly was praised for her prettiness, I was often described as being attractive. It was a distinction I did not find pleasing. I remember once complaining about it to my Aunt Ginny.

'Prettiness is fleeting,' she told me. 'Attractiveness will always endure.' She was right about the fleetingness of Polly McKenzie. Sadly, she was killed in a car accident at the age of twenty-seven.

Like me, Polly wanted to be an actress. Or at least she wanted the glamour and attention that such a career brought. Fortunately for us, a lot of the early British silent films were being made at Shoreham-by-Sea, an hour's bicycle ride from our village. The Shoreham Beach Studios contained a proper production set-up with a large glass house specially built as a film stage in order to capture as much light as possible from the long, smog-free, summer days of the south coast. The studios boasted several hand-cranked cameras, a dark room, a preview theatre, bungalows where the actors and crew could stay during a shoot. A veritable Hollywood by the sea. Polly and I would cycle down there whenever we could, volunteer for odd-jobs around the set in the hope we would be brought in as extras. On one such day, we were watching the legendary Sidney Walcott filming a scene for *On the Pleasure Pier*, a love story between a servant lass and a wealthy business man, when one of the production team sauntered over to where we were standing. He couldn't have been much older than we were, not particularly handsome but he was all swelled up with the confidence that comes from having something desirable to offer two desperate young women.

'We need someone for filming on Brighton Pier tomorrow,' he said, eyeing both of us up and down, then waited until he was sure our interest was snared. 'Cashier girl. Handing out change for the amusements. A couple of lines. Simple. Early morning. Fancy it?'

Oh how my cheeks redden even now at the thought of how that little lure suddenly drove a wedge between Polly and me and our lifelong friendship. I felt her edge me aside so she could show our benefactor a close-up of her prettiness, her back arching slightly to ensure her pert little bosom was on prominent display. As for me, I decided to go for a more sultry look, eyes down, head slightly tilted to the left to show off what I imagined was my best profile.

'You can have it,' he said, pointing at me.

Such was Polly's surprise that she actually grabbed the young man's arm to haul him back as he moved away from us. 'What do you mean, she can have it? I'm the prettier one. Everyone says so.'

'It's not pretty we're after, miss. We want our hero falling in love with the servant lass. Not the cashier girl.' He pulled himself away from her grasp. 'Anyway, your eyes are too blue,' he said, winking at me.

'Too blue? I don't understand.'

'That's the way the film stock is right now. Light blue registers as white. You'd have no pupils at all up there on the screen. Your friend with the nice brown eyes suits us better.'

Well, that was the end of my 'we'll be friends forever' relationship with Polly McKenzie but the beginning of my film career.

I went to see my performance of *On the Pleasure Pier* when it was shown at The Dukes cinema in Brighton. My mother said she was too ill to attend so Aunt Ginny came instead. Somehow I preferred it that way. When that image of myself as the cashier girl came up on the screen, I could feel my cheeks flush and my heart jump with the thrill of it all, seeing that which was me and not me both at the same time. Aunt Ginny grabbed my hand, squeezed it all the way through the minute or so of my scene. After the film was over, we walked down to the sea front. Under the struts of the pier, she slipped off her stockings and shoes, commanded that I do the same even though it was hard to walk on the pebbled beach. She bought us both ice cream cones, then went off to wander joyfully in and out of the surf, I think she was more excited by my appearance on the silver screen than I was.

'You're going to be a star,' she told me, arms outstretched, shoes in one hand, cone in the other. 'I can see it straight away, Georgie. You have such a luminous quality.'

'It was only a small scene.'

'It doesn't matter. Your obvious talent shines through. Your luminosity. Yes, that's the word. Luminosity. It will only be a matter of time before you'll be spotted by one of these directors or whoever it is that chooses actresses for these wonderful new films. You'll see. Your father would have been very proud of you. I'm just sorry Margaret... your mother... wasn't here to see it.'

'She gets these headaches.'

Aunt Ginny sighed, popped the last of her cone into her mouth with a flourish. 'That woman needs to pull herself together. Your father was a remarkable man. But she can't go on mourning him for the rest of her life.' She grabbed my hand and together we tiptoed among the seaweed and the pebbles. 'What about you?' she asked.

'What do you mean?'

'How are you coping?'

'I'm fine.'

'Are you sure? After all, you adored your father.'

'I try not to think about him too much.'

'Hmmm. The two of you, different peas in the same pod.

Well, if you ever need a shoulder…'

I decided to change the subject and asked after Uncle Richard and my two cousins.

'I hardly ever see him these days,' she told me. 'Always out all over the place, managing the estate, only comes back for his tea. Oliver is just about to start prep school and Percy just turned five last week. Too many males for my liking. It would be nice to have a daughter like you to balance the ship.' And with that remark she burrowed into her purse. 'Did you get paid for your acting job?' she asked.

I shook my head.

'Well, here you are,' she said, handing me two half crowns.

'You don't need to…'

'I'm your aunt, Georgie. I'm allowed to do such things.'

Chapter Seven

Lady Caroline's Party

Lady Caroline Hoffman. Or simply Caroline Fletcher as she was in her drama student days. Caroline had done well for herself. Leveraged her few years in the spotlight as one of the sexy stars (blonde, skinny, tight sweaters over perky breasts) of a highly successful sitcom into a marriage to an extremely wealthy businessman. Lew Hoffman, recently dubbed Sir Lewis, no doubt for his contributions to one of the major political parties. Laura wasn't sure which one, it could have been all of them, as Lew liked to spread his bets. A stocky, tensed-up figure of a man, much smaller than Caroline, who had made his money in oil, mining, farming and real estate. As Sir Lew was fond of saying, he liked to invest in things he could put his hands on, dig his fingers into – like his wife. Caroline would give a complicit giggle to this well-worn remark although Laura knew it had been several years since Sir Lew had put his hands, fingers or any other part of his body anywhere near the once-sexy Caroline.

The Hoffmans owned a town house in Knightsbridge in a gorgeous Regency terrace that film companies were always using for period shoots. As Sir Lew tended to be away a lot, Caroline hosted these intimate evenings by herself, embracing her temporary singleton status by only inviting individual guests without their partners (if they had any). Whatever Laura's own relationship status at the time, she usually looked forward to these opportunities to be out by herself and to be herself.

It was dinner for sixteen. Eight men, eight women. The usual balance between business and creative types. Caroline, during a brief hiatus from her hostess duties, pulled Laura aside to explain the seating arrangements.

'I have quite a treat for you this evening,' she said breathlessly, fanning her fingers at the red yoke spread across her neck and bare shoulders. Her low-cut dress revealed most of the infamous breasts that had so excited adolescent television viewers (as well as Sir Lew) in the 1980s. 'To your right, I have put Sal Yerksaw. Heard of him?'

'Should I have?'

'Documentary film maker and theatre producer. American. From California. He's over here doing some project or other. Tanned and good-looking.'

Caroline pointed him out. A rather attractive urbane gentleman with a thick shock of white swept-back hair that gave him a senatorial look. He was casually dressed in a black polo-neck and grey sports jacket while all the other men wore dark suits, various patterned ties to match their personalities.

'And to my left?'

'Fredrik Nilssen. Swedish. He works with Lew. A genius in his field, according to my dear husband. It could be an oil field or a field of clover for all I know. He is officially married but possibly separated. Are you all right? You seem a bit... edgy?'

'I'll be fine. I haven't had a good day.'

'Well, let's hope a little male attention will cheer you up.'

Sal Yerksaw certainly wasn't going to be that male attention. He seemed more interested in the pretty young authoress to his right, the recent winner of some prestigious literary prize. On her more confident days, Laura would have assumed Sal was deliberately ignoring her in a bid to make himself look nonchalant in the company of a well-known actress. The way she was feeling tonight though, she was no longer sure in her assumptions.

Sal's behaviour left her solely in the company of Fredrik Nilssen sitting stiff with his rimless glasses and that cool Nordic stare so hard to read. Everything about him was neat. His hair, his fingers, his grey suit and tie, his movements as he adjusted his place card, spread a napkin on his lap. If there had been an exit route from his dinner companionship, she probably would have taken it. But given their tied proximity for the next hour or so, she decided to be as gracious as possible.

Fredrik turned his head – but not his body – towards her and said: 'Would you like to know when you are going to die?'

She looked back at him. At the candlelight reflecting in his glasses, his pink-spotted, sun-starved skin, his lips formed into a quivering smile. 'I'm sorry?' she said.

'Your age at death. Would you like to know?'

'That's an unusual question...' She glanced at his place card to remind herself. '...Fredrik.'

'You must be asked lots of usual questions, Laura. I was trying to be different.'

'I admit you have my curiosity.'

'Let's say I could predict the month and year of your death with a certain amount of accuracy, would you like to know?'

'I don't think so.'

'Why not?'

She preferred not to ponder the inevitably of her own death. Especially today when dealing with the end of her career was enough demise for her consideration. 'Better the joy of the unknown,' she said, laughing nervously. 'It adds a certain *frisson* to our lives, don't you think?'

'Not really.'

The conversation paused as the waiters moved in to serve the soup. Lobster bisque with a garnish of truffle oil according to the menu propped up at each place setting.

'I love lobster,' she found herself saying to no-one in particular, especially not Sal Yerksaw who still sat quite rudely with his body turned away from her.

Fredrik folded his hands on the table, stared at his soup. 'Would it not be better,' he said, 'if we could properly plan out our lives? Arrange our careers, our finances, our dreams according to a finite schedule. Rather than all this randomness.'

'And what difference would that make?'

'Well, for example, if I knew I were going to die next week, perhaps I would be a little more forthright in this conversation I am having with this very attractive woman. Instead, I am being my usual reserved, risk-averse and boring self.'

Laura smiled, acknowledged the compliment with a graceful nod, happier than Fredrik could imagine for this little boost to her ego on this most awful of days. 'All right then. If you told me I was going to be dead by the time I was sixty I probably wouldn't want to know. But if you said I was going to live until ninety-five, then yes, I would be happy to be told that.'

'So it is the fear of the brevity rather than the certainty?'

'You could say that. What about you?'

'I shall be dead by the age of eighty-two, with a standard deviation of about three months.'

'And how do you know that?'

'Because I am an actuary.'

'And what does that entail?'

'I am involved with the assessment of probability of certain undesirable outcomes and their financial impacts on a company's balance sheet. In short, risk management. For insurance companies, banks, investors, even film production companies.'

'So when you turn up at the office, what do you do?'

'Well, if you really did want to know when you were going to die, I would combine my analytical skills together with complex mathematical theories and algorithms to predict your probable age of death by evaluating a huge amount of statistical data. You wish me to go on? Or am I boring you already?'

'You may continue.'

'This data would include mortality rates for your age group, for someone living in London, the risks arising out of your career, relationship status, family history, diet, life-style, whether you had any children or any health-issues. If I were to hone in on you as a particular case rather than dealing in broad general terms, I would ask questions such as how often you drove a car as opposed to taking public transport, how far you lived from your place of work, how often you travelled overseas, whether you owned a pet. Are your parents still alive?'

'They are actually. Both of them.' Although her father was in a nursing home with hardly a shred of memory remaining to him. Her mother, still agile and attractive in her late-seventies, taking her anonymity in the mind of her husband as a form of release, spent most of her time hopping on and off various cruise ships across the world. Where she was now, Laura had no idea.

Fredrik nodded. 'Longevity in your genes. Obviously a very positive sign.'

'What about the randomness of simple accidents?'

'I could work those into the equation. Road traffic deaths in your area, crime statistics, A&E records and so on.'

'And relationships?' Now she was single, she might as well know if they were good or bad for her health.

'Traditionally, it was always better to be married. Especially for men. They tended to live healthier lifestyles within a relationship. They also took less risks if they knew that there was someone at home waiting for them. However, in recent years, the gap between the single person and the married person is narrowing quite considerably.'

'Why is that?'

'A number of factors. Possibly the most influential these days is that married people end up being more obese than their single counterparts. There is a tendency to eat more as a couple, to let oneself go. A single person is more likely to try to remain thin in order to attract a mate.'

'Are you married, Fredrik?'

'Yes, I am.'

'Yet you seem quite slim to me.'

Fredrik laughed. 'You should also know, Laura, that for marriage to be a positive factor, the union must also be a happy one.'

Chapter Eight

After my brief appearance in *On the Pleasure Pier*, I began
to pick up other small parts in Sidney Walcott films down at
Shoreham Studios, he was churning out about five or six a
year by then. I think people in Britain forget what a thriving
industry we had back in those days, especially down on the
south coast where a lot of the early film camera technology was
pioneered. But inevitably the studios moved up to London – to
Borehamwood and to Lime Grove – and I followed. It was a
life of constant auditions, a few successful, most not. Even the
successful ones were nothing special. Frustration and rejection,
those are the harshest lessons to be learnt by the aspiring artist
whether they be actor, writer or musician.

I took acting lessons, voice lessons and dance lessons, did
bits of theatre back in Brighton at the Theatre Royal or on
the West Pier in the summer to make some money. But my
heart was set on the film business. I wanted to be a star. Not
in any old rubbish, mind you, but real quality films were hard
to find in those days. There was such a voracious appetite for
this new form of entertainment that the studios became like
sausage factories, churning out any old slipshod rubbish to
satisfy the mass audiences. And decent roles for women? Well,
you can forget about those. We were either portrayed as blonde
flibbertigibbets, screaming damsels in distress or dizzy comic
turns.

One film though that really impressed me back then, still
does after all these years, was *The Lure of Crooning Water*
directed by Arthur Rooke. My God, even the title still thrills
me to this day. It was so intelligently and sensitively done. The
formidable Ivy Duke played the female lead as this glamorous

actress who is advised by her doctor to take a rest cure in the countryside where she ends up seducing a married farmer. It was a kind of comedy-drama, a beauty and the beast set-up doomed to fail. It was the type of role I craved.

My first big chance came when I managed to get myself an audition for the part of Daisy, a model and the love interest of the great Ivor Novello in the Alfred Hitchcock film, *The Lodger*, which was being produced by Michael Balcon over at Gainsborough Pictures. I knew one of the assistant directors assigned to the film, Sandy Aitkinson, and he told me he thought I'd be ideal for the role. Sandy even tipped me off to come to the audition wearing a blonde wig as Daisy was scripted as the potential murder victim of a serial killer who only preyed on fair-haired young women.

Hitchcock was only a year older than I, yet he was already gaining something of a reputation as an up-and-coming director thanks to his imaginative use of montage, lighting and unusual camera angles. I think the studio executives and the distributors thought he was a bit too arty for their tastes – 'the problem between the artistic and the commercial is the cost of expression' as he himself would put it – but from what Sandy was telling me, the part of Daisy was a brilliant role for a woman whether the film eventually got widely distributed or not.

Gainsborough Pictures was over in the East End in Shoreditch and I took The Tube rather than the bus which was a mistake as I had a long walk in the rain to get to the studios. I did have an umbrella but I arrived with my shoes wet and all a bit hot and flustered. A secretary showed me into a small waiting area where another woman was sitting. I recognised her from previous auditions – her name was June if I remember correctly. We both gave each other quick polite smiles but were experienced enough to know there would be no small talk. I thought the secretary would provide me with a few pages from the scenario to look at while I waited but nothing was forthcoming. I sat stiff and straight with my hands in my lap, closed my eyes and conjured up an image of my father. That's what I always did at interviews but this time I had a real sense of his presence there with me. I started praying to him: 'Wish me success, wish me success.' I must have been speaking out loud for I heard a sharp cough. I opened my eyes to see June giving me an odd stare. A door into the adjoining room swung ajar and thankfully there was my friend Sandy. He looked at both of us then beckoned me in.

I found myself in a small rehearsal room where the stage was a slightly raised platform area covering about a third of the floor space. Hitchcock was half sitting, half leaning against a wooden crate in the middle of the room facing the stage. He was a roly-poly figure with a weak chin that was already beginning to disappear into his thick neck. His jacket was open and the trousers of his suit were belted high across his stomach. He was only twenty-eighty years old but there was already an air of haughty self-confidence about him. He hardly looked up at me as I came in. I just stood there not knowing what to do.

'Georgina Hepburn,' Sandy said. 'For Daisy.'

Hitchcock eyed me up and down, like a farmer measuring the worth of a horse put up for market, scrunched up his mouth then slowly shook his head. It was as if Caesar himself had turned down his thumb and sentenced me to death.

'What about one of the other victims?' Sandy persisted. 'The blondes.'

'Is that a wig?' Hitchcock asked me in that solemn, deliberate tone of his.

'Yes, it is.'

He grunted, shook his head again, waved his hand in dismissal.

Sandy took me by the elbow, led me back towards the door.

'He doesn't want to see me act?' I whispered as I scampered along beside him.

'That's it, I'm afraid.'

When we are back in the waiting room, he took me aside. 'He's got an exact picture of Daisy in his head. And all the other parts too. You either fit or you don't. He couldn't care two hoots if you can act or not. For him, it's the camera that does all the work.' Sandy turned his attention to June, smiled at her, then escorted her into the rehearsal room.

The rest, as they say, is history. June got the part of Daisy, I missed out on acting with Ivor Novello while Hitchcock's film about a serial killer in the London fog became a huge success, laying down many of the cinematic tropes that would come to establish him as the Master of Suspense. Another opportunity had passed me by. My disappointment was immense but fortunately it was short-lived. For soon after, along came Max.

Chapter Nine

Along Came Sal

By the time coffee was served in the cavernous lounge with its grand piano and several sofas, Laura was slightly tipsy. She had also learned that if she wanted to live longer she would have to do the following: meditate, move to Monaco or Japan (both of which she actually found quite appealing options), travel by train, eat more seeds, buy a dog, try not to oversleep, stop stressing about her career. She should also drink less red wine and have more sex. While Fredrik had turned out to be an interesting dinner companion, this latter activity was definitely not going to involve him.

She had been poised with her cup and saucer desperate for a place to sit when Sal Yerksaw finally approached her.

'I was hoping we could have a chat,' he said.

'You had your chance over dinner,' she scolded in a half-serious, half-mocking tone.

'You seemed more preoccupied with our Swedish friend.'

'And you with that pretty young writer.'

'She has just won a very prestigious prize,' Sal countered, as if this somehow explained his rudeness.

'And Fredrik wanted to predict the date of my death.'

'Well, let's hope it won't be any time soon.' He pointed to the unlit cigar he held between his fingers. 'You don't mind, do you?'

'I actually enjoy the aroma of a good Cuban,' she said, repeating a line from one of her film roles but with a little more swagger than she intended. She really had drunk too much.

'Well, just in case others don't.' He gently took her arm by the elbow, guided her out onto the patio. 'Smoking is a capital crime where I come from.'

'Can I light it for you?' she asked. 'My father used to let me do that all the time. Do you mind?'

'Be my guest.'

She put down her coffee on a patio table. Sal handed over the cigar, then produced one of those old brass petrol lighters, flicked the flame alive.

She put the cut end in her mouth, rotated the cigar slightly as she kissed and puffed the tip into an even burn. That woody, sweet-chocolate flavour immediately reminding her of her father. He might have been unable to recognise his own daughter, but he still smoked the occasional hand-rolled *parejo*. She blew on the lit end to make sure the burn had taken properly, handed it back.

'I'm impressed,' he said.

She dipped her gaze, delivered one of her famous smiles, then a slight dizziness took over and she had to grasp the patio rail for balance.

'Are you all right?' Sal asked from behind a cloud of cigar smoke.

'I'm fine. My heel caught on the decking.' She waved him away. 'Bride or groom?'

'I don't understand.'

'Who do you know? Caroline or Sir Lew?'

'Caroline. I met her last week at a special screening at the British Film Institute. She thought I looked lonely.'

'I can imagine. She's always picking up strays.'

'Your name came up in conversation.' Sal moved in closer, leaned back on the patio rail, drew slowly on his cigar. 'I saw you in that Japanese movie. What was it called again?'

'*Tokyo Winter.*'

'Yeah, that was it.'

'It was awful.'

'You were good in it though.'

'That's kind of you to say.'

'You've pretty much been good in everything I've seen you. You usually make excellent choices.'

'You know how it is. *Tokyo Winter* looked wonderful on the printed page. It just didn't turn out that way on the screen.'

'What are you doing now?'

'I just finished something with Disney.'

'Voice-over?'

'A crab. Not actually high-end stuff.'

Sal smiled. 'Money's good though. Lets you take a bit more risk on the really good stuff.'

'That's a nice way of putting it.' She glanced at his ringless fingers, tried to remember if Caroline said he was married. 'What about you? What are you up to these days?'

'You make it sound as if you know something about me. Is that true?'

'I hold my hands up,' she said, although she had no intention of doing so or she might fall over again. 'I'm afraid I have to plead ignorance.'

He smiled again, a sort of lopsided roguish grin. 'I'm over here producing a documentary for one of the US networks. On the birth of the silent film era. A lot of the pioneers were Brits, lived and worked down on the south coast way back at the turn of last century. Then there were all the studios that opened in London. It was a booming industry.'

'It's not what most people imagine, is it? They usually think. Silent movies. Charlie Chaplin, Buster Keaton, Keystone Cops, Hollywood.'

'Exactly.' Sal sucked on his cigar, flicked it hard so the ash fell away on to the lawn. 'The Brits made some excellent silent movies although many have been lost. I've been at the BFI all week viewing as many as I can fit in.'

'I've only seen a few myself.'

'I'm impressed you've seen any at all. Most people haven't.'

'That's twice I've impressed you then. Are you staying here in London?'

'No, I've shot all the London stuff. I've moved down with the crew to Brighton.'

'Fun place.'

'I guess. If you have the time.'

'Surely it can't be all work and no play?'

'Well, being down there has given me the opportunity to do some research on a pet project of mine.'

'Pray tell.' She took a sip of coffee. It was stone cold. She pretended it wasn't. 'Or is it some great industry secret?'

Sal turned away from her, leaned on the railing, stared out to the garden. 'Have you heard of Georgie Hepburn?'

Chapter Ten

Extract from an unpublished memoir

I met Max Rosen at a party hosted by a couple of communist writers in Soho. Actors, poets and authors crammed together in a small, stuffy flat, the air thick with smoke and seduction, Marxism and other radical talk. He told me he was a scenarist although nothing he had written had yet made it to the screen. When his unusual accent forced me to ask where he came from, he replied:

'I am a Central European.'

'What does that mean?' I said, pursing my cigarette smoke into the air like a gasping fish. Oh how sophisticated I used to think I looked with my raised hemline, my fox stole, my cigarette holder and my red lipstick from metal tubes. 'Don't you have a country?'

'My country keeps changing. Sometimes it is Russia, then Poland, then Germany. Then back to Russia again.'

Max was Jewish. I discovered later he had fled with his family to England prior to the Great War. He had only been fifteen at the time. He compensated for this lack of identity with a homeland by clinging to his ideas with an intensity, an intellect and a charm that was hugely seductive to someone like me. A young woman who at that time was devoid of any strong ideas at all except the one that made me want to be a highly successful actress.

'I envy you,' I said.

'And why is that?'

'The place where I come from never changes.'

'We have nothing in common then,' Max said with a smile. 'But at the same time we share everything.'

'What do we share?'

'A need to rebel.' He touched my bare arm and I felt my body jolt from the contact. I never stood a chance against him.

Max wasn't particularly tall or particularly good-looking in any traditional sense. He boasted an unwieldy mass of thick dark hair that he wore longer than was the fashion in those days. His face was fleshy, his nose crooked from defending his ethnicity in several East End street fights, yet there was a brightness in his eyes that I found totally alluring. He also possessed a vanity that ensured he was always smartly dressed. Except for one peculiar tic in that the corners on the collar of his shirt were constantly bent back. Even if I personally ironed them down, by the end of the evening they had flicked upwards. It was as if there was some raging heat in his upper chest that forced the collar to curl, like paper singed by a flame.

Max was extremely talented, as desperate to be picked up by a major studio as I was. By the end of our first encounter at that Soho party, he told me he had fallen madly in love with me.

'I shall write a scenario just for you,' he declared. 'It will be irresistible to the world. For it will be full of truth and passion.'

And that was what he did. He wrote the screenplay for *The Woman Walks Free*, a tense thriller about a woman charged with a revenge murder she did not commit (or did she?). The script was commissioned, Max insisted I be given an audition for the leading role with the director Cecil Benson and I got the part. The film opened to excellent reviews:

The harshest critics of the British silent film industry have consistently accused its output of being hastily assembled reels of bland and shallow rubbish compared to that of its American rivals. Well, criticise no more. Just take a stroll down to your local picture house to see Cecil Benson's The Woman Walks Free. *A taut, stylish drama with subtle and sensitive characterisation that will have you utterly engaged from start to finish. Georgina Hepburn is mesmerising in the title role. Don't miss it.* (The Stage)

Georgina Hepburn electrifies the screen in The Woman Walks Free. *Move over Lillian Gish. Watch your back Mary Pickford. A new star is born on this side of the Atlantic.* (Picturegoer)

Directed by Cecil Benson and based on a scenario by Max Rosen, The Woman Walks Free *is brought to life by the stunning performance of Georgina Hepburn. Recommended.* (Kinematograph)

I even made it into the gossip pages of *The Tatler*:

Ivor Novello, star of The Lodger, *and Georgina Hepburn, who has been lauded for her debut success in* The Woman Walks Free, *seen here together at Royal Ascot with her beau, the scenarist, Max Rosen. Rumours abound that the happy threesome will be working together in Alfred Hitchcock's next drama but for the time being it is the thrills of the Sport of Kings that attract.*

I may have been denied the opportunity to play opposite Novello in *The Lodger* but I did get to mingle with him socially since he and I shared the same studio. On the day of the races, he came to collect us in a chauffeur-driven limousine. What a handsome, dapper and charming man he was. His success in *The Lodger* was just the icing on the cake of an already successful career as a songwriter, his popularity firmly assured by his song *Keep the Home Fires Burning* which had been the soldiers' anthem of the Great War. He was courteous, generous and attentive to both Max and I on that day. We had our own private box where lunch and afternoon tea were served and the champagne was free flowing. Novello showed me how to place a bet and I actually won. To this day, I even remember the name of the horse. *My True Destiny.* It was one of those days that seemed to be sprinkled with magic dust, the conversation sparkled, luck sparkled, I sparkled. That was until Max and I were driven home in the studio limousine. Feeling quite drunk on all the champagne, cosseted in the luxury of the leather seats, I tried to snuggle up to him. But he pushed me away.

'What's wrong?' I asked.

He didn't answer.

'It's been such a wonderful day,' I said. 'Don't spoil it.'

'Wonderful day? How can you say such a thing? When all we have done is condone the behaviour of the capitalist elite?'

'We had a day at the races, Max. Don't turn everything into a class war.'

'Everything is a class war,' he said.

'Well, I had a lovely time.'

'Gulping down champagne with Novello and the rest of the bourgeoisie.'

'I think you are confusing your politics with your jealousy.' I regretted these last words as soon as they had come out of my mouth.

'What's that supposed to mean?' he snapped.

'Novello was just being attentive. He's like that with everyone.'

'His eyes. They were all over you.' Max grabbed my upper arm, squeezed it tight till it hurt.

'Stop it,' I hissed. I looked through the glass partition to the driver but his attention was firmly on the road.

'I will stop it when you promise you won't do that again.'

'Do what, Max? I didn't do anything.'

He kept on squeezing until my eyes teared but I was determined not to cry out.

'You made a fool out of me. That's what you did.' He pushed me away so hard that I fell over on my side, hitting my head against the door handle. I don't know if I was knocked unconscious or not but the next thing I remember was Max's arms wrapped around me, his fingers running lightly over the burgeoning bruise on my forehead, his mouth next to my ear as he cried: 'I'm sorry, Georgie, I'm sorry, I'm sorry. Forgive me. Please forgive me.'

'Get off of me.'

He did as I asked and I pushed myself upright until we were back sitting side by side, our bodies no longer touching. We stayed like that for a few moments, waiting for our breathing to subside, considering all that had just happened.

'I didn't mean it,' he said, his voice calmer now. 'Forgive me.'

I stared out of the window at the dull streets of London, all the sparkle drained out of my day. 'Just let me be,' I said.

That was Max. He pretended everything was political when really it was personal. He was at odds with the world and he was at odds with himself. He complained about what he called "the system", yet at the same time he craved the success of his scenarios within it.

I remember another instance when our film's director, Cecil Benson, took us to dinner at *Boulestin,* the newly opened French restaurant in Covent Garden. I was terrified of the occasion, I had never been in such an expensive and exquisitely designed restaurant before. The place was peopled with socialites, aristocrats and minor royals, the murals were painted by famous artists, the chef was French, the food was French, the menu was written in French. I was also anxious as to how Max would behave but he seemed to be in his element. As French was a language he knew well, he took care of ordering both the food and the wine. The dishes were nothing like I had ever tasted before. Salmon pie, sautéed tomatoes and peppers, woodcock cooked in its own juices, pancakes flavoured with liqueurs. By the time dessert was finished we were quite drunk and Max was in an ebullient mood.

'What do you have for us next?' Cecil asked. Our director was one of those upper-class, privileged, languid, horsey-faced toffs Max usually hated.

'Revolution,' Max said rather too loudly. 'With my dear Georgie at the heart of it.'

Cecil laughed uncomfortably. 'What do you mean? Revolution?'

'It is time we brought real politics to the screen, Cecil. Instead of all these English classic novels. All this Dickens and Hardy... how do you say?... poppycock. Yes, revolution.'

'And who do you intend to overthrow with these films?'

Cecil looked over at me with an indulgent smile. 'People like me?'

Max cleared the table in front of him, leaned in closer to his director. 'Listen, Cecil. I have just seen the most amazing film. *Battleship Potemkin* it is called. By a young Russian director, Sergei Eisenstein. You have heard of him?'

'I know the name,' Cecil said. 'But not his work.'

'Last week I watched a clandestine copy smuggled in from the United States. Magnificent, it is. Truly magnificent. This is what I want to do. Bring the revolution of the proletariat to the screen. In a subtle way, like Eisenstein did. A small rebellion on a battleship by the crew. But in reality a metaphor for the bigger struggle of labour against capital. I could find something similar for this country. A shipyard. A mining village perhaps. Driven by the women. By my Georgie.'

Here he put an arm around my shoulder and in an unusual display of public affection kissed me sloppily on the cheek.

'I find it amusing to think, dear Max,' Cecil said, 'that you talk of revolution of the proletariat in the most expensive restaurant in London.'

'Hah!' Max responded, throwing down his napkin like some kind of gauntlet. 'Come the revolution, and we'll all be eating in expensive restaurants like this.'

Again that was Max. Full of paradoxes. Which meant he could be generous when he didn't have the means to be and he could be mean when he should have had the sense to be generous. And why did I put up with his behaviour? For he brought to our relationship a passion that excited me. He made me feel we were players at the forefront of great change. And for a brief moment we were. The world was a blank canvas after the war, the old ways had been defeated, a new generation was taking over. We were revolutionaries. Iconoclastic. It wasn't just the film world with Eisenstein, Hitchcock, Novello, Chaplin, Keaton, Fritz Lang, Mary Pickford, Lilian Gish and King Vidor. Everything was changing. Art. Music. Literature. Women. There was Picasso, Chagall, DH Lawrence, TS Eliot,

Joyce, Hemingway, Tolstoy, Kafka, Stravinsky, Magritte and Virginia Woolf. There was jazz with Duke Ellington, Bessie Smith and Louis Armstrong. Women were throwing away their corsets, cutting their hair short and raising their hemlines. It was a glorious time to be young.

Chapter Eleven

Sleepless in Highgate

Laura couldn't sleep. Georgie Hepburn. Perhaps she had been too tipsy to remember the conversation correctly. Georgie Hepburn. She had only drunk two glasses of wine. Although they were quite large ones and possibly a glass of Cristal on entering, then there had been the half bottle with Victoria in the afternoon. Georgie Hepburn. She had adored her, had been obsessed by her, had even sent her a fan letter once, she must have been about sixteen at the time. Nobody really knew that much about her then, so overshadowed had she been by that egotistical bastard of a husband. Georgie Hepburn. She was her secret heroine when everyone else was going for Plath. When all her girlfriends (and some men too) preferred a beautiful brooding poet who'd stuck her head in the oven to a strong and brave woman who hadn't.

She turned to one side, then the other until she ended up in a strangle of duvet and sheets, her legs moving restlessly. She switched on to her back, stared up at the ceiling, tried to recall the conversation with Sal.

'Yes, of course, I know Georgie Hepburn,' she had told him. Sal was staring out towards the lit-up garden with the occasional draw on his cigar, the aroma making her giddy with memories of not just her father, but other men too. 'I had a teenage crush on her,' she said. 'I just wanted to be her.'

'What did you like about her?'

'Her courage. Her willingness to be different. Her authenticity.'

'Ah yes, her authenticity. *The line that goes straight from one's heart to one's art*. Her words, of course.'

'And her integrity,' Laura added. 'Or as Georgie would call it *à la* Hemingway: *authenticity under pressure*.' She had spoken somewhat wistfully, this talk of Georgie reminding her how far she had strayed recently from her own teenage ambitions.

'What makes you think she had integrity?' Sal asked.

'You can see it in her work, the way she led her life.'

'But you don't really know, do you?'

'What does anyone really know about anyone else?'

'I'm a documentary film maker. It's my job to find out.'

'But how do you know they are telling the truth? Maybe someone is fabricating a diary in the hope some day it will be used for posterity.' She had raised her coffee cup to him then in a mock toast and delivered the words: 'I'm not going to write about my life as I've lived it, I'm going to go out there and live the damn thing as I mean to write about it.'

'Did Georgie say that?'

'No. It was a line in one of my movies. I believe it comes from a quote by the writer, André Gide.'

'It obviously resonated if you still remember it.'

'I was just showing off. That's what we actors do, Sal, pluck memorised lines out of thin air to make an impression.'

'Well, you've succeeded,' Sal chuckled, blew another breath of cigar smoke into the night. 'It seems we're on the same page with Georgie, Laura. I didn't write her any fan letters but I did get to meet her once.'

'Oh, please tell.'

'It must have been over thirty years ago now, not long before she died, I was just fresh out of film school. My mentor, a guy called Philip Oswald, wanted to make a documentary about her, so we came over to London to meet her. We thought we'd have to drive up to some little village in Oxfordshire – by that time Georgie had moved in with her god-daughter – but she absolutely insisted she would come down to meet us in London. As long as we treated her to afternoon tea at The Savoy. I always thought it was slightly odd for her to do that. After all, she was about eighty and had to take the train all that way to London in the middle of winter, but she said it was a private gesture to herself. "What is life without these little gestures?" she told us. So afternoon tea at The Savoy it was. Phil did all the talking, I just sat to the side, sipping my tea, stuffing myself with cakes, listening in awe. She'd been a bit of a recluse for most of her later life but was beginning to come out of her shell by the time we met her. She gave us a tentative nod to go ahead with the project but by the time we got any sniff of proper finance, she'd passed away.'

'But you're back doing research on her now?'

'Yeah. I've decided I'd like to produce a one-woman play of her life. Then I'd film it in such a way so that I can present it as a documentary as well.'

'It's long overdue, I'd say.'

Sal ceased his contemplation of the garden, turned to face her, looked at her straight. His eyes were turquoise like Navajo stones. 'I'd like you to play Georgie,' he said.

'Me? Georgie Hepburn?'

'Yeah. I've had you in mind from the beginning. Apart from your obvious competence as an actor, I've always thought you looked a bit like her. I'm sure we can age you up and down to cover her whole adult life from the silent movie days onwards.'

Laura gripped the patio rail. She was actually finding it hard to breathe. 'I'm flattered,' was all she could manage.

'Well, why don't you think about it?' He handed her his card. 'It would be good to hear from you or your agent in the next few days. If it's something you might contemplate in principle, then we can talk details.'

Sal disappeared back into the house after that, having remarked it was becoming a bit chilly for his Californian bones. She said she would remain for a few minutes, it was such a beautiful night. She stared at the stars, waited until she had calmed then left the party as quickly as she could.

Georgie Hepburn. It was too good to be true. After her TV cameos and the crab voice-over, after the acceptance of all the other parts she shouldn't have been accepting, here was a chance to regain her self-respect. Her authenticity. That straight line from heart to art.

She raised herself from her bed, put on her robe, picked up a lipstick from the dresser, walked along to the kitchen where she circled yesterday's date on the calendar in thick red. The day her life changed. Dumped by her agent in the morning, offered dream role by nightfall. 'Eat your heart out, Edy Weinberg – I'm going to revive my career without you.' She made herself a cup of strong coffee, went to her study, powered up her computer, sat down to Google Sal Yerksaw.

There was a short Wikipedia entry. Born Bakersfield, California, three year older than she, father worked in an ice cream plant, mother a nurse, graduated USC School of Cinematic Arts, documentary film maker, theatre producer, married to Dominique Beaumont (Damn! It wasn't as if she was particularly interested in him but the potential would have been nice), two children, film credits:

Children of the Exile (1992): documentary short (directed) – nominated – California Critics Award

The Wind Chasers (1998): documentary (directed and produced) – won – Frankfurt Film Festival

Solly, Molly and Me (2005): documentary (directed and produced) – nominated – Montreal Film Critics Association; nominated – BAFTA

No Profit Under the Sun (2009): play (produced for Sal Yerksaw Productions) – won – Paul Washington Award for Best Emerging Production Company

No Talking Please, We're British (in production): documentary (directed and produced).

She went back into the kitchen to find her evening bag, to retrieve his business card. *Sal Yerksaw Productions*. She would send him an email. Not right now. Christ, it was four in the morning. She would just compose it, then save the draft for later, just so she could get all the excitement out of her system, get back to sleep. After a few attempts, she managed.

Dear Sal

It was great to meet you last night. I always enjoy these evenings at Caroline's – she is such a warm and generous host. It was also wonderful to connect with a fellow Georgie Hepburn fan.

I very quickly wanted to come back to you about your suggestion that I should play her in a film/play about her life. I'm sure you know what it is like in this business but were we just having a casual after-dinner conversation or does your proposal still stand? If it does, I would most definitely like to chat some more. Are you still in London? Perhaps we could meet for coffee. Laura

She re-read it, then satisfied with its tone and content, without thinking she pressed 'Send'. She was half-way along the corridor to her bedroom, still cursing herself for her stupid error when she heard the 'ping' announcing she had mail.

Chapter Twelve

The Hepburn Archives

Extract from an unpublished memoir

The day after my trip to Royal Ascot I received a telegram from Hubert Hoffstetter, a big-time Hollywood producer at Montgomery Studios, requesting a meeting the following day at the Savoy Hotel. Max wanted to come with me but I chose to go on my own. I was still feeling raw from our fight in the limousine.

I arrived at the Savoy just before three o'clock, posed for the usual snapshots at the entrance, it seemed the various London newspapers have photographers stationed there solely for the purpose. I expected we would be having afternoon tea in the Thames Foyer or perhaps a cocktail in the American Bar but there was a message waiting for me to attend Mr Hoffstetter in his suite. I took the electric lift to the third floor and knocked on the door.

Hubert was a skinny man with a skinny moustache, wearing a double-breasted jacket that dwarfed his thin frame. His hair was sparse too and his face shone with sweat. He introduced himself, asked me to call him Hub which I thought was a ridiculous name, then led me through to an ornate sitting room. Hub was not alone. To the rear of the room sat another gentleman, perhaps in his late sixties, tanned, bald, smooth-faced, dressed in a light suit, hands clasped atop his cane. I was not introduced to this person who merely dipped his head graciously at my entrance. I discovered later that he was Mr Montgomery himself. Hub asked me to sit down, offered coffee, tea, sandwiches and cakes from a trolley, all of which I declined. I was too nervous to eat or drink anything and I was getting more nervous by the second. Hub passed me a sheet of paper.

'I wonder if you could read from this,' he said. 'Please project your voice as you do so.'

The words were swimming in front of me at this point but I did what I had been trained to do, breathed into the pit of my abdomen, forced myself not to rush, focused on the text in front of me. It was a menu from the Savoy Grill.

'Go on,' said Hub.

I looked over to Mr Montgomery but he was just sitting there, resting on his cane with his eyes closed.

I did as I was told.

'Soups: Petite Marmite. Consomme Julienne. Cream of Tomato. Hare Soup.

Fish: Northern Trout in a Shrimp Sauce. Halibut in a Hollandaise Sauce. Oyster Patties.

Meats: Roast Sirloin and Ribs of Beef. Roast Turkey and Sausage. Roast Leg of Pork and Apple Sauce. Ox Tongue.

Vegetables: Brussel Sprouts. Potatoes au Gratin. Mashed Potatoes. French Beans...'

Hub put up a hand to stop me, glanced back at Mr Montgomery who nodded.

'Miss Hepburn,' Hub said quite loudly. Considering I was seated only a few feet in front of him, I assumed the raised voice was for Mr Montgomery's benefit. 'Great changes are on the horizon for the movie business. You have probably heard the rumours about "the talkies" over here in Great Britain and I can confirm that the rumours are true. The first feature-length talking motion picture is about to grace our screens in the form of a musical called *The Jazz Singer*. It has been produced by one of our great rivals, Warner Brothers. Congratulations to them for heralding in this new era. In a few years, the silent movie industry will cease to exist. But Montgomery Studios are not to be left behind, will not be left behind. Do you understand, Miss Hepburn?'

Although the question had been addressed to me, Hub had turned to Mr Montgomery who again nodded from his far corner. Hub seemed pleased, returned his attention back to me.

'Montgomery Studios has been very impressed by your performance in *The Woman Walks Free*. However, as you can imagine, actors and actresses will no longer be able to rely solely on their good looks and facial gestures for their success. Fortunately, we are glad to hear that your voice comes across as very pleasant to our American ears. At Montgomery Studios we believe that a British accent could make a very distinct contribution towards gaining the attention of American audiences. For these reasons, we would therefore like to offer you a three year contract with Montgomery Studios over in Hollywood.' Hub produced a briefcase from beside his armchair and extracted what I assumed was the contract. 'As you will see, our terms are most generous.'

I was not able to see as he did not hand over the papers. Instead, he held them back and added: 'However, there are a number of conditions we have not entered specifically into the contract.'

I asked what they were.

'We would like you to use the first name "Georgie" instead of "Georgina".'

I told him that would not be a problem. 'My family and friends call me "Georgie" anyway.'

'I'm afraid we don't like the surname "Hepburn" either. This combination of the "p" and "b", it works as a kind of stumbling block, it doesn't run off the tongue.' Hub licked his lips with said tongue, then pronounced my name, enunciating it as two very strong and separate syllables. "Hep... Burn. We need something classy but snappy as well.'

'What are you suggesting?'

'We have made a list. You can let us know which you prefer. We would have the final say, of course.'

At this point, Mr Montgomery rose on his cane and both Hub and I watched as the elderly gentleman slowly removed himself into an adjoining room. Hub did not seem any more relaxed for the departure although I certainly was.

'What do you say, Miss Hepburn? About the name change?'

'I am not particularly happy about it. But I suppose I could take a look at the list.'

'There is one final matter.'

'And what might that be?'

Hub's moustache twitched as he sucked in a breath through his yellowish teeth. 'My employer would like you to join him in the bedroom.'

Chapter Thirteen

Heading South

The arrangement was to meet south of the river in a coffee shop near Borough Market. She should order a taxi from her usual private hire firm, the charge would be on Sal's dime as he put it. He wanted to be that side of the river, closer to Victoria Station and the train back to Brighton, it would give them more time to talk.

Growing up in north London, Laura rarely used to cross the Thames. All the action in those days had been in the centre of the metropolis. Soho, Oxford Street, Carnaby Street, Leicester Square, Shaftesbury Avenue, the National Gallery, the British Museum. Who ever went south? Then came her interest in the cinema with the National Film Theatre (now the British Film Institute), then the Southbank Centre, then Tate Modern, the Millennium Bridge, the refurbishment of Borough Market and it felt as if the whole city was slipping southwards. She never went to the centre anymore. That was for tourists, politicians, civil servants and the Royal Family.

Sal was waiting for her inside at a table by a large open window. The whole place still boasted the original wood, stacks of jute sacks, the air thick with the smell of roasted beans. She wondered if you could get a caffeine hit from the aroma alone. Sal certainly looked as if he could do with a cup, his face washed out with tiredness under his tan. He stood up on her arrival, held out his hand when she would have expected him to kiss her cheek. She sat down and they ordered.

'So here we are,' she said, trying to find a space for her bag somewhere. She couldn't believe how nervous she was. Eventually, she slung it over the back of her chair.

'Yeah, I'm really glad you're interested in doing this. As I said last night, you're my first choice.'

'And as I said last night, I'm flattered. Did you stay on long at Caroline's?'

'Long enough for Fredrik to tell me when I might die.'

'You probably should tell me then since we might be working together.'

'According to him, I should live past eighty. Apparently Californian males do quite well on the life expectancy stakes provided we don't get killed in an earthquake. Or take our own lives. It seems suicide is the biggest cause of death in The Golden State. It must be all that healthy living pushing us over the edge.'

'Or all those rejected screenplays.'

Sal laughed at that and she finally felt herself beginning to relax. The waiter also arrived with their coffees. She took a quick sip. Too strong. She could be blabbering away in a couple of minutes on a caffeine buzz if she wasn't careful. 'So what's the plan?' she asked.

Sal scratched the back of his neck. Something ursine in the way he moved his body, she thought. As if he might wrap his big arms around her, protect her. It was a comforting thought. This big white-haired, blue-eyed bear come to save her career.

'There is, of course, a lot of stuff about Georgie out there in the public domain,' he said. 'And one really crap unauthorised biography that came out just after she died. However, what I want to do is to tell her story entirely through source material. Letters, diary entries, notebooks, interviews. And of course, there must be the photographs. As many as we can get our hands on. The whole stage plastered with her photographs. Georgie's story in her own words and pictures. *Georgie by Georgie.* I fancy that as the title of the play too.'

'I assume you have access to all this material.'

Sal produced one of his sloppy smiles. 'Actually I don't. Up until now, hardly anyone has. Her literary estate has been fiercely guarded by the trustee.'

'Who is that?'

'A certain Quentin Holloway. He's one of Georgie's cousins. Second or first once removed, I've never really understood these things. The simplest way I can put it is that Georgie's mother and Quentin's grandmother were sisters. Margaret and Ginny.'

'And why has this Quentin been so protective?'

'No idea. It could be the terms of Georgie's will. It could be he's just bloody-minded.'

'I see. What about finance?'

'Nothing in place yet. I thought I'd wait until I gained access to her literary estate before I started hunting down investors.'

Laura gave a short laugh that hid her disappointment. 'So basically you have no source material... and no finance. What about people who actually knew her?'

'Not many left I'm afraid. And those that are still alive are being just as protective as Quentin.'

'That doesn't sound helpful.'

'There is me, of course. I did get to meet her all those years ago.'

'An account of afternoon tea at The Savoy is probably not enough to create *Georgie by Georgie*.'

'Probably not. Getting hold of the source material is paramount.'

'So we're back to square one.'

Sal leaned forward, placed his hand over hers. A gentle, reassuring touch. 'Look,' he said. 'I can see you're beginning to doubt me. But I've got a lot of experience putting these kinds of projects together.'

'I'm sure you have. I just assumed you might be a little bit further along with it.'

'I do have you.'

'What's that supposed to mean?'

'Well, I thought if you and I both went to meet with the reluctant Quentin Holloway, you might be able to charm him into giving us the access we need.'

Chapter Fourteen

I had been renting a room in a flat in Pimlico which I shared with a young woman called Lucy. She worked as a secretary in a lawyer's office, she had a fiancé somewhere across Vauxhall Bridge just south of the river. Apart from dropping in to collect her post or staying over when her parents were in town, I hardly ever saw her. It was an arrangement that suited my relationship with Max who could come and go as he pleased.

On that evening when I returned shaken and angry from my audition at the Savoy, Max was sitting with his typewriter at the kitchen table. He had a habit of attacking his work – his shirtsleeves rolled up, his eyes close in to the paper feed, his forehead a deep trench of clenched lines, his fingers tapping away aggressively on the keyboard. But even thus engrossed in his writing, he quickly realised something was wrong. I told him what had happened at the hotel.

'This is not good,' he said, running a hand back through his thick hair. 'Not good at all.'

'Of course it isn't good. Montgomery Studios was my ticket to America. A career in the talkies.'

'For me too.'

'Yes, for you too,' I said, although to be honest with myself, I wasn't sure if I envisaged Max as part of that future.

Perhaps he sensed my misgivings for he returned to his typewriter, lifted his hands above the keys in readiness, then paused before saying with a snarl of bitterness. 'You only use me.'

'Please don't start with this again.'

'Why not?'

'I've been frightened and humiliated today, Max. This is not the time.'

'Not the time? So it is up to me to make all the time? To write these fabulous scenes. Just for you. Fabulous, fabulous scenes.' He ripped out the sheet of paper from the typewriter, scrunched it into a ball, threw it at me. 'Here. Take it.'

'Stop it, Max.'

'Ah yes, Georgina Hepburn, the glamorous star. What will be my next great scenario for you?'

'I don't want a fight.'

Max sat back from his typewriter, glowered at me. 'You should have gone into the bedroom with him. That is what you should have done.'

'What are you saying?'

'You heard me. You should have slept with Montgomery.'

'I can't believe you said that.'

'And I can't believe you didn't do what you were asked. One time. One little time. That's all. Why the big fuss?'

'You're just trying to hurt me.'

'It is you who are hurting me with all this selfishness.'

'You want me to behave like some kind of prostitute?'

'What is it you think you are doing with me?'

I started yelling at him and he yelled back. The upstairs neighbours banged on their floor for us to shut up. Words were thrown around that should never have been said. I slapped him across the face. Max didn't respond physically, possibly chastened by his behaviour in the limousine. Instead, his punishment came in the form of verbal abuse, often in a language I did not understand. I broke down sobbing. Max went back to attack his typewriter. I slept in Lucy's room that night, in the morning he was gone. He left a note on the kitchen table.

Dear Georgie,
Under the circumstances, I think it is better we stop seeing each other.
    [Signed] Max

'Under the circumstances'. That's what he wrote. He didn't even have the courage to actually tell me directly. A piece of paper left on the kitchen table. A few spartan words, completely devoid of emotion. From a bloody scenario writer. Under the circumstances! What circumstances? Fear, that's what. Frightened of being tainted by the same brush as me. And he was probably right in that respect. To this day, I have no idea what Montgomery or that little weasel of a procurer Hub told everyone about me but their power, influence and reach turned out to be immense. I could not believe how fast they managed to erect this giant wall of rejection in front of me. Hollywood. All the London studios. My film career was over just like that.

Even as I write this all these years later, I realise the anger I have against the studio has never gone away. In fact, as the years have passed, as the stature of women in our society has increased, as my own sense of self-esteem has improved, my disgust at what I was asked to do has accumulated accordingly. But as for Max, devastated as I was that he should abandon me when I really needed him, over time I have become more forgiving. I used to think we were in love, but looking back I see it was our shared ambition that welded us together rather than any profound feelings we had for each other. We used each other, we were hurt by each other and we hurt each other back. We fought constantly and I used to mistake the intensity of these arguments for the intensity of our love.

In the aftermath of my run-in with Montgomery Studios, Max suffered an immediate setback when he was dropped from consideration for the next Hitchcock movie. But he didn't do too badly after that. He was soon signed up to the Cricklewood Studios then moved on to Pinewood where he wrote for some very successful films. I heard he was offered a contract in Hollywood sometime in the mid-Thirties but that he turned it down. He probably thought it was too late by then, his inner light had dimmed, the roots of his career firmly established in this country. And then the war would have intervened.

I never managed to distance myself totally from him, how could I? Under the circumstances. We still had a couple of mutual friends who would pass on information from time to time. He stayed on in London, I learned he had married, a woman called Mabel, she was a secretary at Pinewood ten years his junior, they purchased a house in Twickenham. They didn't have any children. Poor Max, he so wanted to be a father. And I never let him be one. For years after we broke up, I used to linger in the picture house at the end of a film to see if his name appeared among the credits.

Chapter Fifteen

Come on Down to Chipping Something

Sal came to pick her up from her Highgate flat. He prowled around the place like some upmarket estate agent, poking his head into this room and that room, his large frame making the space seem even smaller, until he could eventually stretch out in the garden area.

'Pretty,' he said, standing over by the pond. 'I like carp.'

'Pink Floyd used to live here,' Laura said, wondering whether her discarded mobile was visible through the green slime. 'At least, that's what the previous owner told me. Although I think he meant just one of the band and the rest came round to play. I'm not sure I believed him anyway. Although it's exciting to think *Dark Side of the Moon* might have been written here.'

'I'm sure one day the realtor will say Laura Scott lived here.'

'Perhaps I'll get a blue plaque from English Heritage.'

'I don't understand…'

'It doesn't matter. I think you have to be dead for about a hundred years to get one anyway.'

She led him through the side gate to the front of the house where a yellow sports car awaited her. The roof was down even though the weather was neither particularly warm or sunny.

'Porsche,' he said. 'Rented for the day. I thought we should make an impression.'

'I'd better fetch a scarf then.'

She didn't particularly like sports cars, they were too close to the ground causing her to feel every lurch, jerk, speed bump and pothole as they drove through the streets of north London. Sal didn't look too comfortable either crammed into the driver's seat. But once they were out on the M40 (or the open highway as Sal called it), heading towards Oxford with the engine growling nicely, the sun finally coming out to warm up the day, she found herself relishing the experience.

'Where are we going exactly?' she asked.

'Cotswolds' he said. 'Near Chipping something or other. Funny names you got here.'

'You mean like Schenectady and Poughkeepsie,' she countered, throwing her head back in exaggerated laughter. It was amazing what an open sports car, a handsome driver and a sunny day could do for her mood. She felt like Grace Kelly in *To Catch a Thief* except she was the passenger rather than the driver. She looked across at Sal with his designer sunglasses, his white hair blown back in the wind, drumming his fingers on the leather-clad steering wheel to the beat of some muttered tune. No Cary Grant, but he'd do.

'All these pretty little villages,' Sal said as they meandered through another narrow street lined with ivy covered cottages. 'Reminds me of the England of my filmic youth.'

'I think they make most English people nostalgic for their filmic youth. Hardly any locals can afford to live in these places anymore.'

They stopped for lunch just outside Oxford at a delightful pub with a terrace out by the river. She knew she had been recognised almost as soon as they stepped through the door, she could sense the current of excitement as the information passed throughout the room, the murmured: 'Isn't that...?' 'She's the one from...' 'Look who it is...' from the staff and the other customers. She had to admit to being glad of the attention. *Tokyo Winter* had gone straight to DVD without being released here, *The Bentleys* had taken off worldwide but had been shunted out to a late-night spot on Channel 4, so it had been seven or eight years since she'd done anything high profile in this country. People probably thought she was dead. She sucked in a breath, grabbed Sal's arm, led him straight through the bar area and out to the terrace where a table was hastily being prepared with proper linen.

'I'd forgotten what it feels like to be out with someone famous,' he said as they settled in their chairs.

She wanted to ask who those other "someone famous"

persons might have been but instead said: 'And what does it feel like?'

'Privileged and intoxicating,' he replied.

'Some men find it threatening.'

'Then they have no right to be with you.'

'I'll drink to that.' She ordered a gin and tonic from the owner who had presented himself at their table instead of a waiter. Sal went for mineral water then ordered a steak. 'Blood red raw,' he added.

'Last time I was in California,' she said, 'everyone was into blueberries and black rice.'

'To hell with all that crap. I've just been told I'm going to live till I'm over eighty.'

Laura ordered a poached salmon salad. 'Tell me about Quentin,' she said.

Sal bent down, pulled out a folder from his satchel, passed it over.

'Very professional,' she noted.

'I'm a documentary film maker. Research is what I do. Or at least what my paid researcher does.'

She opened up the file. A photograph of Quentin Holloway was pinned to the inside cover. She glanced at Sal's notes – age 51 – then back to the face. Quentin boasted a full head of (presumably) dyed blonde hair with a schoolboy parting on his left. Clean-shaven, blotchy skin, very thin lips so that his mouth cut meanly like a short scar across the lower part of his face. What struck her the most though was just how small his eyes were. Little wrinkle-free pin-holes that made it difficult to even know what colour they were.

'Do you think he's had Botox?' she asked. 'There are absolutely no lines around the eyes.'

'What do I know about such things?'

'I thought everyone in LA had something done.'

'Well, I haven't.'

'I didn't mean to…' She returned her attention to the photograph. Quentin was wearing a cravat. When was the last time she'd seen someone wear one of those. 'What does he do?'

'I believe he's an art critic.'

'Is that an actual job?'

'It just means he's a wealthy guy with an opinion on all the paintings he's inherited.'

'Is that where the money's from then? Inheritance?'

'Seems like it.'

She resisted taking out her glasses, handed back the folder. 'Just tell me what's in it.'

'Quentin's grandparents, Richard and Virginia, owned a farm with a lot of acreage in Sussex, since sold and split among their three children – Oliver, Percy and the youngest, Quentin's mother, Susan. Susan was married to a very successful financier. Kenneth Holloway. They divorced decades ago. As part of the settlement, she got the place we're driving to now.'

'How do you know all of this?'

Sal raised his eyes in disbelief at her question.

'Sorry,' she said.

Sal went on: 'Susan was also Georgie's god-daughter.'

'Is she still alive?'

'She died four years ago which is a pity for us as she and Georgie were very close. I believe Susan was the sole heir to Georgie's estate and that is why Quentin as her only child ended up as trustee. When I emailed him about meeting up, he replied straight away. Very terse. Like a telegram. *Afternoon tea at Witney Manor. Come on down.*'

'He actually wrote that? Come on down.'

Chapter Sixteen

Extract from an unpublished memoir

I never told anyone except Max about what happened that afternoon at the Savoy Hotel. Throughout my life, it was certainly an episode I tried to forget, some may even say suppress. Many years later when I was being interviewed on a programme for BBC Radio, the presenter, Sir Peter Delaware, asked me why my silent movie career had come to such an abrupt end. I was tempted to tell him then and there. But what was the point? Montgomery was long dead and his studios were defunct. What was to be gained from such a disclosure so late in my life. The truth will be revealed in these memoirs when I myself am gone and my ashes have been scattered across the earth. Until then, whenever I have an opportunity, I stay at The Savoy or enjoy an afternoon tea there. It is my private indulgence and a personal act of defiance.

But sometimes when I hark back to the past as I shuffle towards the end of my days, I wonder – was Max right? Should I have slept with Montgomery? Of course, it would have been morally wrong to do such a thing. But perhaps I should have taken the pragmatic course and compromised my body and my integrity for the sake of my career. Many other aspiring actresses who have gone before and after me have succumbed to such an offer. Where would I have ended up if I too had agreed? As a glamorous star of the Golden Age of Hollywood? As a wartime pin-up? Or as an old hag tormented and disappointed by the follies of her youthful ambition? What is certain is that these moments of decision in a person's life are absolutely crucial. They might come along a mere three or four times in your entire existence. And they will come mainly when you are young. Should I marry this or that person?

Should I live here or there? Should I take that job offer or not? Perhaps like mine it will be a moral choice. Should I fight or flee? Should I speak up or keep quiet? Should I kill or be killed? The decisions you make will forever define who you are. Or the kind of person you aspire to be. The rest of your life is merely coping with the consequences.

Now that Max had left me and I was *persona non grata* as far as all the film studios were concerned, it was to my Aunt Ginny that I turned. If truth be told, I probably loved her more than my own mother, a feeling that always made me feel guilty. But it was hard to recall a moment when I actually felt my mother loved me. Certainly not after my father died. I do remember how she used to teach me things and while there was probably love buried somewhere in these lessons, I felt her efforts were executed more out of duty than any motherly affection.

It was different with Aunt Ginny. Even as I write this, I immediately recall that day we spent together in Brighton after going to see my first film appearance in *On the Pleasure Pier*. How she bought me ice cream, ordered me to take off my shoes so we could walk barefoot on the pebbled beach. Aunt Ginny, so modern, so positive, so independent, so supportive. Always sending me money at every opportunity, here a postal order, there a postal order. For my birthday, for Christmas, for 'just because'. Aunt Ginny on her farm with the horses. Aunt Ginny driving her automobile. Aunt Ginny my saviour, my confidante. Aunt Ginny more like my older sister than my aunt.

I used to marvel how effortlessly she embraced the traditional values of marriage and parenthood but somehow did so in a modern way. It was easy to forget she was a mother and wife at all within that all-male environment of hers. The boys were away most of the time at boarding school while Uncle Richard hovered away happily in the background like some kind of wraith, not capable of being touched or making an impression. He hardly spoke and when he did it was never in an attempt to engage conversation but merely the passing on of information in that inexpressive, matter-of-fact voice of his:

'Going out to the far field. Fence needs fixing.'

'Milking time.'

'Driving over to Loxley for some feed.'

'The tractor. No oil in the hydraulics. Disaster.'

'Early start tomorrow. Lambing.'

'Scraped knee. Broken finger. Boys will be boys, Ginny.'

I was never quite sure what Aunt Ginny saw in him. He was quite good-looking though in that well-built, well-spoken, fair-haired, florid complexion kind of way, like the captain of some English sports team. Perhaps Ginny had just married him for the money. Or for the protection. Or for the independence. While Uncle Richard got on with running the farm, he left her to manage the house and raise the children. Which was just as well, under the circumstances.

The Hepburn Archives

Letter from Mrs Virginia (Ginny) Williams to her niece
Georgina Hepburn dated 10th March 1928

Dear Georgie

I am absolutely delighted this new baby is a girl. Richard though remains unflustered by her arrival. Now that he already has two boys under his belt, he says I can do absolutely anything I want with a female of the species. I am therefore going to call her Susan, even though I know he has a preference for Ethel (such an old-fashioned name, don't you think?). I will spoil her as much as I can before I teach her to be a strong, independent woman with a healthy disregard for the arrogance of men. I trust you will be in agreement with such nurturing.

Ollie and Percy are away at boarding school so they haven't seen their new sister yet. I hope they will treat her kindly as I noticed they have a certain vicious streak towards small animals around the farm. Boys can be such aggressive creatures. I am so glad I now have Susan to balance the boat.

Please don't think it inappropriate of me to ask, but I feel it would be a good idea if you were to be Susan's god-mother. I do hope you agree. However, I also hope you realise that along with acceptance comes the responsibility of attending all birthdays, religious festivals and other important family occasions. You should also expect to be sought after for your advice and expertise. As you can see, I expect you to take your role very, very seriously.

Please accept.

With much love

(Signed) Aunt Ginny

Chapter Seventeen

Quentin

'Wanna know what stinking rich sounds like?' Sal asked Laura.
'Tell me.'
'These tyres on this gravel. The crunch of untold wealth.'
They had already driven about a mile off the main road along a tarmac driveway flanked by ancient oaks, across a moat via a small wooden bridge, before arriving at a pair of impressive wrought-iron gates. There they had encountered one of those self-standing electronic intercoms into which Sal announced their names as if he were ordering a couple of Big Macs with fries. The door opened into a courtyard with a gravel path around the perimeter and at the centre a lawn mowed to within a centimetre of its roots. Off to her right, beyond a high hedge, Laura could see the wire fencing surrounding what she assumed must be tennis courts. To her right there were stables and assorted outbuildings. Sal slowed the Porsche down even more. He seemed both intimidated and enamoured by what he was seeing. This handsome mansion built from that blond Cotswold stone she so admired. The extensive grounds. The sculpted hedges. Laura didn't give a damn about such things. When confronted with such grandeur, she just imagined herself on a film set.

A solitary figure awaited them at the front of the house. Quentin Holloway. Wearing a blue, silk dressing-gown over shirt, slacks and a Paisley pattern cravat in matching blue. He skipped round to her side of the car, very graciously opened the door, held out his arm so that she could extricate herself from the passenger seat with dignity. The touch of his hand was dry and cold despite the day being warm. There was a smell of talc and lemons about him.

'*Mizz* Scott. How delightful to meet you.'
'Laura,' she said. 'Please call me Laura.'

'Laura it is.' He escorted her around the front of the car where Sal grabbed his hand and said: 'Sal Yerksaw. Magnificent place you got here.'

'It has its charms, Mr Yerksaw. The main manor house dates back to the early seventeenth century. Of course, a lot has been added since then. I can give you a tour later. Once you've settled.'

Laura was surprised to see that the interior of the house was not as grand as she had expected. The old beams were varnished and exposed but the rooms were compact, the ceilings quite low so that everything appeared slightly squashed. They were led through room after room, the décor, fittings and art work representing a mixture of the dark and antique (inherited from generations of Holloways) and the light and modern (his ex-wife's taste). They ended up in a large bright conservatory full of cream sofas and plants with a view over an outdoor swimming pool and the hills of the Cotswolds beyond.

'English or Indian?' Quentin asked.

'He means tea,' Laura explained to the perplexed Sal.

'Coffee if you got it,' he said. 'Instant is fine.'

Quentin looked offended. 'I have a machine,' he said as he pressed a bell-button in the wall. 'Laura?'

'Indian is fine.'

'Assam or Darjeeling?'

'I prefer Assam.'

'And so do I.' Quentin clapped his hands together triumphantly as if he had just formed a bond with her for life.

A young maid arrived, kitted out in a proper uniform, took the order, gave the slightest of curtsies and left. Quentin gestured for them to sit.

'So who lives here?' Sal asked, dispensing with any niceties, as he spread out his arms to claim one whole sofa for himself.

'Sadly, just me. There is a dog rustling around somewhere. I have a maid and cook who come in. A landscape company does the gardens. My ex-wife lives in Scotland. My children have jobs in other continents.'

'How many children do you have?' Laura asked.

'Just the two,' Quentin said. 'My son is a hedge fund trader in New York. My daughter digs wells somewhere in Africa. Chalk and cheese. Just like their parents.' He gave Laura a quick smile. 'I've thought about selling up. But you know how it is. I grew up in this place. It would be like dispensing with part of me. What am I saying? Dispensing with all of me. This house occupies me rather than I do it. Do you know what I mean?'

Laura had no idea what he meant. Her whole flat in Highgate could probably fit into this conservatory. 'I'd love to have a pool,' she said, thinking of the small pond in her garden. 'Especially on these warm summer days.'

The conversation stalled at this point, and Laura was grateful when the maid returned with a trolley laden with a tea service, cakes and sandwiches.

'Ah, Mary,' Quentin sighed. 'Please serve.'

Poor Mary, Laura thought. All eyes with nothing to do but be upon her as she laid out the cups and saucers, the teapots, the plates of food.

'I'll just fetch the coffee, sir,' the maid said to Sal, again with a slight curtsy. 'The machine takes time to warm up.'

With Mary gone, there was some polite chat about transport links, the best way to get here, some recent flooding, the facilities available in the nearest village, before the girl was back again with Sal's coffee, served in a silver pot, which he insisted on pouring himself. He then pulled himself into a serious crouch on the sofa, like a bedside vigilant bowed slightly in prayer. Quentin, sitting opposite, took this as a sign to push himself up straight in his own armchair. Battle was about to commence, Laura thought.

Sal looked up from his clasped hands. 'You know why we are here,' he said.

'My lawyer told me. You wish access to the Hepburn estate. But for what purpose?'

Sal outlined his plans for the one-woman play and accompanying documentary. 'Starring the beautiful Laura Scott,' he added.

Both men looked at her at this point as if to check she was still beautiful. They appeared to nod to each other in some kind of masculine pact. She didn't know whether to be angry or flattered. Instead, she took a sip of her Assam. She would harbour her grievances for later.

'So what papers do you need?' Quentin asked.

'Everything.'

'Everything?' Quentin's tiny eyes widened in his otherwise expressionless face. He's definitely had surgery, Laura thought.

'Yeah. Whatever you got.'

'I possess a substantial archive,' Quentin said stiffly. 'Letters, notebooks, tapes, transcripts and so on. Thousands of photographs, of course. I've documented everything myself over the last thirty years. A task I took upon myself after Aunt Georgie passed away.'

'Your aunt?' Laura said.

'That's what I would call her,' he said, his tone immediately softening for her. 'Technically she was my elderly cousin but we always knew her as Aunt Georgie.' He then turned his attention back to Sal. 'I certainly cannot give you access to all of the estate.'

'Why not?' Sal asked.

Quentin visibly recoiled then in a raised voice he said: 'Because I don't want every...' He paused to search for probably the least offensive word. 'Every Tom, Dick and Harry to exploit her memory. She was very precious to me. Very precious to the whole family.'

Sal tried on one of his sloppy smiles. 'Well, I'm not every Tom, Dick and Harry. I am a serious documentarist. I would be preserving rather than exploiting her legacy. She was very precious to a lot of people.'

'That may well be but...'

'I met her once, you know. Must have been not long before she died. The Savoy, London. My boss wanted to do a documentary about her back then. She seemed to be up for it...'

'Up for it?' Quentin exclaimed. 'Up for it? I doubt that. She was probably just humouring you. Anyway, a documentary when she was alive to monitor the content is very different from allowing you *carte blanche* to an archive I have taken years to assemble.'

'You've allowed access to some of this material before.'

'That is true. But only a few letters. For academic purposes. To clear up some discrepancy in matters between Georgie and her late husband.'

'You mean Douglas. Uncle Doug.'

'He was most definitely not Uncle Doug.'

Sal sighed, sat back on the sofa, looked across at Laura. *Now it's your turn,* his eyes seemed to say.

'This tea is delicious,' she commented to no-one in particular.

'It comes exclusively from the Numalighur estate,' Quentin said. 'It was Aunt Georgie's favourite too.'

'You must tell me where I can buy some.'

'I am happy to give you a few packets when you leave. It would be my pleasure.'

'That is very kind of you,' she said. She laid down her cup and saucer, rose to her feet, walked over to the window, stared out across the countryside. How quintessentially English she thought. The rolling landscape. The church spires. The cultivated fields divided up by their stone walls and hedges. It was like being in a Thomas Hardy novel. Although here was Oxfordshire and not Dorset. She used to love this part of the world, yet today she found it stifling. 'How I envy you,' she said. 'It is so peaceful here. Did your Aunt Georgie come here a lot?'

Quentin drew up beside her, a little too close perhaps, the rather acrid smell of his citrus cologne biting into her nostrils. In the reflection of the glass, she could see Sal moving restlessly on the sofa.

'She came to live here not long after I was born,' Quentin told her. 'My mother was her god-daughter after all.'

'You must remember her well.'

'I was in my early twenties when she died. I have many memories.'

'What was she like?'

'A magnificent woman. Even in her old age, she was still carving out her own path. Only a few people can do that. For everyone else, life just seems to swallow them up in the end. Don't you agree?'

She did agree. Or at least that was how her life felt like right now. All chewed up and spat out. When had she lost control of her own destiny?

'What about your own work?' she asked. 'Sal told me you are an art critic.'

'I don't do so much of that any more. The occasional article or exhibition review. I am concentrating on my own writing now. Short stories. A play.'

Laura turned from the window, gave Sal a look with the visual message: *See. This is how it is done. In the English manner. Softened up and calmed down. It's back to you now.*

Sal tipped his head in acknowledgement, reassembled his large body into his bedside praying posture. Quentin returned to his armchair.

'Tell me, Quentin' Sal said. 'When you granted permission for the publication of the letters, what were your conditions?'

'There were no conditions. Just a price.'

'And what was that?'

'Three pounds per word.'

Sal actually whistled his surprise. 'What? Five dollars a word?'

'If that is the current exchange rate.'

'That's a bit excessive.'

Quentin smiled condescendingly. 'I found it helped the publishers to be precise in their request.'

'That kind of price tag is way beyond anything we could afford,' Sal said. 'I mean we would want thousands of words of original texts.'

'Use of the photographs would cost a lot more.'

'Any room for negotiation here?'

'I wish to remain consistent in my response to all approaches for access. And anyway, I would not consider a request for access to the entire estate.'

'I'm offering you a quality production here.'

'I appreciate your good intentions, Mister Yerksaw. And I have no doubt Laura could provide us with an excellent portrayal of Aunt Georgie. But those are my terms.'

'Come on. Can we not be a little bit more flexible?'

Quentin rose abruptly, rubbed his hands together as if he were washing himself clean of the whole matter. 'Would you like a tour of the house, Laura? I have some lovely pieces of porcelain from Aunt Georgie which may interest you.'

Sal was also back up on his feet. 'We need to get back to London,' he said.

Chapter Eighteen

The Hepburn Archives

Extract from an unpublished memoir

I still rented the flat in Pimlico with the little money I had left over from *The Woman Walks Free*. It was an empty, lonely place with Max gone and room-mate Lucy married and moved out. There had been a terrible flood that winter and my property, close to the Thames as it was, had just managed to escape undamaged. Somehow the threat of those dirty swollen waters lapping at my doorstep summed up the darkness at the edges of my moods. Even when I found the energy to extricate myself from my bed and the flat, the streets were awfully dull and quiet. I think the area was populated mainly by civil servants who led sombre and secret lives. The jazz clubs and dance halls in the city centre were packed but London in all its imperial magnificence offered me nothing. Hubert Hoffstetter had been right in one respect though. The talkies killed off the silent movies. Al Jolson in *The Jazz Singer* – the first full length feature film with synchronised sound – had taken the city by storm. But the last thing I felt like doing was going into the West End to see it. Instead, I finally convinced myself to take the train down to Five Elms Down to visit my mother.

'You don't look well, Georgie,' she told me almost as soon as I had entered the cottage. She began to trim a bunch of flowers recently plucked from her garden. In the years since my father had died, she had this tendency only to speak to me when she was distracted by doing something else.

'I'm tired. That's all.'

'Are you still stepping out with that Jew?'

'That finished over a year ago. I told you that already.'

She started to arrange the flowers in a tall glass vase. Freesias, long-stemmed roses, baby's breath, she was really good at that kind of thing. 'I never liked them,' she said.

'Freesias?'

'Jews.'

'What Jews do you know? There are certainly none around here.'

'Just as well then.' She stood back to view her handiwork. 'Are you staying for long?'

'I'm not sure.'

'I have a schedule, you know. The Women's Institute. The church, of course. I can't be expected to stop everything at the drop of a hat. When you turn up like this with hardly any notice.'

'I realise that.'

'Will you be going over to see your Aunt Ginny and the new baby?'

'I came to see you.'

My words actually made my mother stop on her journey between sorting out the flowers in the vase and some as yet undefined task. 'I see,' she said. 'Well, I went over.'

'Why wouldn't you? You have a niece now.'

'I never know what to say,' she said picking up a dust rag. 'I don't really like them very much when they're that age.'

I was tempted to say that she didn't really like them very much at any age. Instead I asked: 'How is she?'

'Oh, you know what she's like. Takes these things in her stride. She's always been good at that.'

'I meant the baby. Susan.'

My mother picked up a photograph of my father, wiped the glass. A pilot in his uniform. 'As I said. I never know what to say. I did take her over some of your old dresses.'

'You've kept my baby things?'

'Why not? Someone in the family was going to need them at some time. Shame to waste.'

I stayed for a week. I went for long walks on the Downs, visited places my father used to take me to, my mood would lift from the fresh air, the views and the exercise only to be brought down again as soon as I returned to the cottage. My mother's comments went something like this, often repeated throughout my stay:

'I'm so pleased your acting days are over,' she said as she boiled up a pot of raspberries for her jam jars. 'Simply not the right kind of vocation for any decent young woman.'

And while she stitched away at her embroidery. 'Dorothy Wheatley finally got married last month. You remember Dorothy? She was in your class at school. To think I was barely eighteen when I was wed.'

Or when I helped her prune the roses. 'It's a pity you didn't let me teach you properly about working with flowers. A florist is a good job for a young woman these days. Missus Dorward's daughter helps her out in the shop now.'

Or during her evening tea and biscuits. 'I see Robbie Longland has returned to the village. His mother's not so well, needs looking after. And appreciates the company as well, no doubt.'

I could never work out whether these were simply throwaway remarks that I in my vulnerable state took as veiled criticisms or if she was really trying to upset me. She never mentioned my father even though his presence still looked out at us from the various photographs displayed throughout the house. Ten years after his death and his clothes still hung in the bedroom wardrobe. Eventually I had to stop my mother in whatever task she was engaged in, got her to sit down and listen to me properly.

'What's happened to us?' I asked.

My mother fiddled with her wedding ring. 'What do you mean? We get on just fine.'

'You never talk to me.'

'We talk all the time.'

'You don't even look at me when you are speaking.'

She raised her eyes from her fiddling. I could see her desperately trying to hold my gaze from behind her spectacles. It was a fearful look. 'What do you want to talk about?'

'About you and me. After Papa died.'

'What is it you want to know?'

'You seemed to disappear from me then.'

'I disappeared from you? Where were you when suddenly I had a house to run, bills to pay? I'll tell you. Out with that Penny... what's her name? Both your heads full of nonsense about being stars of the silver screen? Look where it's got you, Georgie. Just look where it's got you.' My mother stood up, smoothed down her apron. 'I have too much to do,' she announced before disappearing into the kitchen.

I returned to London feeling worse than when I had left. I had reached rock bottom. That was exactly how it felt. Such a cliché. To reach a point from where it was not possible to descend further. To arrive at that hard pebble of a place inside myself where nothing else could hurt me. Nowadays I would probably have been diagnosed with depression. Back then I was said to be suffering from melancholia. Or nerves. Such a woman's complaint. Especially for one without a husband, children or any hope for the future. Rock bottom. From where there was nowhere else to go but up. Or out. To leave this world behind. But what I discovered was that having been stripped naked by my despair, I actually possessed the strength and will to rebuild myself. It was a resilience, an emotional and mental toughness, an inner strength that I felt had been instilled into me by my father. The power to start again. To start again armed with the knowledge that having descended into this deep and dark place, I had the ability to survive. That there was nothing left in this world that could defeat me. Yes, I could start again. But how would I do this? And then it came to me. It was so obvious. So bloody obvious. It was, as my dear Papa used to say, a universal truth.

Chapter Nineteen

The Play's the Thing

Laura had not slept well but somehow she had awoken full of energy. Or was it just the backed-up flow of frustration? She had argued with Sal all the way back to London on the basis he had not handled Quentin at all well.

'You could see he's a delicate being,' she had said. 'He needed to be caressed not mauled into giving us what we wanted.'

Sal had laughed at that, pressed down harder on the accelerator, swerved into the outside lane. 'Delicate being?' he shouted into the wind. 'Delicate being? Well, if you call a toad a delicate being I suppose he is. But that guy... there's something... I don't know... he's the trustee of Georgie's estate after all... he should be trying to promote her memory. Not erasing it.'

'That's very American of you. Marketing her memory.'

'And that's very English of you. All this pussy-footing around. Getting us nowhere.'

Either way, Sal was right. They had gotten nowhere. And now, that brief feeling of elation she had experienced at finally being able to take on her dream project was slowly evaporating. She decided not to think about it. Instead, she would use all this pent-up energy to do some gardening. She would start by retrieving her mobile phone from the fish pond. She had already bought a new one which now sat on her patio table. But she worried that some kind of chemical corrosion or seepage from the battery of her old one could be destroying her poor carp. Although they seemed to be swimming around healthily enough. She rolled up a sleeve, was just about to plunge her arm into the water when the message alert went off on her new phone. She hesitated. Probably Sal with an apology. Let him wait then. She looked down at the green slime, then stood up, walked over to the patio table. A text from Quentin Holloway. There had been an exchange of numbers before they had left his manor house but somehow she couldn't imagine Quentin in his dressing gown and cravat punching out letters on a tiny keypad. Yet here he was:

'Coming to London Thursday. Meet for lunch? Members Room. Tate Modern. 1 PM. Q.'

She immediately called Sal.

'He's all yours,' he told her.

'What do you mean, he's all mine?'

'I've gotta get back to the States to edit my film.'

'When did your pet project become my pet project?'

'When I realised how desperate you were.'

'That's not fair.'

'I guess it isn't. But you'll do a good job. Passion and desperation are good qualities to bring to the table.'

'I thought we were in this together.'

'Don't worry. I'll be back over here as soon as possible. In the meantime, I'm sure you can hold the fort with Quentin. He's only a delicate being after all.'

'Maybe he just wants lunch.'

'I doubt it.'

So there she was, back down south of the river, twice in the space of a week. She was surprised at Quentin's choice of venue. She would have put him down as a Tate Britain kind of gallery member. Or better still, the Royal Academy. But a patron of the industrial cathedral that was Tate Modern? She didn't think that was his style at all.

She managed her arrival so that she was ten minutes late but to her annoyance discovered Quentin hadn't turned up either. She was able to persuade the door attendant to let her into the Members' Room and was led to a reserved table with breathtaking views of the Thames and St Paul's, the Inns of Court, Unilever House and the rest of the skyline she considered as her London. She tended to ignore the new London to the east with its Docklands, gherkins, shards and domes spreading upriver in all its youthful exuberance. She sat down, was just about to pretend she had some important emails to deal with when Quentin arrived. He was dressed in a cream suit draped over an open-necked Hawaiian shirt that was printed in deep blue with large white floral patterns. He wore a pink rose in his lapel, held a straw sunhat in one hand, a briefcase in the other. She had been mistaken. Tate Modern was an ideal venue for him. She stood up to greet him.

'I hope you don't mind sitting inside on such a beautiful day,' he said, kissing her on both cheeks without an apology for his lateness. 'But I find these marble benches out on the deck quite uncomfortable. And I do want that we should be comfortable for our little chat.'

'So we're having a little chat?'

'And a very pleasant lunch I hope.'

They agreed to skip the starters, they both opted for the hake as a main, Quentin suggested a white Burgundy (Chassagne-Montrachet 2011). When the wine came, Quentin raised and clinked his glass with hers.

'To Aunt Georgie,' he said.

'To Aunt Georgie.'

'If you don't mind me saying,' he said. 'You do look a bit like her.'

'So I've been told.'

'Is that what attracted you to her? The likeness.'

'It was the other way around. She made such a huge impression on me when I was young. So I guess my face tried to morph itself into hers.'

He laughed at that. 'I think you would make a wonderful Georgie. You have the same sense of humour.'

'I thought that wasn't going to happen.'

Quentin pulled his briefcase on to his lap, extracted a rather bulky envelope.

'Are these her papers?' she asked excitedly.

'No. These are my papers.'

'What do you mean?'

Quentin placed the envelope by his side-plate. 'This is my

play,' he said with an affectionate pat on the manila.

'I don't understand.'

'I told you I was writing a play.'

'I think you did mention it.'

'Well, here it is.'

'I see.'

'It is called *Maimonides*.'

'*Maimonides*?'

'He was a famous philosopher from around the twelfth century.'

'So this is a play about him?'

'Not so much about him as about his philosophy. He is well known for what is commonly called his doctrine of negative attributes.' Quentin paused, pulled back to give her a schoolmasterly stare with those little eyes of his. 'Have you heard about him before?'

'I'm afraid twelfth century philosophers weren't on the curriculum at my drama school.'

Quentin sniffed in a manner that suggested perhaps they should have been and then went on. 'In his doctrine of negative attributes, Maimonides says you should think of God in terms of what He isn't, rather than what He is. Do you believe in God, Laura?'

'Not really.' Why were people asking her all these questions recently? Did she want to know when she was going to die? Did God exist? 'What I mean is that I don't know.'

Quentin folded his hands under his chin. 'I see. Well, Maimonides thought that if you try to describe God positively – in terms of what He is – then you merely end up limiting the limitless by your language and your concept.'

'I have no idea what you are talking about.'

'In simple terms, it means that if you say God is good, you are limiting God by your definition and idea of what 'good' is. It would be better to say 'God is not bad' because the concept of what is 'not bad' is limitless.' Quentin spread his arms as if to indicate the infinite nature of God and the universe. 'Such is the doctrine of negative attributes.'

Laura sipped her wine as she pondered what had been said. The aroma was discreet, hints of citrus and vanilla, exactly as described on the wine list. No negative attributes about it. Suitably refreshed, she ventured. 'So, instead of saying God is powerful, I should say God is not weak.'

'Exactly.'

'God is not cruel. Rather than God is merciful.'

'Correct again.'

'And what has this got to do with your play?'

'Well my play uses this doctrine of negative attributes as a kind of fun metaphor. Not that my play is a comedy exactly. Perhaps you could say it is a dark comedy.'

'Or not a light drama.'

'That is very funny, Laura. I've already said you share Aunt Georgie's sense of humour. Ah look, here comes our food. Some more wine?'

She shook her head. 'Look, Quentin. Can you just tell me what is going on here?'

'We are hopefully having a pleasant lunch.'

'You know what I mean.' It was her turn to pat the manila envelope.

'I have a proposition to make to you. And to your American friend.'

'And that is?'

'I would like you to arrange for a proper run-through of my play with professional actors.'

'Really?'

'Yes. And I would like it all to be properly filmed in the same way as you intend to make your documentary about Aunt Georgie.'

'That's quite a large undertaking. What's in it for me?' My God, she thought, I'm beginning to sound like Sal.

Quentin sat back smugly in his chair, placed his hands into a steeple formation. 'In exchange, I will permit you access to all of the Hepburn archives. Everything. Absolutely everything. Free of charge. Gratis.'

Chapter Twenty

Extract from an unpublished memoir

As with the century, I was also thirty at the beginning of that particular decade. Like almost all women of my age and of my era, I should have been married with a family rather than being a lonely spinster. My mother – as she was so proud of telling me – was only eighteen when she gave birth to me. But I had learned a very important lesson during the Roaring Twenties. And that was I would no longer rely on fame or the vagaries of men to make me happy. I was a strong, healthy, intelligent and independent woman. I was determined not to let anyone or anything undermine my worth. I was going to live to my full potential. I was going to fly.

With some financial assistance from my dear, ever-supportive Aunt Ginny and the gift of flying time from a couple of wartime pilots turned flight trainers who had flown with my late father, I took my certificate out of Hanworth Club in Hounslow on a de Havilland 60G Gypsy Moth in June 1931. The Moth was an aircraft not that dissimilar from the Sopwith Camel my father flew when he was shot down over the Western Front. It was still a flimsy open-cockpit bi-plane, its wings and fuselage made mostly out of plywood and fabric, but the engine was lighter and extremely reliable. It was also a two-seater which made it ideal for training purposes and gave room for a co-pilot on those long flights. I discovered I had a real sense for manoeuvring a craft within three dimensions rather than two (I didn't learn to drive a motor car until much later) and it didn't take me long to get my wings.

However, if you think I was some kind of female pioneer in what has become known as the Golden Age of Flight you would be most mistaken. There were so many brave and wonderful women aviators in those heady days, I think nearly one hundred and fifty of us had licences by then. Dear Amy Johnson, of course, she was probably the most famous but there were lots of others too. The fearless Pauline Gower, the glorious and notorious Beryl Markham, that beautiful Kiwi, Jean Batten, and the irreverent speedster Mildred Bruce. And how could I forget the formidable Mary Russell, the 'Winged' Duchess of Bedford, who learned to fly at the ripe old age of sixty-one? Or Winnie Brown, the Lancashire butcher's daughter, the first woman to win the King's Cup, the 700 miles air-race around England?

It is hard to describe the excitement and freedom we felt. We were the suffragettes of the air, competing with men as equals, swishing around in our goggles, helmets and those marvellous long leather coats. And it wasn't just in Britain that we were gobbling up the attention of the press. Amy was flying all over the place, breaking and making records in the process. Russia, Japan, Australia, South Africa, the United States, where didn't that girl fly to? She probably would have been one of the first to fly to the moon if she hadn't been killed in the war. The Winged Duchess was no slouch either making it to India and South Africa in her sixties while Kiwi Jean flew to Brazil and broke records from England back home to New Zealand. Over in East Africa, Beryl was quite the mistress of the air, pioneering routes where no man, woman or road had ever gone, scouting out the elephant herds for the wealthy hunters.

As for me, I guess I was a stay-at-home girl most of the time, confining my flights to the British Isles for I neither had the private wealth nor the sponsors to take me further. Still there was money to be made as a pilot in those Wild West times. The public were only too happy to pay to be taken skywards for a bit of joyriding. I worked part-time for an air-taxi firm, hooked up with an air circus on a tour of the country, performing fly-pasts, taking up stunt men for wing-walking and parachute jumps.

And the male pilots? What a bunch of handsome, daring rogues they were, these knights of the sky, ferrying their titled lady passengers here and there, forever cited as co-respondents in divorce cases, pushing the boundaries of height and distance, inventing new manoeuvres with which to dazzle the public, testing the latest aeronautic innovations, racing each other (and we women) all over the globe. I had experienced this kind of ebullient dynamism and glamorous excitement before as an actress but as an aviatrix there was an added ingredient... and that was danger. So many of the people I knew around that time lost their lives in crashes or just literally disappeared into thin air. Brave pioneers who were prepared to prove the limits of their skill and their equipment like trapeze artists without the benefit of a safety net. That extra element of peril added an edge to everything we did, forced us to live out our lives as if there were no tomorrow. Down at the Hanworth Club, we were renowned for the zeal and zest we threw into our parties and pageants where pilots and engineers mingled with royalty, diplomats, politicians and celebrities in a fabulous combustive mix. It was at one of these parties at Hanworth Park House that I met my own knight of the sky.

I had just come down from my plane after a fly-past, literally dropping into a party on a sunny, dusty afternoon, tea and drinks on the balconies, picnics on the lawn, guests sitting on the broad front steps or stretched out in deckchairs in front of the House. I was buzzing and tingling from my flight, my blood pumping hot, all my senses working at full throttle when this gentleman appeared from under my wing with an ease that showed a familiarity around aircraft, and stepped out to block my path. No introduction. Just the statement:

'I've a proposition for you, young lady,' he said. Which was a compliment in itself as I no longer considered myself particularly young.

He was tall, taller than me at least, and quite handsome – not in that dashing, strong-chinned, sleekly groomed, moustachioed look of the time – he had quite a long face, clean-shaven, soft brown eyes. His mouth creased into a broad smile as if he had found something amusing about me rather than in the strangeness of the question just asked.

'Don't you think we should get acquainted first?' I said, feeling all swaggering and confident in my leather jacket, jodhpurs and high boots, twirling my goggles as if they were a string of pearls.

'What would you like to know?'

'Name, please.'

'Roland Paxton-Jones. Call me Rollo.'

'Are you married?'

'That's a rather forthright question, don't you think?' he said. 'It takes the conversation along a route I was not initially intending.'

'Well, there you are then,' I said, still feeling all swelled up and reckless from the obvious tension passing between us. 'As long as your intentions are honourable.'

'I'm not sure that they are now.'

In my memory, it seemed only a matter of minutes before we were smooching on the back stairs of the House but I imagine it had to be longer than that for I was able to ascertain the following additional information before any hanky-panky occurred:

Rollo was two years older than me, also an only child, who had recently inherited a fortune on the death of his mother. His late father had made his money importing indigo from India for textile dyeing until the Germans came along with a synthetic version, forcing him into a wealthy retirement but early death. Rollo was passionate about photography and was training to be a photographic officer over at the RAF School of Photography in Farnborough. He had borrowed (I later discovered it was stolen) a state-of-the-art Fairchild F-8 Aerial camera from an American aircrew, was desperate to use it. He had his own airplane, wanted to hire me to take him up on it so that he could take pictures from the air.

'Where do you want to go?' I asked him, anticipating a joyride over the city.

'The Holy Land,' he said, with that same smile of amusement.

'The Holy Land. As in Palestine?'

'Is there any other?'

'And why the Holy Land?' I asked, trying to keep the surprise out of my voice.

'Nothing like a bit of an adventure.'

'Why choose me? I'm not really a long-distance flyer.'

'I've had my eye on you for a while,' was his vague reply. And then he kissed me.

Unlike Max, Rollo was not a talkative man. While Max used to smother silences with his various harangues and polemics, Rollo relished the quiet. It was the legacy of being a pilot I suppose, the drone of the engine making speech redundant, the wonders of this planet from above rendering worldly chatter below insignificant. It was a talent I had begun to acquire myself which meant Rollo and I could enjoy each other's physical presence without constant conversation. Also unlike Max, Rollo was extremely rich. He took me to the best London restaurants. Not only a return to *Boulestin,* but also *Quaglino's* and *L'Aperitif Grill.* He had a box at the Opera House but avoided the glamour and gossip of the London night clubs. Instead, he drove me out to the countryside or down to the coast in his sleek automobile where we would go on long walks, hand-in-hand, very little spoken between us. It was a whirlwind romance that lasted just ten days before we had to prepare earnestly for the trip to Palestine.

Chapter Twenty-One

Matinee Idol

After what turned out to be a stilted lunch at the Tate Modern, Laura abandoned Quentin in a Blackfriars side-street to take a taxi back up north. She had the manila envelope with his play in her shoulder bag as well as a whole lot of pent-up anger in her gut. Sal had been right. Quentin was not a delicate being. He was a hard-nosed toad of a man who knew exactly what he wanted and how to get it. What right had he to make these demands? Was this how the trustee of an estate behaved? How could he manipulate her in this way? Because she was desperate. That was why. He could probably smell it off her in the same way Sal had. Perhaps she should market it as her own fragrance. *Desperation. It will allow a man to do exactly what he wants with you.*

The traffic was all snarled up going along Charing Cross Road, the interior glass panel was slid open so she could hear the afternoon DJ providing her with everything but music, the driver busy eyeing her up in his mirror and she just knew he was about to ask her if she was on the telly or something. She tied up her hair in a silk headscarf, slipped on her sunglasses, paid him off with twice what it said on the meter, stepped out on to the street just past the National Portrait Gallery. She immediately regretted her decision. The hot air was thick with vehicle fumes and the aroma of fast food, the taut atmosphere from the frustrations of trapped drivers seeping into her own mood. Crowds of mainly young people – or at least younger than she – moved in swarms across traffic lights, forcing her to choose one particular throng that pulled her along into Leicester Square towards another mass of bodies. It was only when she saw the lit-up arc lamps (even though it was still daylight), the crash barriers, the police cordons, the hysterical fans, the held-up mobile phones, the film crews on their cranes, the porcupine bristling of camera lenses, the red carpet, did she realise she had walked into the middle of a film premiere. She quickly turned away from the madness towards one of the other cinemas in the Square. A giant poster read: *An Exquisite Sense of What is Beautiful*. Starring Jack Muirhead. Her Jack. She escaped inside.

She hadn't seen Jack for over a year, knew that he had returned to Japan to complete the shoot on the very movie she was about to watch. She wondered what he had felt being back there among the backdrop scenery to the beginning of their love affair. Not much, knowing Jack. For Jack, life rolled on easy. He was one of the lucky ones, there were very few of them about in her profession, probably in any profession. He was one of those remarkably gifted and charismatic persons who could just sit back, let the world come to him. Rather than the other way around for those mere mortals – of which she was one – who had to work so hard for every morsel of work or money or recognition or reward that was granted them. After every movie, Jack would retire to his small estate in Athens, Georgia, where he would read, meditate, practise yoga, swim in his lap-pool, tend his garden, smoke a bit of dope, drink the finest malt whisky, entertain his friends, play guitar, hang out with rock stars, send out cheques to various charities, convince the woman he was with that she was the most important person in his world. He might grow his hair long, stop shaving, dress up in grubby clothes and sandals, head off to India or South America where a few people might say 'Isn't that Jack Muirhead?' but then dismiss as preposterous the idea this old hippie could possibly be a cinema A-lister. That was Jack. Eschewing the world of the movie star, yet every time he opened up his inbox or picked up his mail there would be script offers, festival invites, interview requests, nominations for this, awards for that. How did he do it? And the answer was that Jack didn't do anything. Jack was Jack was Jack. And everyone – including herself – loved him for it.

She was glad to find the cinema almost empty, settled into her Premier seat, draped her headscarf over her bare shoulders to ward off the air-conditioned chill. The film opened with some plinky-plonky music played out on the strings of a Japanese *koto* and the camera swooping over a majestic curved-roof building cascading out of the hillsides. She had read the book on which the film was based. An ageing writer returns to the hotel in the Japanese mountains where many years previously he had written his most famous novel and fallen in love with a young chambermaid. If she remembered correctly, the novelist in the book was in his mid-seventies. The role must have been aged-down for Jack for there he was, still managing to stir up her feelings as he stepped out of a taxi in the hotel forecourt. He was fifty-two years old. Two months younger than she was. That was their running gag when they were together, that she was a baby-snatcher, that he was her toyboy.

'It must be really weird to see your lover up there on the screen?' That was a question her friend Victoria always used to ask her for Jack was merely one of a handful of ex-lovers who had been film actors. It was a good question, one with no easy answer. She reckoned her response depended on two criteria – how strong were her feelings and how good was the actor? If she was really besotted with someone and all loved-up when she came across one of their movies while idly flicking through the channels, then yes, she probably did see the actor more than the role he was playing. But once she had emerged from the first excited throes of a new love then it would be his qualities as an actor that were more important. She looked at Jack now, his face taking up most of the screen, searching and searching for him in his giant eyes and he was just not there. He had disappeared completely and in his place was some ageing writer, full of remorse, weary of life, trying to find the love and the creative spark that had once so invigorated him. My God, you're good, Jack, you're so bloody good. He had never won an Oscar though, said it was because he didn't play nice with the Academy. He said he didn't care but she thought he really did.

She missed him. How could you not miss someone like that? They had been good together although not for very long. The month of the movie shoot then a few weeks back at his place in

Georgia. It was unusual for either of them to be seeing someone their own age and in the end they turned into each other's mentors rather than lovers. When he wanted to take her on a trip down to Central America, she decided instead to go back to London. There was no heart-rending farewell. It wasn't as though the relationship had officially ended but it seemed they had tacitly agreed it wouldn't go any further. If their coupling had been filmed as a movie it would be high-quality indie with two excellent leads and no chance of a sequel.

And yet, deep within herself, in that place where the secret truth is told, she knew that her retreat from Jack hadn't been as simple as that. She remembered once when the two of them were lazing out on the deck of his Georgia property as the day began to cool, the evening shadows had started to creep in, the air thick with the sweet pineapple fragrance of Cherokee Rose – the white flower of the native shrub – that scrambled up one side of the porch. She was laid out on a hammock, Jack seated not far away, reading Tolstoy, wearing nothing but a pair of tattered shorts and horn-rimmed glasses. As the gentle rock of the hammock brought Jack in and out of her view, she watched him wrapped up in the intensity of his reading. He was probably capable of attracting any women on the planet from legal age of consent upwards with an interest in the Western concept of what constituted a good-looking man. Jack sat there bare-chested (albeit with a fair amount of tufts of grey hairs), not an ounce of flab on him, his strong legs stretched out before him while she was wearing loose cotton pants, a smock top and an extremely helpful push-up bra. For her age, she knew she was still an attractive women but she knew she would never be able to compete with the younger, more beautiful members of her gender who constantly flirted with him. She might be able to fend off this competition for a while but she would be exhausted by it and someone was bound to eventually break through. Better to bail now while things were still good between them, better to sabotage their relationship now before she got hurt.

'I'm going back to London,' she told him.

He looked up from his book with no more concern than if she had said she was going to take a shower. 'Why spoil things?' he asked.

'That's the point. I don't want to spoil things.'

He took off his glasses, stared thoughtfully across at her. It was just the kind of thing an actor would do in the same situation. Sometimes with Jack she wondered if she was playing out her real life or just a part in his movie. 'I don't get it,' he said softly. 'We're doing well here.'

'That's why I want to leave now. Before we're not doing well.'

'What are you frightened of?'

'I'm not frightened of anything,' she said, although she could hear the sudden lift in her voice betraying her fear. 'I just want to get out before we hurt each other.'

'Well, I've no intention of hurting you. So it must be you who's out to hurt me. Is that what you're telling me here?'

'See, we're spoiling things already.'

'I'm just trying to understand what's going on.'

'And you're not listening. It's time for me to go. *Capisce?*'

He put his glasses back on. 'Have it your way then.'

She left the next day.

It was still light when she emerged from the cinema, brighter still for the contrast with the darkness inside. It had been a good decision to see the movie, to take her mind off the awful lunch. She fumbled in her bag for her sunglasses, was unfortunately reminded of Quentin by the presence of the bulky envelope hosting his play, realised she had left her scarf back on the seat. Suddenly, she heard her name being called. She looked up into the flash of a camera from a paparazzo who must have stayed back in the Square for the end of the premiere. Her photograph – hair dishevelled, eyes wide open like a startled fawn, her knees crooked and bent as she searched for her sunglasses, the poster for the movie smack bang behind her head – was all over the online edition by the time she got home. The tag line read: *Lonely Laura Desperately Seeking Jack.*

Chapter Twenty-Two

The Hepburn Archives

Extract from an unpublished memoir

According to my old aviation logbook, Rollo and I set off in his Gypsy Moth 60G from London Air Park on a 2,000-plus mile trip to Palestine at 10.30am on the 12th September 1934. Rollo had the route all mapped out. Le Bourget (just outside Paris), Marseilles, Rome, Naples, Taranto, Athens, Crete, Alexandria, Cairo, then across the Sinai to Kalandia, a tiny airport situated between Ramallah and Jerusalem. Altogether the trip was meant to take ten days. That was all theory, of course. The weather would play an important factor, as would the availability of fuel and our ability to maximise its use. Some sections of the trip were way beyond the basic range of a Gypsy Moth (300 miles) so we often had to take on an overload of petrol. This extra fluid weight together with all the camera equipment and baggage made some of our take-offs quite scary at times. It turned out I was the better pilot so it was up to me to handle these manoeuvres but Rollo was a whizz with navigation. With a few basic maps, watch, compass and altimeter, we never once lost our way.

Rollo and I might have had our share of romance before we started on this adventure but once we set off from London, our relationship was all business-like and practical. It had to be. We had so many dangers and challenges to face on a daily basis. We could be airborne from four to eight hours per day (although we had decided beforehand there would be no night-flying unless in an emergency), we were confined to a very small space in a cockpit open to the mercy of the elements and the quality of visibility the weather granted us. Concentration was another factor. It was so easy to drift off into daydreams with the constant hum of the engine, especially over monotonous terrain. Then there were our ablutions. Urination and bowel movements all had to be attended to before we set off on each leg. A few days into our trip, I had to cope with menstruation cramp. My period pains were never too bad but I often wondered how other women managed. It was something I very rarely hear talked about even now after all the feminist advances of the 60s. How did women deal with their menses on climbing expeditions, playing in sports tournaments, flying into space? How did you manage, Amy Johnson, when you first flew solo all the way to Australia? Did you plan the journey around the weather or the moon?

Even when the flying was over for the day, exhausted yet elated at safely reaching our destination, we had to think about accommodation, stocking up on our food and water, making sure we had access to petrol, finding out about the weather, checking over the aircraft, filling in the log book, reviewing the route for our onward leg. We were lucky though. Apart from a couple of days holed up in Marseilles waiting for a storm to pass, it was plain flying all the way to Cairo where thanks to one of Rollo's old university chums we dined at the British Consulate on ox-tail soup, roast beef and potatoes. For the first time in ten days, I felt myself relax. We drank fine wine, we danced, we made love, we slept in a four-poster under mosquito nets. Yet we still managed to be up and airborne by mid-morning for the final part of our journey.

After stopping off to re-fuel in Suez, the plan was to strike a path north-east up to Palestine and the Holy City of Jerusalem. But after about a half-hour up in the air with me as pilot and Rollo taking photographs with the aerial camera, he signalled for me to keep going due east over the Sinai. As far as I knew there was absolutely nothing in that direction for a hundred miles or so until the port town of Aquaba on the Red Sea but Rollo kept on with his signalling. I gave him a shrug, banked the aircraft into an easterly path, continued out over barren desert. The landscape was quite mesmerizing. Endless shimmering plains and mountain ranges, pale yellow and pink, set off against a cloudless blue sky. No movement, no birds, no sound except for the puttering of our engine. As time passed and the angle of the sun changed, shadows would come into play, creating different contours across this blank canvas in the most fascinating of waves. I was not religious although flying could definitely bring out the spiritual side of a person – or provide insights into universal truths as my father used to tell me – but looking down at the markings in the desert it was if God Himself were drawing pictures in the sand. I was sure Rollo felt this too as he swung from side to side with his camera in a frenzy of photo-taking.

I was keeping the altitude steady for him, cruising at about 75 knots when I spotted some kind of encampment below. I indicated the site to Rollo, thought we might give the place a lower pass. He responded with an excited thumbs-up, then pointed downwards for us to land. I wasn't sure about this at all. The desert dust could clog up our engines, I had no idea about the suitability of the terrain for a landing or how we would be received by a tribe of nomads. I shook my head at him but he continued with his pointing. In the end, I gave in – after all, he who pays the piper picks the tune.

I picked out a flat, hopefully rock-free area far away enough I hoped from the encampment not to arouse any fears from its residents. To my relief, the Moth bounced down easy and solid on the ground and I brought it up to a halt pretty quick even without a headwind. We climbed down from our cockpits, stretched our limbs, dusted ourselves off. I looked towards the encampment, nothing more than a collection of black-cloth tents.

'Right on time,' Rollo said, as a small group came riding out to meet us. He tore off his helmet and goggles. His skin was pink along his hairline, round his eyes, his forehead and cheeks desert-dusted.

'That face will be enough to scare them off,' I said laughing, although I wasn't sure why. Six riders were coming towards us, two of them with rifles strapped across their back.

'We should walk towards them,' he said. 'Hands above our heads. Show them we're unarmed.'

'Good idea.'

'I have a pistol. In my boot. Just in case.'

The riders, all men, completed a couple of circuits of the Moth, before drawing up in front of us. We stood there with our arms up in the air, while they just leaned over in their saddles staring back. Eventually, one of them gave us a wide toothy smile, said something presumably in Arabic which sounded friendly enough and we all relaxed. Then came an exchange of hand-gestures indicating that Rollo and I were invited to eat back at the encampment. Arms were outstretched and we were pulled up roughly on to horseback.

It was only when I took off my helmet back at the encampment did the Bedouin men realise I was a woman. The discovery led to a lot of laughter, some lewd gestures made for Rollo's benefit. I was then led outside the main tent to sit under one of the raised flaps with the rest of my sex. The older women had their hair tied up with headscarves, a few of the younger girls wore long plaits right down to their waist, some bore elaborate brown markings on their skin. Their clothes were mainly dark and baggy set off with the occasional colourful embroidery to add a prettiness. They all tried to touch me, feel the leather of my jacket, rub their rough hands along my cheeks. All this was done in a friendly, feminine way and I did not once feel intimidated. After the inspection was over, they attended to the needs of the men. Plates of goat meat, flatbread and a moist paste made from ground beans (I learned later that this was called *hummus*). Dates, coffee and a clear alcohol (known locally as *arak*) were also served. It was then the turn of we women to eat. I looked inside the tent at Rollo. He was thoroughly enjoying himself, seated within a pile of cushions, sharing out his cigarettes, trying to explain the workings of a Fairchild F-8 Aerial camera to a fascinated audience.

There was a quiet period after lunch when a heavy heat descended, the men dozed, the women cleared up the dishes.

I walked out to the plane, laid down with my back against one of the wheels, fell asleep. I was woken with the arrival of Rollo accompanied by three of the Bedouin men.

'We're going joyriding,' he said. 'Short hops.'

'Do you want me to fly them?'

'No need. They won't go up with a woman.' He gave me his Leica camera. 'Take some snaps. Back at the camp. Memories of lunch.'

And that was what I did. No-one seemed to mind either as I walked around by the tents clicking away. There was no posing, everyone just getting on with what they were doing, tending to the livestock, grinding beans, churning butter in sacks swung on tripods, baking bread on hot stones, trusting me, allowing me to get up close. What marvellous faces the men had, so burnished and weather-beaten, their eyes narrowed from sun-glare and tobacco smoke. The women, smooth-skinned despite the sun, sometimes girlish in their shyness, at other times imbued with an aura of peaceful resignation that seemed to come from living so close to the rhythms of nature. When I was finished, I was taken for my own private ride, not on an airplane but on a camel. I bounced along atop that beast with so much laughter, nervousness and childish excitement. It was one of the most wonderful occasions of my life. To laugh, not at some silly joke or at someone else's misfortune, but out of pure joy.

Night came and the temperature cooled quite dramatically. Rollo and I were given blankets, a reed basket of bread, cheese, dates, a goatskin pouch of *arak*, and escorted back to the Moth by two men with lanterns although the moon and the stars would have been sufficient to light our way. After much hand-shaking and back-slapping we were left alone. We lay down in our blankets by the side of our trusty plane, stared up at the most magnificent canopy of stars I had ever seen.

'It is so quiet,' I said.

'Good not to hear the old engine. Rattling away.'

'I keep having to remind myself where we are. Out here in the middle of the desert, in the middle of nowhere, jammed into a corner between Europe, Africa and Asia.'

'Happy?'

'Very.'

We made love, slowly and gently, sinking into such a closeness, a smallness, consumed by the majesty of the nature that surrounded us – the galaxies, the continents, the desert, the mountains, the stillness, the silence. Two tiny souls, clinging together for warmth and tenderness in the loneliness of a vast universe. Afterwards, we swigged *arak* from the pouch, shared the last of our cigarettes.

'I don't want to go on,' Rollo said.

'What do you mean?'

'I feel we have already reached the apex. It is so perfect. This place. Do you mind?'

'Not seeing Jerusalem?'

'This is our holy city. Right here. The two of us.'

Rollo was not a man of many words but these ones moved me deeply. How could they fail to?

We followed the exact same route back to England. For the most part the journey was uneventful except for a few weather delays and when the wind ripped away Rollo's maps over France. Altogether it took us 22 days to complete the round-trip. It was one of the most adventurous and exciting undertakings of my entire life. We were pioneers of the sky in the same way astronauts today are the pioneers of space or captains of yesteryear were the pioneers of the seas. I have flown to the Middle East since on passenger jets. I have even been to see Jerusalem. I have had the privilege of being asked to join the pilots in their cockpits to wonder at the array of instruments at their disposal when back then I had no more than a compass, an altimeter and my instinct to guide me. Whenever I have looked out from the air-conditioned comfort of my window seat (always a window seat) at the vast expanse of cloud and sky over the Mediterranean or the Sinai or North Africa, I imagine myself and my dear Rollo bobbing around in our little Tiger Moth, and I am consumed with tears of profound happiness.

On our return to England, Rollo took all the film we had shot back to the lab at Farnborough. A few days later he turned up with the prints of the photographs I had taken with the Leica.

'These are damn good,' he said as he handed them over. 'Hidden talents.'

Chapter Twenty-Three

The Kenwood Ladies' Pond

No Men Allowed Beyond This Point. What bliss, Laura thought. A summer's day at Kenwood Ladies' Pond on Hampstead Heath. With Victoria and many other fine women of all ages, shapes, sizes, race and class who were happy to host a variety of exposed breasts, unwaxed legs and several famous faces (writers, TV presenters, journalists, actors like herself) without any fuss. She preferred the cooler, misty, less crowded days of the other seasons but what better way to spend a hot London afternoon than in the safe company of one's own sex, especially when the opposite gender had emerged as her enemy. Or one particular man. Quentin Holloway. Although she was sure she could throw a few others into the mix if she put her mind to it.

She had already taken her brief plunge into the cold waters among the frogs, ducks, lilies and pond slime. She wasn't much of a swimmer, considered these dips more as a baptism in nature rather than for any physical benefits. Unlike Victoria who swooped off with those wonderfully long, languid strokes of hers, hardly breaking the surface, returning breathless, pink-glowing, exhilarated, her feet and calves smeared with mud. The two of them then stretched out like stiff dummies on their respective blankets, still with their one-piece bathing suits in proper position. Gone were their topless days, suspended by a tacit mutual agreement some time ago. After the sun had succeeded in warming them up, drying them off, they plundered the contents of the picnic basket. As usual Laura had brought the food – cheeses, breads, olives and spreads – leaving Victoria to take care of the wine and bottles of mineral water. Birds sang, insects danced, sunlight glistened on the leaves, all worries had ceased for Laura until Victoria reminded her by saying:

'That Quentin Holloway is a manipulative bastard.'

Laura looked up from the little bouquet of daisies she had been happily assembling. Victoria went on: 'You should have nothing to do with him. Absolutely nothing.'

'I agree.'

'You need to surround yourself with positive people. People who support you rather than put obstacles in your way.'

'I'm on your side with that. But it's a tricky situation.'

'People like that are poisonous. Toxic.' Victoria popped a Kalamata olive into her mouth, washed it down with a gulp of white wine. 'Men,' she said bitterly.

One simple word but Laura knew the leaden history it carried for her friend, recently and unwillingly accorded the status of single mother. She stroked Victoria's forearm in sympathy, the fair hairs still matted from the swim. 'Yes, men,' she said, although the word generally held more kindly thoughts for her. She had enjoyed those couple of hours spent the previous day watching Jack up on the big screen. Despite it leading to her photo being splashed around the less glamorous sections of the media. 'To be fair though, Quentin's behaviour has nothing to do with his gender.'

'You don't think so? I'd say his desire to control access to the estate – and therefore to control you – is very much a male characteristic.'

'You really are in a mood about this.'

'I don't like to see you messed around.'

'Trust me, I don't want to be messed around either.'

'At least, he didn't suggest you should sleep with him.' Victoria visibly shivered. 'At least, not yet.'

'Perish the thought.'

'So what are you going to do about his play?'

'I haven't decided yet.'

'Oh, Laura.'

'It's not that simple. The Georgie Hepburn thing is so perfect for me.'

'Even if it means allowing this Quentin character to manipulate you?'

'I wouldn't have minded so much if his play had been any good. But it's awful.'

'What's it about?'

Laura outlined the plot to *Maimonides*. 'It's all centred around something called a doctrine of negative attributes.'

'Hmmm. Doesn't exactly grab my attention. What does your pal Sal think?'

'He's fast asleep in LA. I've emailed to tell him I'll Skype later.'

She re-filled her wine glass, turned over on her back, closed her eyes against the glare. Female voices all around, the subdued banter of well-behaved children (all above the age of eight, such were the rules of entrance for the Kenwood Ladies' Pond Association), the splash of the water, the drone of a jet flying off to who knows where. The uprush of air as Victoria lay down beside her, their shoulders, upper arms and hips touching, warm and sticky.

'Sleepy?' her friend asked.

'Just thinking.'

'Penny for them.'

'Do you know what's funny about this whole Quentin thing?' She could feel herself slurring her words as she spoke – the sun, the wine.

''Tell me.'

'One of the qualities I admired most about Georgie was her integrity. And now here I am with one of her own family challenging my own integrity. It feels like some kind of test. Maybe that's what Quentin's doing. Testing me.'

'What is the poor girl to do?'

'The question I really need to ask myself is… what would Georgie Hepburn do?'

Laura actually found herself dressing herself up for the Skype call. There had been a whole wardrobe of sun-frocks strewn across her bed until she found the right one. Not too colourful, just the right amount of cleavage, show off her skin glowing and sun-kissed from the hours at the pond. She did up her face, again not too much, she wanted to look as if she had just come off a beach, toasty and tingling, ready for some late afternoon sex. What the hell was she thinking? Sal was a happily-married man as far as she knew. Or at least according to his Wikipedia entry. She wrapped herself in a simple silk shawl. She could always let it drop if the occasion demanded. She clicked her mouse, listened to the harsh ring-tone, watched the diagram of little pulses joining her name to his, wriggled up straight, wetted her lips with her tongue. Then came the connection, the picture, Sal's large frame settling down in front of his screen, his usual deliberate movements slowed down even more by the slight video delay. He wore a light-blue, short-sleeved shirt completely unbuttoned, tufts of grey hair, tanned chest. He obviously hadn't dressed up for her.

'Hey,' he said.

'Hey,' she echoed as he drew up closer to the screen. She saw that his hair was wet. 'Got you out of the shower?'

'Naw. Swim.'

'Me too. Earlier. London's boiling hot.'

'Here too. You OK?'

'Fine.'

'How was lunch with my pal Quentin?'

She told him what had happened.

Sal wagged a finger at her. 'I said he wasn't to be trusted.'

'What should we do?'

'Exactly as he wants.'

'I can't ask actors to put on a shitty play.'

'I thought actors did that all the time.'

'That's not funny.'

'Anyway, it's only a run-through.'

'He wants it filmed as well.'

'Yeah, I got that. So what's the problem?'

'I feel as if I'm being blackmailed.'

'You are being blackmailed.'

'It's not what I wanted this project to be. I wanted to get away from all these compromises. From feeling used. Manipulated. I wanted *Georgie by Georgie* to be full of integrity.'

'It will be, it will be. We just gotta get over this little hurdle.'

'Isn't there anything else we could do?'

'Well, we could check out the terms of Georgie's will, get an extract, see if Quentin is acting appropriately, bring the lawyers on board if he's not, force him to back down with his conditions, then we'd be back to square one, probably still paying five dollars a word for the price of your integrity. Which is money I don't have. The show wouldn't go on.' Sal moved closer to the screen so it was just his face she was seeing. 'Is that what you want?'

'I feel defeated already. And we haven't even started yet.'

Sal pulled back so that he became a less threatening headshot. 'Look, I get it that Quentin is exploiting Georgie's estate for his own benefit. But he'd be saving us a helluva lot of money.'

'I know.'

'And this integrity stuff. It's not like he's asking to have sex with you.'

'That's what my friend Victoria said too. As if that makes his proposal any less of a blackmail.'

'You've just got to set the bar a bit lower. Otherwise nothing'll get done.'

She'd thought the voice-over for a crab had set the bar low enough. 'It just doesn't sit right with me.'

'It's not a question of right or wrong, Laura. It's a question of the end justifying the means. We both want the same ending, don't we?' Sal's image slowed down, then froze on the screen. That was her moment, her chance to say 'no'. But she wanted this too much. He stuttered back into life. 'Can we move ahead on this now?' he drawled.

'OK.' She let out a half laugh. 'After all, it's just a shitty play between friends.'

'Good. I'll put together a crew for the filming. Camera, sound, lighting. How many actors do you need?'

She did a quick count with her fingers. 'Eight. Six at a pinch, if I double up a couple of the small roles. Not sure if Quentin would be happy with that. Especially since it's being filmed for posterity.'

'Do the eight then. Can I leave you to get the venue and the cast?'

'Sure. But who's going to pay for all this? Crew. Venue. Equity rates.'

'I'll sort out the filming. Can you front the acting and theatre costs? Once we have access to all the papers, we shouldn't have any problem with funding. I'll pay you back then. Is that OK?'

'I can just about manage that. But that's all, Sal. Cash flow is a serious issue for me right now.'

'I thought you were one big success story.'

'Tax problems,' she said, allowing her brain to release that one anxious phrase for a millisecond before shutting it back down.

'Oh yeah, that'll do it for you.' Sal ran his palm over a bristled chin. She could hear the friction all the way from California. 'One other thing,' he said. 'This play. Is there a role in it for someone around your age?'

'There's the wife of one of the main characters. But I don't want a part in this. Doing all the organization and direction is enough for me.'

'I wasn't thinking of you. What about our friend Lady Caroline?'

'Caroline? Seriously?'

'She used to be an actress, didn't she?'

'Thirty years ago.'

'Well, maybe she'd like to revive her career.'

'I'm sure she would. But why her?'

'I'm just thinking ahead, that's all.'

Chapter Twenty-Four

The Hepburn Archives

Extract from an unpublished memoir

There was a Hollywood film out around this time with Fred Astaire and Ginger Rogers called *Flying Down to Rio*. Rollo and I absolutely loved it mainly because it contained all these ridiculously impossible flying scenes. Ginger sitting astride the fuselage of a monoplane in a silk aviator's suit flying over Rio as if she were riding into town in her pyjamas on some fine horse. Up in the skies, twenty dancing girls high-kicking across an airplane wing, a routine so top heavy that the plane would never have gotten off the ground. Another shot showed five wing-riding young women having their dresses ripped off to their underwear by the wind. Astaire would sing something about spinning the plane's propeller and getting to Rio on time and Rollo would substitute the place name of our destination so we had to get to Bristol or Swindon or Woking, or wherever we were going, on time. By then, Rollo had ditched the Gipsy Moth for a spanking new Percival Gull Four with a three-seater glazed cabin. No need for goggles or helmet. Rollo sitting just ahead of me singing his head off over the sound of the engine and I knew he was spinning that old propeller, heading off for somewhere else in his mind. Perhaps even Rio with one of those stripped-off wing-riding girls.

Ours was definitely the flying life. We were not as illustrious a couple as *The Flying Sweethearts* – Amy Johnson and her husband Jim Mollison (until they got divorced, of course). We weren't interested in long-distance flying or trying to break aviation records. But our flight over to the Sinai and back had provided us with a solid reputation among those in the flying circuit.

Rollo decided to focus on his aerial photography, a skill gaining in importance now that the threat of war against Germany was becoming more serious by the day. The RAF were determined to properly map as much of the potential theatres of conflict as possible with the result that Rollo ended up spending a lot of time photographing along the coast of North Africa. As for me, I would use his Percival Gull to take the general public up on joyrides or carry out post delivery and private passenger transport for a small commercial company. When our free-time coincided, Rollo and I would fly up to Scotland or over to Ireland. We enjoyed going to the cinema too. Not just the Astaire-Rogers musicals but fabulous thrillers like Hitchcock's *The 39 Steps* when I could regale Rollo about my encounter with the now famous director and to remind my beau that he was now stepping out with a once briefly successful film star.

We never did much talking about our plans for each other, I suppose our relationship was a bit like a silent movie in itself. But when Rollo did speak about us, he came out with words of such measured gravity that all I wanted to do was pin my future to him.

'Love is an active verb,' he told me once. 'Judge me on what I do for you rather than what I say.' Or when he had returned from a solo flight, he said: 'I feel the Gull is heavier without you in it.' Or when we hadn't seen each other for a while: 'You are like a print negative coming alive in my hands.' He would have that faraway look in his eyes as he spoke. Most aviators had it. I probably did too. As did sailors. A gaze cultivated from forever scouring the wide horizons. And then he would smile that broad smile of his, as he did when we first met, in private amusement (and perhaps a little disbelief) at what he had just said out loud.

And what words of endearment would I say to him? For the life of me, I cannot remember. When I try to recall the past and its conversations, it is usually that which is spoken to me that I remember (probably inaccurately) rather than the words I myself say. I was no longer the gushing young woman from when I was with Max but if I did not actually tell Rollo I loved him, I certainly felt it in my heart.

I was down in the hangars at London Air Park, working with the mechanics getting my plane ready for a post delivery down to Ipswich. The sky was clear but I had a funny feeling in my bones that some kind of change was looming. All aviators have a nose and a wariness for the weather, always with a glance upwards or a sniff of the air to detect the slightest movement or dampness in the atmosphere. I remember Davy the mechanic saying to me: 'Looks like yer man o'er there. Getting ready for the off.'

I strode out of the hangar, held up my arm against the weak sunlight, and there was Rollo taxiing off in the Gull. I waved at him, strained to get a good look at his face in the cockpit, not sure if he waved back but I'd like to think he did. Like me, he was headed off east, although for him it was to Norfolk and the Broads for some aerial shots. It was a routine job, especially with a cloudless sky and a full tank of fuel. It turned out that I should have listened to my bones that day for a couple of hours later conditions had changed dramatically with a heavy mist coming in off the coast and I had to postpone my own scheduled flight across to Ipswich.

For a couple of hours or so I pretended I wasn't worried, then I got our radio operator to call around the other airfields out east. There hadn't been any sightings of Rollo's Gull or any radio contact at all and I began to get more anxious. The police and coastguard were alerted. I took a chair outside the women's changing hut and just sat there, scouring the skies for any sign of him coming out of the clouds. I closed my eyes and tried to imagine the scene. I could see the glint of the sunlight off the glass of the cockpit, that little dip of the wings from side to side in greeting, that particular sound you get from the 6-cylinder Napier Javelin engine that Rollo preferred. And there was me running out to wave him down, the tension all draining out of me, wiping my greasy hands on my overalls, all ready to grab him as soon as he stepped out of the Gull.

But it wasn't to be like that at all. No more sightings either on land or out to sea. No radio contact. The hour had long passed when he would have run out of fuel. The sun was gone from the day and Davy the mechanic came out with a jacket for me.

'Come on in, lass,' he said with a fatherly hand on my shoulder. 'No point you catching cold.'

But I stayed out in the twilight. The clouds had lifted and I watched the firmament come alive, praying that the birth of each star might be the light of his plane arriving back from the coast.

Lost in fog over sea was the official report. Once the petrol had gone he would have crashed into the icy waters alone. Although I never saw it that way myself. I'd like to think he found a crack in the sky and just disappeared into it – into a better world.

I still think of him. That perhaps he might be at home waiting for me. Or just around the corner ready to surprise. Or look, over there, strolling along the pavement, whistling *Flying Down to Rio*, with a little shimmy of a side-step like Fred Astaire. Spinning that old propeller. Trying to make up time.

Chapter Twenty-Five

The Director's Cut

Laura had always fancied herself as a producer. A Cameron Mackintosh, a Jeffrey Katzenberg, a Kathryn Bigelow, a George Lucas, a Kathleen Kennedy. Assembling all the essential ingredients like a dedicated alchemist before handing them over to a director and cast to wield their magic. Although in this case, she lacked one essential part of the recipe. A decent script. But with her inner eye fixed firmly on access to all of Georgie Hepburn's papers, she did the very best she could.

She arranged the venue, managing to book a plush little theatre at the back of a north Islington pub on a rare day-off between other productions. She called up all the jobbing actors she knew who might be in need of work, explained the set-up of the run-through, apologised for the quality of the play. She received immediate acceptances to all her requests. 'Oh we poor, poor actors', she thought. 'We'd do anything to be up there in the limelight.' She produced multiple copies of the script, had them properly bound, then sent out to the members of the cast. She paid for both a sound and lighting engineer from the theatre to be there on the day, co-ordinated the arrival of the film crew with Sal, organized a buffet lunch, ensured the pub would supply a constant supply of coffee, tea and sandwiches. She then instructed her lawyer to draw up a contract between herself and Quentin, granting her full access to the Hepburn papers on completion of a run-through of his play together with the delivery of a digital video recording of the performance. She had only one item left on her to-do list before she printed off the final playbill. To ask Caroline to play the part of Hannah, a Holocaust survivor and wife of the main character.

Caroline had servants. Maids, gardeners, a chef, a house-keeper and the butler who answered the door, whom Laura believed was called "Robert". 'It's nice to see you again, Robert,' she said, consciously using his name to show she was a decent human being who made the effort to remember such personal details.

'You too, ma'am,' he said as he directed her towards a gorgeous sun-lit sitting room, all pale blues and yellows, the air thick with the scent of iris (also pale blues and yellows), a bit too sickly sweet for her liking. 'Lady Caroline will be with you shortly.' Which turned out to be a matter of seconds for Caroline immediately appeared from behind her butler in a gorgeous multi-coloured maxi dress, her once-blonde hair dyed the reddish brown of the Australian desert.

'Thank you, Ronald,' Caroline said, immediately causing Laura to flush at her error.

Ronald remained impassive. 'Should I tell the kitchen to serve tea?'

'We'll have ten minutes to settle first.' Then to Laura. 'Sit, sit, sit. Marvellous to see you.'

Laura did as she was told. 'Love the dress,' she remarked.

'Nothing really.'

It may have been nothing to Caroline but Laura had recently seen the very same outfit at Harvey Nichols. She simply hadn't been able to justify the price-tag to an actress recently dumped by her agent. Which was probably just as well, as they both could have ended up meeting today like a set of twins.

'So hot,' Caroline said, fanning her face with her fingers even though the room was air-conditioned cool. 'Sunning in the garden. You'll just catch Lew. He's on his way to somewhere. South Africa I think.'

And again, as if the mention of his name had the effect of conjuring him up, Sir Lew Hoffman himself arrived, full of brusqueness and tight efficiency, his too-tanned face the colour of his wife's hair. A stocky man with a thick neck, Lew always seemed to wear suits and shirts too tight for him which Laura thought was odd because his clothes must surely be custom-made. Yet here he was, all buttoned-up and ready to burst, dispensing with his briefcase, taking both her hands, kissing her on one cheek then the other, smelling of an expensive cologne that rivalled the roomful of flowers in its pungency.

'Good to see you,' he said, pulling back, still holding on to her, inspecting her as if she were a piece of real estate. Everything was a commodity for Lew. That was why she always thought of him as being unfaithful. Not with lovers but with high-end call girls. 'Heard you met one of my number crunchers,' he said. 'Freddy Nilssen. Hope he didn't bore you?'

'He was quite charming actually. In his own way.'

'His own way is usually very intense. Someone who can't seem to switch off from his work.'

'Takes one to know one,' Caroline said.

Lew ignored the comment. 'And where is life taking you these days, Laura?'

'Trying to get a new project off the ground.'

'Film?'

'Play and documentary.'

'I wish you'd put Caroline in it.'

'I might do just that.'

'Excellent. She needs something to do.' He glanced at his wife – who scowled back at him – then his watch. 'Well, I'll leave you to chat. Off to South America. Maybe catch one of your films on the plane. Anything recent?'

She shook her head, decided against mentioning the Disney thing.

Lew pecked at his wife's cheek, retrieved his briefcase from the sofa, Ronald was at the door to let him out, and he was gone, leaving behind the residue of his cologne, lingering like a canine scent.

Caroline snorted an acknowledgement of her husband's departure, her head still tilted towards the front door. 'I don't know,' she said. 'I don't know.'

About what Caroline didn't know, Laura decided not to ask. Instead she remarked: 'The flowers are beautiful.' She wasn't sure why she always spoke to Caroline like this. The flowers are beautiful. Your dress is lovely. Such gorgeous curtains, wallpaper, cushions, paintings, antimacassars, sculptures, sconces, coffee table. Was it for a lack of something to say, a bland recognition they no longer had anything in common? Even though they had been at drama college together, slummed and slutted around Europe along with Victoria, stuck out their thumbs in short skirts at the side of French autoroutes, the three of them a perky little triumvirate, soaking up the vodka, marijuana and one-night stands as if their world was about to end in a nuclear holocaust, Caroline generally ending up with the best looking of whichever young studs they had set their greedy sights on. Or did she really think the flowers were beautiful?

'They match the room,' Caroline noted off-handedly, as if the sole purpose of Mother Nature was to chime with the decor. Or Victoria's taste, for it was she who had been the interior designer of this sumptuous property. 'Is it true?'

'What?'

'You might have something for me.'

'That's why I'm here.'

'How exciting. It's been decades since I've done any real acting.'

'It's just a run-through,' she said brightly. 'A chance to catch up with some of our old drama school chums.' Chums? When did she ever use a word like 'chums'? It was Lew. Something about his bullish, self-assuredness that always put her off-balance, stripped away her own self-confidence until she was gushing away like an awkward teenager, trying to impress, commenting on the flowers. 'Some of the old crowd.'

'Do tell.'

She reeled off a list of names, then told her about the play.

'A Holocaust survivor?'

'It's a decent-sized role.'

'Don't you think I'm a bit full-figured to have been in a concentration camp?'

'It was thirty years ago in this woman's past. She will have filled out since then.'

'I don't think these people ever fill out.'

'Caroline. It's only a bloody run-through.'

'Still. I like to feel I fit the part.'

'I've brought the script. Read it through and let me know.'

'It's fine. I'll do it, I'll do it.'

'Good.'

'It was nice of you to think of me.'

'To be honest, it wasn't my idea. It was Sal's.'

'Oh really. Sal. How thoughtful of him. Tea?'

Chapter Twenty-Six

Extract from an unpublished memoir

When is a person dead? When the heart stops? When the breath ceases? When the brain shuts down? When the body is recovered? When the coffin is buried? When the pyre is lit? When he or she no longer exists in our hearts or our memories? I have no idea when Rollo died. I could have been grieving for him while he was still alive somewhere, cast adrift on a piece of wreckage, washed ashore on some Scandinavian coastline. Unlikely I know, but not impossible. Of course, the law had a different attitude. Rollo was declared dead once the police and the coroner had submitted their reports. It was necessary for the winding-up of the estate. Rollo had made a will. As had I. As had most of the aviators I knew. It made sense with death forever nudging at our wingtips. He left a large estate, most of it inherited, and I was named as one of the beneficiaries. He had no parents, brothers or sisters, but my share was small enough to ensure distant cousins wouldn't contest a scandalous bequest to his lover. He had also bequeathed me his Percival Gull Four, the plane he had disappeared in. I now possessed sufficient funds to buy myself a new one but I decided against it. I never wanted to fly again.

> *Now that my ladder's gone,*
> *I must lie down where all ladders start,*
> *In the foul rag-and-bone shop of the heart*
> —WB Yeats

My own desire to be grounded became irrelevant anyway. With the threat of war looming, all civilian flying was suspended and most of the aircraft in private hands were impounded by the Air Ministry. I considered a number of landed options if I was to make myself useful in the war effort. I thought about being a plotter, working in a data control centre marking out the positions of enemy aircraft crossing over into Britain. Well, I was irked to discover I was too old for that. The RAF only wanted eager young girls with lots of stamina, nerve and a head for figures, a bit like female equivalents of stock market traders. I toyed with being a barrage balloon operator but I realised I simply wasn't strong enough for all the hoisting and pulley work. Instead, I volunteered for the Observer Corps.

It made a lot of sense really, standing at my operations post scouring the sky with binoculars in the middle of the Sussex countryside, the dutiful part of me trying to identify the type and number of German aircraft moving in from the coast while I still held on to the absurd notion I might spot Rollo too, coming back through a crack in the sky from who knows where. It was usually a case of ears first, eyes second as I listened out for the threatening grumble of enemy bombers. I would then point out the location of anything I spotted to my partner on duty who would use a sighting arm to calculate the height and direction of the incoming aircraft. We would then call in the information to our district ops centre. There they would use our data along with that collected from other observation posts together with anything that had come in from the coastal radar stations to decide whether to scramble our own planes, alert anti-aircraft sites, the barrage balloon operators and the ARP. It was important work but it was also a soothing task for me as well, spending hours each day focused on the sky with its drifting clouds and starlit firmaments.

I remember working a shift towards the end of a cold afternoon in January 1941. All the observation posts were on high alert as London had been badly bombed a few nights before but I had nothing to report and called in an "all clear" to the operations centre.

'Amy Johnson's gone missing,' the communications officer on the other end of the phone told me. 'News just coming in.

Unlikely she'd be anywhere near you, Georgie. But be on the look-out anyway.'

'What was she flying?'

'Airspeed Oxford. On her way to RAF Kidlington, I believe.'

'How long has she been gone?'

'She set off at ten thirty this morning.'

I looked at my watch. Three o'clock. I made the calculation knowing the Airspeed. Amy would be running out of petrol just about now. If she was still all right, she'd be searching out an airfield to land and refuel.

I made the change-over on my own shift and headed off home. I hadn't seen Amy for years. Our paths used to cross often in my early days of flying when we were both hanging out at the Hanworth Park base. But more often than not she was off trying to break long-distance records, flying to India, Japan, Australia or the United States with that daredevil husband of hers, Jim Mollison, until they got divorced a couple of years ago. She had joined up with the Air Transport Auxiliary (ATA) when the war broke out. I hadn't heard much about her since. I called up a friend of mine at the Ministry of Aircraft Production as soon as I got in.

'Amy's plane came down over the Thames Estuary,' he told me. 'Parachute spotted in the water though. Naval vessel nearby. But there's a heavy swell over there on the Essex coast. That's all that's been radioed in so far. Fingers crossed she'll be rescued.'

She never was. Drowned at sea was the official report. Neither her body or her plane were ever recovered.

It seems Amy had been ferrying her Airspeed Oxford back from Prestwick in Ayrshire, stopping overnight in Lancashire before going on to deliver her plane to the RAF base at Kidlington. The weather had been pretty murky that day and the likelihood was she got lost in the clouds, ran out of fuel as she was looking for some clean air. In the end she probably thought she was baling out over land rather than sea. I think it was as simple as that. There were a lot of rumours about her death, I suppose that is what happens when you are famous and beloved by a nation. Some said she was shot down mistakenly by our own gunners. Others said they had seen someone else jumping out of the aircraft alongside her – an important passenger or perhaps even a lover. And why shouldn't she have a lover? She was a single, attractive, 37-year-old woman. But that 'mysterious passenger' was more likely the pigskin overnight bag she often carried or even the door of the aircraft which she could have jettisoned to get out of the cockpit. Just pity the poor seaman from HMS Haselmere who drowned trying to rescue the 'mysterious passenger.' And pity poor Amy. An astonishingly courageous woman who was such a source of inspiration to me and many other aspiring pilots.

Her death had a profound effect on me, shaking me out of my own flying lethargy. By May 1941, I had surrendered my observation duties and signed up with the Air Transport Auxiliary.

Chapter Twenty-Seven

A Dress Rehearsal

'Laura, you look divine...'

'But did you see him in *Othello*...?'

'I'm sure she's had something done, she couldn't possibly...'

'And who do you think he slept with to get that...?'

'I loved you in that Japanese thing. Was it true you and Jack...?'

'Half the audience just got up and left...'

'Lady Caroline is it now? I always said your cleavage would get you a peerage...'

To Laura's relief, the cast had arrived on time, in full complement, and to much squealing, kissing and hugging. Several years, decades even, had passed since many of them had met, the intervening period being cruel to some, kinder to others. Caroline might have obtained a title along the way but Laura was aware she had been the most successful in the acting stakes. There were some people like ex-lover Jack who were just born to succeed, for whom nature or society or some divine force conspired to create a glorious path to inevitable stardom. Laura had realised early on she was merely one of a supporting cast who occasionally received a helping hand. A reward for good deeds done in a previous life? A simple victim of positive circumstance? A belief in an equitable universe providing a fair return for hard work? Who knew? Perhaps it was all down simply and purely to luck. During her early career, Edy had got her a part at the last minute when another actress had pulled out, the film she had thought was awful turned out to be a huge critical success. But Laura's appreciation of her own good fortune meant that while internally she obsessed about her success, on the outside she always appeared modest. This humility endeared her to her peers when they might have been forgiven for harbouring more envious or bitter thoughts.

She made a little speech, apologised for the poor quality of the script: 'Too many flashbacks,' she said. 'I always think flashbacks dilute the dramatic tension.' No-one seemed to care. As the morning moved on to her direction of the first read-through, she was genuinely moved by the display of real effort, professionalism and affection shown towards her by these colleagues and friends as they worked on the play.

She had arranged that Quentin should arrive in time for lunch. Which he did with a strut down the aisle in the company of a slobbering labrador. He also brought with him a basket containing jars of caviar, crackers and cheeses which he placed on the tables already laid out with salads, sandwiches and cold sausage rolls.

'To supplement the feast,' he announced, applauding the cast seated on chairs across the stage.

'Our playwright,' Laura told her fellow players who enthusiastically returned Quentin's clapping, some even giving a slight bow as if it were Noel Coward himself who had just appeared with the victuals. Now that there had been this interruption, she stood up and declared: 'Lunch is served.'

The film crew also turned up (three strapping young Australians with a couple of digital cameras and an array of lighting equipment) as did Victoria (for support and to wind-up Caroline). On being introduced to Caroline, Quentin became all gushing: 'Oh, my, my. I remember you. Caroline Fletcher. You were Charlie in that sitcom... what was it called again?... *Tightly Knit.*'

Caroline laughed. A bit too loudly, Laura thought, the rest of the cast turning to look. 'The only thing tightly knit was my sweater,' she said, thrusting out her bosom by way of emphasis.

'Well, well,' he said. 'But who are you to be today?'

'I shall be Hannah. Your Holocaust survivor.'

'Ah yes, Hannah. A woman scarred by her past.'

Caroline pressed a hand against her surgically enhanced chest. 'As I have been,' she said.

'I'm sorry. I don't understand...'

Seeing Quentin's confused look, Laura intervened by introducing Victoria.

To Victoria's astonishment, Quentin grasped her hand, kissed it. 'Such a bounty of natural beauty,' he said.

'He thinks he can charm me,' Victoria told Laura afterwards.

'I saw your harsh demeanour crumble.'

'I've warned you already. He's a manipulative bastard.'

'I know, I know. I'm trying to get through this the best I can. I just wish it wasn't such an awful play. I'm embarrassed for myself. I'm embarrassed for the actors.'

'Don't worry. They're only too happy to have some paid work.'

Laura left Victoria at the buffet table, pulled Quentin aside.

'I thought I'd explain the schedule,' she said.

'Shoot,' he said as he fed his hound another caviar-smothered cracker.

'We've had one read-through this morning. After lunch, there will be a proper rehearsal, then a break, then the final performance which will be filmed. Two cameras – one static to take in the whole stage, the other mobile for close-ups, different angles, back-stage and so on. I'd also like the film crew to interview you about the play. I've prepared a list of questions. Sal will then edit the whole lot down into your final production.'

'You've done a swell job, Laura.'

'Wait until you see the final result.'

'I'm sure it will be just fine. And thank you for the tea.' He toasted her with a cup of his favourite Assam from the Numalighur estate. 'That was thoughtful.'

It wasn't until late afternoon that the final performance was ready to begin, by which time Laura was exhausted. She gave the last instructions to the camera crew, then sat centre stalls with Victoria on one side, Quentin on the other with his hound straddling his feet. She could see he was anxious, seated stiff, tiny eyes unblinking, fixed on the stage, his breathing rapid.

Such a strange man with his cravats, dyed-blonde hair, old-fashioned manners and misplaced American slang. She suddenly felt sorry for him. She wondered if he would see how bad his play really was. Or would he just be blinded by his own vanity? In the end, what did she care? As long as she got access to the Hepburn estate. 'Action!' she shouted.

It was the first time she was witnessing the whole play properly unfold. Up until that point, she had just been working on little chunks of it, out of sequence, never really getting any sense of the total production. As her friends on stage began to disappear into their roles, as the various characters and their complexities began to emerge, what she had dismissed as a dull manuscript was coming alive before her eyes. She started to realise that this was not such an awful play after all. It wasn't vanity that had blinded Quentin to its merits but rather her own anger towards him that had blinded her. She looked across at him. He was all perched up on his seat like an eager puppy. She leaned into Victoria.

'What do you think?' she whispered.

Her friend shrugged. 'I hate to say it. But it's rather good.'

'I'm not imagining things?'

'No, really.'

'Pinch me. I'm dreaming this.'

'Seriously, Laura. Relax. It's fine. Absolutely fine.'

She turned her attention back to the stage. The cast seemed to be enjoying themselves. They really were superb, she had chosen well. Even Caroline, as the filled-out Holocaust survivor, was turning out to be an inspired choice. The cameraman scuttling about among them added a certain gravitas to the event, some spot-on lighting contributed to the drama. She was finding it hard to admit but everything seemed to be falling into place. There was a rhythm, an intensity, a tension, as the play moved towards its climax. And when it did, Quentin was on his feet, shouting 'Bravo! Bravo!' while the cast clapped, congratulated each other. Victoria beside her was muttering: 'Well, what do you know? What do you bloody well know?'

When everyone had calmed, Quentin ordered in champagne from the bar next door.

'This has been absolutely delightful, Laura,' he squealed.

'It went better than expected.'

'A dream come true. To see *Maimonides* performed on stage like that. With such a wonderful cast. How can I thank you?'

'Well, you could sign the consent form.'

'Of course. Of course. Just lay it on me.'

As Quentin appended his signature, one of the Australian film crew came over.

'Sorry to bother you, Laura. But we need to be paid.'

'What do you mean?'

'Cash on the day.'

'How much?'

'Six-fifty.'

'Six-fifty an hour?'

'Six hundred and fifty pounds. As agreed.'

'With Sal?'

'Yeah.'

'I thought he was paying you.'

'Naw. He said you would sort us out.'

'Will you take a cheque?'

Chapter Twenty-Eight

The Hepburn Archives

Transcript from BBC Radio 4 interview
Broadcasting House, London
16ᵗʰ May 1982
Interviewer: Sir Peter Delamere
Interviewee: Georgie Hepburn

PD: I'd like to talk about your flying career now. I'm sure not many of our listeners know this but you were one of the very first women to take to the air. What inspired you to do that?

GH: It seemed very natural for me. After all, my father had been a fighter pilot in the Great War.

PD: You make it sound very matter of fact. But flying in those days was an extremely dangerous occupation.

GH: I suppose it was. But I wasn't one of those pilots who was constantly trying to break records or test the boundaries of aviation mechanics. I was a kind of flying courier. Delivering mail, ferrying personnel, towing banner advertisements, things like that.

PD: But what about that flight you made to the Sinai with Roland Paxton-Jones? That was well-documented as a famous pioneering trip at the time.

GH: Oh that. Yes, that was quite an adventure. One of the greatest things I ever did in my life. Many good memories.

PD: And you and Roland became quite the celebrated couple after that.

GH: Oh, I think Amy and Jim – Amy Johnson and Jim Mollison – were the Flying Sweethearts in those days.

PD: Aren't you being a bit modest here, Georgie? After all, Roland was the wealthy playboy, you were the glamorous actress.

GH: I never thought of it that way. By the time Roland and I were together, his playing-the-field days were over and I was no longer acting. He was an aerial photographer. I was a flying postwoman. Nothing celebrated in that.

PD: You do credit Roland with being one of the most important influences in your life.

GH: Absolutely. The flying was just part of it though. Rollo gave me my first camera. In fact, I still have it. A Leica Mark II.

PD: And tragically, he was killed in an airplane accident.

GH: He wasn't killed, Peter. He just disappeared.

PD: I believe that neither his body nor his plane were ever recovered. That must have been very hard for you. Not to have any kind of closure.

GH: On the contrary. When there is no concrete evidence of death, it gives one hope.

PD: Even after forty years?

GH: I know it's illogical but yes, even after forty years. It's hard to explain to those who have never suffered from such an experience. It is like that famous philosophical question – if a tree falls in the forest and no-one is around to hear it, does it make a sound? If an event like Rollo's supposed death goes unobserved, goes unproven, did it really happen? So yes, there has always been a hallowed space deep inside of me that still harbours a little hope, irrational as it may seem.

PD: I see. Now those kind of tragedies... perhaps I should say events... were quite a normal occurrence in those early days of flight. Much more so, of course, than they are now. Amy Johnson being the most famous.

GH: It was an occupational hazard, I suppose.

PD: That's a brave way of putting it.

GH: Not really. All we early aviators accepted that risk. Both Rollo and Amy would be the first to admit that. These were glorious times. The Golden Age of Flight. But a dangerous time too. I suppose that is what made it so glorious. So glamorous even. The danger. But despite being aware of all of that, these tragedies still have an effect. Of course they do. After Rollo disappeared I stopped flying for a while. When Amy was killed I enlisted with the ATA.

PD: *Are you OK to go on? We could take a break for a few minutes.*

GH: *It's fine, I'm happy to continue. But no more about Rollo, please.*

PD: Well, let's move on to the outbreak of war and the establishment of what you just mentioned there, the ATA or the Air Transport Auxiliary. I'm sure many of our listeners will never have heard of it. Would you mind explaining?

GH: The ATA was formed when it looked like war with Germany was imminent. The idea was to create a back-up air service to the fighting squadrons for things like transport, ferrying planes around between factories and bases, non-operational stuff. Initially, it was only for men who were experienced flyers but too old or infirm to be fighter pilots. It was Pauline – Pauline Gower – a very experienced flyer with lots of high-up connections – who managed to get the women on board as well. I wasn't involved in the initial batch though. *The First Eight* as they were called.

PD: Was there any resistance to women being part of the RAF?

GH: [LAUGHTER] What do you think, Peter? Of course there was. Many people thought women were incapable of doing such a job, and even if we were capable, we were accused of taking the toys away from the boys. Pauline persisted though. It made so much sense. Some of us were very experienced pilots and instructors. Pauline herself had over two thousand hours in the air. I had twelve hundred myself. You know, Peter, I am old enough now to have lived through both the suffragette movement and the feminist movement of the 1960s, both worthy advances of women's causes in their own right. But I can tell you something – I have never felt prouder, freer, more liberated, more joyous, more exhilarated and yes, more equal – after all we ATA female pilots ended up getting paid the same as the men – as I did in the company of those courageous women.

PD: What kind of work did you do?

GH: At the very beginning, *The First Eight* were just given the light, single-engined aircraft to ferry around from the factories or to pick up those impounded from civilian bases. By the time I came along, we were starting to be allowed to fly Hurricanes and Spitfires as well. Not in combat, of course. God forbid the RAF would actually allow a woman to fly into battle. The Russians to their credit were the only ones to have female fighter pilots during the war. The Night Witches they were called.

PD: Night Witches?

GH: The Germans dubbed them that. These Russian women used to carry out harassment bombing at night in these old wooden bi-planes, cutting their engines before the target area and gliding in very low with their bombs. The sound of the wind through the struts and canvas would give a swishing sound. The Germans thought it sounded like broomsticks rushing through the air. And so... Night Witches. Brave women but a bit mad too, flying these crop dusters into a sky full of Messerschmitts. I wouldn't have done it myself. For love or country. Or the ATA.

PD: It was also around this time you met the film director, Douglas Mitchell.

GH: It seems many of the men in my life were involved with airplanes in one way or another. My father was shot down in one, Rollo disappeared in one, and yes, as you say, I met Doug in one.

Chapter Twenty-Nine

Entering the Vaults

Laura didn't know if it was the video delay or Sal was moving slower than usual but it did seem to take him quite a while to get settled in front of his computer screen.

'Howdy,' he said.

'Good afternoon. Or I guess I should say "good morning".'

'Whatever it is, it's too early for me.'

'Bad mood?'

'Editing into the small hours. How did things go with my pal Quentin?'

'Surprisingly well.'

'I thought you said the play was awful.'

'My critical faculties were blinded by my distaste for the man.'

'Well, that should make you feel better.'

'What do you mean?'

'That you weren't blackmailed into producing something crap.'

'It doesn't excuse his manipulation of me. Nor yours.'

'What do you mean by that?'

'The film crew.'

'They didn't show?'

'They turned up all right. And I had to pay them.'

'A thousand dollars.'

'Six hundred and fifty pounds.'

'Sounds about right.'

'You said you would cover their cost.'

'And so I will.'

'Sal. This is your production. I'm your cast. It's not up to me to finance this. Especially the way my career is at the moment.'

'I thought we were partners.'

'That's never been discussed.'

'Well, we can discuss it now.'

'Go ahead.'

'Did Quentin sign the access consent?'

'On the dotted line.'

'Everything?'

'All that is in his possession. Letters, papers, all the photographs, radio interviews, some video. The lot. Total access.'

'That means we can start bringing in the investors.'

'You can start bringing in investors.'

'What do you think about Caroline?'

'What about her?'

'Her husband – that Sir Lew guy – he's loaded.'

'There's no way I'm going to ask Caroline for money.'

'She kind of owes you a favour now.'

'Owes *you* a favour. If you want to approach her, that's up to you. Just keep me out of it.'

'I thought you wanted we should be partners.'

'I wanted that we should talk it through properly. When are you going to be back over here?'

'A couple of weeks tops.'

'I prefer we discuss it then. Face to face.'

'What do you think this is?'

'Skype to Skype. It's not the same.'

'What will you do in the meantime?'

'I'm going to see Quentin.'

She drove over to the Cotswolds in her own little Mini which felt incredibly small as she entered through Quentin's estate gates and up the gravel path towards the manor house. Victoria had offered to accompany her – *you should not allow yourself to be left alone with that man.* She declined the offer. She was sure she could handle Quentin Holloway all by herself.

'Come to claim the spoils,' he said by way of a greeting.

'You make it sound sordid.'

'I apologise, I apologise. My permission was fairly won. I was absolutely delighted with the performance. I've been watching the video all morning.'

'I'm glad it made you happy.'

'Would you like something to eat or drink before we begin?'

'I'd like to see what's ahead of me first.'

'I have a special room.'

He led her upstairs. Thick carpet, brass rods, dark ceiling beams set off by white walls, a series of Tudor doors, possibly original, in dark oak with black ornate latches and handles. Quentin stopped before one of them.

'A couple of things before we go in.'

'Yes?'

'This is my study,' he said, pointing to the adjacent door. 'Inside there is a photocopier and scanner. I am quite happy for you to copy certain documents. But it will be in my sole discretion which ones.'

'It was agreed I should have total access.'

'That is the key word, Laura. "Access". That you will have. But I will not allow any secondary material to leave here without my permission.'

'Agreed. Anything else?'

'Your mobile phone.'

'Really?'

'Yes. I don't want you taking photographs of any documents without my permission either.'

She handed over her phone.

'Shall we go in?' he said.

She stared at the door. It was as if she was about to reveal herself to Georgie than the other way around.

'Laura?'

'I'm ready.'

The room was set out as the study it no doubt had been for Georgie. A large desk sat by the window with a view out to the garden and the fields beyond. A leather chair, two grey-metal filing cabinets, a typewriter, a computer, a telephone. All the usual fittings for a home office. Except for the photographs.

Every section of wall space was covered with Georgie's work. It was an exhibition. An homage. An exposé. Many of them iconic images of the previous century. A lot of nature photography she had never seen before, even though she thought she possessed every single book released of her work. It took Laura's breath away in her excitement of it all.

'Oh, look at these,' she said at the sight of some small, black and white headshots.

'Bedouin,' Quentin said. 'The very first photographs she ever took.'

'When would that be?'

'September nineteen thirty four. Sinai Desert. A trip she made with Roland Paxton-Jones. It's all in the archive.'

'These faces. So natural.'

'They really trusted her. She had that way about her. You felt you could tell her anything.'

'You could see she had a talent. Even then.'

'She was more interested in flying in those days. But she could have been so many things.'

'Do you mind?' she asked, signalling the chair.

'Go ahead. You may treat this room as your own. Everything is in the filing cabinets. Beginning top left, in chronological order. I've made a CD of her nineteen eighty-two radio interview with the BBC which you can play through the computer. There are transcripts as well, if you prefer. The extracts from her unpublished memoir will probably be the most useful to you, again in chronological order. I've left pad and paper for notes. Dial zero for an outside line. Dial nine for internal. The numbers are all there. Please order anything you want from the kitchen. Cook is on hand until eight every evening.'

As Laura rocked gently in Georgie's chair, she noticed the small framed black and white photograph on the desk. Nothing more than a snapshot really. Two women sitting in an open-top sports car, the older one being Georgie.

'Who's that with her?' Laura asked.

'Oh, that's my mother.'

'Susan?'

'Yes, Susan. That would have been just after the war. Down at Grandma Ginny's farm in Sussex. My mother would only have been about eighteen then.'

'The two of them look so happy together.'

'That photograph has acquired a bit of a mythical quality in our family. Seemingly Grandma Ginny clambered up on to the bonnet to take it. I don't remember her myself but she did have a reputation for being a feisty lady.'

'It's unusual even to see a picture of Georgie.'

'I know. That's the case, isn't it? Always the photographer, never the photographed.'

Chapter Thirty

The Hepburn Archives

Extract from an unpublished memoir

The First Eight group of female ATA pilots attracted a lot of press attention when they started out, glamour girls of the sky, all that sort of thing. After all, there wasn't much good news around in those early days of the war so what better way of boosting morale than by having a few snaps of the 'ATA-girls' brightening up the breakfast table. Even when I joined up a year and a half later, there were still a lot of photographers snooping around for a story. Some of my crowd would encourage the attention, rushing off to the London clubs and parties as soon as a day's flying was over, drumming up a few headlines for the next day's papers yet still making it back to base in time for the first morning flight. That kind of life wasn't for me though, I was always thinking of Rollo every time I took to the sky, I still do.

Anything to Anywhere. That was the unofficial slogan of the ATA and that pretty much was the job I had to do, ferrying all kinds of aircraft here, there and everywhere. The main ferry pool was at White Waltham near Maidenhead, I was stationed at Hamble in Hampshire but basically we could be sent all over the country, even as far as Lossiemouth up in the north of Scotland. Sometimes in an open cockpit bi-plane with only basic instruments and without radios, the only method of navigation was by following landmarks, not a particularly safe way to fly through low clouds which could be most of the time.

The factories were churning out fighter planes as fast as they could, perhaps as many as thirty a week, and one of our tasks was to get them away from these manufacturers as quickly as possible, prime targets for the Luftwaffe that they were, and over to the M.U.s (Maintenance Units) for armament and munitions to be installed. I never knew what I would be flying one day to the next, it could be a Spitfire or a Hurricane or a Mosquito or even one of my old Tiger Moths. It was a ride in the Spitfires I savoured the most, I absolutely loved them, we all did, it was like slipping into a bespoke suit, that plane really felt a part of me as I swung it through the sky. It was like dancing with a lover.

It must have been around mid-1943, I was commissioned to fly a group of pilots up to the aircraft factory at Castle Bromwich in an Avro Anson to collect some ready-for-battle Spitfires. I was a bit miffed for being the one to do the ferrying, missing out on my own chance to have a dance with one of the new Spits but orders were orders. After dropping off the pilots, I then had to go on to the RAF station at Ringway near Manchester to pick up a film crew on some propaganda shoot for the Ministry of Information, take them back to London.

There were five of them in the crew, all men, the director and his four minions with a whole load of equipment. I didn't usually have anyone sitting up beside me on a short hop like this one but the Anson only has four seats at the back so it would have been churlish of me not to let one of them come up front unless the poor man wanted to spend the entire journey jammed into the gun turret. That person turned out to be the director himself, Douglas Mitchell.

Doug must have been close to fifty then, still a good-looking man in the Douglas Fairbanks mould, grey-blue eyes, a good shock of hair, a thin moustache topping a wide, wide smile that could charm even a hollowed-out woman like me. We introduced ourselves, he made himself comfortable in the co-pilot seat as if he were a born flyer, strapped himself in and was chatting away even as the Anson was speeding along the runway. The conversation as I remember it went something like this:

'So, tell me, Second Officer Hepburn,' he said. 'I heard some of the male pilots don't like being ferried around by a woman. Is that true?'

'It's been known to happen,' I replied as I lifted the Anson clean into the air with that familiar creaking sound these twin-engined beauties were renowned for. The noise didn't faze Doug a bit.

'I pity the poor buggers then.' He glanced at me when he swore, probably wondering whether I could take a bit of cursing like a man. 'I prefer a woman driver myself.'

'Why is that?'

'A lot more attractive for a start.'

I was hoping the view of Manchester off to his right was grabbing his attention for I felt myself suddenly redden to my roots at his comment. My reaction surprised me. After all, I was used to having my fair share of male gibe and innuendo thrown at me on a daily basis. But there was something about this man that caught me off-guard.

'Is that all you can say about the wonderful women of the ATA?' I said, trying to keep the conversation professional, even though we were huddled together, our shoulders and knees touching.

'I have nothing but admiration for you all,' he said. 'The sooner you women take over the planet, the better off we'll be. No more damned wars for a start. Can't see a woman trying to take us into war, can you?'

I wasn't so sure I agreed but I kept my opinion to myself, I knew quite a few women in my squadron who'd only be too happy to gun down a few Jerries from the Luftwaffe. Doug went quiet for a while himself until he said: 'You look familiar.'

'We've never met,' I replied.

'Are you sure?'

'I would have remembered.'

'I'll take that as a compliment,' he said with a chuckle and again I felt myself flush. What the hell was happening to me? I loosened my belt so I could lean forward to make an unnecessary check of the various gauges on my instrument panel.

'Haven't been in the film business, have you?' he asked once I had settled back in my seat.

Even hard-hearted me couldn't resist that bait. 'Way back in the Stone Age,' I said.

'When was that?'

'Before the talkies.'

'It wasn't that long ago.' Doug turned towards me, drew himself back so he could have a full view of my profile. 'I recognize you now, Second Officer Hepburn,' he said.

'I doubt that.' I gave the controls a little jiggle so he'd sit back properly in his seat. I heard a groan from back in the passenger area.

'*The Woman Walks Free.* Is that it?'

I actually felt my chest swell up under my safety belt from the sheer joy of being remembered. 'Well done,' I said evenly, trying to remain unflustered by his interest.

'I loved that film... now, give me a second and I'll just get your first name, memory isn't as good as it used to be... Jean?... Grace?... Georgina... Georgina Hepburn. Am I right?'

'Bingo again.'

'Well, what do you know,' Doug said, slapping his thigh. 'What happened to you after that? I don't remember seeing you in anything else.'

'Talkies killed me.'

'Killed a lot of people,' he said. 'That was a great film though. One of the best roles for a woman around at the time. A Max Rosen script.'

'You remember Max?'

'I don't need to. I know him now.'

'Really?'

'He works with me at the Ministry. Writes a lot of this propaganda stuff that I direct. It's pretty mindless work compared to being a proper scenarist. But there's a war on...'

I asked Doug more questions about Max but I didn't glean very much, just that he was still married, still living in London.

'How often do you see him?' I asked.

'Just when I get anchored in the office. Which isn't much.'

'Will you see him now that you're back in London?'

'Probably.'

'Would you give him a message… a letter for me?'

'Of course.'

'He's an old friend.'

'No harm in catching up with old friends,' he said, with just a tinge of sarcasm. 'In times like these.'

After we landed at White Waltham, Doug said he could give me half an hour to write out my letter, he didn't want to keep his own crew hanging around much longer than that, they had a van waiting to take them back into central London. It was actually good I was under a little bit of pressure, it made me stick to the essentials, plenty of time for details later if Max decided he wanted to see me. I gave Doug the envelope, he said he'd probably catch up with Max the following day.

Chapter Thirty-One

Let's Spend the Night Together

With Quentin gone, Laura swivelled in Georgie's well-worn chair, feeling possessed of a sense that her heroine's spirit was hovering behind and above her, embracing her, whispering into her ear. '*I am watching you,*' she imagined Georgie saying. '*I am watching you. Can I trust you?*' 'Of course, you can,' Laura said out loud. 'Of course, you can.' In her excitement, she felt playful, swinging herself quickly from side to side like a little girl, before settling into a more sombre, more respectful, more adult mood. She steadied herself, then moved gently in an arc, surveying as she did so the panorama of photographs adorning every inch of wall space, some framed, others simply pinned into place. There didn't seem to be any order to their positioning, more a mosaic than any sequence of a career. She wondered whether Georgie herself had organized them or whether this was Quentin's own homage. *Where to begin?* She swung round to address the filing cabinets. *At the beginning, of course.* The thought intrigued her for she was aware of the little known fact that Georgina Hepburn had once been an actress in the silent movies. She had always wondered why Georgie had not pursued that particular career and now here was her chance to find out. Filing cabinet number one. Top left. Cue lights. Cue curtains. The story of *Georgie by Georgie* was about to unfold.

She became absolutely enthralled by the details that emerged from Georgie's early career. How she used to hang around the studio sets waiting to be picked up as an extra, her first minor role as a simple cashier girl in *On the Pleasure Pier*, acting lessons, bit parts, taking on summer jobs just to survive, typical of an actress as much back then as it was now. She read about her relationship with the screenwriter Max Rosen and how it led to her success in *The Woman Walks Free*, the press clippings, a day out at Ascot with the great Ivor Novello. She found the CD of her interview with the BBC which she played through the computer. It was wonderful to just sit there in Georgie's study, in Georgie's chair, with her eyes closed, listening to Georgie talk about her life. There was so much richness in her voice, an accent hard to determine, somewhere between refined English and American drawl, the kind of throaty timbre a smoker might possess, yet as far as Laura knew Georgie didn't smoke. She rocked gently in her chair, let Georgie talk on, it was as if she were in the same room. So engrossed was she with the interview that she didn't hear Quentin's arrival.

'I did knock,' he said. 'But there was no answer.'

'I was just so absorbed,' she said, clicking off the recording. 'I feel... I don't know... so emotional about all of this.'

'The silent movie years. She could have been such a star.'

'Why did she give it up?'

'Never talked about it.'

'Was she always like that? Without a mind to the past?'

'Not at all. She would chat about her time as a pilot for days on end. But about her film career? Not a word. She forbade the subject even being mentioned.'

'It does seem odd though. One minute she was riding high. And then nothing. Was it something to do with her relationship with Max Rosen?'

'Perhaps.' He clapped his hands to bring an end to that particular strand of conversation. 'I didn't want to disturb you. But it is late.'

'What time is it?'

'Just after nine.'

'Really. The hours just flew by.'

'Hungry?'

'To be honest, I'm starving.'

'Cook has gone home. But I brought you something.' Quentin stepped back out through the doorway then returned holding a tray which he managed to slip onto the table beside the various scattered documents. 'Roast beef sandwiches,' he announced with a mock flourish. 'You're not veggie, are you?'

'Roast beef is perfect.'

'And a glass of Beaujolais. A Juliénas.'

'This is all very kind of you.'

'All part of the service. I can bring up the bottle if you want?'

'One glass is fine at this time of night.'

He hung about in front of her, seemingly unsure what to do next. There was no other chair in the room. He placed a hand on the desk, started to drum away with his fingers. 'I was wondering if you would like to stay the night.'

Laura picked up her glass, gently allowed the wine to swirl beneath her nostrils, breathed in the vanilla scent, paused to admire the red ruby hue. If this were a scene in a movie, this is exactly what she would do to add to the tension. It was such a heavily laden question. What did Quentin actually mean by his offer? Was he literally providing her with a bed for the night? Or was there a more subtle proposal embedded in his question? After all, here was a divorced man, one who had declared himself a fan of hers, a man no doubt still full of sexual urges, although she did not put him down as being a great seducer. She sipped at the Juliénas. It was her favourite of the Cru Beaujolais, rich and spicy, the taste for which she had acquired from her father. Good cigars and good wine, that was about all she had to thank him for. She said nothing. She certainly wasn't going to flatter Quentin with his fortuitous choice of vineyard.

Her host moved into a proper lean on the desk, perhaps unnerved by the delay which could be turning what might have been a simple gentlemanly suggestion into one laden with meaning. 'The roads are quite badly lit in this part of the world,' he said.

She put down her wine, reached for the roast beef sandwich, took a bite. Thick crusts, French mustard, just the way she liked it. She chewed slowly. 'I didn't bring an overnight bag,' she said once she had swallowed.

'Oh, don't worry about that. The guest room has everything you need. *En suite*. Toothbrush. Night clothes.'

Night clothes? What an odd choice of words, she thought. She really was making Quentin nervous. She glanced out of the window. A summer's eve but the light was fading fast. Red sky at night and all that. It would be dark by the time she set off. She looked back at Quentin who had turned one of the papers on the desk round towards himself. The playbill for *The Woman Walks Free. Yes*, she thought. *I can definitely handle him.*

'I shall stay,' she announced. 'I can continue with some more of my research in the morning.'

'That's settled then,' Quentin said, breathing out a huge sigh.

The bedroom was lovely, adorned with fabrics of muted grey and pinks, the *en suite* bathroom tiled in the same colours. There was a view to the front of the house with its massive lawn and gravelled driveway. She opened one of the hinged lead-paned windows, set it fully on its stay, sucked in the air with its dewy moisture and smell of pine. Down below, she could see the outline of her little Mini fading away into the darkness, the glass of the headlights just catching the glint of the rising moon. The hoot of an owl then a thick silence. Apart from these night creatures, there was probably nothing around for miles to make a sound. She turned back to the room. The night clothes Quentin had referred to were contained in a sealed plastic bag from M&S – checked pyjama bottoms and a loose cotton T-shirt. But she had ignored those in favour of the luxurious bathrobe she had donned after her shower. She laid down on top of the queen size bed, stared at the ceiling. She thought of Georgie's exploits as a pilot.

She had read somewhere before that Georgie had worked for the Air Transport Auxiliary during the war but imagined her in some kind of role as an aerial photographer not as an actual pilot. Yet now she had discovered that Georgie had been one of the actual pioneers in the Golden Age of Flight. Laura still possessed a certain squeamishness about flying even in the present era, how hard must the conditions have been then.

A tiny aircraft, some simple navigation aids, exposed to the elements, crammed into a tiny cockpit with only the drone of the engine for company. And these weren't just little joyrides above London, but flights of thousands of miles, not knowing if there was enough fuel to get you to the next destination, not even knowing if there was a place to properly land. Or if the welcome would be friendly or hostile. And here she was, Laura Scott, wrapped up in a warm bathrobe, worried about driving back to London in the darkness because of the absence of a few street lights. She inwardly chastised herself for her own temerity.

A couple of hours later, still unable to sleep, she returned to the open window. She had abandoned her duvet cover, thrown off her bathrobe and tried to sleep naked through the sultry night but that hadn't worked either. She had then put on the M&S sleep-suit which she wore now as she stared out into the darkness. She would have loved a cigarette, hadn't smoked for years apart from the occasional cigar, but she craved one right now to calm her moody restlessness. She was hungry too. That one roast beef sandwich had not been nearly enough. Perhaps it was the acid in her stomach that was keeping her awake. She would go downstairs, try to find something to eat.

She hated wandering around other people's houses like this, fearful of waking up her host, not knowing whether to switch on lights, not even knowing where the switches were even if she wanted to, trying to remember where the kitchen was, careful not to trip over the stair rods. She eventually made it down to the bottom of the stairway, the moonlight through a window in the eaves helping her up until that point. But here in the narrow dark corridor she needed to search for the nipple of a light switch, stumbling into a low table in the process. Which apart from hurting her knee did turn out to be supporting a large lamp. She felt her way up the base until she found the toggle, turned it on. She recognized where she was. The kitchen lay ahead of her then through there to the conservatory where she and Sal had taken tea on their first visit. It was also at this point she remembered Quentin owned a large dog.

She played with the handle of the kitchen door without opening it, waited for a bark or a growl but none came. She eased the door slightly ajar, inserted her hand, felt up and down the wall on the other side, until she found the dimmer knob, turned it up. The dog basket was empty. The hound must be sleeping with its master.

She found a plate of cold cuts and cheeses in the fridge, added butter, crackers and a glass of milk to a tray then took it through to the moonlit conservatory. She moved across to one of the sofas, turned on a table lamp, started to work on her post-midnight feast. Once she had satisfied her hunger, she took up her glass of milk, walked over to the wall of windows. The moon and stars had clouded over, there was not much to be seen, she could hardly even make out the swimming pool. A slight movement in the glass distracted her. She realised she was looking at Quentin's reflection.

'It seems I have disturbed you again,' he said quietly.

She didn't turn round, just watched on as he stepped up close beside her, almost shoulder to shoulder.

'I couldn't sleep,' she said, addressing his image in the glass. He wore a blue silk dressing-gown, his hair was slightly mussed which seemed so out of character for him. 'Same?'

'I'm something of a night person,' he confessed. 'It's not unusual for me to be wandering around at this hour.'

'I hope you don't mind, but I helped myself to something out of the fridge.'

'*Mi casa es su casa.*'

'I appreciate that.'

She felt that he had inched even closer to her, she wasn't sure. Then moonlight broke through the clouds and she saw that the swimming pool had been drained. She shivered at the sight of it.

'Are you all right?' Quentin asked, briefly touching her forearm.

'I have a phobia about empty swimming pools,' she said. 'I

don't know why. It must come from some suppressed childhood memory.'

'There were some cracks in the tiles,' he said. 'I had to drain it. I don't use it much anyway these days.'

She felt rooted to her spot. Even with this view of the empty pool, she couldn't pull away. It was as if Quentin – or at least his reflection – had hypnotized her.

'I love this garden,' he said eventually. 'Georgie moved into her nature photography phase not long after she came to live here.'

'I noticed all those close-up prints of flowers up in her study. I'd never seen any of those before.'

'It was the portraits that made her famous, of course. But it was nature rather than people that fascinated her in the end. I used to follow her around the garden helping carry her equipment. I would have been five or six at the time.'

'You must have many wonderful memories of her.'

'You can't see it from here in the dark. But there is a small orchard over there to the left. That is where she died.'

'I only know she passed away at home. What happened exactly?'

'She loved to pick the apples,' he said. 'She had her own small step-ladder. Even in her eighties, nothing could stop her from getting up on it and foraging among the branches. I discovered her lying on the ground at the foot of one of the trees. No life in her at all.'

'That must have been quite traumatic for you.'

'Traumatic indeed. But for Georgie, it was a good way to die. Quickly. In the garden she loved. My mother was devastated though. Are your parents still alive, Laura?'

'They both are. My father unfortunately has latter-stage dementia. He is in a home now, doesn't know who I am.'

'How awful for you. And for him too, of course. Your mother?'

'Oh, she's having the time of her life. She's become one of these cruise junkies. Just loves to hop from one ship to the next.

I hardly ever see her these days. But then again I very rarely did.'

'Ah yes, parents,' Quentin sighed. 'I never knew my father at all. He left almost as soon as I was born.'

'Your mother lived to a ripe old age though.'

'She was also in her eighties when she passed.'

Laura suddenly felt very cold. And very tired. 'I think I'll go back to bed,' she said. But as she turned away from the window, Quentin caught her by the arm.

'I know you don't like me very much,' he said.

The question startled her but she quickly regained her composure. 'Why do you think that?'

'I have an instinct for such things. Anyway, it doesn't matter. What's important is that we have a good professional relationship. I was impressed by the work you did for my play. And I'm sure you'll do a good job with Georgie.'

'Thank you.'

'I also hope that as time progresses, you might begin to think more kindly towards me. After all, my only interest is in protecting Georgie.'

'I can see that.' Although protecting Georgie from what, she wasn't sure.

Chapter Thirty-Two

Extract from an unpublished memoir

I remember I was filling in my daily logbook in the hut at the White Waltham base where we female pilots used to change in and out of our uniforms. I had just flown down from somewhere up north in one of the brand-new Spits and I was feeling as high as a kite. Perhaps we wouldn't have described it in such a way back then but there was a kind of sexual ecstasy experienced from flying one of these planes. The control, the speed, the manoeuvrability, the power, the thrum and thrust of the engine, the sensitivity of the throttle, the potential (one denied we women pilots) to shoot another aircraft out of the sky. To put it simply – and I can say this now – it was like having a bloody orgasm flying one of those things. So there I was, all flushed and buzzing, finding it difficult to keep my pen focused on the narrow lines and little boxes to be filled in when I looked up and there was Doug Mitchell standing in the doorway. It had been three days since I had given the film director my letter for Max so it was with a little bit of a disappointment that it was Doug who was blocking out my light and not my ex-lover.

'Busy?' he asked with the same ease as if it were my own senior commander standing there putting the question.

'Boring paperwork.'

'Can I come in?'

'Please enter,' I said, surprised by his reticence then remembering the *Women Only* sign on the door.

He was dressed casually in a sports jacket and open shirt collar, something manly and slightly predatory about him which made me both excited and wary at the same time. Although having just jumped down off a Spit, any male, even

Old Tom our mechanic, would probably have had the same effect. 'I didn't think I'd see you again,' I said, all primed up for a bit of banter until I picked up that Doug's mood was sombre. 'Did you see Max?' I asked.

He shook his head, then moved in a bit closer to where I sat. 'It's bad news, I'm afraid.'

'What do you mean?' Although I knew perfectly well what he meant. How many times had a person heard that phrase – *it's bad news, I'm afraid* – over the course of the war?

Doug came and sat down beside me, placed his hand over my hand, the one that held the pen. I had a desperate desire to continue filling in my logbook, I was annoyed Doug's clasp was stopping me. 'Georgie,' he said softly. 'A bombing raid. Only a few days ago. I'm sorry.'

'A bombing raid,' I repeated.

'Some loose ordnance. Luftwaffe happy to risk some flak by dumping its load over London. Doesn't happen much these days. Unlucky.'

'Unlucky,' I said, not sure whether it was me or Max who was unlucky.

'I brought you back the letter.'

'Thank you.'

'I have a car,' he said.

I looked up from my uncompleted logbook. I was unsure what he meant by that statement. He must have seen my puzzlement for he added: 'I can take you into London. We could have a drink somewhere. Cheer you up.'

'Yes. Cheer me up.'

'Well?'

'I'll need a few minutes to fill this in.'

Doug took me to a pub in a narrow lane just off Curzon Street near Green Park. Plush red leather banquettes, huge bar with little on offer, all a bit tattered but what wasn't in those days. Doug brought over a beer for himself, a gin and tonic for me. I hadn't said much during the ride over, Doug being kind enough to leave me alone with my thoughts, but now he seemed anxious to talk.

'I'm divorced,' he said. 'I thought you should know.'

I didn't think I should know at all, my mind being more occupied with my remorse rather than on Doug's marital status. That didn't stop him going on.

'A couple of children. One boy and one girl,' he added. 'They're with their mother, of course. Down in Guildford. I don't get to see them very often. My work takes me all over the place. Not much time.' He took a large gulp of beer. 'Growing up without me. Perhaps not a bad thing. And you?'

I now realised what was going on. I was supposed to participate in a conversation rather than sit there all quiet and reflective, possibly because Doug had no idea how to treat a grieving woman. It had been a long time since I'd been out like this with a man who wasn't a flying officer or my senior commander. 'What do you want to know?'

'Tell me about you and Max. Were you close?'

'We were an item back in my silent film days. It didn't last too long. Just over a year. He was very intense about everything. Politics, ideas, literature, me. He was a good writer though.'

'Yes. *The Woman Walks Free* was excellent, ahead of its time really. Even all these silly Ministry of Information films he wrote for. He always did professional work. So what happened with the two of you?'

'He was ambitious. We both were. Then, when I could no longer be a vehicle for his ambition, he... buggered off.'

Doug smiled yet he seemed slightly taken aback by my swearing. To be honest, I had surprised myself but it showed me how angry I was with Max. For buggering off in the first place. And now, after all these years, getting himself killed before I had a chance to talk to him.

'One of the chaps,' Doug said.

'Who? Max?'

'No, you,' he said. 'Too much time spent with the troopers.'

'I can swear if I want to.'

'I'm sure you can. And you will, no doubt. But why did you want to see him again? If all he did was bugger off the last time.'

'Unfinished business.'

'I see.' Doug moved in closer, stretched his arm along the top of the banquette above me. There was a smell from him that was so familiar. It came as a shock to me when I remembered what it was. Citrus shaving soap. The same as my father used. 'And are you stepping out with someone now?' he asked.

I laughed at his remark. Perhaps a little too loudly, for a lonely old codger at the bar turned round, gave me a look for disturbing his solace. 'Me?' I said. 'I'm a middle-aged spinster.' Oh how I hated that word. Spinster. There I should be, sitting at home, spinning thread, rather than up in the skies putting a Spit through it's paces. 'No, not spinster. Spitster. That's what I am.' It must have been the gin talking for I laughed, raised my glass to the skies. 'To all the great female Spitsters.'

Doug passed me his handkerchief. It was only then that I realised I had been crying.

'Perhaps we should go,' he said.

'Go where?'

Doug took me back to his tiny flat in Shepherd's Bush. He cooked me a rubbery omelette from dried eggs and I drank too much gin. We made love on damp sheets wrapped around a sagging mattress while sirens wailed outside and I let a middle-aged woman's memory of one man be replaced by the comfort of – and perhaps hopes for – another.

But it didn't work out that way. We didn't see too much of each other after that interlude. He was busy making propaganda films all over the country for the Ministry of Information while I was ferrying planes daily for the ATA. If luck had it and his break in filming coincided with a few days leave for me, then we might manage to see each other. But an affair that started out with a lot of initial passion soon died away through lack of care and attention. Wartime might have been a benign background for desperate lovers but not for long-term relationships. So that was the end of Doug. At least for the time being.

Chapter Thirty-Three

Absent Fathers

Working on Georgie's early memoirs had put Laura in a nostalgic mood, sending her on a guilt-ridden trip down to visit her father in Eastbourne. The day was warm with only a light sea-breeze so his care nurse had placed him outside in a wheelchair, lined up alongside other naval veterans on the gravel path fronting the cream Regency-style building that faced southwards to the Channel. Nurse Donovan was a young Irish woman with a plain, round oatcake of a face who gave Laura a little dip of a curtsey as she approached as if she were welcoming royalty itself to her parish.

'That's your daughter Laura here to see you,' Nurse Donovan said bending down close to her father. 'Remember Laura? The famous film star. Of course you do.' And then to Laura herself. 'I'll just leave you with the Captain then.'

The rank was not some kind of patronising honorific. Her father had indeed been a captain, commanding ocean liners out of Southampton until he retired. Laura always remembered him as a gentle mast of a man, tall and straight-backed, red-cheeked like a drinker although he hardly touched a drop, his face forever tilted slightly upwards as if he were constantly checking the direction of the wind. Hidden behind his back in large hands cuffed with lines of gold braid there would always be some exotic gift – a handmade doll from Peru, a coral necklace from Hawaii, a child's dress made from Shanghai silkworms – items she still treasured as compensation for the time with him she never had. Now here he was with all the time in the world for her and he had no idea who she was.

She pulled up a rickety metal chair rusted in places from the salty air and sat down beside him. She waited until she felt he was aware of her presence. Good eye contact, plenty of touching, the simplest of language, that was what she had been told. It was her turn to give him a gift. She took out the small aluminium tube from her handbag, unscrewed the top and tipped out the cigar, placed it within her father's fingers, then guided his hand so he could run the *parejo* under his nose.

'Smells,' Nurse Donovan had told her. 'Smells is always something that can bring them back.' As the brown leathery wrapped-up leaves passed beneath his nostrils, she was irritated to see a patch of grey stubble just above his upper lip where the nurse's razor had missed a stroke, a lack of precision so unbecoming in a man who prided himself on smooth-cheeked perfection. She would 'have a word' – as her mother would put it – with the carer later, although her mother barely came to see the Captain these days, off as she was on her own ocean voyages, possibly as revenge for the loss of precious time in her marriage to this seafaring man.

'Chocolate,' her father said, although Laura wasn't sure if he was referring to the aroma from the cigar or if he actually wanted some chocolate.

'Yes, chocolate,' she echoed. She would have liked to have lit up the cigar for him but smoking was forbidden on the premises even out here in the grounds. She retrieved the *parejo* from the clutch of his fingers, returned it to its tube, slid it into his top pocket. She then delved back into her handbag for the print-outs she'd run off from her computer.

'Football,' Nurse Donovan had also told her. 'They don't remember nothing but they can tell you about a goal scored fifty years ago. See if you can talk to your father about football. That way you might feel you've had some meaningful conversation.'

Laura didn't know the first thing about the sport although she did know the Captain had supported Southampton. An obvious choice really, her father managing to sneak in a home game whenever his ship was docked in the city's harbour. Thanks to the wonder of the Internet, she was able to locate a website that contained all kinds of memories of famous games at the club's ground, The Dell as it was called in her father's day, even she knew that now.

'Here's a game for you, Daddy,' she said. 'March sixteenth, ninety eighty four. Southampton versus Liverpool. Two-nil for Southampton. Both goals scored by Daniel Wallace. One of them an overhead kick. It was the first ever televised match from The Dell. Were you there?'

Her father just stared out to sea, his once vibrant brown eyes faded to a kind of dull yellow. She thought again of Georgie's photographs, how she had managed to capture the essence of her elderly subjects yet now when she observed her own father she could locate nothing of the person she once knew. If only Georgie had been around to photograph her father while his own essence still remained, she would have treasured it forever. A breeze came up and she shivered. She lifted up a fold of the blanket on her father's lap so that it covered his chest. She tried again:

'Southampton defeated Manchester United one goal to nil to win the FA Cup Final in 1976. Do you remember that game, Daddy?' She looked across at him but again no response. She was just about to search for another stand-out piece of information from her print-outs when her father said:

'Turner.'

'Turner? Who's Turner?

'Turner, Rodrigues, Peach, Holmes, Blyth, Steele, Gilchrist, Channon, Osgood, McCalliog, Stokes.'

'Who are they, Daddy?'

He shook his head.

'Were they your friends? Your crew?'

Her father jabbed a finger at the paper in her hand. She looked down the sheet. He had just recited the names of every player in that Southampton Cup-winning team of 1976. 'Oh, Daddy,' she cried.

She sat quietly with him after that, watching his face in its scan of the sea, listening to his hoarse breathing. She really didn't know this man at all, off as he had been on his long haul seafaring stints that took him away from home three or four weeks at a time. She remembered the excitement of awaiting his return on shore leave, the anticipation of the presents that would be the envy of her young classmates, but beyond that she hardly recalled his visits. What did he do during his time at home? She had no memory of him together with her mother or of him taking her anywhere. He had no interest in the garden or the pub. He walked a lot, she remembered that. Across Hampstead Heath, over Parliament Hill and on down to Camden where he would follow the towpath on the Regent's Canal for miles. He never took her with him, too far for a young girl he'd say, she guessed he just wanted to be alone, close to the barges and to the water. She thought back to Georgie and the loss of her father in the war. Perhaps that is why both she and Georgie had become actresses, seeking the attention they never had from absent fathers, trying hard not to feel alone.

'I'm doing a one-woman play about the life of Georgie Hepburn,' she told him. 'Do you know who she is?'

Her father just looked at her, then his eyes wavered to focus on what was behind her. The beach and the sea.

Nurse Donovan returned with her usual patronising manner that so irritated Laura but which she stopped herself from criticising as the nurse really was an excellent carer. Apart from the sloppy shaving which she had decided to forgive.

'Did he behave himself then?' Nurse Donovan asked.

'Good as gold.'

'He's such a gentleman he is, aren't you, Captain?'

'Has my mother been down recently?'

'Oh yes, she was here only last week. Must have been… let me see…Wednesday was it? No, Thursday. Yes, Thursday. She looked so well. All tanned and healthy. Didn't she, Captain? All nice and tanned and healthy. Your wife. Been on holiday.'

Her father just continued to stare out to sea.

'She brought you a nice gift, didn't she?' Nurse Donovan went on. 'She's always bringing you presents.'

'What did she give him?' Laura asked.

'Oh, a nice honey cake all the way from Madeira. And a straw hat. I forgot about that. I could have had him wearing it today. Just the right weather for a hat, don't you think? Smart. For such a gentleman.'

Chapter Thirty-Four

The Hepburn Archives

Extract from an unpublished memoir

8th May 1945 was a public holiday to celebrate victory over the Germans. I remember it well. How could anyone forget? The war in Europe was over but for me, another war had began. The battle with my mother. My Aunt Ginny had called me.

'The police found her,' she told me. 'Wandering round the fields in a neighbouring village. How she got there I do not know. She was in her nightdress, wearing wellington boots. I can't stay with her, Georgie. I need to go back to the farm. You have to come down.'

It was easier said than done. As soon as war was officially declared over, the citizens of London had burst into spontaneous celebration, masses of them rushing to converge around Trafalgar Square and Buckingham Palace. Everything and everywhere was festooned with red, white and blue ribbons, the church bells were ringing, the river craft were hooting their horns, people were singing and dancing in the streets. I was on the top deck of a bus which was trying to plough its way through all of this just as dusk was falling. What I remember most were the windows, the lights coming on behind the glass, the black-out blinds all taken down, a city blinking awake from its war-weary slumber. Who would have thought my soul could receive such a boost from these storeys of unobstructed glass? Such a symbol of hope those windows were, of optimism, of the future. I got off the bus, walked the rest of the way to Victoria Station, pushing against the crowd.

I hadn't seen my mother for two years. The difference in her appearance over that time was horrific. When I had left she was a healthy, robust woman actively engaged in a social whirl of village fêtes, garden parties, community meetings and church affairs. I returned to find her shrunk, skinny and ashen-faced, sitting stiff-backed and expressionless in her favourite armchair. The worst of all was the terrified look in her eyes.

'You finally came to visit, Georgie,' she said as I pecked her sparsely powdered cheek.

'Yes, I am here.'

Aunt Ginny hugged me, shepherded me away into another room.

'You have to be very patient with her,' she said.

'What exactly is wrong?'

'She's losing her memory.'

'She seemed to remember my lack of visits.'

'She has quite lucid periods when it seems she is just fine. But the doctor says these lucid periods will become shorter and shorter over time.'

'Over how much time?'

'That he doesn't know. Now remember, try to be patient. I can say this as your aunt but it is not one of your better qualities.' She hugged me again. 'You must come over to see us. You've become very lax in your duties as a god-parent.'

'Now that this damn war is over. And once things settle down here.'

'I hope so. Susan is a very lovely young woman. And she has your independent streak.'

Things started off as usual. My mother worked away in her garden most of the day, her friends came to visit, I shopped for groceries in the village, cooked the meals, we listened to the radio after dinner, my mother had some brandy with her tea and biscuits, then she went off to bed. We didn't talk much, and if we did, it was about innocuous subjects, village gossip, the radio programmes, how various plants were progressing in her garden, she seemed calm. She still made the occasional undermining comment about me – my lack of a husband and family, a proper career, the failure of my filial duties as a daughter. But I felt I was in carer mode rather than in resentful daughter mode, and these barbed remarks passed over me without much reaction on my part. Sometimes she would forget or become confused about the simplest detail – the wrong day for someone she had invited for tea, whether or not she had just watered the flowers, losing her knitting and accusing me of hiding it – but generally I felt she was coping. Four nights into my stay, her screaming woke me. I rushed into her room. The bed was stripped and she lay naked in the centre of it, balled up into a foetal position, her body shaking from her sobs.

'I want to die,' she kept saying, over and over again. 'I want to die.'

I went over to the edge of the bed, I didn't know what to do. I had never seen my mother naked before and in such a terrified and vulnerable state. This pale shrivelled up, shivering creature with her sagging flesh webbed with bruised-blue veins. I tried to prise a hand away from her face but she shook me away. 'I can't stand it any more,' she wailed.

'What can't you stand?'

'Can't you see it? Can't you smell it?'

I didn't think I could see or smell anything special. Until I realised that what I had mistaken for a shadow across the mattress was in fact a large stain. My mother was lying in the damp of her own urine.

'We need to clean you up,' I said.

She moved her head slightly from the crook of her arms, so that there was this one dark brown eye looking up at me, like the terrified glance of a beached whale. 'Nothing left,' she said.

'What do you mean?'

'The cupboard.'

It was more than a cupboard, rather a small shelved room for linen, space enough for an adult to stand in and sort the folding of the laundry. As a child, it was my favourite place in which to hide away from a hostile world. I opened the door. Instead of the usual neat rows of stacked towels, blankets and bed linen, there was a mound of stinking sheets topped off with several discarded nightgowns. I went back over to the bed, gently took my mother's hand. She responded by gripping me tightly.

'Come,' I said.

I took her to the bathroom where she let me bathe her. I dried her off, dressed her in one of my nightgowns, led her like a little girl to my own room, tucked her into my bed. I slept on the settee in the lounge.

In the morning, she came down to breakfast all bright and cheerful, behaved as if nothing had happened. She looked at me straight, didn't pull away from my gaze in the slightest, not even a hint of shame or embarrassment. I remembered the London windows devoid of black-out curtains, my mother's eyes possessed that same clarity, the awful night before erased, forgotten.

With a spring sun and a light breeze, it was an ideal day for washing so I tackled what I could of the soiled sheets and my mother's nightgowns, pinned them out to dry while my mother sat in the garden, face to the sun, ignoring what was going on. I telephoned Aunt Ginny, told her what had happened. She said she would drive over, 'come to the rescue' as she put it. I quietly blessed her.

After lunch, I was ready for a nap after all my exertions of the morning. My mother hadn't spoken a word to me up until then but just as I was clearing away the dishes, she piped up and said:

'Let's pick some apples.'

I said that I would and she instructed me to keep my pinny on or bring out a bucket if I preferred. There were four heavily-laden trees to the side of the garden, a small three-step ladder resting against one of them.

'Up you go,' my mother said, pointing to the ladder. 'After all, you're the pilot.'

I looked over at her. The colour was back in her cheeks and she was smiling at me. I couldn't remember the last time she had ever acknowledged that I flew aeroplanes.

We worked away together, with me on top of the ladder,

picking apples into my bucket, my mother pointing here and there to the best ones to be plucked. She remained below, taking whatever was in reach into the nest of her pinny. It was the reverse of our positions when I used to pick with her as a child. I glanced down at her and for a moment I felt I could see right through to the heart of her. Through the layers of skin lined and loosened by age and experience, through lens clouded by cataracts, through the despair of losing a loving husband in battle, to the bright-eyed, fresh-skinned beauty of a young girl full of her own hopes and joys. I felt my own eyes tear up from the sheer brutal truth of a lifetime contained in those few moments and my love for her came streaming back to me.

During a break in our efforts, I went into the house for my Leica, came back, took some photographs of her resting against the tree. She became quite animated by my efforts, stood up and even performed some exaggerated poses as if she were a professional model showing off the latest country wear. I never was quite able to capture that essence of her I had observed earlier from the top of the ladder but the photographs turned out well nevertheless. It was into this rare scene of mother-daughter bliss that Aunt Ginny arrived. She had come equipped with a rubber sheet from her own children's bed-wetting days, some adult diapers she had acquired from a friend who was a nurse, and a promise to get her hands on some rubber pants as well.

'This is a quick turn-around,' she said. 'I'll explain to sis how to put these on, then I'm off.'

I made my own promise that I would visit her and Susan the following week once I felt my mother was settled.

I sat with my mother in front of the radio that night to listen to the BBC Home Service and her favourite show, *It's That Man Again*. Her bed was all properly made-up upstairs with fresh linen and a rubber sheet, she wore diapers under her clean nightgown. She stirred a drop of brandy into her tea, blew on her cup as she always did before taking a sip.

'I remember when you played Pocahontas in the Festival of Empire pageant,' she said. 'You could only have been eight or nine.'

'I was eleven, mother.'

'Robert and Viv Shaw's son, Eddie, he played the part of King James. He went on to become a doctor somewhere.'

My mother's sudden lucidity surprised me. I tried to keep the conversation going. 'Canada, I think it was,' I said, although I had no idea if that was true.

'Yes, Canada. Lucky for him. Missing the war.'

'Oh, I don't know about that. Lots of Canadians signed up.'

My mother sighed, blew on her tea again. 'Your father and I were so proud of you that day.'

'The day of the pageant?'

'Yes, of course, the day of the pageant. That was what I was talking about.'

'I don't remember Papa being there.'

'That's because you were too busy with your young friends. But I remember clearly how you came over to us after your performance, your face was beaming with the excitement of it all and your father twirled you around like a ballet dancer on a music box and said: *Look, at our beautiful young actress. One day you'll be a star.* How could you forget a thing like that?' My mother chuckled. 'You're worse than me.'

'I don't know. I must have blocked it out somehow.'

'Hmm. Strange to think that.'

It was also strange to hear my mother talk about my father at all.

Chapter Thirty-Five

A Tête-à-Tête on the Terrace

Laura had Sal on her mobile. 'Where are you?' she asked.

'A pal gave me his London pad for a month.'

'That's kind of him. But whereabouts?'

'Kensington somewhere.'

'Where should we meet?'

'Hey, Laura. This is your city.'

She knew a million places. That was the problem, honing in on just one when she was put on the spot. 'How about Somerset House?'

'In Somerset?'

'No, silly. It's just off the Strand. I'm not sure what the nearest tube is.'

'I'll take a cab.'

'Once you're there, go right through to the river. There's a smart restaurant on the terrace. Lunch at one?'

'See ya then.'

And she did see him then, saw him first, for she decided to get there before him, settle herself down nice and relaxed for their business meeting. It was a good choice. Even though the restaurant was outside on the terrace, it boasted covered awnings that not only offered shade but protected her from prying eyes. She had ordered a glass of Prosecco and some mixed nuts, was sitting back, admiring the view of the river when Sal arrived. He was looking rather cool and casual, all dressed in linen – blue suit, white collarless shirt – no socks, sunglasses. *Very Californian*, she thought.

'You're paying,' she told him as he pulled out his chair.

'It's customary to wait until offered,' he said.

'I'll take it as an advance. You still owe me for the camera crew.'

'You're annoyed with me?'

'What do you think?'

'Fair enough.' He held up his hands in mock surrender. 'What are you drinking?'

'Prosecco.'

'Another two of the same,' he told a passing waiter, then sat down.

'When did you get in?' she asked.

'Yesterday afternoon.'

'Sleep last night?'

'Not too bad. Still a bit lagged though. Fell asleep in the cab on the way over. The driver could have taken me on a tour of the sights and I wouldn't have known. By the way, you look fantastic.'

The compliment threw her. She couldn't recall Sal ever flattering her before. Her acting perhaps, but not her looks. 'It takes a lot longer to achieve these days.'

'Damn you English women.'

'What's that supposed to mean?'

'Can't just accept a compliment straight off.'

'Modesty is welded into our DNA. I thought you'd know that by now.'

Sal sat back, spread out in his seat. 'You're not still with Jack Muirhead, are you?'

'No.'

'I saw his latest movie on the plane. Some Japanese thing. I remembered reading somewhere how you two used to be... connected.'

'Well, our connection finished a while ago. By mutual consent.'

'Really?'

'Mature adults are quite capable of making such decisions, Sal.'

'Are you saying I'm not a mature adult?'

'I'm saying you don't have to be so cynical. Have you come across him out there in LaLa land?'

'Met him once at a party. Must have been quite something

going out with a guy like him?'

'We had our moments.'

'Are you still in touch?'

'We could be if we wanted to be,' she said, not entirely convinced of the truth of that statement. She finished off her Prosecco. Bad move. She was feeling quite tipsy already and there was another one coming. But Sal's rather aggressive questioning was bothering her. 'What about you, Sal? I don't hear you talking much about Dominique.'

'How do you know about her?'

'A little Wikipedia told me.'

Sal laughed. 'Don't believe everything you read on that. Dominique and I split a year or so back.'

'I'm sorry to hear that.'

'No need to be. We were beating the hell out of each other. Psychologically, not physically. Only stayed together for the sake of the kids. Until it was time to move apart... for the sake of the kids.'

'Do you get to see them?'

'Not as often as I would like. What about you? Ever married?'

'It seems I forgot to.' Fortunately, before this line of conversation could go further, the waiter came with their drinks. They clinked glasses. She took a sip, she would leave the rest until she had some food in her stomach. 'I thought we were here to discuss business,' she said.

'I was just making small talk.'

'If this is your small talk, I'd hate to be around when you get serious.'

'I guess I just wanted to rock your boat a little.'

'Why would you want to do that?'

'I don't know, Laura. Maybe it's because you always seem so cool and aloof.'

'Can we talk about what we came here for?'

'Apologies. Put it down to the jetlag. What have you got for me?'

She placed a memory stick on the table. 'First instalment.'

'What's on it?'

'My notes on Georgie's early years. Growing up in a small village in Sussex. Her brief career in the silent movie business. But I guess you knew most of that stuff already from your documentary.'

'Yeah, I just finished the editing before I got on the plane. It's going to be called *No Talking, Please – We're British*.' He smiled at her, as he waited to be congratulated on his choice of title. She ignored him so he went on. 'Any info on why she gave up on her film career?'

'Not a thing.'

'Strange. Did you ask Quentin?'

'He says she refused to talk about those days.'

'Do you believe him?'

'Not so sure. He seemed a bit touchy on the subject.'

'Well, keep digging. It would be good if we could put some meat on the bones of her early life. What about her relationship with Max Rosen?'

'Pretty stormy by all accounts. Dumped her as soon as she left the movie business. Killed in the war during a London bombing raid.'

'Anything else?'

'Did you know she was one of those pioneering female pilots?'

'You mean like Amelia Earhart?'

'Same era. Georgie was one of the first aviators to fly to Palestine. Co-pilot was the millionaire playboy Roland Paxton-Jones. Rollo, to his friends. They were a bit of a celebrity flying couple.'

'Did they marry?'

'I guess they would have but Rollo died flying. Plane disappeared in fog over the Norfolk coast. Body never found. Georgie never really got over that. She even gave up flying for a while... until the war came along.'

'Excellent. All good dramatic material. Is that it?'

'So far. I've scanned in a few documents as well. Photographs, playbills, interview transcripts.'

'How are you managing with Quentin?'

'He gets a little too close for comfort. But I can handle him.'

'I'm sure you can.' Sal sat up straight, clapped his hands together. 'Here's my proposal. I say we go with a straightforward fifty-fifty.'

'Can we be a bit more precise?'

'You keep on with all the research stuff, I'll write the script. You act, I produce. A small tour to iron out the kinks, then we'll try to push for a London run. Get it all down on film interwoven with some talking heads. I've got plenty of silent screen footage to throw into the mix and I'm sure I can get hold of newsreels on the early flying years as well. I'll tout the documentary around to the festivals, I've got a lot of contacts there. Anything you can add from people you know on the film side much appreciated. We split the costs and the profit right down the middle. How does that sound to you?'

'I want it all in writing.'

'I'll get my lawyers on to it.'

'What about start-up funding?'

'I guess we'll need about ten grand up front to keep you and me going for a couple of months. Another fifteen for when we move into rehearsal. Let's say twenty five to get us off the ground. Make it thirty to keep us cosy.'

'Dollars?'

'Let's stick with your local currency.'

'And where's this money coming from?'

'Now we've got our hands on all this original material, I can start talking to investors. I had a chat with your Lady Caroline.'

'I told you I wasn't going to go begging to her.'

'And I told you that I'd sort it out by myself. I've arranged a meeting with Sir Lew.'

'I don't think he'll be interested. He's into oil, real estate, mining, Sal. Plays are not his kind of thing. I doubt he's ever been to one.'

'I thought I'd get Caroline to sweeten him up. After all, she kind of owes us for getting her back on the boards again. She was telling me how much she loved the other day.'

'I'm sure she did. She managed to make herself the centre of attention in a play that wasn't about her.'

'Jesus, Laura. What is it about you two?'

'We go back a long way.'

'To where exactly?'

'Oh, where do I start with Caroline? Our early twenties.'

'Rivals in love?'

'In just about everything.'

'Well, you just leave Caroline to me. What about Quentin?'

'What about him?'

'As a backer. It's his dear Aunt Georgie after all. And especially now the two of you are such great buddies.'

'It's a possibility.'

'Well, give it a try. I'm sure he's got money to burn living in that fancy place of his. Forty thousand sterling is probably small change to him.'

'I thought you said thirty?'

'Might as well go for broke.'

'I'll speak to him.'

'Perfect.' Sal took off his sunglasses, held out his hand. 'We gotta deal, partner?'

'We've got a deal.'

Chapter Thirty-Six

Extract from an unpublished memoir

I took the country bus across Sussex to Aunt Ginny's farm, for the trains ran only back into London and out again for such a trip. It would be just the three of us – Ginny, Susan and me. I preferred it that way. The three girls. Uncle Richard I hardly ever saw anyway, he was always off managing the estate. As for the boys, my cousins Oliver and Percy, when I had visited previously they had either been at boarding school, university, or surviving the war – Oliver as part of essential food production, Percy for the Royal Engineers in India. Where they were now, I had no idea.

Aunt Ginny picked me up in a gorgeous royal blue open-top motor car.

'It's a Triumph Dolomite Roadster Coupé,' she informed me with a little flourish of her gloved hand.

'I know nothing about cars.'

'I'm surprised you don't drive,' she said, as the vehicle spun up the dirt and dust close to a roadside ditch. 'You being a pilot.'

'I prefer the open skies to the open road.'

'You should let me teach you. Out on the farm.'

'You're right. I probably should learn.'

Aunt Ginny, her eyes hidden behind her fashionable sunglasses, turned to look at me while I preferred she kept her attention on the road. I might not have been a motorist myself but I could see she was a terrible driver. 'And how is my big sister?' she asked.

'She's much more comfortable. I'm so grateful to you for sending over the rubber pants. They've made a big difference. It's her memory that I worry about now.'

'We'll need to arrange for some help once you've gone.'

'I can organise that. She has friends in the village… Aunt Ginny, there's a tractor up ahead…'

'Yes, yes, I see it… these country roads… so narrow. What were you saying?'

'She has friends in the village who will come in.'

'I'll try to take her eventually. When the time comes. Unless she goes totally doolally. Then we'll need to think about a nursing home.'

'I realise that.'

'But for now, you need to start spending more time with Susan. You've been very lax in your godmotherly duties.'

'I'm sorry. But my work with the ATA…'

'The war is over now, Georgie. New beginnings.'

'I understand. New beginnings.'

Susan was all grown-up, appearing older than her eighteen years, not in her outward appearance but I could see it in her eyes. That same clouded look of all those youngsters who had lost their childhood and adolescence to a war. Aunt Ginny told me Susan had spent the last few months before armistice working in a London hospital, scrubbing up the bodies brought in from the rocket bombings, scraping off the blood and dust ready for medical inspection or the morgue. Not a sight for a teenage girl who should have had eyes for boys, lips for kissing and feet for dancing.

'I did the same as you,' Susan told me.

'I was a pilot.'

'I meant in the Great War. Mother told me you also worked in the hospitals.'

'I suppose I did. But I was an actress then. We were putting on performances for the wounded. Not cleaning up their bodies.'

We went out together to the stables, Aunt Ginny staying behind to prepare lunch. Susan had brought with her a bunch of carrots and was feeding each horse in turn as we passed by the stalls. I watched her as she attended to them, standing up on tip-toes to wrap her arms around the animals' necks, soft words in their ears. Susan never bothered much with the way she looked, her clothes always baggy, the way she had her hair cut in an almost boyish style. That's what she was really – a tomboy – I couldn't remember her being dressed up otherwise. But there was an openness about her that I could see would be attractive in other ways.

'Do you mind if I ask you a personal question?' she asked.

'Go ahead.'

'Have you ever been in love?'

Both she and the horse she was caressing turned to look at me, causing me to feel quite discomfited by their combined teenage and equine stares. 'I suppose I have,' I admitted.

Susan abandoned her grasp of the querulous beast, bounded over, linked her arm in mine, guided me over to sit on some bales. 'Do tell,' she said.

It wasn't just her forthrightness that charmed me, I realised I also had a need to tell a story I had long suppressed. Not just a story but a name as well. 'Rollo,' I said softly. Then more firmly: 'Roland. Roland Paxton Jones, if you want the complete mouthful.'

'And?'

'And what?'

'What did he look like?'

'Well, he was tall but I wouldn't describe him as very handsome. Quite handsome perhaps. Clean-shaven, which was unusual for the men of those days, especially the pilots who loved to play with their moustaches. And he always had a smile in his eyes. We flew in his plane to Palestine together a couple of weeks after we first met. We ate with the Bedouin in the desert, we slept under the stars.'

'Oh, Georgie, that sounds so romantic.'

'It was. I think it was the happiest time of my life.'

'What happened to him?'

'Sadly, he disappeared.'

'He left you?'

'No, he and his aircraft disappeared into fog over the Norfolk coast. He was never seen again.'

'I'm so sorry.'

'I still imagine sometimes that I might bump into him. Coming around the corner, across the street, on a station platform. Funny that, still looking for him. A face in the crowd.'

Susan clasped my hand tight, I think she might have seen me tear up at the memory.

'I have another question,' she said.

'Yes?'

'Why did you never have children?'

'I don't know. Too many other things were happening. And then it was too late. Why all these questions?'

'I was just thinking of my own life. Mother and Father always pushing me towards marriage and a family. Well, Father mostly. He'd love me to be a farmer's wife. But I want to be like you.'

I laughed. 'A childless spinster?'

'No. A strong, independent woman who does what she wants.'

'Well, what is it you want to do?'

'I don't know exactly. But I think I'd like to be connected to the arts.'

'I didn't know you were creative.'

'I'm not at all. But I'd like to be around creative people. I want to do an art history degree. If Father will let me.'

'Well, we women will just have to team up to persuade him then. But first, go back and stand over by your horse.'

I had Rollo's Leica with me, thought it would be fun to take some photographs. Susan by her favourite mare, Susan up in the saddle, Susan posing on the bales. Quite the little model she turned out to be, a good figure on her too once she had tightened up her loose shirt, pulled in her belt, a wide smile that enchanted. So busy was I with her that I didn't notice Aunt Ginny's approach with glasses of lemonade on a tray.

'Taking pictures for *Woman's Illustrated*, are we?' she said.

'Susan's a natural.'

'So it seems.' Aunt Ginny put down the tray on one of the bales. 'Show me what to do, Georgie. And I'll take a picture of the two of you.'

'Let's have one with the car,' Susan suggested.

So we all strolled over to the front of the house where the coupé was parked, Susan and I in the front seats, Aunt Ginny being quite ridiculous by crawling on to the bonnet so she could photograph us over the windscreen. Click! The two of us. Susan and I. Black and white. Frozen in time. Laughing.

Chapter Thirty-Seven

A Big, Small Part

It was a late summer's day and Laura sat out in her little Highgate garden with her laptop, putting together another batch of research to send over to Sal for his script. She loved this time of year, the turn of the leaves, the comforting smell of woodsmoke from a neighbouring garden, the squirrels scampering up tree trunks and along the stone walls, the sun still warm enough for her to linger outdoors, a time for reflection, to harvest what she had sown over the last few weeks. She realised she felt happy. Or at least content. A contentment she had not felt for a long time. She was engrossed in a project that she really cared about, that had meaning for her and most importantly – that properly defined her. Yes, that was the essential quality, this one of definition. She had learnt that from Georgie. To spend one's life doing the work that truly reflected and described one's inner nature, one's creativity. That was what would give her integrity and authenticity. That was what would draw the straight line from her heart to her art. Being a serious actress immersing herself in the character of someone she totally admired. She couldn't wait to bring the role to the public. She sipped on her coffee, nibbled on her Portuguese custard tart.

Ping!

An email from Quentin. *A favour to ask*, he wrote.

Me too! she replied, although asking for a contribution towards £40,000 of start-up costs was probably stretching the concept of favour.

Ping! *Oh good, tit for tat. Let's meet to talk.*

My place or yours?

Ping! *Prefer a neutral venue. Do you know All Saints' Church in Tudeley? It's near Tunbridge Wells.*

Never been there.

Ping! *You're in for a big surprise then.*

I like surprises.

Ping! *Excellent.*

They arranged a day and time, and no sooner had she signed off than her mobile started to thrum. She glanced at the number. All the way from America. Edy.

'Laura, Laura, Laura. I said I wouldn't forget you.'

'It's been a while since your cull.'

'Since I what?... since I called?'

'Since you dumped me.' She heard Edy suck hard on a cigarette. Then the inevitable bout of horrible coughing. She took another bite of her custard tart while she waited for her former agent to recover.

'I didn't dump you,' Edy went on. 'I merely effected a pause in our relationship.'

'Same thing.'

'Please don't be so curt. We used to be friends.' Suck, suck, cough, cough. 'Still are, I hope. Aren't we?'

'Why did you call, Edy?'

'I got something for you.'

'What?'

'A big, small part.'

'What's that supposed to mean? A cameo?'

'Remember Dame Judi in *Shakespeare in Love*. It's a bit like that. An Oscar for eight minutes' work. This is the same. Trust me, it's juicy.'

'What is it?'

'A hundred million dollar mega movie. It's called – wait for it... *The Boston Tea Party*. Can't believe they haven't done that before, can you?'

'What's the part?'

'Elizabeth Wells. Boston-born daughter of an English merchant family. Wife of Samuel Adams.'

'Who was Samuel Adams?'

'One of the founding fathers of this great and noble land. An architect of the Revolution. It's so perfect for you, Laura. You'll be one of an all-star cast.'

'Who's playing Adams?'

A pause. Another drag of her cigarette. 'Does it matter?'

'Of course it matters.'

'Jack. Jack Muirhead.'

'Jack.'

'Yes, Jack.'

'You know something, Edy? I was having a perfectly enjoyable afternoon. Until you called.'

'You told me it was an amicable split.'

'Jack and I. We're fine. It's just that… I'm feeling so balanced right now. Working with Jack would be so… disruptive.'

'This is a big movie, Laura. A serious part. Not some stupid voice-over…'

'The voice-over was your idea.'

'It was? Anyway, a chance for you to shine again in front of the camera. And the money's decent too. I thought you needed some cash.'

'I do, I do, I do. But you know what, Edy? I'm doing exactly what you told me to do when you dumped me. I'm involved in a project I really care about.'

'Nobody is saying you should give up what you're doing. Fly over to LA. Shoot your few scenes with Jack. Go back with a few bucks in your pocket and a top-class movie under your belt. What's not to like?'

'Who else is in this all-star cast?'

'Nothing's finalised.'

'Come on, Edy. What are you not telling me?'

'OK then. If you have to know. Kate.'

'Kate,' Laura shrieked. 'Fucking Kate. She's a drunken wreck. You told me you'd axed her the same time as me.'

'What could I do? She was desperate. She begged me. She actually came round to my apartment, got down on her knees, hugged my ankles and begged me. What could I do? I have a heart you know.'

Laura seriously doubted this was true. 'What part has *she* got?'

'George Washington's wife. Martha. It's only a small role.'

'How small?... forget it. You know what, Edy. I don't want to be dragged back into this. It's all bubbling up inside me again. I can feel it as we speak. The ego, the jealousy, the bitchiness. I don't want it.'

'I'm trying to mend broken bridges here.'

'I didn't ask you to.'

'I was anticipating your needs. That's what an agent is for.'

'I'm turning you down.'

'Why? Because of Jack? Because of Kate?'

'No. Because of me.'

A pause. Edy's heavy breathing. Then her soft but threatening voice. 'I called in a lot of favours to get you this. Don't let me down.'

'I'm afraid I have to.'

'Fuck you, Laura.'

'And fuck you, Edy.'

She would have liked to have slammed the phone down, that was the problem with mobiles, no facility for dramatic endings. Unless she dropped it in the pond like the last time. She found herself instead clicking off in a rather lady-like fashion, her hand shaking but feeling exhilarated nonetheless. She couldn't remember the last time she had sworn at someone like that.

The sound of the entrance buzzer.

She waltzed down the hallway, quietly singing to herself. She opened the front door to be greeted by the postman with a recorded delivery envelope.

Chapter Thirty-Eight

The Hepburn Archives

Transcript from BBC Radio 4 interview
Broadcasting House, London
16th May 1982
Interviewer: Sir Peter Delamere
Interviewee: Georgie Hepburn

PD: The war was over, Georgie. And you survived, of course...

GH: I was one of the lucky ones. A lot of ATA pilots lost their lives. Planes going down in bad weather. Engine failure. We might have just been ferrying aircraft around but it was a dangerous business.

PD: You could have gone on to be an instructor or some other job in aviation but you chose not to. Why was that?

GH: I would have loved to have done something like that. But my mother's health had started to deteriorate by then. Senility they called it in those days. She wasn't even that old. Mid-sixties it was when it started. I went down to the cottage at Five Elms Down to look after her. It wasn't easy as we never got on at the best of times.

PD: It was around this time you started taking photographs.

GH: I didn't have that much to do around the cottage when I wasn't looking after mother. I dug out the Leica camera Rollo had given me on our trip to Palestine, started playing around with that. I took photographs of my mother mainly. I wanted to preserve my memory of her, that was all. I had no idea I was sowing the seeds for a new career.

PD: These photographs of her became iconic, didn't they?

GH: Well, no-one was really taking pictures of the elderly in those days. It was all glamour or war photography. Robert Capa was the biggest instigator of that, of course, with his Magnum Photos outfit and photo-journalism.

PD: Were you ever tempted yourself?

GH: Robert and I did have a chat about it once. In the very early days. But I told him I had experienced enough of war without having to go off and take pictures of it. He gave me the impression he was pretty fed up with it all himself. Yet, he couldn't resist. All that excitement. All that adrenalin. It was addictive. I knew that myself from just flying the Spits. In the end Robert was blown up by a landmine. How tragic. He could only have been in his early forties. A handsome man. Very intense. Very intellectual about his work. We don't really respect intellectuals in this country. Britain is more of an emotional nation. [LAUGHING] Sorry, I'm rambling on here. Getting a bit senile myself. Where were we?

PD: Well, your resistance to Capa's style of photojournalism certainly paid off as you ended up carving out your own niche.

GH: I've often thought about that. I used to think it was just pure luck. But I believe it was more than that. It was about staying true to myself. It was about taking the photographs I wanted to take. The line that goes straight from one's heart to one's art.

PD: That's a fine way of putting it.

GH: I am merely paraphrasing the words of Marc Chagall,

my favourite painter. He used to say: *If I create from my heart, nearly everything works.*

PD: Well, there is certainly an authenticity to your work that the public has responded to. Myself included.

GH: That's very kind of you to say.

PD: I'm sure it's true.

GH: My subjects were a lost generation, Peter. A generation trapped between the end of the Second World War and the Swinging Sixties. Once David Bailey and the rest of his gang came along, it became all about fashion and celebrity after that. Still is.

PD: How did you feel about that?

GH: I have no problem with it at all. They captured the *zeitgeist* of their generation and I suppose I captured the *zeitgeist* of mine. That surely is what the contemporary artist must strive to do.

PD: Would you say that the *zeitgeist* you captured in your work was this feeling of being lost? Of being abandoned?

GH: Not only 'of being lost' in that sense of not knowing where you're going because everything ahead of you has changed. But also the sense of 'loss' for what had been. People of our generation, we all lost something or someone in that damn war. It was certainly a feeling I could relate to myself. We're contemporaries, Peter. Didn't you feel it yourself?

PD: I suppose I did.

Chapter Thirty-Nine

Her Majesty's Inspector Calls

'There are two basic rules that a self-employed person should follow.' That is what Marcus Green, Laura's former accountant used to tell her, a giant wardrobe of a man speaking from his uncomfortable wedge behind his tiny desk. Marcus was not fat, he was just tall and wide, very wide. Visiting him was like visiting Gulliver in the land of Lilliput. Clothing that frame in the expensive fabrics he enjoyed must have cost him a fortune. He had been recommended to Laura as someone well-versed in the erratic earnings and lifestyle of the modern-day artiste. 'If there is no other advice you take from me, Laura.' Marcus' voice would rumble threateningly from deep within his cavernous belly. 'Please let it be Marcus Green's two commandments. They are set in stone.'

Marcus's two basic rules for the self-employed were as follows: One – keep handy a large container for receipts. 'Before you retire for the night, you must be able to easily empty your wallet, purse, handbag, pockets, satchels, envelopes, parcels, packages and plastic bags of all relevant receipts and place them in this receptacle. Now this container must not be kept in a cupboard or under a coffee table or behind some ornament, but nestle out there in the open, in full view, so that in one simple swoop you can place your receipts therein. A box, a vase with a wide neck, a bowl, it doesn't matter, any easily accessible container will do. And at the end of the financial year, all that you need to do is collect these bits of paper and deliver them to me. How simple is that? The more paper, the less tax. That's rule number one.'

And basic rule number two? 'Take thirty percent of everything you earn and place it in a separate bank account marked TAX. In that way, Her Majesty's Revenues and Customs will never surprise you.'

Unfortunately for Laura, HMRC was surprising her now. No, in all honesty, she could not say that. For lodged in the back of her mind was always the thought that one day the very recorded delivery manila envelope she was presently holding in her hand would eventually arrive. It was just that she had been in denial. Marcus Green, her former accountant, would have been very pleased to learn that she had indeed trained herself to save all her receipts daily in an accessible receptacle. The problem was that she had failed for a number of years to follow basic rule number two to any extent whatsoever. She had also failed to follow Marcus Green's basic rule number three – and that was to retain his services as an accountant.

She walked back out to the garden, sat down at her patio table, tore open the envelope. The figures appeared as a jumble before her eyes. She put on her glasses. It was worse than she had expected. All that text in red, the capital letters, the penalties, the final figure. She wished she had Marcus Green in her employ now, protecting her with his enormous bulk from these demands of the tax authorities. She thought about phoning Edy again, getting down on her knees, begging for the part the same way as shameless Kate had done, regretting the finality of their 'fuck you' exchange. She picked up her mobile, retrieved Edy's contact number, let her thumb hover over the green icon of the call button. Swallow her pride, that was what she should do. Instead she swallowed the bile of terror that had risen in her throat, replaced the phone on the patio table.

She looked around her garden, then back through the open doors into her bedroom, viewing her property not as a home-owner but as an estate agent might. *Two bedroom ground floor flat situated in quiet cul-de-sac in sought-after part of Highgate. Recently refurbished to exceptionally high standard. Both bedrooms en-suite. Large handcrafted kitchen-dining area. Italian marble worktops. Delightful private garden and patio area. Owner desperate to sell due to slump in career and horrendous tax problems.* She glanced back down at the form in her lap, the sum total of her arrears, then called for help. Victoria arrived within the hour. Laura was at the ready with a chilled bottle of white wine and two large glasses.

'What happened to the thirty percent rule?' Victoria, also a client of the formidable Marcus Green, asked.

'I followed it for a while and then...'

'Then what?'

'Things came up.'

'Like what?'

'Holidays. The fees for my father's nursing home. Those in themselves are almost £3,000 a month. Renovating this place. The new Mini. Hotels. Meals out. You know me, Victoria, I'm not an extravagant person but money just seems to slip through my fingers. Like water down a drain.'

Victoria shook her head solemnly in the same way Marcus Green used to do when confronted with the economic frailties of his clients. 'Receipts?'

'Somewhere.'

'In an accessible container?'

'I have a box.'

'Well, that's a start. You could take it over to Marcus, get one of his minions to sort out the paperwork.'

'It's not going to make much difference. This bill is for money already owed.'

Victoria whistled then took a slug of wine. 'Any work?' she asked.

'Only the Georgie Hepburn project.'

'I hope your pal Sal is paying you for that.'

'We're approaching a couple of investors for some seed money.'

Victoria gave one of her patient sighs that made Laura feel like a child.

'What about a proper *paid* acting job, Laura?'

'That's not going to happen.'

'Why not?'

She recounted the telephone conversation with Edy.

'Not the best of moves,' Victoria noted. 'At the worst of times.'

'You know what? I don't regret it.'

'You might when the bailiffs start pressing your buzzer. What about June? Can she help you?'

It was always strange to hear Victoria use her mother's first name like that. When they were at drama school, Victoria would always call her Mrs Scott when she visited. But then somewhere along the line, Mrs Scott became June. When did that happen? When Victoria became a wife, a mother, reached a certain age? It was as if they were the best of friends now. Or at the very least, it suggested that Victoria had a different, more intimate relationship with her mother than she, her own daughter, could ever have.

'I've never asked my mother for money. And I never will.'

'Even in a crisis situation?'

'Especially in a crisis situation. She'd just lecture me until her dying breath on what a mess I've made of my life. Anyway, I doubt if she has that kind of cash lying around.'

'How is she anyway? June.'

'Still cruising the world. Probably having more sex than I am.'

'That wouldn't be difficult. How old is she now… seventy-two?

'Seventy-five.'

'I hope I can be like her at that age.'

'What? A self-centred old bag with no time for her only child.'

'I was thinking of her *joie de vivre*.'

'And I thought you were here to talk about me.'

'Sorry.' Victoria leaned forward, poured herself another glass of wine. 'What will you do then?'

'There is only one thing I can do. I'll have to sell this place.'

'But you love it here.'

'I know.'

Victoria surveyed the space in which they sat and sighed.

'It's so nice to have a garden.'

Laura knew that whenever Victoria talked about anyone else's garden she was using it as a metaphor for the break-up of her marriage and the loss of her own family home. A three-bedroom Victorian semi with extensive acreage at the rear that had to be down-sized for the modern garden-less flat she and her two children now occupied. 'We had rabbits,' Victoria recalled. 'And tortoises.'

Laura refused to be drawn. 'Jobless and homeless,' she said of her own situation. 'Who would've thought it?'

'I wish I could help you. But you know my own position is…'

'That's sweet of you. But I need to work this out by myself.'

'What about Jack?'

Laura stared at her fingernails, the lack of varnish here and there. That was what happened when she wasn't working, no make-up artist to keep her right. 'I'm not going to ask Jack for money.'

'I didn't mean that. I was just wondering if you could get him to lean on the producers of that *Boston Tea Party* film to give you back the part. He's bound to have influence.'

'I don't want Jack to help me. And I don't want that part.'

'God, Laura, you're impossible sometimes. You told me just a few weeks ago that being a film actress was what gave your life meaning.'

'I told you that since I hadn't fulfilled my biological function by having children, I needed to fulfil my life in other ways. This is what I am doing with this play about Georgie.'

'You'd better call the estate agents then.'

Chapter Forty

The Hepburn Archives

Transcript from BBC Radio 4 interview
Broadcasting House, London
16th May 1982
Interviewer: Sir Peter Delamere
Interviewee: Georgie Hepburn

PD: *Are you ready to start again, Georgie?*

GH: *I think so. I really needed that cup of tea.*

PD: *I'm sorry for turning it into such a long day but we wanted to make the most of your time while we had you.*

GH: *[LAUGHING] You mean in case I pop my clogs sooner rather than later.*

PD: *[ALSO LAUGHING] You know what I mean. [PAUSE] What are you doing afterwards? We can have dinner if you would like? Or are you heading back to Oxfordshire?*

GH: *That's kind of you, Peter, but I'm meeting up with my god-daughter once we're finished here.*

PD: *Ah yes. Susan. Well, next time you're in town then. Helen and I would love to have you over... oh, there's the signal from the producer. Shall we begin?*

GH: *Ready when you are.*

PD: *OK. We'll just pick up from when you were talking about this lost generation trapped between the end of the Second World*

War and the Swinging Sixties... I'll count us in... one, two, three and... What do you mean by that exactly? A lost generation?

GH: Well, if I can go back first to the Great War. When that was over, things changed very quickly. There was an immediate reaction to all that had gone before. I think women were a great driving force because they had become used to going out to work, earning a wage. Of course, there was the suffragette movement as well. And then along came the movies and the radio and jazz and the telephone. We had iconoclasts like James Joyce, DH Lawrence, TS Eliot, Louis Armstrong, Picasso, Chagall. The Dadaists. I don't think it was like that after the Second World War. It was a slower process. The old values like loyalty and civility and class division and honour and collective responsibility and sexual modesty, well they were being eroded more slowly. Until *The Beatles* came along. And bang! Everything changed overnight.

PD: What about Elvis?

GH: He could have been the trailblazer. But then the army sucked him in and that was the end of any real influence he had on transforming the prevailing culture.

PD: So you blame everything on *The Beatles*?

GH: Only in so far as they were the focus, the headliners, the star act. Of course, there were lots of others too. Jagger and the *Stones*, Warhol, Dylan, Mary Quant, Twiggy, Hendrix, David Bailey and many, many more. But *The Beatles* became the poster boys for the revolution. They just seemed to wipe out everything that had gone before. Not just in music. But fashion, art, photography. Attitudes to sex, attitudes to government, to war, to authority, to religion, to the previous generation. There was no sense of shame anymore. The young had money in their pockets and they were going to make the most of it. It was brutal if you were of that previous generation.

PD: And that's what made your work so important. You photographed that lost generation.

GH: I was part of that lost generation, Peter. But as I said before, I just got lucky I suppose. I started off taking photographs of my mother because she was dying and it just grew from there. I had to put her in a home where many of the residents were ex-servicemen and women or just plain elderly. I ended up spending time with many of them, listening to their stories, gaining their trust. And eventually, they would let me photograph them. At first, it was just simple snapshots. In the end, I would visit with lighting equipment and back-drops. Proper portraits. Black and white.

PD: I have a copy of your latest book in front of me. It's quite a remarkable collection.

GH: Well, Susan was responsible for that. She curates all of my photographs for me.

PD: Susan, of course, for the benefit of our listeners being...?

GH: My god-daughter. Susan Holloway. But not just my god-daughter. She has a fine arts degree. And many years experience working in the art world. Also very good taste.

PD: As is evident in this collection. We also have a few fascinating photographs of big time movie stars. Cary Grant. Audrey Hepburn. Gary Cooper. Just to mention a few.

GH: They were all around me at the time. Susan insisted I put them in.

PD: It sounds as if you were against that?

GH: I never wanted to be known for these kind of celebrity shots. But Susan says I need to think of them as my Trojan horse. Drawing the audience in before I reveal the true nature of my work.

PD: That sounds like a reasonable tactic.

GH: Perhaps.

PD: I sense a reluctance there.

GH: It's always been a touchy subject with me.

Chapter Forty-One

Hidden Treasure

Laura tried to put all thoughts of tax bills behind her as she drove down to Kent, destination All Saints' Church in the village of Tudeley. Quentin had sent her one of his usual enigmatic emails just before she set out: *Church location challenging. Lane to left, off B2017. Eyes peeled. Q.*

He was right. Her destination wasn't easy to find. Her satnav had no knowledge of such a place and she ended up passing the entrance lane twice before finally noticing it. Fifteen minutes later than expected, she drove into a car park adjoining a grassy graveyard and a modest stone church. Quentin was waiting for her, all in a lean against a beautiful, vintage open-top motor car. He had dressed for the occasion in a tweed suit and peaked motoring cap. She had to smile. All he needed was a pair of goggles and his touring outfit was complete. He waved her in to park beside him, gallantly opened her door.

'So is this the surprise?' she said, pointing to his car.

'What? The automobile? No, no, no. Although it is a beauty. It was Grandma Ginny's. A nineteen thirty-eight Triumph Dolomite Roadster Coupé. Exceptionally rare these days.'

'It's the one from the photograph with Georgie and your mother. Grandma Ginny on the bonnet with the camera.'

'Well spotted,' he said. 'I take her out for a run whenever the sun shines. We can go for a spin later if you want.'

'I'd like that.'

'Excellent. But first the real surprise.'

She looked around her. The tiny medieval church was typical of many an English village but for a non-descript red brick tower apparently added much later than the original stonework. The building itself was surrounded by well-kept lawns hosting a smattering of ancient gravestones. A few other unremarkable outbuildings were dispersed around the perimeter. What could he mean?

Quentin guided her towards the small porch entrance to the church, also constructed in red brick. In the vestibule, the usual busy mosaic of community posters for church services, fêtes, planning meetings, nothing to prepare her for what awaited inside. Quentin pushed open the stout wooden door. As she stepped forward onto the cold stone floor, her first visual sweep of the interior caused her to gasp.

'My goodness,' she whispered. 'The windows. Are they...? Chagall? Marc Chagall?'

Quentin was smiling, nodding gleefully, like a parent watching a child open a longed-for present. 'Yes, indeed,' he said. 'The one and only.'

She counted them off. There were twelve of them, all done in stained glass by the famous Russian-French artist. She hadn't noticed them from the outside because they had been covered in mesh and bars. But from the inside they were spectacular. One giant centre piece graced the apse behind the altar, the other smaller windows were scattered throughout the church. Blue was the predominant colour, not that dissimilar in shade from Quentin's roadster, those rich and bold indigo hues so typical of the artist but various pale yellows and greens had crept into the designs as well. The main window depicted a compassionate-looking Christ in crucifixion hovering in the sky above two figures awash in a stormy sea. Quentin explained that this window had been commissioned by one of the parishioners whose daughter and a friend had drowned in a tragic boating accident in the 1960s.

'Chagall was so impressed on seeing this window *in situ*,' Quentin told her, 'that he immediately decided to create stained glass designs for the other eleven windows as well.'

She wandered around the rest of the interior. With no-one else in the building, it was like a private viewing. She had always loved Chagall's work. She had seen his windows at the Hadassah University Medical Centre in Jerusalem but it was impossible to get anywhere near them. Here, because the windows were not positioned high up in the walls, she was able to inspect them quite closely. It was remarkable that she could approach such priceless works of art in this way – not in a museum or a gallery but in a simple English village church. The side windows were not so figurative as the main east window, being inlaid mainly with petal, lozenge or butterfly shapes. But she was quite overwhelmed by the beauty of them all. She sat down on one of the pews, watched the subtle change in the colour of the sunlight as it became diffused through the stained glass. Perhaps it was her emotional state from so much going on in her life but she felt so moved by what she was seeing that she actually felt like crying. Quentin came to sit beside her. She was grateful they could sit together silently for a while until he said:

'Aunt Georgie used to bring me here when I was little. She loved this place. Chagall was her favourite painter.'

'It's not difficult to see why.'

'*If I create from the heart, nearly everything works.* A quote of his she was fond of repeating.'

'Words you could apply to her work as much as his. In the end, I believe that's what people respond most to. Honest, heartfelt creation.'

'I agree. And the situation of these glorious windows in such a humble place only adds to the majesty of it all.'

Quentin was right, she thought. This was how art should be seen. Not shut away in some museum or gallery. But in everyday settings like this. She looked across at him. He had closed his eyes, tilted his face so that the light through one of the windows could bathe his pale skin.

'Thank you for bringing me here,' she said.

He stirred from his reverie. 'My pleasure. All part of my devious plan to make you like me.' He patted her hand. 'Now, I believe we have favours to exchange.'

'Shall we go outside? It seems sacrilegious to discuss such matters in here.'

'I see our privacy is about to be invaded anyway,' Quentin

noted as several members of a coach party began to funnel into the church.

They sat in Quentin's car. Even though she had no particular interest in matters automobile, she couldn't help but be seduced by the blue, cracked leather seats, the mahogany dashboard with its old-fashioned dials and switches – it all seemed so hand-crafted and bespoke, so well-used but yet lovingly preserved – belonging to a world of care and attention that didn't seem to exist any more. Quentin drummed his fingers against the large steering wheel.

'How shall we do this?' she asked.

'Ladies first?'

'I don't mind.' She sat up in her seat, turned towards him, their closeness slightly disconcerting for such a negotiation. 'I won't beat about the bush, Quentin…'

'That's fine with me. I prefer we should be straight-talking. Shoot from the hip, as they say.'

'All right then. It's funding we're after. This play… *Georgie by Georgie*. Sal and I were wondering whether you'd be interested in investing.'

Quentin sucked in a breath. 'I see. How much?'

'We need around forty thousand pounds for start-up costs. So a contribution towards that. We didn't think it was inappropriate to ask. After all, you've had so much involvement in the project already.'

Quentin swivelled so that he was properly facing her. He moved his arm along the back of the seat, started to pick at the fabric of her blouse, just at the shoulder. It was an odd gesture, something a tailor or a seamstress might do with a loose thread. She didn't know what to make of it. It didn't feel like his action had any sexual undertones, he just seemed absorbed in his task.

'Not inappropriate at all,' he said eventually. 'But I'm afraid I can't oblige.'

'Oh,' was all she managed to say. Perhaps it was her own secret arrogance but somehow she had convinced herself

Quentin would agree to her request. 'Can I ask why not?'

'Of course you can.' He pulled away from his touching of her blouse as if he had just noticed his actions for the first time. 'I'm sorry,' he said with a look to his offending fingers. 'Don't get me wrong, Laura. From what I've seen so far, I think you'll do an absolutely sterling job with the play. But I do not wish to get involved for a couple of reasons.'

'And these are?'

'First of all I just don't feel comfortable having a financial involvement in this material which I am so close to. It would seem like... I don't know... like a vanity project. I hope you can respect that. And secondly...' Quentin was back fingering her blouse. 'Yes, secondly. Secondly, I've decided to invest what spare cash I have in backing my own play.'

'*Maimonides*?'

'Yes, *Maimonides*. You did such a wonderful job with the run-through, I thought – why not take a risk on something I really care about? I've spoken to some theatre producers and we're looking at the whole package. Rehearsals, provincial touring with the possibility of staging it somewhere in London if reviews are positive. And that is why I would like to ask you my favour.'

'Which is?'

'I was wondering if you would be kind enough to give me the contact details for your wonderful cast. I'd like to offer them all parts in my new production.'

Chapter Forty-Two

The Hepburn Archives

Extract from an unpublished memoir

I notice it's been a while now since I mentioned the film director, Doug Mitchell. Doug who brought me the news that Max had been killed in a bombing raid. Doug who briefly became my wartime lover until we no longer had the time nor the inclination to keep our liaison alive. Ours wasn't an instant or brutal separation. We simply and slowly starved our relationship to death.

I was therefore surprised one day to find that on answering the insistent knocking on the door of my mother's cottage, Doug was standing there with a bunch of flowers in his hand and a wide smile on his still handsome face.

'What the bloody hell are you doing here?' was all I could say.

Doug pushed the bouquet at me. 'A peace offering,' he said. His hair and moustache were grey and he had filled out a bit, as had most people now that the war was over. Looking back at those years of conflict, I understood how we all had been such pale, thin rations of our real physical selves.

'I didn't realise you and I had been at war,' I said, taking his gift.

'A war of attrition.'

'Still the charmer.' I noticed that almost subconsciously I had placed my hand on my hip to adopt some coquettish pose. 'How did you know where I was?'

'I'm making a film not far from here. I remembered you came from Five Elms Down, it's not a name I could easily forget. Drove over on the off-chance. The florist told me where you lived. Are you letting me in?'

'Of course, of course. Please enter.'

I took him out to the garden. I could feel myself trembling as I walked him through, feeling his gaze on the back of me. It had been a long time since I had entertained male company and here I was behaving like a teenage girl as I rushed to pull out the garden chairs, mumbled lots of things at once about my mother being asleep upstairs, and if he wanted a cup of tea or perhaps something stronger and if he could just give me a minute while I tidied up, put the flowers in a vase. He just stood back and watched me with that stupid smile on his face which just made me twitter on all the more. I got him settled then went into the downstairs bathroom, powdered my cheeks, applied some lipstick, talked to myself in the mirror. 'For Christ's sake, Georgie. You're a forty-six-year-old woman behaving like an adolescent.' I just prayed my mother wouldn't wake up for a while.

I went into the kitchen, made up afternoon tea for two, took the tray through towards the garden. Just as I was approaching, I saw Doug sitting there, smoking a pipe, gazing out across the lawn, and I recalled an image of my father sitting in that very same position smoking his pipe so many years ago. The memory was quite overwhelming and I had to stop for a moment, regain my composure. I thought of my mother upstairs asleep in her room, looked back again at Doug, the present and past images somehow fusing together into one, and I realised I felt immensely happy. No. 'Happy' would be the wrong word. I felt content. As if finally this was how my life was supposed to be.

'I've made tea,' I said, scolding myself quietly for stating the bloody obvious.

My words seemed to have shaken Doug out of some reverie. 'I was just thinking…' His voice drifted away.

'Penny for them.'

'I've always wanted a place like this. Cottage in the country. Quite the English dream, eh? Apple trees and trimmed lawns. Village green. The birds singing. Do birds sing in the city? I've never noticed. Do they?'

'I'm sure they do.'

'And horses. I'd have stables, go riding every day. Do you ride, Georgie?

'I used to when I was young. I suppose we all did round here. What about you?'

'Me too. When I was young. Pony trekking holidays in Scotland. Magnificent memories. But don't you get lonely out here?'

'There's my mother, of course. Although she hardly registers who I am these days. I know people in the village. And my aunt and god-daughter live not too far away. What about you? Are you still in that little flat in Shepherd's Bush?'

'I'm afraid so. My former spouse still has the house. Which is fine for the children, of course. But my hope is that this film I'm working on takes off and it will be goodbye to poverty forever.'

'Not another war film?'

'Absolutely not. And I'm not one for Ealing comedies either. Or Dickens or Shakespeare. You know that film you did? *The Woman Walks Free*. It's a bit like that. Dark, gritty, a strong female lead. I've got a young actress called Marion MacDonald playing the role. She might not be famous now but this girl is bound for stardom.'

'Who wrote it?'

'I did actually. It's called *Limehouse*. Most of it takes place in London's East End. But the young woman moves in from the country. That's why I'm down here filming.'

I poured out the tea and listened as Doug talked animatedly about his film. Of course, my own career in that industry had come to a halt twenty years previously but I still took an interest, keeping up-to-date with my monthly dose of *Picturegoer* magazine. I became quite animated myself when I told Doug about my day out at Royal Ascot with Ivor Novello, my encounter with the great Alfred Hitchcock. The light began to fade and the air cooled but we chatted on and I realised that we had never talked like this before. Our previous encounters had been precious moments of physical pleasure snatched out of the fear and drama of a war. Here we were now actually communicating with each other, sharing our passions. Darkness and the coldness of the night eventually forced us inside. I prepared dinner, my mother came down to join us, hardly seeming to notice there was a male guest at her table. When it finally came for Doug to leave, I walked with him out to the car. We kissed briefly, it had been such a long time, I felt I had forgotten how to. I pulled away and just buried my face in his shoulder and he held me warm and close. He told me he would come back to visit again as soon as there was another break in filming.

When I returned to the house, I asked my mother what she thought of him.

'You know I've always liked Douglas Fairbanks,' she said. 'I'm just surprised he came for dinner.'

Chapter Forty-Three

A Benchmark

Laura didn't take up Quentin's offer of a drive in his vintage roadster. It wasn't that she was angry with him. After all, the man had every right to do what he wanted with his money, even if it meant funding a play she had helped him put on. Or providing work for a cast she had assembled – including bloody Caroline – while leaving her empty-handed. It all just felt like another let-down at a time when everything else was going wrong in her life. She thanked him for introducing her to the wonder of the Chagall windows and drove off a little too fast for these winding country lanes. She noted that Sal had texted her several times wanting to know the outcome of their meeting. She waited until she got back to London before she called him.

'How's my pal Quentin?' he asked.

'He took me to a tiny Kent village to see some stained glass windows.'

'Are you guys going on dates now?'

'Don't be silly. And the windows were by Chagall. Absolutely stunning.'

'I'm sure they were. Did you ask him about funding?'

'He turned us down.'

'Ouch. You couldn't twist his arm?'

'He wouldn't budge.'

'Did he say why?'

'He said he felt too close to the production. Although I'm not sure I understood what he meant by that.'

'That was his reason?'

'He's also decided to put his money into his own play. That *Maimonides* production I organized for him.'

'I thought you said it was crap.'

'I told you it wasn't as bad as I first thought. Although my opinion doesn't matter here. Quentin intends to put together a full-blown production. And he wants to use my cast.'

'Jesus Christ, Laura. You don't have to help him with that. We've already come up with our side of the bargain.'

'We? You mean *I've* come up with our side of the bargain, Sal. I'd be interested to know what *you've* done.'

'OK, I get you're annoyed with Quentin. But no need to take it out on me. We're partners, remember. Which is just as well. Since I got your back covered.'

'What have you done?'

'I had a meeting with Sir Lew.'

'I'm impressed. And?'

'He said investing in the arts wasn't really his thing.'

'I could have told you that.'

'He didn't dismiss me out of hand though. He said he'd run it by one of his advisers. Remember that guy you sat beside at Caroline's dinner party?'

'The Swede. Fredrik something.'

'Fredrik Nilssen.'

'The one who predicts the age of your death.'

'Yeah, that's him.'

'I thought he just worked out risk for insurance companies, banks, things like that.'

'And for all kinds of Lew's potential investments. Like our play.'

'Doesn't make sense. We must be small-fry compared to his other projects.'

'You underestimate my powers of presentation, Laura. I told him that if we can get our little play to the West End, then to Broadway, license the rights overseas, we could be raking in the dollars. Andrew Lloyd Webber territory.'

'You told him that?'

'Maybe not the Andrew Lloyd Webber line. Anyway, you seemed to get on well with Fredrik that night.'

'Well enough.'

'I thought he had the hots for you.'

'How would you know? You had your back to me all through dinner.'

'I was playing hard to get.'

Laura ignored the comment. 'When will we know?'

'A couple of days. Tops.'

It had been a boozy lunch as usual with Victoria in Hampstead. Afterwards, the two of them strolled through Highgate Wood, Laura taking her friend's arm more for support than out of affection. Too much wine in the afternoon? So what? She had nothing else to do for the rest of the day although Victoria had an appointment with a client at three. She snatched in a couple of deep breaths, hoping the oxygen would clear her head, moved in a little closer to her friend. She loved these woods with their clusters of oaks, hornbeams and holly. She loved the word 'wood'. There was something comforting and magical about it, better than the word 'forest' which always seemed to contain an element of darkness and fear. Although Highgate Wood was probably a forest at one time before Muswell Hill and Finchley and Highgate itself crept in.

'When I die,' she announced with a grand flourish of her free arm. 'I'm going to leave money for a bench to be placed here in my memory.'

'No star on the Hollywood Walk of Fame?'

'Those days are over.'

'A blue plaque from English Heritage?'

'Just a bench. And I'd like you, Victoria, my dear bestest friend, to deal with it.'

'Only if I get to choose the inscription.'

'Something simple then. Name. Year of birth and death. And then a short sentence like: *She loved this place.*'

'Oh, I was thinking more along the lines of: *Laura Scott. Died in denial about her tax bill.*'

'Are you still going on about that?'

'Laura, you've got to do something about it. Go and see Marcus. Please.'

'He'll just scold me like I was some naughty schoolgirl.'

'Better that than ending up in prison. Swallow your pride and call him.'

Laura pulled her friend to a stop. 'I'd like you to place the bench up there.' She pointed towards a rise in the woodlands. 'That's my favourite spot.'

Victoria stamped her feet. 'You're not listening to me.'

'I always listen to you and your wonderful words of wisdom.'

'Yeah, yeah, yeah.'

'Some of your advice has stayed with me all my life.'

'Be serious.'

'I am being serious. Remember when we were in Greece together, you, me and Caroline? Somewhere on Crete.'

'Paleochora.'

'That was it. It was in your more "hippy dippy" days.'

'I don't know why you keep saying that. You were as much a dippy hippy as I was.'

Laura stood back from her friend, looked her up and down from her white lace headband, past her Indian kurti top to her tie-dye baggy yoga pants. 'I really don't think so.'

Victoria shrugged. 'You were saying about Paleochora.'

Laura hooked herself back into Victoria's arm and they continued walking. 'We were sitting around a fire on the beach with some others, I don't remember any of them, young men, Greeks, one was playing a guitar, good-looking he was, Caroline all over him like a rash as usual. Do you remember that?'

'Vaguely.'

'Full moon, canopy of stars, warm night. We were all drunk or stoned, singing something about not saying goodbye to the summer. Still with me?'

'I kind of remember.'

'I was feeling immensely happy and content, probably haven't ever felt better since if I were to be truthful. And then you turned to me and said, completely out of the blue, in a sort of far-off voice as if you had just experienced some kind of an epiphany: *The most important thing, Laura, is to follow your dream.'*

'That would be my Martin Luther King moment.'

'Will you let me finish. And then you said: *If you do that, the universe will take care of you. And all the pieces will fall into place.'*

Victoria laughed. 'That was very profound of my younger self.'

'You are very profound.'

'And you're a little bit drunk.'

'Seriously, that's what you said to me. And the intensity of the way you spoke then was frightening.'

'You just felt that way because you were stoned.'

'Perhaps. But your words stayed with me even after all these years.' Laura tried to imitate Victoria's otherworldly tone. *'Follow your dream and the universe will take care of you.* And that's what I'm doing now.'

'By not going to see Marcus?'

'No, by believing in myself. I'm convinced that by committing myself to this project about Georgie, everything will work out just fine. Sal will come up with the finance, the play will be a huge success, I will pay off my tax bill and Marcus Green can go fuck himself with his rules number one, two and whatever. After all, that's what happened to you.'

'What do you mean?'

'Well, you persisted with all your *feng shui* stuff when everyone else thought you were mad.'

'You never told me you thought I was mad.'

'So I lied to support you. And just look at you now. Designer to the rich and famous.'

'You're missing out the part about the unfaithful husband and the broken marriage.'

'That's another aspect altogether. That involves the vagaries of another person. I'm talking about individual choice.'

'Well, my individual choice is that I have to see a client at three. Do you want to stay or shall we share a taxi?'

'I'd like to stay for a while. At my favourite place. Where you shall put my bench.'

'Are you sure you wouldn't rather go home and sleep off lunch?'

'I'll be fine.'

With Victoria gone, Laura wandered off among the trees, away from the pathways to find her own private spot. She still felt a bit light-headed and it took a while for her to locate her destination. When she found it, she took off her suede jacket, folded it up to serve as a cushion and sat down on it with her back against her favourite oak. The sun had just begun to slant through the branches sending out fingers of light everywhere. It was that gorgeous time of year when the last of the summer lingered but autumn was most definitely in the air, the temperature cooling, the colours changing, the faint whiff of mulch from the damp earth and the early fallen leaves.

Her phone started thrumming away on mute from somewhere inside her satchel but she had neither the desire nor the energy to go foraging to find it. What she really needed to do was pee. She surveyed her location. She was out of sight from any of the paths, it was hardly likely that anyone else would be stumbling around in this part of the woods. She had some tissues in her pocket. So after another quick look around, she pulled down her jeans and her knickers, squatted down close at the earth. She could feel the draft on her bum. Was this how other middle-aged women behaved after a few glasses of wine and with a full bladder? She actually found herself smirking at the thought of some rogue paparazzo snapping away at her white arse and the flapping tails of her shirt. What a headline – or bottom line – that would make. She wiped herself off, zipped herself up, sat back down on her jacket, closed her eyes. Peeing in the woods had made her feel so…? So liberated. Like the pot-smoking rebellious youth she once was. She thought again about Victoria's ancient advice. Could she seriously believe that the universe would take care of her if she followed her true destiny? Well, all it needed was for Sir Lew to come up with the money and she could find out.

The awful sound of a police siren woke her. Was it her imagination, or had the sound of these emergency vehicles become more urgent, more strident these days? She had a dull ache behind her eyes, her mouth felt incredibly dry, she wondered how long she had been asleep. She fumbled inside her bag for her phone. She had several messages All from Sal:

Important news. Can we speak?
We need to talk.
Where are you?
Where the hell are you?
Christ, Laura. Turn on your cell.

Chapter Forty-Four

The Hepburn Archives

Extract from an unpublished memoir

I often wondered why I married Doug. Perhaps when it came to my encounters with men, he was my last temptation, my final dip in the relationship pool before I decided that an independent, single life would be best for me. Certainly on rational reflection I should never have done it. But sometimes life catches us off-guard and we end up making decisions we shouldn't have. There were certainly a lot of things pushing me towards him at the time. I was lonely and Doug was there. I was vulnerable as I tried to deal with the deterioration in my mother's health and Doug was there. I missed the excitement of wartime flying and Doug was there. I was at a loss about what to do with my life and Doug was there. He could also connect me to the world of film and acting that in some part of me I still missed. Fundamentally, there was a huge vacuum in my life and Doug was able to fill it. It was a decision based on need not love. And that is never a good basis for a healthy marriage. Or maybe it is, depending on whether you both need the same things.

The wedding was a small affair in the village church. My family were there, of course. Aunt Ginny, Uncle Richard, the two boys Oliver and Percy, Susan was my maid of honour. My mother was in a wheelchair by then, she didn't really know what was going on but she did seem happy enough, probably because she still thought it was Douglas Fairbanks Jr. I was marrying. From Doug's side, there were his two children, William and Kathleen, both in their early twenties thank God, too old to care too much about the presence of a wicked stepmother stealing their father away. A few villagers, some film people from London, a couple of the ATA girls and that was it.

After all, I was a middle-aged spinster and Doug was a divorcé – the quicker we were in and out of that church the better.

There had been talk of Aunt Ginny taking my mother but she needed round-the-clock attention so we moved her into a care home. Doug settled in with me at the cottage, neither of us having much money, it appeared the best arrangement. As Doug spent a lot of time commuting into London, he kept on his flat in Shepherd's Bush. I suppose I was happy in those first few years as we struggled financially waiting to see what would happen with Doug's great film project. I spent a lot of time going back and forward to the care home, taking my camera with me, photographing my mother then later many of the residents, listening to their stories, gaining their trust.

The young are so impatient with the elderly these days, always dismissing them, never stopping to hear what they have to say. Yet we – I can say 'we' for I am old now myself as I write these words – yet we carry with us so much history, knowledge, experience and wisdom, it is a shame that the young allow themselves to waste all of that. I suppose that is the great tragedy of human existence in that the old know what it is like to be young but the young don't know what it is like to be old. Of course, there are those who say that the young need to create their own histories, knowledge, experience and wisdom, and there is some truth in that. But for me, I have gained so much from listening to the wisdom of my elders. It has infused my work, helped me to create three dimensional portraits of them in my photographs, for I was able to capture who they really were.

My mother died relatively peacefully. Of pneumonia, the death certificate said. I was at her bedside when she breathed her last brittle breath. It wasn't so much that she died, it was just that she finally disappeared, just like that little white dot you used to see when switching off the black-and-white television set. Over the years the person she had been was vanishing bit by bit right in front of me until 'click' she was no longer there. It had been such a slow process that it was almost as if I had indeed switched off the TV programme of her life and said: 'Oh well, off to bed then.' I had seen people at the care home become quite angry and frustrated as their lives closed down on them. My mother didn't really know who I was by the time she went but she was kinder and gentler to me in her deteriorating years than she had ever been since my father died. It was as if she had returned to being that little girl I had once espied as I looked down on her from my perch in the apple tree.

Oh yes, I was writing about Doug. You see, every time his name comes up in my mind I want to veer off somewhere else. I must concentrate now. Write everything down.

His film was a huge success, we all know that now. *Limehouse*. An absolute triumph. The heralding of a new era in film-making. No more war films, no more silly comedies, no more adaptations of historical novels. Modern, gritty dramas on an epic scale. Six Oscar nominations, Doug winning his two for Best Director and Best Screenplay. Our lives changed overnight. Suddenly I was thrown back into that glamorous world I had been evicted from in my youth.

Those first couple of years, I really enjoyed being on the coat-tails of Doug's success. The focus was all on him and I didn't mind that at all. In fact, I preferred it that way. I would turn up at these premieres and charity balls and house parties and snap away with my camera. No-one seemed to mind or at least they didn't say anything for fear of offending Doug. Doug who was planning his next great picture, Doug who was looking around for his new cast, Doug who was the darling of producers in search of the next fruitful investment.

I had access to all the great stars of that era on both sides of the Atlantic. Audrey Hepburn, Marlon Brando, Cary Grant, James Stewart, James Dean. Click, click, click. Vivien Leigh, Ava Gardner, Laurence Olivier, Gary Cooper. Click, click, click. Never posed shots. Lying by the pool (Brando), playing cards (Leigh), powdering her nose (Bacall), sprawled out on the sofa (Dean), playing with our dog (a labrador called

Rollo, everyone loved him, especially Bardot). I kept them all, intimate moments – without make-up, without guile – stashed away in a box in the basement of a beach house we were renting in Malibu. But I always felt these photographs of the stars were a form of cheating when it came to my work, the viewer being drawn more to the celebrity of the subject than to the essence of the person. Even in their most casual moments, their stardom somehow acted as a filter between the viewer and the viewed. That was the opposite of what I was trying to do in my work. I remember once saying to Susan that it would be interesting if one day in the future, when these actors and actresses had been forgotten, to display their photographs alongside those of ordinary people. Would their star quality still shine through?

Where was I? Rambling on, anything but Doug. Nothing succeeds like success. That's what they say. And that's what carried us through those first few years. Of course, Doug had affairs. I would have had to have been a fool not to see that coming. He may have been in his fifties, but he was still good-looking. He was what they call these days an Alpha-male. He had money, he had power, he had access to all the young actresses desperate to please him. Marion MacDonald was one of them, the star of *Limehouse*, nominated for an Oscar for her performance, didn't win (much to my not-so-secret glee). It didn't really matter to me. Doug and I hardly had sex that much anyway in those days, why should I blame him for seeking satisfaction elsewhere? It was what happened later that I never forgave him for. When he entered what I called 'the trough', that period of five years or so after his career went into a downward spiral and before he was able to resurrect it again with his last great film. Aptly entitled *To Rise Again*.

Chapter Forty-Five

A Slap in the Face

Jack once told Laura that the best way to avoid being hounded by the general public as a celebrity was paradoxically to go out and mix with the general public.

'Take the subway, take the bus,' he would say. 'Go to the mall, the park, the deli. Wear your ordinary clothes. That way people will say – *Isn't that the actress, Laura Scott? Naw, it couldn't be. What would she be doing flying economy, eating in a diner, browsing in a bookshop?*'

So here she was now, stumbling through the trees in Highgate Wood with a splitting headache, her jacket all covered in mulch and leaves, her sunglasses nowhere to be found, her heels catching in the earth causing her feet to twist painfully, and a couple of young mums harassed by their toddlers scooting around on an array of miniature vehicles, looking at each other and mouthing words she couldn't hear but guessing one of them was saying: 'Isn't that Laura Scott?' While the other was responding: 'But it couldn't be. What would she be doing staggering around half-drunk in Highgate Wood in the middle of the afternoon?'

It was with some relief therefore that she managed to find herself an unoccupied bench far away from the gaze of Jack's general public. She brushed off the leaves and other muck, discovered her lost sunglasses in her jacket pocket, tied on a headscarf, pressed down on Sal's name on her contact list. He answered immediately.

'Where you been?' he asked.

'Lunch,' she drawled.

'It's five in the afternoon. I've been trying to get hold of you all day.'

'I see that. What's all the fuss about?'

'I got some news.'

'Good or bad?'

'Good *and* bad. What do you want first?'

'Is this a joke?'

'No, I'm serious.'

'I'll take the good then.'

'Sir Lew's going to fund the play.'

'Oh, that's fantastic. I'm so happy. I was just saying to Victoria, you have to follow your dream and the universe will take care of you. See, the pieces are falling into place.'

'Laura?'

'What?'

'You're forgetting the bad news.'

'What bad news?'

'Are you sitting down?'

'I suppose I am.'

'He doesn't want to do it with you.'

'Who doesn't want to do what with who?'

'Lew. He doesn't want you to do *Georgie by Georgie*.'

'What do you mean?'

'He wants to use it as a return vehicle for Caroline.'

'You can't be serious.'

'That's what he wants. Remember I told you about him taking advice from the actuary guy. Well, that was the advice. To go with Caroline.'

'I can't believe I'm hearing this. Caroline as Georgie? Fucking Caroline as Georgie. Sitcom Caroline who was just a pair of tits in a tight sweater about a hundred years ago. Don't tell me Fredrik thinks she's more bankable than I am?'

'Yep. I'm afraid that's what he's saying. Look, Laura, there's no better way to put this than just to tell you the truth. According to Fredrik, the play stands a better chance of success if it is used as a platform for the return of an extremely popular sitcom star from the late nineteen seventies. Rather than as the stage for a fading film actress. His words not mine.'

'And you supported him?'

'Of course, I argued your corner. You were always my first

choice, Laura, you know that. But we… I need the funding. Lew's the one calling the shots.'

'Surely we can get the money elsewhere?'

'If we waited long enough perhaps. But Lew's offering very generous terms right now. Business is business, Laura. You know how tough this industry is. You're a far better fit for Georgie than Caroline. A million times better. But I've got to take Lew's offer.'

'Fuck Lew.'

'Laura…'

'And fuck you, Sal.'

Still with an aching head, Laura paid off the taxi, stomped up the steps of the Regency terrace mansion with its cream pillars and glossy black door so shiny it might have been a mirror she was looking at rather than a panel of painted wood. She buzzed on the intercom and almost gave the 'V' sign to the eye of the discreet camera tucked away in a top corner of the portico. The butler Robert or Ronald or whatever his name was answered the door but kept an arm across the threshold so she couldn't brush past.

'Where is she?' Laura shouted.

'I'm afraid, Madam isn't…'

'Where is…?'

Caroline's voice interrupted from up in the stairway. 'It's all right, Ronald. You can let her in.'

Laura strode into the spacious marble hallway, catching her heel on some fabulous Persian rug which possibly cost more than her entire debt to Her Majesty's Revenue and Customs, causing her to stumble forward. It was Ronald who stopped her falling, grabbing her arm, easing her upright.

'Let me show you into the lounge,' he said as if nothing had happened.

Laura found herself gently coaxed along into the stunningly bright blue and yellow room of her previous visit.

'Can I get you something to drink?' the butler asked.

'She doesn't want anything to drink, Ronald,' Caroline said, waving away her servant as she entered. 'She just wants to harangue me.'

'Actually, I'd quite like a gin and tonic, if you don't mind,' Laura said, although the last thing she needed was another quantity of alcohol to add to her lunchtime intake.

Ronald looked over at his mistress and Laura saw a slight twitch develop at the corner of his left eye as he was caught between Caroline's command and the demands of the guest.

'Oh, very well then,' Caroline said. 'Make that two.'

Laura chose to sit in an enormous armchair which was a mistake as it immediately engulfed her, forcing her back into what she saw as a defensive position. She pushed herself upright, then had to wriggle to the front edge of the cushion just so that she could face Caroline with a straight back and neatly folded ankles. Now that she was here, she felt the strength of her anger begin to ebb. She was no longer in the mood for confrontation. All she felt like doing was taking a couple of aspirins, putting on her sunglasses against the blinding brightness of the room, falling asleep where she sat.

'Are you all right?' Caroline asked. 'You look a bit pale.'

'I'm fine,' she snapped back.

'So?'

'I thought we were friends.'

'Of course we are.'

'Then why are you stabbing me in the back?'

'What did Sal tell you?'

'That Lew would only invest in the play if you got the title role.'

'What else?'

'Apparently that Swedish actuary you placed beside me at dinner advised him it was better to have a comeback queen rather than a fading star.'

Caroline threw her head back, laughed like a neighing horse. 'Is that what he told you?' she said, as she shivered herself back into some sort of composure.

Before Laura could respond, the conversation was forced to stall as Ronald returned to the room with their drinks which he placed on little tables beside where they sat. Caroline flicked her fingers against the thigh of her cream trousers while Laura contemplated the expensive art work that adorned the walls, none of which reflected Caroline or Lew's own tastes, but instead the abstract designs of their mutual friend Victoria. Within this tense silence, Ronald stepped away from his finished task, dipped his head slightly, and left.

Caroline reached forward but instead of taking her drink, she plucked a cigarette out of a box of Marlboros, lit it with a bulky silver lighter in the shape of a genie's lamp. She sucked at it nervously then picked up her glass. 'Old friends,' she said with a slight slur.

Laura raised her own glass but ignored the toast. As she began to emerge from the haze of her own lunchtime over-indulgence, she realised Caroline might have been slightly drunk herself, here in this vast house in the early evening with only her servants for company. She was immediately reminded of the unhappy, insecure student she had once known Caroline to be, the young woman who feared men were only after her for her body, a fact of life she had eventually succumbed to. Laura had only to look around at this expensive home to see what Caroline's physical attributes had achieved.

'So is that what he said?' Caroline asked again.

Laura had lost the thread of a conversation she felt she should be controlling. 'Who?'

'Sal. Comeback queen versus fading star.'

'Fredrik told him that.'

'What a coward.'

'Who? Fredrik?'

'Sal. Fredrik has nothing to do with this.'

'I thought he advised Lew on his investments?'

'Laura. This is a tiny production. A minuscule speck of a thing. Why would Lew want to get involved in something like this, never mind bring Fredrik on board? The amount of money that Swedish calculator charges per hour would be enough to take care of your box office for a year. Lew turned down Sal right from the off.'

'So, who is…?'

'Who do you think?'

And then the truth became so obvious to her. 'Fuck, Caroline. You. You're putting up the money.'

Caroline sipped on her drink, drew on her cigarette, then back to her drink again. 'I suppose I am.'

'Why are you doing this to me?'

'Oh come on, Laura. You can't always have everything your own way.'

'And you haven't?' Laura stretched out her arm to the room and its art work in an indication of some of Caroline's wealth, causing a slosh of gin and tonic to spill on her hand.

'All this means nothing to me.' Caroline tried snapping her fingers to illustrate the vacuousness of her existence but failed. 'I always wanted what you have. Right from the start. When we were back in drama school.'

'I had a bit of luck in the beginning that's all.'

'Well, I'm going to make my own luck now.'

'Even it means screwing over an old friend?'

'You've had your glittering career. I just want one last chance. That *Maimonides* thing reminded me of what really makes me happy.'

'Quentin's turning *Maimonides* into a proper production. I suggest you stick with that.'

'Oh, Laura. I'd merely be supporting. *Georgie by Georgie*, I've read Sal's script… it's just so wonderful.'

'I'm not letting you do this to me, Caroline. I'm not going to let you bribe Sal into giving you this part.'

Caroline smirked at her. 'Sal didn't need any bribe to do that.'

Laura stood up quickly, knocking over the little table that supported her drink. She watched as the clear alcohol seeped into the expensive carpet, regretting for a moment that she had not asked for a large glass of red wine. 'Christ, Caroline. You never change, do you? You're sleeping with him. That's what this is all about.'

'So what if it is?'

'You conniving bitch.'

'Jealous? He is rather good-looking.'

'Well, two can play at that game.'

'What are you going to do about it, Laura?'

'I'll tell Lew.'

Caroline laughed. 'Go on. Tell him. Do you think Lew gives a shit who I'm fucking? He's got a trail of whores lined up from here to Acapulco. Go on, Laura. Give him some dirt on me. You'll be doing the bastard a favour.'

Chapter Forty-Six

The Hepburn Archives

Extract from an unpublished memoir

The period I call 'the trough' began after we moved to the States – 'to be closer to the action' as Doug decreed it. We rented a beach house out in Malibu, Los Angeles County, California. It was a gorgeous place to live, ocean view, miles and miles of sand, acres of mountains, chaparral and canyons, no wonder so many of the Hollywood rich and famous chose to locate their homes there. But what I loved most was the light. Even when it was sunny in England, everything still seemed so drab and dreary in those post-war years. Here in California, that never-ending bucketload of sunshine dazzled me every day, charged up my batteries, filled me with hope.

I certainly needed to cling to that feeling of hope. Doug had directed two movies in the wake of the success of *Limelight* but they had both bombed at the box office and his calling card at the various studios was gradually losing its sheen. He had always been a bit of a drinker but he took up the alcohol then with a vengeance. Thankfully, he was never a violent drunk. I can say that about him, despite all that he did, he never once raised a hand to me. Alcohol would just make him incredibly maudlin, then boring, then full of self-pity, then he would collapse. I would find him passed out on the beach, floating around inside a rubber ring in the pool, flat out in a puddle of his own vomit on the bathroom floor (several times), head down on the steering wheel in the garage. Drugs crept into his life too, cocaine for sure, marijuana was just coming into its own, I doubt if he injected any of the really hard stuff, Doug was always afraid of needles.

I helped him to his bed, cleaned up after him, ignored the alcohol on his breath, the smell of another woman's perfume on his clothes, the semen stains on his underpants, the receipts for flowers and jewellery I never saw. I nursed his ego, nursed him through the script he was writing that would eventually prove to be his resurrection. I treated him more like a naughty little boy with homework to be done rather than as my husband.

In the meantime I got on with my own life, continued taking my photographs, managed to organize a few exhibitions of my work, obtained several commissions for portraits of wealthy clients. I made enough money not to have to ask Doug for anything for myself. It was Doug though who paid the rent on the beach house and all the associated utilities. I never thought to ask him where the money came from, I assumed funds still remained from the heady *Limehouse* days.

I had been commissioned to do some portraits for an oil executive and his family about 100 miles up the coast in Santa Barbara, a place I'd never been to before. Frank Monaghan was the name of the client, he told me he had seen my work in a small gallery exhibition I'd held in Ventura a few months previously where he had even bought some of my photographs. I thought this was rather odd at the time as I didn't recognise Frank's name as one of my buyers but then again he might have purchased them through a corporate account. Frank was courteous enough to send a car down to Malibu to pick me up. It was a pleasure to be chauffeured up the coast, the surfers out in the ocean, the cool breezes through the parklands, the eternal sunshine. I had work, I had purpose, I had nothing to do but sit back in leather-ensconced luxury and enjoy the ride.

Santa Barbara, hemmed in as it was between the mountains and the ocean, had a distinct Mediterranean feel about it. I mentioned this to the driver who looked at me through his sunglasses and his rearview mirror. 'We call it the American Riviera,' he said. He went on to tell me that where Frank Monaghan lived was called Mission Canyon. 'Much cooler up there,' he said. 'But plenty wild fires. Especially at this time of year.'

The Monaghan house was all timber and glass built on one

level, hidden behind palm trees, pink and purple bougainvillea, an array of succulents in giant terracotta pots. There was a natural, cool feel to the place, views over Santa Barbara and out to the ocean. Frank was waiting for me on the steps, a big, florid hunk of a man in a coffee-cream short-sleeve shirt and matching slacks, all ironed into razor-sharp edges. While the driver unloaded my equipment, he guided me into the house.

It turned out the assignment was not as I thought it to be. There were to be no family shots. Looking around at the open-plan lounge-dining area – all dark wood and leather chairs – I even wondered if there was a family at all. Frank just wanted some corporate photos for his company brochure as well as some more casual portraits that he might have enlarged and framed for his study.

'Arty stuff,' he said. 'Like those other ones you did.'

'To be honest, Frank, I'm not sure what you purchased.'

'You'd better come with me then.'

I followed him through a long wood-panelled corridor adorned with black and white photographs, all of Frank engaged in some sort of sporting activity – golf, hunting, fishing, bowling. Some of his companions were known to me – a couple of actor friends of Doug's, the Governor of the State. I looked ahead to where he was waiting for me, the door to his study wide open. I entered the room which in turn looked out on to an enormous swimming pool. Frank stood framed against this blue, blue backdrop, his arm held out in presentation pose.

'That's what I want you to do for me,' Frank said.

I looked across the room to the back wall. I was shocked by what I saw. Three of my photographs that I thought were stashed away somewhere in my Malibu basement hanging there on Frank's wall. A famous triptych. Brando by the pool, Jimmy Dean on the sofa, and in between the two of them, John Wayne in a dinner suit trying with great difficulty to eat a large slice of cake. The Duke was smiling, there was cream all over his chin and fingers. It was one of my favourite photographs, that big hunk of a hero undone by an unwieldy gateau.

'Where did you get these?' I asked.

'What do you mean? I bought them.'

'From who?'

'Your Ventura exhibition. The gallery owner.'

'But these photographs weren't in the exhibition. I've never even mounted or framed them.'

Frank scratched the side of his neck. 'That guy...'

'What guy?'

'The gallery owner. Schulz, I think he was called.'

'Yes, Mike Schulz.'

'Well, Mike showed them to me. Back of the gallery. Special clients only. I love them, Georgie. Even though they are big shot stars, you've captured the humanity in them. The essence of who they really are. That's what I want you to do with me.'

'How much did you pay for them? If you don't mind me asking?'

'Five thousand a pop,' he said, then back to scratching the side of his neck again. 'Aren't they kosher?'

'What do you mean?'

'Their provenance is good, yeah?'

'Don't worry. Their provenance is just fine.'

I don't know if it was through my anger or my talent, but those photographs I took of Frank Monaghan that day were among the best I'd ever done. (I don't own them myself but I often came across them years later, Frank lending them out to exhibitions or for albums). After the shoot was over though, I didn't hang around for any niceties but got the driver to take me straight back to Malibu. I went down to the basement. Out of my whole collection there were only a few photographs left – Cary Grant, Gary Cooper, Audrey Hepburn, some other lesser knowns.

I found Doug asleep by the pool. He was snoring loudly, a half bottle of Jack Daniels by the side of his lounger. I stopped to look at him for a few moments. He had put on quite a bit of weight since we'd moved from ration-stricken England to all-you-can-eat California. His fat belly disgusted me, struggling as it was to fit into the waist band of his tight little trunks. His mouth was half-open, he was snoring away, there was dribble on his chin. I kicked at the leg of the lounger and he lurched awake with a snort.

'What the fuck is going on?' I said. I remember that these were my exact words for I hardly ever swear.

Doug knew that too. His head spun here and there like some kind of mad cock on a weather-vane as he tried to figure out what had happened. 'Wha?' was all he could say.

'My photographs. The ones in the basement.'

He eased himself upright on the lounger, his face red and blotchy from the sun. He never did tan well in the Californian sunshine.

'So that's what this is about.'

'You had no permission to sell those photographs, Doug.'

'How do you think I've been paying for this place the last year?'

'Paying for this place? You mean paying for your drugs and whisky.'

'They're just photographs, Georgie,' he said, his voice softening slightly.

'I never wanted them displayed.'

'Why not? What's the point of letting them rot away in the basement?'

'I have my reasons.'

'Because the subject happens to be more important than the photographer.'

'That's not the point. You breached my trust. You breached the trust of all these people. You've ruined my reputation as a photographer.'

'No-one is going to know. They were all sold to private collectors.'

'You think that makes me feel better.'

Doug snorted, lifted himself off the lounger, picked up the bottle of Jack Daniels, walked back towards the house. I had to run after him.

'I'm fed up supporting you,' I shouted.

Doug spun on his heels, turned to face me, his mouth curled, his expression ugly. 'You supporting me?' he said, laughing. 'Who got you access to all this Hollywood royalty? Who got you that gallery exhibition in the first place? I'm doing you a fucking favour, Georgie. If I want to sell off these photos, then that's my right. You're my wife after all.'

'And who picks you up off the floor when you're drowning in your own vomit? You're a mess, Doug. Can't you see that? A fat, drugged-up, drunken mess.'

Doug pulled in his stomach, straightened himself to his full height. 'You'd be nothing without me,' he said.

'Well, that's how it's going to be from now on, Doug. Life without me.'

'Yeah, sure,' he said, as he turned back towards the house. 'Nothing, Georgie. You'll be fucking nothing.'

I watched him go, his sandaled feet flopping away on the wet tiles, his elbow cocked back as he took a few gulps of whisky straight from the bottle. I flew back to England two days later.

Chapter Forty-Seven

The Three Envelopes

When Laura returned home from her run-in with Caroline, there was a note pinned to her front door. At first, she thought it was a writ from the bailiffs for the non-payment of her tax bill. It turned out to be from Quentin.

Dropped by but you weren't in. Tried your mobile. No answer. Give me a call. Q

'To hell with you, Quentin,' she said to herself as she pulled a bottle of sparkling mineral water from the fridge. 'To hell with the lot of you.'

She unscrewed the top, drank straight from the bottle until all the water started bubbling up against her lips, spilling down her chin, onto her shirt, between her breasts, she didn't care. She went through to her bedroom, unlocked the French windows, stepped out into the garden. There had been a heavy rain, now eased down to a drizzle but it was still warm. The surfaces of her garden furniture were pooled up wet so she went over to sit on the wall by the pond, trailed her fingers across the slime, caught a glimpse of her mobile phone still resting below among the rocks and the silt. She could have rolled up her shirt sleeve and fished it out but preferred to leave it there, a souvenir of her call from Edy and the end of her career. Her new phone buzzed inside the pocket of her jeans. She dragged it out, squinted at the name and number. Quentin.

'You're a persistent bugger, aren't you?' she said.

'Charming.'

'I'm sorry. I've been dumped from *Georgie by Georgie*. Did you know that?'

'Let's not talk about that now. I'm here in London.'

'I guessed that from your note.'

'Come over for tea tomorrow.'

'I'm in no mood for company.'

'Stop feeling sorry for yourself. I need to talk to you.'

'It's too late, Quentin. The play's finished as far as I'm concerned. I don't need your money.'

'I still think we should talk. Come on, Laura. Tea for two.'

'Where are you staying?'

'At the Savoy.'

'Just like Georgie.'

'Yes. Just like Georgie.'

She had expected the reception clerk to point her in the direction of the Thames Foyer but instead she was told that Mr Quentin Holloway would see her in his suite. Apart from the annoyance at not being able to have tea in one of her favourite salons in the whole of London, it irked her that Quentin was quite happy to take a suite in one of the best hotels yet had not been prepared to fund the play. Quentin, however, showed no such remorse when he opened the door.

'Ah, my dear Laura,' he squealed. 'I am so glad you could come.'

He wore a white shirt with a broad blue pinstripe and a pair of pale yellow trousers, the combination reminding Laura of the colours of Caroline's front room. He guided her into the sitting area all laid out in the Art Deco style. 'If you don't mind I thought we might chat first, have tea later,' he said.

'That's fine with me.'

'Good.' Quentin beckoned her over to the window where there was an oblique view across the river to the south bank. 'It's hard to recognise the old city these days.'

'I guess we have to move with the times.'

'Paris has managed to retain its identity. But London... London is becoming something else altogether. Some of it I quite like. The Tate Modern, of course, where we had lunch. But sometimes I look across the skyline at say the London Eye over there and I think... where am I? Blackpool?'

'I'm a London girl born and bred but I actually prefer the new London. The old London is just so full of tourists.'

Quentin turned away from the window to survey the room. 'Georgie always used to stay here whenever she was in the city. Unfortunately, she had a love-hate relationship with the place.'

'Why would she hate it?'

'Memories, memories,' he said wistfully. 'Perhaps we should sit down.'

Laura chose an armchair while Quentin sat on the nearby sofa. Arranged across the table between them was a magnificent bowl of fruit still in its cellophane wrapping, several luxury travel magazines and three envelopes.

'I have a confession to make,' he said, not looking in any way contrite. He paused, waited, forcing her to intervene for the sake of her curiosity.

'Go on,' she said.

He dipped his head as if she had just given him permission to repent. He cleared his throat and continued. 'In exchange for putting on my play, I granted you full access to Georgie's papers. I'm afraid I was not entirely forthcoming in that respect.' Another pause. 'There were certain items I withheld.'

'Such as.'

'You asked me once why Georgie abandoned her acting career. I told you I didn't know when in fact I do.' Quentin folded his hands in his lap and sighed. 'It would have been around nineteen twenty-seven. Georgie was quite a star at the time what with the success of *The Woman Walks Free*. But her rise to fame came at an important transition point in the film industry as it moved from silent movies to the talkies. She was asked to come here to this very hotel, in fact to this very suite, for an interview with the highly prestigious, now defunct, Montgomery Studios, to find out if her voice – not just her face – would be pleasing to an American audience in this new era. Mister Montgomery, the studio head, was in attendance as was his producer, Hubert Hoffstetter or Hub as he preferred to be called. To check out her voice they asked her to read from the Savoy Grill menu. I found Georgie's written account of the incident among her papers.'

'Is that what you held back from me?'

Quentin picked up one of the envelopes. 'Here,' he said. The word *Savoy* was written on the front.

Inside she found not only Georgie's notes but the menu too. The paper on the latter was quite yellowish, not surprising considering it was over eighty years old, slightly stained at one corner with what she assumed was red wine. A small crest was printed on the front above the words: *The Savoy. Grill Room.*

'I hope you don't mind, Laura. But I wonder if you would read it out.'

'What's going on here, Quentin?

'Please. Indulge me.'

She looked at the words on the page, imagining for a moment that she was the excited yet scared young actress, twenty-seven years old she would have been, ushered before this famous Hollywood producer for an audition that could change her whole career, her whole life. 'All right,' she said.

'Do you mind standing up?'

She did as she was requested, held out the menu and read: 'Soups: Petite Marmite. Consomme Julienne. Cream of Tomato. Hare Soup. Fish: Northern Trout in a Shrimp Sauce. Halibut in a Hollandaise Sauce. Oyster Patties. Meats: Roast Sirloin and Ribs of Beef. Roast Turkey and Sausage. Roast Leg of Pork and Apple Sauce. Ox Tongue...'

Quentin clapped his hands together. 'Enough, enough,' he shouted. 'No more.'

Laura was beginning to lose her patience. 'Can we stop with these games, Quentin? And just tell me what happened here.'

'Montgomery was sitting over there in the corner of the room.' He pointed to the supposed chair which had no doubt been replaced several times during the last eight decades. 'He must have been nearly seventy by then. He rose on his cane and walked into the bedroom. Hub then suggested that she join him.' Quentin's tiny eyes widened with rage. 'A young woman with a golden future ahead of her. What could she do?'

'What did she do?'

Quentin looked up at her in disbelief. 'I imagine most other women at that time would have felt they had no choice.' He held up his hand, wagged a finger. 'But no, no, no. Georgie didn't go into the bedroom. She had too much dignity, too much integrity, for that. And Montgomery destroyed her for it. I never found out what he told people about her, but the studios wouldn't touch her with a barge pole after that day. She insisted though that she would still come back to this hotel whenever she could, despite what had happened. An act of defiance. Bitter-sweet. So bitter-sweet.'

Laura sat down beside him. 'That kind of thing happened a lot in those days,' she said. 'It happened in my day too. I'm sure it goes on even now. The casting couch.'

'I know, I know. But she could have been a star.'

'Perhaps it worked out best for her in the end. Look at the fantastic career she made for herself as a photographer.'

'I realise that's true. But whenever I spoke to her about her film days, I could see the brightness in her eyes. A sudden sparkle as if she were lit up from within, and then that clouding over of regret.'

'Perhaps we should have tea now,' Laura suggested.

'That might be a good idea.'

Quentin called down and ordered afternoon tea with a specific request for his Numalighur estate brand. This did not seem to present the slightest problem for soon after Quentin had replaced the receiver there was a knock on the door of the suite. In came a butler who resembled quite closely the Ronald in Caroline's service – they could have been brothers, Laura thought – followed by a trolley and a waiter. There then proceeded a quasi military-style operation presided over by the butler as the waiter distributed the plates of sandwiches, scones with jam and clotted cream, pastries and cakes along with various pots and jugs.

A snap of the fingers from the Ronald look-alike indicated that everything was in position.

'Shall I serve, madam?' the butler asked.

'That will be all,' Quentin called over from his stance at the window. 'We can manage the rest ourselves.'

With the butler and waiter gone, Quentin came over to sit beside her again, began to fill his plate with a selection of sandwiches while she poured out the tea.

'I'd like to think that we have become friends,' he said.

Laura reflected for a moment on the truth of this comment and then said: 'I suppose we have.'

'Good. I'm glad. And that we can trust each other?'

'Oh I'm not so sure about that, Quentin. Today has already been a day of secrets.'

'Well, I trust *you*,' he said, picking up one of the other envelopes from the table. 'I would like you to have this. One more secret to be revealed, I'm afraid, but I promise this is the last.' He made to hand it over but then held back. 'First let me explain.'

'I hope this isn't some kind of game,' she said.

'No, no, no. Not a game at all.'

'What's in the envelope then?'

'You have read about Max Rosen in Georgie's memoirs?'

'One of her former lovers. A screenwriter from her acting days.'

'Exactly. Do you recall that when she first met Doug Mitchell she asked him to deliver a letter to Max?'

'I do.'

'Well, you may also recall that Doug was unable to deliver the letter because Max had been killed in a London bombing raid a few days previously. The letter was subsequently returned to Georgie and remained unopened until I found it among her papers.'

'What does it say?'

'I'll let you read it for yourself. But I shall take my tea and sandwiches through to the bedroom while you do so. I don't think I could stand to watch you read it in my presence.'

Left on her own, Laura stared at the envelope. Her first

instinct was to smell it. Silly really, she thought, as if Georgie's scent would have lingered after all these years but she did so nevertheless. She then extracted the contents, nothing more than a folded sheet of paper, not even lined for writing but crisscrossed with empty squares, probably torn from an arithmetic jotter or from some notebook Georgie used to log her flight details. She unfolded the sheet, immediately recognised the distinctive slope and curl of Georgie's handwriting and read:

My dear Max

I realise this letter must come as something of a shock to you. It is nearly seventeen years since we last saw each other. I have often thought of you during those years. Many times I used to wait for the credits at the end of a picture just to see if you were the scenarist. If you were, I would be so proud of you. Until now, I have had no way of contacting you. Douglas Mitchell has given me that opportunity but he is in a hurry to go so I need to be quick and concise.

I know that you are married but I don't know if you have any children. Neither do I know how what I have to say will impact on your life but I feel I have to tell you. We have a child, Max. A beautiful daughter.

I was at my lowest ebb when you left me, cutting me off with hardly a word when that whole business with Montgomery had ruined my career and shattered my dreams. I only discovered after you left that I was pregnant. I didn't know what to do. My nerves were in such a state, I was at such a low point, it seemed impossible to look after an infant. So I gave her away, Max. I gave her away to someone who was better able to look after her, to give her a good home. Not to any stranger, Max. To my Aunt Ginny. Do you remember her? So vibrant and gay. A good choice, Max. I couldn't have looked after her myself. Her name is Susan. She is sixteen years old. She looks so much like you.

I don't know how you will react to what I have told you but I felt I needed to let you know. We are living in such terrible times never knowing whether death is around the corner that I felt it best you know the truth. I have no idea how you will take this news. If you want to see me to talk about it, Doug can tell you where I am. If you want to bury this information and never want to see me, I will understand that too.

Please forgive me, Max.

With remembered love and affection,

Georgie

'Laura.'

She looked up. Quentin was standing in front of her, cup and saucer in hand. So entrenched had she been in the letter that she was unaware of his return from the bedroom. She let out a breath she seemed to have been holding for a very long time.

'Your mother was really Georgie's daughter,' she said, stating the obvious but she was so shocked by the information she didn't know what else to say. 'And you're her grandson.'

He nodded.

'When did you find out about this?'

'A couple of years ago. The letter was hidden among her papers.'

'You never suspected anything before?'

'There were some vague references to what happened in other parts of her biographical notes. But this letter is definite proof.'

'Did your mother know?'

'I have no idea.'

'She never mentioned it?'

'Grandma Ginny was always her mother. Georgie her godmother. Never a hint of anything different.'

'I'm trying to think how Georgie managed to pass Susan off like this in the first place. Someone must have known.'

'Well, there would have been Grandma Ginny, of course.

And Grandpa Richard would have had to agree to it as well. But the two boys, Oliver and Percy, they were off in boarding school most of the time, they were probably never told. Ginny and Richard lived on quite an isolated farm so it wouldn't have been difficult to keep a pretend pregnancy quiet for a few months. A few cushions up the dress if need be, Ginny would have no qualms about doing that. And bingo! A brand new daughter to go along with the two boys. No-one ever knew. Anyone else who might have been in on the act long dead by now.'

'How do you feel about it?'

'I remember exactly the moment I came across this letter. It was like uncovering the missing piece of a jigsaw. This great secret revealed. Somehow everything seemed to make sense. As if all the fragments of our lives – mine, my mother's, Georgie's – finally fitted properly together. So in many ways I feel quite blessed.'

'And you're sure your mother didn't know about Georgie?'

'I doubt it would have mattered. The two of them behaved just like mother and daughter anyway.'

He sat down beside her, placed his cup and saucer on the table, she noticed his hand shaking as he did so. He took out a handkerchief from his trouser pocket, wiped his lips. 'Sal called me,' he said. 'He explained what's happening with the play.'

'Did he tell you he's replaced me with his lover?'

'Perhaps you should have a look at this.' He leaned over, picked up the last of the envelopes from the table. 'This might perk you up.'

She looked at the envelope. The words 'Letter of Consent' were written on the front. She took out the document contained inside.

'Well?' Quentin said.

'Well what?'

'Take a look.'

'I know what it says, Quentin. My own lawyer wrote it on my instructions. Signed and dated by you. It grants access to all of

Georgie's papers in exchange for me organising a run-through of your play.'

'Look again.'

'Jesus Christ, Quentin. Why didn't I think of this?'

'I imagine you have been too upset.'

'Have you told Sal?'

'Oh, I thought you might like to do that yourself.'

Chapter Forty-Eight

The Hepburn Archives

Transcript from BBC Radio 4 interview
Broadcasting House, London
16ᵗʰ May 1982
Interviewer: Sir Peter Delamere
Interviewee: Georgie Hepburn

PD: I was wondering if we could talk a little about your marriage to Doug Mitchell. As you are probably aware, I interviewed Doug several times throughout his career and got to know him quite well. You were never divorced. Is that right?

GH: It was just out of laziness more than anything else, Peter. He was in LA, I was in England. I wasn't seeing him anyway, there were no financial issues between us so an extra piece of paper to confirm legally what was going on in reality hardly seemed worth the bother, time or money.

PD: I noticed he barely mentioned you in his autobiography…

GH: …just over one thousand words. I counted them myself. He wrote more about his horses.

PD: Yet you were together for eight years. That strikes me as rather odd, don't you think?

GH: [LAUGHING] I would say that is typical Doug. He was such a vain man. He wouldn't want to give too much space to anyone else in his life.

PD: I've just re-read his book where he claims he played a pivotal part in your early career. Is that true?

GH: If you call stealing my photographs, peddling them to art dealers to pay for his drug habit, then yes he helped launch my career.

PD: When was this?

GH: We were living in California at the time, a beach house in Malibu. You know, everyone tip-toes around Doug's memory. Especially in this country. What a great British film-maker he was with his three Oscars. Well, he wasn't that great to me. I'm over eighty now, Peter. Too old not to tell things how they were.

PD: And how were they?

GH: They were pretty awful actually. Doug had made two terrible movies, his career was in free fall. He was drinking a lot, taking drugs. His life and our marriage were in a mess. It was me who helped him through that. I used to have to pick him off the floor as he lay there in a pool of his own sick. And as you know, Doug was not exactly a lightweight. If it wasn't for me, he would never have written the screenplay for *To Rise Again*. And even to this day, it irks me that he wants to take so much credit for my career yet never gave me one ounce of credit for helping him with his.

PD: I appreciate your frankness.

GH: Frankness? I'm just being truthful, that's all.

PD: Despite these... how can I say... these acrimonies between you, there is a sense that for many years after you split up, in the public eye at least, he overshadowed you. I mean, for a long time you were forgotten about and it is only in these last few years with these hugely successful exhibitions you're finally getting the recognition you deserve.

GH: I never resented Doug his fame. There's no doubt that *Limehouse* and *To Rise Again* were great films. I don't deny that. Doug was one of those larger-than-life personalities. The public adored him. And he was quick to seek their adoration as well. I never courted that kind of existence. I just wanted to get on with my work. If the public responded to what I was doing, that was all good and well. And if they didn't... well, it didn't really matter.

PD: If you don't mind me asking, how did you feel when he died?

GH: Oh, it was such a stupid, stupid death.

PD: I wonder if you could remind us what happened.

GH: Doug loved horses. He went out and bought a ranch somewhere up in northern California after the success of *To Rise Again*. He was out riding with his daughter, Kathleen, I guess he wasn't paying attention and he struck his head on an overhanging branch. Died instantly, I believe.

PD: Did you go out to the funeral?

GH: What was the point? Doug and I never kept in touch. I wasn't close to his children.

PD: Yet you were still married to him?

GH: I suppose I was. Technically speaking, I'm his widow. Although I never think of myself in that way.

PD: And you never stayed in touch throughout the years after your break-up?

GH: No need to really. Although I did bump into him once in

London, not that long before he died, he was over here seeing his family. I remember it was in Covent Garden, he was buying presents for his grandchildren. The great Doug Mitchell out shopping by himself, that alone showed me he had changed. We ended up having afternoon tea back at The Savoy. He was quite sweet then. All the bitterness of our marriage forgotten. He even told me he was going to leave me something in his will. A special bequest.

PD: And did he?

GH: Oh yes. He left me all his memorabilia. Reels of films, stills, contact sheets, posters, scripts. I was quite shocked as you can imagine. But he said – or at least his will said – that I would know what to do with it all.

PD: And what was that?

GH: I think he was hoping I would get my god-daughter Susan to catalogue and exhibit his work the same way as she did mine.

PD: And did you?

GH: [LAUGHING] Not at all. I burnt everything.

Chapter Forty-Nine

An Evening Out with Sal

After tea with Quentin at the Savoy, Laura went for a walk along the Embankment. It was a grey, misty, Turner-painting of a late London afternoon, the cold, weak light of an autumn sun struggling for attention behind a low blanket of clouds. The river ran murky and sluggish and only the most stubborn of leaves remained on the trees. It was that time of year when the first grasp of winter was about to take hold and she might as well forget about long days and warm sunshine for the next few months unless she flew off to more southern climes. Which was highly unlikely given her current financial predicament. Christmas lights were strung up but unlit between the lamp-posts, the festive reds and greens of holly, Santas, crackers and pine had already been unwrapped for shop-front display. Somewhere in the back of her mind she remembered the clocks had to be set back an hour at the weekend. But at the forefront of her thoughts were all these new revelations about Georgie. Discoveries that not only made her want to rewrite the screenplay to Georgie's life but also to her own. She reached into her coat pocket for her mobile.

She was actually shaking as she pressed her finger on Sal's contact number. She wasn't sure if it was from nerves or anger. But she managed to keep her voice calm, years of acting experience had taught her that.

'Hey,' he said. 'Didn't expect to hear from you.'

'Well, here I am.'

'You spoke to Caroline?'

'You know I did.'

'What's with the call then?'

'I want to move on from this.'

'Which means?'

'I'm not going to scream at you.'

'That's very generous of you. What *do* you want?'

'This Thursday night. Are you free?'

'For what? A hanging?'

'We can be civilized about this, Sal. I thought we'd have dinner.'

'You're kidding?'

'Why not?'

'I can think of a lot of reasons. Like you hate me for what I did to you.'

'I told you. I want to move on.'

'Let it be on my dime then.'

'Bloody right it is.'

'I'll even let you choose.'

'That's very generous of you.'

'The least I can do.'

'I'll text you the details once I've picked a place.'

The restaurant was tucked away on a quiet street in Notting Hill, relatively new, but Laura had become a regular ever since it had opened. It was Victoria who had originally recommended it, being as it was so close to her new flat. Even though the place was tiny – only twenty covers – the attractive feature was that the high-profile chef didn't just lend her name to the frontage but actually worked in the kitchen. Laura loved the menu in its lean towards French cuisine, always fresh yet never too fancy.

'I expected something more upmarket,' Sal said, standing up as she took a seat. She had kept him waiting fifteen minutes, getting the taxi to let her off early for the very purpose. 'A couple of Michelin stars at least.'

'For revenge?'

'Yeah. Something like that.'

'I did think about it. But I really like this place. Cosy. The food's good. And don't worry, I'll get my own back with the drinks.'

As if to prove her point, she picked up the wine list, passed on the first couple of pages.

'How do you want to do this?' he asked.

'What do you mean?'

'There's obviously some air that needs to be cleared here. We can get it out of the way early. Or wait until after we've eaten.'

'I prefer the latter option. I want to enjoy my food first.'

Sal sat back in his chair, unbuttoned his jacket, as if to signify the first round was over. He was wearing a black polo neck which set off his white hair and blue eyes very nicely. Was she jealous of Caroline? If she could dispense with her anger with both of them then probably just a little bit. The waiter came over with a jug of iced water, asked about their choice of wine.

'We'll go with the Saint Julien,' she said. It was £120 a bottle.

The problem Laura had about being angry with Sal was that she actually enjoyed his company. He was extremely personable, charming, entertaining, a sympathetic listener but could also make her laugh. She liked the slow ursine way about him, a man in charge of his movements, a quality that any actor would admire. So she was happy to let the evening unfold in a pleasant manner, enjoy the food and wine, and leave her *coup de grace* until coffee time. Sal seemed glad to do the same. They talked about film mostly, Sal had produced some interesting documentaries, they gossiped about people in the industry. It was only when her dessert arrived – a soufflé of vanilla and fresh fruit – that Sal pre-empted her preferred schedule by bringing up the subject that had been the elephant in the room since the moment she had sat down.

'This is all very nicey nicey,' he said. 'But don't you think it's time to talk about the play?'

'Oh,' she said, puncturing the soufflé with her spoon, then easing through to the warm strawberries. 'I'll let you start.'

Sal sat back in his chair, folded his arms. 'Let me say from the outset that it was you I always wanted for Georgie.'

'So you used to tell me.'

'You're perfect for the part.'

'Did you tell Caroline that as well?'

'Of course not.'

'When did you start fucking her then?'

Sal visibly shuddered from her question then composed himself, looked at her straight with those clear blue eyes of his. That was the problem with blue eyes, Laura thought, she could never tell the meaning behind them.

'I met her at a special screening at the BFI. Things developed from there.'

'Before or after I met you at her dinner party?"

'Before.'

'Whose idea was it for her to fund the play?"

'Hers. After Lew turned me down.'

'And she came along as part of the package?'

'I wasn't expecting her to ask for that. I thought her little stint in Quentin's play would be enough to satisfy her acting ambitions. But she made it a condition.'

'An offer you couldn't refuse?'

'I'm afraid not.'

'Especially as you were sleeping with her?'

'I agree that made matters more complicated.'

'And all that stuff about Fredrik Nilssen?'

'I made it up.'

'You were both a liar and a coward then.'

'Yes, I was. I apologize for that.'

'You could have refused to go along with Caroline. I thought the whole idea about wanting to do the play was how much you admired Georgie's integrity.'

'Sometimes expediency has to trump integrity.'

'I don't think Georgie would have seen it that way.'

'I imagine you would like to think so.'

'I know so.'

'What makes you so sure?'

'Remember how we wondered why she had given up her screen career? Well, back in the nineteen twenties, she had a chance to go off to Hollywood just when the talkies were starting up. There was an audition at the Savoy with Montgomery

Studios. The deal was that she got the contract if she slept with old man Montgomery himself.'

'I take it she refused?'

'Of course she did.'

'Wow. That'll make for some excellent drama.'

Laura was convinced he was already writing the dialogue for the scene in his head as he went on: 'I assume there's material in the archives to back this up?'

'Quentin's just handed it over.'

'Good. I'll use it then.'

'You're missing my point, Sal.'

'Which is?'

'I'm trying to show you that in Georgie's case, she let her integrity trump expediency. But you wouldn't know about that.'

'OK. I agree most people would've done differently. And become big stars.'

'Yet the choice she made back then won out in the end. After all, here we are still talking about her... after what... eighty years? How many silent screen stars do we know from that era?'

'True. But I need Caroline's money, Laura. Simple as that. And she'll do a good job. I know you dismiss her because of her TV fame. But you know it yourself, she did a lot of theatre before that. Caroline can do this. Not as well as you. But she'll be fine.'

'Perhaps.'

He leaned forward, elbows on the table. 'I must admit though that I find your composure in this whole matter to be... very mature.'

'That's very patronising of you to say so.'

'Sorry. Heartening then.'

'That's because your play's not going to happen.'

'Oh, I think it will. Fabulous script. Investment in place. Production ready to go.'

'I don't think so.' She leaned back, retrieved her handbag from its hang on her chair, extracted the envelope. 'This is for you,' she said, making to hand it over, then pulling back. It wasn't just Quentin who could play the envelope game.

'What is it?'

'A letter from my solicitor.'

'Stating?'

'A demand for the return of any material you may hold in connection with the play *Georgie by Georgie*.'

'On what grounds?'

'On the grounds that you do not have any authority to exploit Georgie's papers either now or in the future.'

'Quentin signed the consent form. That's an irrevocable agreement. He can't just go back on it because you want the part. I'd sue his butt off.'

'The consent only gave *me* access to the archive, Sal. Your name was never mentioned.'

He snatched the envelope away from her, extracted the letter, fumbled away for his glasses in an inside pocket. While he scanned the pages, she poured herself out the rest of the wine. At £120 a bottle, it would be a shame to waste.

'If you want to play hardball, Laura, I can lawyer up too. We're partners after all.'

She stood up with a certain amount of reluctance as the wine and the soufflé were delicious. 'There is absolutely nothing in writing to that effect,' she said, reiterating the phrase her solicitor had told her to say about any implied partnership with Sal. 'The only document we have about this project is the one you are holding.'

And with that remark she stepped away from the table only to turn back for one last flourish. 'By the way,' she said. 'My solicitor also requests payment of the six hundred and fifty pounds you owe me for the film crew on Quentin's play. You might want to lawyer up for that too.'

Chapter Fifty

The Hepburn Archives

Extract from an unpublished memoir

I returned to England and the cottage at Five Elms Down. It was not a happy place for me with its memories of my mother and my relationship with Doug but I had nowhere else to go. Aunt Ginny who had always been my saviour at such times was ailing. Susan had married a rich banker while I was away in America and was living up in Oxfordshire in the throes of early marital bliss. I occasionally visited the nursing home where my mother had stayed to take photographs of some of the residents but otherwise I pottered aimlessly around the village, tended the cottage garden, read a lot of biographies with the radio as my constant companion (our little village was not yet tuned in to the early days of black and white television reception). These were my limbo years where I felt that I had nothing much left to do except wait for death. I was still only in my mid-fifties yet I felt ancient.

I went to see Aunt Ginny. She was dying of cancer. Although in those days no-one ever mentioned the 'C' word outright. She was sat up in bed, her face done up with a bit of powder and rouge but she was all bone and stretched skin by then, her gown struggling to remain on her shoulders, eyes large in their sockets, trying to put on a brave smile for me. Uncle Richard was there too, a sad and stoic witness in the background, reading magazines, never saying much, but he was there for her all the time nevertheless.

I sat quietly at her bedside, Aunt Ginny drifting in and out of some morphine-induced haze, as I thought of how I would like to remember her. If I could just fix one image in my mind that would flash up before my eyes whenever I thought about her, what would it be?

The vision came to me very quickly. That day not long after the war when I took the country bus over to the farm and Aunt Ginny was waiting to collect me at the bus stop in that gorgeous royal-blue open-top motor car she had. Her hair was tied up inside a light-blue headscarf (had she chosen the colour especially to match the car?). She was wearing sunglasses – very fashionable for the time – and white gloves. What age would she have been then? Probably close to what I am now yet she still seemed so young. She was laughing, and driving terribly, and I was trying to make sure she kept her eyes on the road, and her head was thrown back slightly and somehow if I could just capture that moment, capture all that joy and zest and vigour and warmth and openness in her face, the fun in her eyes and in her expression. I clicked my own eyes closed on the light of that image just like a camera lens. There it was. My eternal memory of Aunt Ginny.

Then it became clear to me that this is what we all did. We distilled the memory of a person down to this one portrait on an index card in our minds by which we would forever remember them by. That was why photographs were important. That was why *my* photographs were important.

Aunt Ginny's weak voice interrupted my thoughts.

'Susan is not happy,' she said.

I drew my chair in closer. 'What do you mean?'

Aunt Ginny moved her hand nearer to mine. I grasped it. It was like clutching a nest of winter twigs. 'Go to her,' was all she said.

These were her last words to me. She drifted back into sleep after that, passed away the next day. It was as if my mother had died all over again.

After the funeral service, Uncle Richard cornered me back at the reception in the farmhouse. I could see that he had been drinking, his cheeks more flushed than usual, slightly unsteady on his feet as his whisky sloshed around in its glass. His pale blue eyes shone watery.

'It's only me left,' he said.

'What do you mean?'

'Now that Ginny's gone.'

'Left here on the farm?'

'No, no. It's only me left that knows. About Susan.'

We had never ever talked about this before. We had hardly ever talked about anything before. Sometimes I even wondered whether Aunt Ginny had even told Richard about Susan at all. Given his disinterest in anything that wasn't to do with the farm, the sudden arrival of a baby daughter might not have surprised him in the slightest. 'What are you trying to say, Uncle Richard?'

'I don't want you to tell her. Please. I want her to still think of me as her father while I'm still here.' His eyes teared up as he spoke and I started to get all emotional myself.

'It's all right. I wouldn't do that.'

'After I'm dead would be fine. It won't be long now until I join her.' He tipped his head up to the sky where I imagine he thought Aunt Ginny's spirit was lingering. His glass tilted over slightly, the whisky dribbling on to his fingers then on to his mustard corduroy trousers. I put out my hand, steadied his arm.

'I know I'm a quiet one,' he said, his voice quavering. 'But I really loved her. Susan too.'

After the days had closed back around the hole in life that a death can bring, I did go to see Susan. She lived in an Oxfordshire manor house that seemed to upset the taxi driver's sensibilities as he quietly cursed the grind of the tyres on the gravelly drive. Susan came out to greet me. She was holding her baby son, Quentin. It was a name I hated, I had no idea where she had unearthed it from, I assumed it must have been her husband Kenneth's idea. I wasn't fond of that name either, always wanted to call him 'Ken' or 'Kenny' but Susan insisted he didn't like any abbreviation at all. Fortunately for Quentin it was only his name I despised – he was a gorgeous little boy whom I would come to adore. After all, he was my grandson.

Susan deposited Quentin in a pram and we strolled with him out into the garden into the shade of the apple trees. Susan had arranged for a picnic spread out on a blanket on the grass. A maid came out with a pitcher of lemonade and glasses on a tray.

Susan poured out the drinks and we chatted quietly about Ginny. I noticed how wan and drawn Susan looked but I soon realised that her distraught appearance had nothing to do with her recent bereavement.

'It's all over,' Susan said once the maid had gone. 'Kenneth has left me.'

'Don't be ridiculous,' I said, immediately regretting the harshness of my remark. 'You've just had a child together.'

'I think Quentin has just made things worse.'

'What are you talking about?'

She subsided into tears at this point and it was difficult to get an answer about anything but finally she confided in me. Apart from the obvious intercourse that had taken place to create the child, there had been no further intimacy between them. She later discovered that Kenneth had been having an affair – with an American, Elspeth was her name – before the marriage and it had continued afterwards as well. He told her that it was Elspeth whom he really loved, the marriage had been an awful mistake and he wanted out. She could keep the child in whom he had no interest at all and this house in the grounds of which they now sat. He would stay at the apartment in London, Elspeth had her own place in New York. He would make sure she and Quentin never wanted for money but he wanted a divorce as quickly and as quietly as possible.

'What did I do wrong?' Susan asked me.

'You did nothing wrong,' I responded severely. 'Please don't blame yourself for the failings of men. Women have been doing that for centuries and it has got to stop.'

With her story told, Susan calmed. She got up and went over to the pram where she checked on Quentin. She was twenty-seven years old, the same age as I had been when Max left me. Did history just repeat itself, from generation to generation? She was still an attractive woman, she had lost all the tomboyishness of her youth, the wealth that Kenneth had brought into their marriage allowing her to be decked out in the finest and most fashionable of clothes which she wore with a quiet elegance. She had an art history degree which she had parlayed into a career in the mysterious world of galleries and auction houses and curatorships. She came back to sit beside me on the blanket, sorting out her long limbs gracefully, her fingers plucking at daisies.

'I've a big favour to ask,' she said.

'Go on.'

'I want you to come live with me.'

Before I had time to respond she went on quickly. 'I mean you are all alone down there in that little cottage. And I have this huge house. You could help me with Quentin. Of course, I have a nanny for him and everything but you could help me bring him up, educate him, you have so much experience and knowledge to give. It would be company for me and you can keep taking all your photographs. There is plenty of room for you to have a studio in the house. Oh, please, Georgie. Please.'

Chapter Fifty-One

A Break in Proceedings

Laura got the taxi driver to drop her off about half a mile from her home. She knew most Londoners would shirk from walking these quiet streets at night but she had always felt safe in this part of the city. She had been born in Muswell Hill, moved across to Highgate when she had started to earn decent money. She was a north London girl in her heart and bones and if she couldn't stroll these avenues in the dark what was the point of living here. She loved this ancient village where Coleridge, Dickens and Marx once took their daily constitutionals, the self-satisfaction of the Georgian architecture, the old-style pubs, the lack of litter and high-rise buildings, homes hidden safe and settled behind stout walls and ivy shrouds. Barristers, authors, TV personalities and retired comedians. It was all very comfortably middle-class, sometimes a bit too smug for her liking, but it suited her just fine. As Georgie would say, it properly defined her.

She was still feeling giddy from the way she had dealt with Sal over dinner, ordering the expensive wine, managing the conversation, delivering her solicitor's letter, timing her exit, taking control. Yes, that was it – taking control. Of the play. Of her life. Deciding what was important for her own happiness, then embarking on the necessary steps to achieve that. This was the new Laura Scott. Or perhaps it was just the young Laura Scott, the Laura Scott she had been as an aspiring teenager, now resurrected.

It was with a head full of these thoughts that she rounded the corner, the entrance to her flat came into view, and she could see her security lamp highlighting the figure of a man sitting, possibly even asleep, on her doorstep. He wore a pulled-down trilby and a long overcoat, a garment still too warm for this late autumn night. Her first instinct was to reach inside her bag for her mobile phone, call the police. For the person waiting for her was quite possibly Braden O'Sullivan, an individual forbidden by law to knowingly approach within 500 metres of her home or place of work. Also forbidden by law to communicate with her by telephone, fax, letter, text, electronic mail or Internet. Up until two years ago when the restraining order came into force, Braden O'Sullivan, a 35 year-old unemployed mechanic from the town of Chicopee, Massachusetts, USA, had been her stalker. A man who used to send her a barrage of fan mail along with countless CDs burned with his favourite tracks, the first one always being *Tell Laura I Love Her*, the Ricky Vallance version. A man who had once even crossed the Atlantic, and inveigled himself past a security guard to visit her on a London film set. Hence the necessity to obtain a restraining order. Could this be him here again...?

She wasn't quite sure. Braden was a stocky individual, yet the shape on the doorstep appeared to be quite tall, the legs sneaking out from under the hem of the overcoat rather slim. She moved forwards toward the open gate, one hand on her mobile, the other on the can of mace she always kept in her bag even though it was illegal to possess such a deterrent in this country. The figure stirred and she stepped backwards. This man had a beard, the hair long beneath his hat streaked with grey. This wasn't Braden, this was some drunken lout loitering on her doorstep, probably having pissed in her plant pots or all over her front door. She thought again about phoning the police until the man removed his hat, she saw the familiar dark eyes above the beard and recognised immediately the voice that called her name.

'Jack. What the hell are you doing here?'

Jack scrambled to his feet. 'Waiting for you.'

'How long have you been here?'

'Dunno. Must have fallen asleep. Jet-lag.'

'You could have called.'

'I thought I'd surprise you.'

'You certainly did that. How did you know I was even in London?'

'No milk bottles.'

She laughed at that. 'Oh, Jack. I think they stopped delivering milk in bottles about thirty years ago.' She looked him up and down now that he was at full stretch. The overcoat worn over a faded blue T-shirt bearing some Japanese lettering, tattered jeans, sandals. No luggage. Typical Jack. An A-list movie star on her doorstep and no-one would have recognized him. 'I thought you were a tramp. You look like... I don't know. Tom Cruise in that Vietnam movie.'

'*Born on the Fourth of July.*'

'That's the one.'

'I'm on my way back from India. Stop-over in London. You're my go-to girl for a haircut.'

Laura didn't have a lot to thank her mother for but she did have to grant her credit for that skill. To win over her parents to the giant leap of faith that made her want to be an actress, she had let her mother persuade her into learning to cut hair at Vidal Sassoon's hairdressing school. 'Better you have something to fall back on,' her mother had told her with no sense of optimism whatsoever about her chosen career path. She had been right, of course. When money and acting roles were scarce, Laura had temped out at the salons at a time when Sassoon's cuts were all the rage. She actually enjoyed the work, the snip, snip, snipping of another person's hair acting as a meditation, as something of an escape from herself. In the few months she and Jack had been together, she had cut his hair quite often, it becoming a bit of an in-joke between them, she being his personal hairdresser rather than live-in girlfriend.

'You'd better come in then,' she said, laughing again. 'But I'm not touching that beard.'

Once inside, he tried to embrace her but she pointed to the bathroom. 'Shower first.'

'Come on, Laura.'

'Get yourself clean.'

Jack disappeared into the main bathroom while she went into her own en-suite to tidy herself up. What an evening it had been. First Sal. And now here was Jack in London. Jack London. *The Call of the Wild*. Quite appropriate really. She was actually tingling from excitement, couldn't remember the last time she had felt this way. Probably the last time she had seen him in the States. She stripped down to her bra and panties, wrapped herself up in the *yukata* he had bought for her in Japan, went searching for her old hairdressing kit.

Jack stepped out of the bathroom about twenty minutes later, dressed in her white towelling bathrobe, rubbing a clean-shaven but scored chin, his hair still lank and wet.

'Hope you don't mind,' he said. 'Used one of your razors in there.'

'My scraper is your scraper.'

Jack grinned at her and she looked back at him, hand cocked on her hip, thinking to herself (because there was no way she was actually going to tell him): 'My God, Jack. You just light up a room.' She had met many of the big time movie stars in her time and yes there was definitely a sense of awe about being in their presence. But Jack really did brighten up a room, brighten up her life. It wasn't just his star quality but there was something else – a certain humanity – that shone through as well. The only other person she had met who bore that same quality was the late, great, Paul Newman.

'Sit,' she said, pointing to the chair she had placed in the centre of a sea of newspaper sheets.

Jack saluted. 'Yes, ma'am.'

She did the usual hairdresser routine as she clipped away at his wet locks, asking questions, just letting the customer ramble away so she could concentrate on her task. Jack told her he had just completed a ten-day meditation retreat in India, a silent retreat it was too so she had to excuse him if he was babbling on as he hadn't really spoken to anyone else since it had finished. He told her about the upcoming *Boston Tea Party* shoot and she declined to inform him about Edy's offer to be involved. He asked her what she was up to. She told him a little bit about Georgie.

'She was married to that director guy, Doug Mitchell, wasn't she?'

'That's the whole problem right there, Jack. Everyone puts her together with Doug. He kind of overshadows her. A bit like Hemingway and Martha Gellhorn. But Georgie was a spectacular person in her own right. And a great photographer too.'

'Don't remember seeing her work.'

'You probably have, you just didn't know it. Lots of iconic portraits taken between the end of the war and the Swinging Sixties.'

'Film stars?'

'Some. Cary Grant. Audrey Hepburn. She had access through Doug, of course. But mostly ordinary people. A lost generation, she called them.'

'We were the lucky ones, I suppose. The Baby Boomers.'

It was such an intimate job really, cutting hair. There she was touching Jack's head, moving it around as she pleased, her fingers running through his long locks, his hair still thick, snip, snip, snip, Jack complaining about all the grey he was seeing in the shorn pieces landing on the sheet she had wrapped around him. 'Not grey, Jack. White.' Snip, snip, snip. Normally, when she was cutting a man's hair, she would be careful how she moved her body around the customer, not leaning in with the breasts, keeping the groin area pushed back, that was how she had been taught. But with Jack, she found that her body was rebelling against her training, letting herself step in close, allowing her hair to brush his face, almost sitting astride him at one point as she moved across the front of him. She caught herself breathing heavily, sensed the flush in her neck, Jack seemingly oblivious to all of this until she felt his fingers slipping between her lower thighs where the *yukata* had fallen open.

'Stop it,' she said, pushing his hand away. 'I need to finish this. Or you're going to be all lop-sided.'

'I'm all lop-sided all ready.'

'I'm not sure I know what you mean by that.'

'It doesn't matter. Come here.'

He gripped her round the waist, pulled her into him. It was an awkward embrace because he was sitting down, kissing her stomach through the gap in her robe, while she was bent over his head, scissors in one hand, comb in another. But in one swift movement, he had lifted himself off from the chair, taking her with him, so she was hung over his shoulder, kicking away like some captured cavewoman, as he swung her around and shouted:

'Bedroom. Where?'

She threw away her scissors and comb, balanced herself with her hands on his shoulders and shouted out, half laughing, half breathless with excitement. 'Over there. Next to the bathroom.'

Afterwards, she wanted a cigarette. No use wanting Jack to ease that craving, his lifestyle was too healthy for that, unless it was a grass-filled joint, without tobacco of course. She turned to look at him. He was fast asleep, zonked out by sex and jet-lag, the skin along his jawline red raw from her razor, his hair cut shorter on one side than the other, she'd fix that later. She recalled a remark she had once heard Priscilla Presley say in an interview. It went along the lines of: 'I used to wake up next to Elvis and gaze at him and think he was the most gorgeous man I had ever seen.' She felt the same way about Jack. Even now that he was in his fifties, he was still immensely attractive. But there was also another feeling present in her beyond this physical attraction. Not love but a lightness. Most of her lovers felt like a burden after sex. Or to put it to herself crudely, they had served their function and now she just wanted to be left alone. It didn't feel like that with Jack. She wasn't weighed down by him at all. He was like air beside her, hardly leaving an imprint on her pillow, sheets and mattress. Perhaps it was to do with the ephemeral quality of their relationship, the no-strings, no-future, no-nonsense approach. Jack would probably put it down to some kind of Buddhist non-attachment. Or maybe it was the opposite. Perhaps she was attached in more ways than she thought. Perhaps this was what real love should be. Weightless, timeless, purely in the moment. And then it was gone.

Chapter Fifty-Two

Extract from an unpublished memoir

I sold the cottage at Five Elms Down and moved to Oxfordshire to be with Susan and baby Quentin. It was an idyllic time really, an unimaginable blessing on my life to be able to enjoy these years with my daughter and grandson. Susan's was a magnificent house where I had my own bedroom, study and darkroom. I swam every day in the pool, I played tennis with my daughter and her friends, I went for long walks in the grounds and the surrounding woodlands – I can't remember feeling fitter. Once Susan had stopped breast-feeding Quentin, she went back to work in London, curating exhibitions for a small, high-end gallery, leaving Quentin to be looked after primarily by a succession of nannies, mostly from the Continent, Susan wanting her son to be proficient in French and Spanish. Sometimes I would steal Quentin from their charge so that I could spend my own precious time with the boy. Although he was obviously unaware I was his actual grandmother, I believe a special relationship existed between us. If each child rebels against their parent then logic dictates that the grandparent and grandchild will end up in tune. I certainly felt an exquisite harmony between us. As he grew older, it was to me he loved to show off. I recall how he would entertain me by performing little vignettes he'd written by himself, acting out all the parts from an assembly of low tables arranged as his stage, a couple of powerful torches on broom handles serving as the lighting. My grandson – quite the little actor and dramatist.

The early years of the 1960s came and went. The building of the Berlin War, the Adolf Eichmann trial, the Cuban Missile Crisis, Yuri Gagarin becoming the first man in space, the assassination of John F Kennedy, The Beatles taking the US by storm. Susan and I together, watching history unfold on the television. Around this time, I stopped taking portraits, concentrating my attention mainly on nature photography. Camera technology had come a long way since I had first picked up Rollo's Leica at that Bedouin camp in the Sinai so many years ago. I began experimenting with some of the latest equipment, honing in on my subjects with various close-up lenses and micro-filters. Perhaps that was the ultimate sign of old age, when we start to lose interest in people and become fascinated with nature instead.

I loved taking sharp focus shots of flowers. Never having been good at biology, I learned a whole new vocabulary beyond petal and stamen to describe the plants I was photographing – words like *sepal* and *carpel, anther* and *stigma*. I would creep around the bushes in Susan's estate, seeking out the exact flower in bloom, a drop of dew on the petal or if I was lucky a foraging bee, a caterpillar, the light shining on it just so. Quentin enjoyed accompanying me on these expeditions, my satchels of lenses strung across his little body so that he resembled some kind of intrepid explorer. Later, I would return to my darkroom to process the negatives, Quentin sitting quietly in a corner, happy to watch me work away in the glow of the amber safelight. I had also rigged up a red/green lighting system outside the door so that Susan, Quentin or anyone else in the household with an interest would know whether I was inside working or not. It was on one such occasion when I had just tidied away all my trays and chemicals that I switched my outside light to green. Susan came in immediately, as if she had been outside waiting, ready to pounce.

'You're home early,' I said. I was standing at my angled desktop, hovering with a large magnifying glass over a contact sheet of floral shots I'd taken that afternoon. The magnifying glass had been my father's, all that was left to me apart from his love of flying. The prints were in black-and-white which I still favoured over colour even when it came to flowers, an attempt to imitate, mostly unsuccessfully, the wonderful work of Ansel

Adams.

'Everyone went off to some cocktail party,' she said. 'I decided not to go with them.'

'Pity. It's always a chance to meet new people.'

I could hear Susan rummaging around at the back of the room where I kept a stack of old prints. 'You're always saying that,' she said. 'You don't know what these things are like. Bores me to tears. And I'm useless with small talk.'

'You never know. Sometimes an absolute gem of a person who thinks just like you can turn up at one of these events.' I looked up from my desk. 'And by the way, I do know what these things can be like. I went to my fair share of these parties with Doug Mitchell.'

'That's what I was thinking.'

'What do you mean?'

'All these photos you took then. Where are they?'

'Somewhere back there, I suppose.'

'Everything is such a mess. I'm surprised you don't keep your work in better order.'

'There's more order to my work than you think.'

'Not back here, there isn't.'

'Those are just the prints. All my negatives and contact sheets are properly catalogued.'

Susan came forward to stand by me. She was dressed in a cream blouse, short beige skirt and knee-length brown leather boots. It was hard to believe what passed for office clothes these days. She gave me a little kiss on my cheek. Oh, how I cherished these moments. 'Really, Georgie,' she said sweetly. 'Show me.'

'Over there,' I said, nodding to another dark corner. 'Under that dust sheet.'

Susan went over, lifted the sheet to reveal a mountain of catalogue drawers. I'd bought them years ago as a job lot when the local library had closed. 'This is brilliant,' she exclaimed. 'When exactly were you out in California with Doug?'

'Why the sudden interest?'

She floated back to me again. 'I was just thinking... '

'Yes?'

'Have you still got the photographs of all those film stars?'

'Some. Doug sold off most of them.'

'You know how I love all your other work. Those portraits of your mother. The elderly patients in the care home. Well, I was thinking... maybe I could arrange for you to have a small exhibition.'

'And the film stars?'

'Those could be our way in. Our Trojan horse. Our lure to bring in the general public. Then we can expose them to the rest of your oeuvre. These photographs of the post-war generation are fascinating. When did you go to California?'

'Beginning of the fifties.'

'I know that. But when exactly?'

'I'm not sure about this, Susan. Going public again.'

'Just let me show a few of your photographs to Michael.'

Michael was her boss, not someone I immediately warmed to. He reminded me a bit of my director Cecil Benson on *The Woman Walks Free* – one of those horsey-faced toffs with an immense sense of privilege that Max would have hated. Perhaps that was why I wasn't a big fan of Michael's either. Then as if she was reading my mind, Susan said: 'I know you don't like Michael very much. But he's got very good taste. He thinks retro-photography is going to be the next in-thing in the art world. And I agree. That's what got me thinking about your work. Let me show him some. Please.'

'Retro-photography?' I said with disdain. I glanced over at her. Her hands and face were already smudged with dust from her rummaging. Her voice was all soft and pleading but there was a determined look in her eyes, her lips tight with resolve. I knew that expression. I just had to look at myself in the mirror to see the same image once I had made up my mind to do something. 'All right,' I said. 'You might want to start with 1954.'

And so it was that Susan did show some of my photographs to Michael, and Michael loved my so-called retro-photography, agreed to put on a show at his gallery which Susan curated. To my surprise – but not Susan's – the exhibition was a great success. Fortunately, although my photographs began to take on a life of their own I was still able to lead my own quiet existence in Oxfordshire. As time went by and the past began to form itself into distinct periods of history, my work gained a reputation for portraying a certain era. It was Susan who came up with the term *The Lost Generation* for the subjects displayed in my work. It was a term that eventually became firmly fixed in the minds of the public. I didn't mind the recognition my portraits gained as long as people weren't interested in the person behind the lens.

Chapter Fifty-Three

Jack in a Box

Laura prepared lunch while Jack sat out in her small garden area reading. They hadn't left the flat for nearly three days, Jack had his luggage sent over from the airport, practically moved in. She had switched off her computer, turned off her mobile, shut her back on the world and opened herself up to him. They made love, slept, ate, read, slept, made love. Jack would meditate for an hour in the morning and again in the evening. Sometimes she sat up in bed and watched him. So peaceful, so self-contained, she had no patience for such things although she envied those who had. They didn't reflect on the past, they didn't discuss the future, sometimes when she thought back on their conversations she wondered what they had talked about.

'What the hell is this?' Jack was standing by the French windows holding up a drenched and dripping mobile phone.

'Oh that.'

'In your carp pond?'

'A sunken memorial to my previous career.'

'What?'

'I was pissed off with Edy'

'Sure ain't good for the fish. All those seeping chemicals.'

'I actually thought they were looking healthier than usual. And they glow in the dark.'

He chuckled as he moved towards the kitchen area, dropped the phone in a bin, kissed her on the cheek. 'What's for lunch?'

'Making a salad. Plus last night's left-over fish pie. OK?'

Jack nodded, went over and lay down across the sofa. She placed a tomato on the chopping board, began to slice away. Then a red pepper, or bell pepper as Jack would call it. Followed by a courgette or zucchini depending on which side of the Atlantic you were on. She started making up her own lyrics as she hummed away at that old Gershwin song.

You say freeway and I say motorway. You say sidewalk and I say pavement. She didn't want to break the spell but there was a question she needed to ask. No, it was probably better not to. Chop, chop, chop. But she couldn't keep her life on hold like this forever. Chop, chop, chop. *You say jelly, and I say jam.* She took the plunge:

'How long do you think you'll be staying?' She had tried to make the question sound casual but she heard the tremor in her voice, that slight inflection at the end of the sentence that had insecurity written all over it.

'Dunno,' Jack said, with no more interest than if she had asked if he wanted *still* or *sparkling*. 'What do *you* think?'

'What? You're leaving this up to me?' Shit, she thought. That's the spell broken. 'Actually, I'm sorry I asked. Let's forget I said anything.'

'Sure.'

'Is that it?'

'You told me to forget what you said.'

She picked up a cucumber, chopped it in half. 'Fuck you, Jack.'

He hadn't moved an inch from his sprawl on the sofa. 'I thought that's what you were doing?'

'You know what I mean. All this Buddhist non-attachment shit.'

This time he finally moved, sat up to look at her. 'Where's all this coming from?'

She realised she was crying. 'Oh God, Jack. I just don't know.'

'Come over here.'

'No, you come to me.'

Which he did, put his arms around her while she sobbed into his shoulder. 'What do you want from me, Jack?'

'I want what we've got now. I think you need to ask yourself what you want from me.'

'I don't know, I don't know. I'm just so happy right now. But I know it has to stop.'

'I can give you another week, Laura. Then I gotta go back for the *Tea Party* shoot.'

She drove him up to Scotland, he had never been before. They rented a cottage in the Western Highlands, long walks, wood fires even though it wasn't that cold, just for the romance of it all. 'October and November are the best months to be in Scotland,' she told him. 'Crisp sunny days and no bloody midges.' Civilization was a village ten miles away with a shop that stocked most things they needed, a pub whose customers left them alone (probably because they had no idea who they were, the nearest cinema being forty miles away), fresh salmon farmed from a nearby loch, same with the oysters and mussels. No broadband, mobile phone reception patchy, they left the rest of the world behind. She tried to put a kind of glass dome over everything, the place where they were staying, the days they had together, her feelings for Jack, so nothing would expand beyond this precious space and time. It wasn't easy for her to do, her natural instinct was to try and fast forward, to imagine a future. The situation didn't seem to trouble Jack at all. Jack was Jack was Jack. That's what everyone said about him. That's what she said about him. That's what she loved about him. And that's what would probably hurt her in the end too.

It was the close of the day, she sat side by side with him on a wooden bench outside their cottage with its view down to the loch, a glass of white wine in her hand, Jack with a glass of malt, both of them wrapped up cosy in tartan blankets. A scattering of geese flew over the water, disappeared over the hillside, the sky darkening, the occasional ripple in the water.

'We call this the gloaming,' she said. 'Twilight time.'

'We? I thought you were a London girl through and through.'

'So I am, Jack. But the name's Laura Scott. Does that not give you a clue to my roots?'

'I thought that was your stage name. Seemed too neat to be real.'

'And what's Jack Muirhead then? That sounds pretty

Scottish to me too.'

'And so it is. My father's grandfather came from this fair land.'

'I'm surprised you never told me that before.'

'I'm not really into all the genealogy stuff. Anyway, you never mentioned your Scottish ancestry to me either.'

'That's the problem with you and me. We never talk about things like that.'

'Things like what?'

'I don't know. Things outside our little bubble. About our past. Our future.'

'You know me, Laura. I'm a living-in-the-present kind of guy.'

'That's the problem.' She made to get up from her chair but Jack put out a hand, held her back.

'Stay,' he said. 'Stay and we'll talk.'

She sat back down.

'What do you want to say?' he said, swirling his whisky in the glass, his face fading into darkness as the sun set behind him.

'I don't have an agenda.'

'Tell me about the play then.'

'I've already told you what it's about.'

'I meant the production.'

'That's the hard part.'

'Yeah. Just you on stage for a couple of hours isn't going to be enough. Even if the script is fantastic.'

'I've got some ideas though.'

'Like what?"

'They're rough.'

'That's OK.'

'Well, I imagine a backdrop plastered with her photographs. Just black and white. I'll be in black too. And lots of mirrors that will help with the flashbacks. So when Georgie looks back at her past, images of those times will appear in the mirror... but in colour. The young actress, the pilot and so on.'

'What else?'

'I was thinking of using mannequins dressed up like her, talking to them, dancing with them. I don't know, Jack, it's all new for me this production for the theatre stuff.'

'I know someone in London who could help you, give you some ideas.'

'I can't even afford sound and lighting, never mind my own producer.'

'You don't have to hire him. I'll give him a call. I'm sure he'll be happy to have a chat with you.'

'I'd appreciate that.'

He reached across, touched her hand, gave her one of those sincere Jack Muirhead looks a million female film fans across three decades would die for. 'I can give you the money for all of this,' he said.

'I know you would.'

'I'd be happy to support you. You just need to ask.'

'The thought had crossed my mind.'

'It doesn't have to be a gift. I could make it a loan if that would make you feel better.'

She pulled her eyes away from his gaze. 'Thank you. But I don't want a knight in shining armour. I want to do this on my own, Jack.'

Chapter Fifty Four

The Hepburn Archives

Extract from an unpublished memoir

People often tell you that change is important in life. After all, change is the essence of all living things. It is therefore essential to keep challenging yourself, to learn a new language, to travel to different places, to take up a hobby. It is sound advice I've tried to follow myself. But as we grow older, routines do become necessary. Perhaps it is because we have figured out what makes us happy, perhaps we need certainty in a constantly shifting world, perhaps we need something to cling on to as death approaches, or perhaps it is simply because we are getting lazy. I certainly had my little schedules that I enjoyed. And one of them was meeting Susan for tea in the village on Thursday afternoons. It was her half-day off, she would take the train back from London to Oxford, then by bus into the village while I would walk down from the house stopping off at Kennedy's General Store which also hosted the local post office to pick up our mail. On this particular cold day in early winter, Bill Kennedy exchanged the usual pleasantries with me about the weather before handing over our bundle of letters and magazines with an unusual degree of solemnity.

'Looks like something special there, Georgie,' he said. 'From the powers that be.'

'What do you mean?'

'Top of the pile.'

I laid down the bundle on the counter, extracted the first envelope from under the trap of the postal rubber band. I felt the heft of the quality stationery, observed the fancy crest embossed in the corner, my name and address laid out in exquisite handwriting. The powers that be indeed.

I could see Susan from the street, grateful to note she'd managed to bag my favourite table by the window. I still called the place a 'tearoom' for that's how I remember it with its odd assortment of tables, linen cloths, cake stands and floral-patterned tea service. But it had undergone several revamps since I had first come to the village emerging finally as this bright café with its gleaming coffee machine, the management no longer consisting of elderly ladies but a long-haired young man called Leo with his rainbow coloured clothes and a hippy happy attitude. That attitude, however, seemed to preclude the taking away of the original bell which tinkled every time someone entered. Somehow my current anger and irritation succeeded in transferring itself to the ring of this bell for Susan immediately looked up and frowned concern at me as I came in the door.

'What's the matter?' she asked.

'You'll see,' I said. But before I even had a chance to sit down, Leo was already at our table, notepad in hand.

'Black coffee for me,' Susan said. 'And the usual pot of Earl Grey.'

'I'll have a double espresso,' I said.

Susan raised her eyebrows at me. 'Really? You never have coffee.'

'Well, I want one now.'

Leo nodded with a sort of Jesus-like humility before going off to attend to our order. I pulled off my gloves, hung my coat on the back of the chair.

'Someone's in a mood,' Susan said.

'Take a look at this.' I passed over the opened envelope. 'It seems my past has caught up with me.'

'Bloody hell. Ten Downing Street. What does the Prime Minister want from you?'

'Go on. Read the damn thing.'

Susan clapped her hands on finishing her reading. 'Congratulations. An MBE.'

'I'm not happy about it.'

'What do you mean? This is a great honour, Georgie. Recognition for all your fantastic work. Not just as a photographer. But flying with the ATA. How could you not be happy?'

'I'm not accepting it.'

'When have you ever been a republican?'

'I'm neither a royalist nor a republican. I just can't be bothered with such things.'

'I don't understand you.'

'I thought you did understand me. I'm a very private person. I just want to be left alone to get on with my work. Once I accept something like this, I'll be dragged into the public eye. Or even worse – appropriated by the Establishment.'

'And would that be so terrible?'

'Yes, it would. It would feel elitist. I don't want to be part of this private club that binds our business, political and judicial leaders. I don't think most creative people do. It sets them above their peers.'

'Lots of artists have accepted honours from our kings and queens.'

'And many have turned them down.'

'How would you know something like that? As your letter says, these offers are all made in the strictest of confidence.'

'That may be so. But I remember when I was over in Hollywood, Doug telling me he'd heard Hitchcock had turned down a gong. Henry Moore also. And Lowry.'

'Just rumours.'

'Well, I'm turning it down.'

'I think you're being very selfish.'

'Selfish? Don't be ridiculous, Susan.'

'What about me? What about all the work I've put into your career. I pushed you into exhibiting your photographs in the first place. Curating everything. All the promotions. Working with publishers on your albums. Don't you think I deserve some proxy recognition for all that I've done for you?'

And it was there I saw it. It's funny how you can pretend that it doesn't exist, that the child is the daughter of the mother and that the father has disappeared, his biological function completed. Of course, Max was always there in Susan's physical appearance but when it came to her character and her nature, I had persuaded myself those were wholly mine. 'You know, you're just like...'

'Just like what? Like who? Tell me.'

I could have just said it there and then. Those words I had

often ached to tell. *Your father. And I am your mother.* But I had made a promise to dear Uncle Richard who was still very much alive, albeit in his doddery nineties. Why upset things now? 'Nothing. Nobody. It doesn't matter.'

We settled back into a silence, so unusual for the two of us, as Leo returned with our coffees. Even he refrained from his usual banter such was the obvious tension in the air. Susan sat, staring out of the window, I tried to control my own anger. It felt as though I was back in my little flat in Pimlico, I had just returned from that awful meeting with Hub and Montgomery at the Savoy, and there was Max telling me how I had ruined his career. What was happening now did not possess the same gravity but somehow the issue was the same. My integrity was being challenged for the sake of someone else's career. Of course, Susan had no idea what was going on. As far as she was concerned, I was just a stubborn old woman.

'Susan.'

She didn't flinch, her teeth in a bite of her bottom lip.

I continued. 'I appreciate everything you've done for me. I know it might not seem like that sometimes because fame is not something I have courted. But it does really please me that my work is out there in the public domain. And hopefully these photographs will endure long after I'm gone. It's just that my work – even my time served with the ATA – has never been about me. That's why this honour confuses me, even threatens me. You have to understand that.'

Susan turned from the window, looked at me with those deep brown eyes of hers. She placed one hand on top of mine. I softened to her touch, looked down at our clasp. 'You don't have to accept the honour,' she said. 'I really do understand.'

Perhaps she didn't possess Max's nature after all.

Chapter Fifty-Five

All Beginnings Are Hard

Jack left. In the early hours of the morning, she hadn't heard him go. After the Scotland trip, she had taken him down to see the Chagall windows, she had so enjoyed sharing them with him. They ate out at a country pub, came back to London, made love, she had fallen asleep. And just as suddenly as he had arrived, he was gone. She found the note on her computer keyboard. He had written down the contact details of his producer friend, some words of gratitude for her hospitality and the simple sentence – *I love you now*. She went back to bed, slept the morning through. When she awoke with the sun streaming through the windows, she realised she didn't feel miserable at all. Surprisingly no sense of loss but rather of gain. She felt light, invigorated, full of energy and purpose. 'Oh Jack, I love you now.' She was going to start anew. She was going to start now.

Marcus Green was doing well, Laura thought, as she sat in the reception area of the new offices of her former accountant. A frosted-green glass desk with the words *Marcus Green Associates* etched on the front with an emerald swirl dominated the green-carpeted space. Behind this icy fortress sat not one but two equally frosty receptionists citing the name of the firm into the mouthpieces of their headsets before clicking through their callers in rapid succession. Beyond the desk, a wall of leafy plants. Green, green, green everywhere. She wondered if Marcus voted for the Greens just to remain consistent. She actually laughed out loud at the thought, snaring a glance from one of the receptionists. She picked up a magazine, put it down again. One half hour previously she had been told Mr Green would see her in ten minutes. In the past, she hardly had to wait thirty seconds. She guessed she was being punished for her customer disloyalty.

To his credit, Marcus actually came out himself to collect her from reception. His mammoth arms held out as he approached, she feared he was going to swallow her up into the crush of an embrace. Instead, just as he reached her, he brought his hands together and made a slight bow in front of her as in the Japanese tradition. She wasn't sure if he was being respectful or ironic.

'Laura, Laura, Laura,' he boomed. 'How wonderful to see you again. It has been such a long time.'

'You know how it is. Shooting schedules. America. Japan.'

'Such a glamorous life,' he said. 'We boring accountants can only tremble with awe and jealousy. Now, let me guide you to my humble office.'

Marcus's office was anything but humble. A wide glassy space with fabulous views of the Thames. A work area with a giant mahogany desk, slick computers and thick silver ornaments; a lounge area with glass table tops, abstract art and dark brown leather sofas. She was heartened to find herself invited to sit on one of these sofas, an informality she hoped was a sign of forgiveness. Marcus sat opposite, his enormous bulk sinking deep into the leather. Victoria had told her that Marcus's wife had just given birth to a baby girl. Laura tried to imagine what his wife might look like in such a copulation. Would she be of similar mammoth proportions, two giant whales in a blubbery embrace? Or was she some tiny creature perched on top of him like a child on a bouncy castle. Probably stressed out too, with dark circles under her eyes and sick all over her clothes. While Marcus, all fresh-faced and rosy, looked far from being a partner in the parental chores. Although in all fairness to Marcus given his current surroundings, there was probably a whole staff of nannies and maids back at Green mansion.

Marcus stretched his arms out across the back ledge of the sofa like some giant on a cross. 'Laura, Laura, Laura,' he said. 'You look marvellous.'

'I believe congratulations are in order.'

Marcus's face brightened as if a vision of his daughter had just appeared before him. 'Three months old. A little beauty. You never had children did you?'

'It appears that I forgot to.'

Marcus gave a condescending chuckle. 'Now what can I do for you?'

'I have to confess to putting my financial affairs on the back-burner for a number of years.'

'Five years, Laura. Five years. I retrieved your file. I thought you had abandoned me.'

'Well, here I am.'

'So you are.'

'I'd like to engage you again to look into my tax affairs.'

'You know my rules, Laura. Number one, you must...'

'You'll be pleased to know I've been very good with rule number one. I've kept all my receipts for the last five years.'

'Excellent.'

'It is rule number two that is the problem. I've made no provision for any tax.'

Marcus withdrew his arms from their stretch along the sofa, drew himself into a posture of concern, nodded sagely. A pose that no doubt was costing her several pounds per second. 'I see.'

'I received a letter from the tax authorities.'

'What's the damage?'

She opened her handbag, passed Marcus the manila envelope from Her Majesty's Customs and Excise. He extracted the payment demand, scanned it until he arrived at his destination. He let out a breathy whistle, looked up at her. 'Do you have the money for this?'

She shook her head.

'Some of it?'

She shook her head again.

'Where has it all gone? To attract this kind of liability, you need to earn the money too.'

'I don't know, Marcus. It just goes. You know what it's like in my business. Feast or famine. When it's feast I tend to spend. Holidays, hotels, clothes, renovations, flights, new car. My father is in a care home. That's three thousand pounds a month before I even start on myself.'

'Assets?'

'My flat in Highgate.'

'What do you think it's worth? Ballpark.'

She reported the price range the estate agent had given her earlier.

'Mortgage?'

'Still quite a bit to pay off.'

Marcus quickly snapped his fingers at her. 'Figures, Laura. I need figures.'

Again she told him.

'What about work? Are those blank Tinsel Town cheque books still opening for you?'

'I'm working on a smaller project over here.'

'How small?'

'Very.'

'I see, I see.'

Marcus stood up, casting a frightening shadow over her. He then walked over to the window, surveyed the aspect of his domain as he continued speaking, his words bouncing off the glass back at her. 'Fortunately, Laura, there are things we can do here. But first of all, I would like you to describe your ideal scenario.' He turned back round to face her. 'What would you like to happen here?'

'I'm going to have to sell the flat, I realise that.'

'Downsizing would be helpful.'

'I'd need a deposit for something new. Say a hundred and fifty thousand.'

'For a broom cupboard in Peckham perhaps.'

'I'd move out of the city.'

'Let's call it two hundred and fifty thousand for starters with stamp duty, fees and so on. What else?'

'I need about forty thousand to fund my play – set design, production, sound and lighting, venue, insurance. Maybe another thirty to keep me going for a year, same again to pay for my father's care. Your fees, of course. Anything else above that would be a bonus.'

'Hmmmm. So basically you would like to emerge from your sale and this tax fiasco with a minimum of say around four hundred thousand to kickstart this new life of yours for the next year or so.'

'If that's how the figures add up.'

'And after that?'

'I'm going to work on the assumption my play is going to be a huge success.'

'Is that a reasonable assumption?'

'Probably not.'

Marcus walked over from the window, this time to sit down beside her. She felt the cushion on which she sat rise slightly beneath her to counterbalance his weight. Again he crouched forward in a worried pose. 'Can I ask you something personal?' he said.

Having just disclosed to him the whole of her financial affairs, she wondered how much more personal he could get. 'Whatever you want.'

'You have been a very successful actress, Laura. My wife absolutely adores you as I'm sure many millions of fans around the world do also. I have seen some of the fees you commanded in the past. What has happened? Is the work no longer out there for you?'

She was genuinely moved by his concern, so out of character for a man only usually interested in the certainty of numbers. The birth of his baby daughter must have softened him. 'It's certainly getting harder for a woman of my vintage,' she said. 'But yes, I could take a part in a big blockbuster movie if I wanted to.'

'So why don't you? It would solve so many of your problems.'

'What can I tell you, Marcus? I've made up my mind about doing this play. It means a lot to me. And I am willing to make the necessary sacrifices. Can you help me?'

Marcus nodded. 'Since you are a member of a creative profession whose earnings are generally erratic, I can propose an amortization of your debt.'

Amortization. She didn't like the sound of a word that seemed to imply death. Mortal. Mortuary. Mortician. 'What do you mean?'

'I mean that I can defray payment by spreading your income, expenses and allowances over a period of several years. In this way, we can reduce the amount of liability. This should give you the amount of equity you need to fund your new project and reduced lifestyle. It would also buy you a little more time.'

'That sounds excellent,' she said, although she only had a vague idea what he meant.

Marcus turned to face her and smiled. 'What is excellent is that you have followed rule number one and kept your receipts.'

Chapter Fifty-Six

The Hepburn Archives

Transcript from BBC Radio 4 interview
Broadcasting House, London
16*th* May 1982
Interviewer: Sir Peter Delamere
Interviewee: Georgie Hepburn

PD: Before we wind down, Georgie, I wonder if we could talk for a few moments about the scandal that occurred when you turned down your MBE.

GH: Oh, Peter. I wouldn't call it a scandal. A slight *faux pas* perhaps on my part.

PD: Even so. It caused a bit of an uproar at the time. I've pulled some of the newspaper articles commenting on the issue. If you don't mind I'll read them out for the benefit of our listeners. Is that all right?

GH: It's all water under the bridge now.

PD: Well, the Sun had the headline *Sorry Ma'am – but I don't accept gifts from strangers.* The Daily Mail led with *Surly Snapper Snubs Her Maj* while the News of the World didn't hold back with *Going, Going, Gong* then underneath *MBE not good enough for Hepburn (and we don't mean Audrey or Katherine)*

GH: I wasn't the first person to do it. Far more important men and women than myself have refused honours.

PD: As you know yourself, that is only hearsay. John Lennon is the only person I am aware of officially who sent his back.

And I don't believe he was ever vilified for doing so in the same way you were.

GH: I just think it was a quiet day in the London press offices.

PD: What happened exactly?

GH: Well, the Prime Minister's office asked me if I would be prepared to accept an honour for my services to the art world as well as with the ATA. Only two other female pilots in the ATA have been awarded MBEs – Joan Hughes and Pauline Gower. And quite rightly so. Far more deserving than I was. They were awarded theirs right after the war. I believe the ATA connection was only cited for me in order to bolster up my photography work.

PD: Is that why you turned it down?

GH: Not at all. I just wanted to get on with my life away from the public eye. I wanted my photographs to be known for themselves and not because of who was behind the lens. Accepting an honour would have changed that.

PD: Unfortunately, the press saw it differently. Can you tell us how that all occurred?

GH: If I remember correctly I was coming out of a restaurant in Covent Garden when someone from the papers confronted me. *We heard you've turned down an honour*, he shouted at me. *How does it feel to snub Her Majesty?* Something like that. Well, first of all, I don't recall telling anyone but my nearest and dearest I'd been offered an honour in the first place. You're not supposed to say anything publicly about these things until the official list is published. And secondly, how they found out I had turned down the damn thing was a mystery to me too.

PD: Any ideas?

GH: I can only think it was some clerk somewhere who saw my very polite and gracious note of refusal to the Prime Minister, then passed on the content to some contact in Fleet Street for a few bob.

PD: So what happened after that? With the reporter?

GH: Well, I was a bit put off by his question and mumbled something like: *Well, Her Majesty probably doesn't know me and I certainly don't know her, so I decided to save her any awkwardness.* It was meant as a silly, throw-away remark and it was blown out of all proportions. All those headlines that you mentioned.

PD: That wasn't all, was it?

GH: I got quite a lot of hate mail. You'd think people had better things to do with their time.

PD: Matters got a lot worse than that.

GH: Well, there was that incident when someone spray-painted *Traitor* over several of my photos at one of my exhibitions. He also cut up a few of the others with a Stanley knife.

PD: That was all over the papers too. It must have been hurtful. For someone who flew Spitfires during the war to be called a traitor. Do you regret it?

GH: The remark? I could have phrased it better.

PD: I meant not accepting the honour.

GH: Look, it was very nice of Prime Minister Wilson to

consider me. Of course, anyone would be flattered by such a gesture. I remember my father was awarded a DSO for shooting down enemy aircraft over the battlefields of France in the Great War. That was a medal for extraordinary bravery. I'd done very little compared to that.

PD: Are you really saying you turned down an MBE because you felt you didn't deserve it?

GH: No, as I mentioned earlier, I felt it would end up being an intrusion into my private life. Ironically, turning it down caused far more of an intrusion than if I had accepted it.

PD: I've been trying to get you on this programme for years yet you have always turned me down. I suspect for the same reason – that you felt it was an intrusion.

GH: Yes, that's true.

PD: So what made you change your mind this time?

GH: It's a good question, Peter. I suppose I'm old enough now not to care much about protecting my private life. I have tried writing a memoir because I did live through some interesting times. But I would never dream about trying to get it published. There have been a few approaches from people wanting to do biographies, once even for a documentary, but I have always refused. As for this interview? I think you just wore me down.

PD: [LAUGHING] I don't believe that for a moment.

GH: I suppose it was vanity that got to me in the end. The idea that I could leave a record of this conversation for my daughter was appealing.

PD: Your daughter?

GH: I'm sorry?

PD: You said *daughter.*

GH: I meant my god-daughter. Susan. I'm sorry, Peter. I'm beginning to tire here.

PD: *Don't worry. We'll take care of that in the final edit.* And just to finish off on this topic, do you think if you were offered another honour, you would accept one, now that you appear to have become less protective about your private life?

GH: [CHUCKLES] Oh, I don't think so. I just couldn't be bothered now with all the dressing up.

PD: *OK. Georgie, let me just wind this up for the producers... five, four, three, two, one...* Well, I'm really glad that you finally succumbed to coming on to this programme whatever the reason. It has been such a pleasure talking to you. If our listeners would like to catch some of your work there is currently a retrospective running at the National Portrait Gallery in London. If you can't get to London, a fine album of the collection is also available from your nearest bookstore. Georgie Hepburn, star of the silent screen, wartime ferry pilot and renowned photographer, I thank you for being with us this evening.

GH: Thank you, Peter.

PD: *OK. We're off-air now. I'm sorry for bringing up all that MBE stuff. Orders from above. They think it makes for good listening. Don't agree, of course.*

GH: *I'm too old to worry about these things these days. It's just that it's a story that's hounded me for the last few years. I suppose it's a pity if all that people remember is that I turned down a silly medal.*

PD: *I'm sure that won't be the case. Especially now that the retrospective seems to be doing so well. Now are you positive, you don't want to stay and let me take you out for dinner?*

GH: *Not this time, Peter. I'm meeting Susan in... oh, is it that time already? Well, thank you so much for having me. I hope you have everything you need.*

Chapter Fifty-Seven

A Night Out at the Theatre

'Theatreland,' Laura half-sang. 'Walking hand in hand. Along the Strand. Oh, Theatreland.'

'Nice rhyme, darling,' Victoria said. 'But we're arm in arm, not hand in hand.'

Laura ignored the correction. 'Hand in hand, along the Strand, in Theatreland.'

'How about round the bend in the West End?'

Laura laughed at that, they both did, spirits were high, after a fine early supper in Covent Garden that included two gin and tonics. 'I love the West End in winter. At night, all bundled up like we are now. The frosty air, the lit-up buildings, chestnuts roasting on a pavement grill, skating in the courtyard of Somerset House, things like that. I don't mind the cold as long as it's dry.'

'My sentiments exactly,' Victoria said, huddling in closer.

'Round the bend in the West End,' Laura sang again. 'Off to see a play. By a friend. Such is the trend.'

'Who'd have thought it? Quentin Holloway. Name in lights.'

'Quentin at the Adelphi. He'll be positively beaming.'

'Like a bloody lighthouse.'

'There he is now.'

'What *is* he wearing?'

Quentin stood outside the steps of the theatre in a long black fur coat with matching Russian *ushanka* and a bright yellow scarf. His arms were held out wide to greet them. 'Welcome, welcome,' he said, kissing each of them on both cheeks.

'Quite the showman,' Laura said, rubbing the lapel of his coat.

'Don't worry, none of it's real,' he said. 'I've got enough to worry about without animal rights activists boycotting me.'

'We're sorry we couldn't make opening night,' Victoria said.

'It's just as well you weren't here. I was a nervous wreck. Not worth speaking to. Not worth speaking to at all. Stockport, Sheffield and Oxford I could manage. But London. It just overwhelms me.'

'First reviews were fabulous,' Laura chipped in.

'Who reads reviews?' he said, although Laura was quite sure Quentin did. He clapped his hands together. 'Come, come, come. Box seats await.'

Laura was ambivalent about box seats, she didn't like the angle of the view but enjoyed the privacy, the lack of heads in front. It was just the three of them in this red velvet splendour together with a seat for Quentin's hat and coat. A bottle of champagne on ice. A toast. To *Maimonides*.

'I'm proud of you,' Laura said.

'Well, I am grateful to you,' Quentin said. 'Had it not been for your well-organized run-through of my little play, I would never have had the courage to go on. I salute you.' He raised his glass, then downed his champagne in one gulp 'I don't think I can stand all this excitement,' he said as the curtain was raised.

For Laura, there was something fascinating seeing the transformation of *Maimonides* from her tiny stage offering in a London pub into a full-blown production in a West End theatre. She looked over the balcony, hardly an empty seat in the house, must be close to 1,500 eager souls. It reminded her of what acting at this level was all about. The initial readings, the tour of the provinces, ironing out the kinks, mollifying the cast, the elation on the discovery that there will be a West End run, extra investment coming in, tarting up the costumes and the set, the dress rehearsals for London, the nerves, the crises of confidence, the flowers, the telegrams (now it's just a flurry of texts), opening night, the reviews, the magic of it all. She was glad for the friends she'd managed to provide a decent run of work for but she wondered how she would take to seeing Caroline perform again. For after the collapse of Sal's involvement in *Georgie by Georgie*, Caroline had persuaded

Quentin to let her back into her role in *Maimonides*. And here she was now, the mother still scarred by her Holocaust past, trying to find it in herself to give love to her ageing husband and their young son.

Three encores, Quentin sitting back in his seat, tears running down his face, Laura up on her feet, Victoria there beside her, both a little tipsy on all the champagne, clapping their hands high in the air along the line of the cast as they took their bows.

'Let's go see Caroline,' Victoria said once the lights had come up.

'I don't really want to,' Laura said.

'Oh, for God's sake, Laura. Show a little generosity of spirit. She's one of your oldest friends.'

'She tried to stab me in the back.'

'But it all worked out in the end,' Victoria countered. 'You got *Georgie*, she got this. Give her a break. She made a mistake. A bad one. But she'd appreciate your support right now. With the divorce and everything.'

'It's not like she'll be left a pauper.'

Victoria wrapped an arm round her shoulder, pulled her in close. 'Come on. The three of us. For old times sake.'

Laura couldn't help but be irked to see that Caroline had her own dressing room even though she didn't have a starring role in the play. She pointed this out to Victoria just as Quentin poked his head through the door to see if Caroline was available for visitors.

'It's not her fault,' Victoria said. 'The press just love her. A sit-com goddess making a theatrical comeback. Or as yesterday's Sun put it – *Lady Tightly Knit Dazzles in West End Debut*.'

'That's a bit inappropriate for someone playing a Holocaust survivor.'

'Who's she to worry?'

'Lady Caroline is available,' Quentin announced, holding wide the dressing room door.

'As she always has been,' Laura whispered to a chuckling Victoria as they stepped through.

The room was filled with flowers in vases, fruit in their baskets, cards of congratulation perched here and there. Laura held back as Caroline stood up from her dressing table, pecked Quentin with a light kiss to each cheek then a big hug for Victoria. Caroline hesitated then, Laura sensed the feelings of uncertainty and embarrassment pass between them for a few moments before the shared history of an old friendship erased all that and they embraced.

'I'm sorry,' Caroline whispered to her.

'I'm fine with it,' Laura said. 'After all, you've done far worse to me in the past.'

Caroline laughed, a big throaty laugh that dissipated any final traces of tension between them. 'Don't tell me you're still pissed off about Marco...'

'...Marco? Who the hell's Marco?'

'That waiter in Venice. Who were you thinking of?'

'That time when we were in Crete... Paleachora'

'...now, now, ladies,' Quentin said 'This is a time for celebrating the present. Not excavating the past.'

Caroline sat back down at her mirror, pulled out some tissues from a box, started to clean the make-up from her face. Victoria moved in behind her, massaged her shoulders. 'You were great,' she said. 'A powerful performance.'

'You really were good,' Laura conceded. 'I'd forgotten what a presence you had on stage.'

'Some actresses just have it,' Quentin added. 'Magnetic. Absolutely magnetic.'

'I was sorry to hear about you and Lew,' Laura said.

Caroline ceased the dabbing away at her cheeks. 'It's for the best.'

'Twenty-five years together. It still must be hard for you.'

'I consider myself lucky. I'll be left very comfortably off. A lot of women stay in marriages for fear of poverty.'

'And does Sal still fit into the equation?'

'Oh, that little stray. Just a passing phase really.' Caroline waved a hand in dismissal although Laura detected a slight waver of insecurity in her voice as she went on to ask: 'And you?'

'He's disappeared off the map as far as I'm concerned.'

'Good. Good for both of us then.' Caroline moved right up close to the mirror as she wiped the makeup from around her eyes. 'I hear you've moved down to Brighton.'

'London has become so expensive, don't you think?' Laura replied, although she found it hard to imagine Caroline thinking anywhere was too expensive.

'I loved your place in Highgate,' Caroline went on. 'It must have been a wrench to sell.'

'I like where I am now. Regency terrace. View of the sea.'

'Permanent?'

'We'll see. I'm renting for now.'

Caroline scrunched up her lips. 'It's funny how things work out. Me doing this and… you must be so excited about your play?'

'She's all a-tremble,' said Victoria, still massaging Caroline's shoulders.

'It's been tough,' Laura added. 'Don't know what I'd have done without dear Victoria here.'

'Lots of wine and ego boosting involved,' Victoria said.

'Who's producing?' Caroline asked.

'I've had some help from a friend of Jack's. But mostly it's just me.'

'And the script?'

'Also me.'

'Well done, darling. That's very brave of you. No wonder you look so… so anxious.'

Laura sneaked a glance at Caroline's mirror. 'Just opening night nerves.'

'Which is when?'

'Next week. In Brighton.'

'The Theatre Royal. How lovely.'

'Nothing so grand. Just the Studio Theatre at the Dome.'

'Oh well,' Caroline said. 'I'm sorry I won't be able to attend. What with this little thing on every night.'

'I'll be there,' Quentin said. '*Georgie by Georgie.* I wouldn't miss it for the world.'

Chapter Fifty-Eight

*Handwritten notes by Georgie Hepburn, on guest stationery of
The Savoy hotel, Strand, London. Date: 16th May 1982*

The interview with Peter Delamere at the Beeb was gruelling
but I'm glad I did it. And Peter knows me so well, he is able
to tease things out of me I promised I would never talk about
in public. I can't believe he had me happily regaling Radio 4
listeners with the news that I went out and burnt everything
Doug left me. They must think I am crazy. How did he get
me to admit that? Susan and I had an enormous bonfire in the
garden. We needed to make one anyway with all the autumn
leaves swept, trees and bushes pruned for the winter. There
we were like a couple of mad Banshees chucking all of Doug's
posters and reels of film on to the fire. We didn't anticipate all
the black smoke from the celluloid though, a police helicopter
diverted from its traffic patrol flying over to have a look. As we
were dancing there around the pyre, I did reflect for a moment
that perhaps this is exactly what Doug had hoped for – that
I would want to burn away his memory, leaving nothing but
that self-aggrandising autobiography of his – as well as his two
Oscar-winning films, of course – as the only testament to his
life and career. Perhaps, he won out over me after all.

I was exhausted after I left the BBC and really would liked to
have come back here for a nap, but there was Susan waiting to
take me for dinner. How could I resist? We went to a charming
French restaurant in Notting Hill where she was so full of news
about the exhibition at the National Portrait Gallery, sales of
the book, interviews, press coverage. I am so pleased for her. I
wouldn't want to tell her that for myself I don't care a hoot. My
work is done. Some of these photographs I took so long ago I
don't even remember the slightest thing about them. Of course,

I am glad that people have responded in the way that they have. But as long as my work gives Susan a sense of purpose I am happy. To be honest, my photographs of plants and flowers are the ones that give me the most pleasure now.

I watched her as we ate. All I can see in her face is Max, nothing that resembles me at all – which is probably a good thing. Sometimes when I look at the faces of children of friends, I can see a kind of morphing effect where the features of the father transform into the face of the mother and vice versa. But I don't experience that with Susan. All I see is Max. Those deep brown eyes belonging to some ancient soul, that dark unruly hair Susan has always cursed, never knowing where it came from, confounded by the straight locks of her so-called parents. 'Sometimes I feel as though I'm adopted,' she'd often complain. She possesses that same restless intensity as Max. If Max were to walk into this restaurant right now, I'm sure Susan would know immediately who he was. And sometimes the temptation to confess is almost too great.

Many a viewer or critic of my work has congratulated me for my authenticity, my integrity, the truth in my work. Yet, here I am, not speaking the greatest truth of my life. And with both Ginny and Richard gone now, there is only me left with this truth to tell. But what good would it do? What is wrong with creating these myths and false narratives if they only bring happiness to people. Would Susan be any better for growing up with me when I was at the deepest and darkest and most despairing point of my life? Would I have been a pilot? Would I have met Rollo? Would I have flown to Palestine? Lived in Hollywood? Would Susan still be the beautiful, well-rounded and well-grounded woman that she is now thanks to Aunt Ginny and Uncle Richard taking her in? Or would she instead have emerged as a troubled soul whose mother was too distraught and insecure and self-obsessed to provide her with a loving and stable childhood? Would we even be sitting at this very table, talking about my photographic exhibition?

I recall when I first set out to write my memoirs, I mentioned the thoughts of an astrologer friend of mine, Kipling Jones. He once told me that while we think we make these significant decisions in our lives – about marriage, relationships, careers – in astrological terms these huge turning points mean absolutely nothing at all. If you believe your life to be ordained by the stars, it will always end up being exactly as it is now – here, in this pleasant little restaurant, with my lovely Susan, waving her hands about with the same flamboyance as her father used to do. Do I believe what Kip told me? I don't think I believe in anything these days, I have become an agnostic like my father. But I suppose there would be something reassuring in knowing that this intimate conversation I am having now would be the exact same conversation that would have taken place whatever good or bad decisions I made in my life.

'Georgie, you're not listening to me,' Susan said.

'I was hanging on your every word.'

'Liar,' she said laughing, squashing out her cigarette in the ashtray with the same vehemence as her father. 'I want you to pay attention. It's important. We need to continue while we have the momentum.'

'What momentum?'

'The exhibition, the book, all this media coverage. That interview with Peter. Fabulous.'

'I'll do whatever you want. Just remember that I am an old woman.'

'Oh, Georgie. You're the youngest old woman I have ever met.'

'It doesn't feel like that to me.'

'I didn't want to tell you this until it's for sure but it seems your exhibition is going to the States. New York, Chicago, Los Angeles, Miami.'

'I don't need to go with it, do I?'

'It would be good if you were in New York to start it off. After that, it's up to you. I thought you might like to take in some Californian sun.'

'You know, I've never been back there since I left Doug.'

'Long overdue then. Some tea?'

'Not this late. I'd be running to the loo all night.'

'Well, I'm going to be up all night with these calls to the States. You don't mind if I have a coffee, do you?'

'I'm happy to wait.'

'You're always happy.'

'Such an illusion you have about me.'

'Oh, come on. I can't remember the last time I saw you being miserable. I always wondered – what is your secret?'

'There is no secret, Susan. I'm just fortunate that I've ended up doing exactly what I want to be doing.'

'Without the comfort of men. That is perhaps your secret.'

'I did have my great love. It's still not too late for you to have yours.'

'Oh, I think those days are over.' She reached out and placed her hand over mine. 'I've always got you, Georgie. You've been like a mother to me.'

Chapter Fifty-Nine

The Apple Tree

The day before *Georgie by Georgie* was due to open, Laura drove up from Brighton to Quentin's house in the country. It should have been a two-hour drive but the traffic around London had been awful due to an accident. She had passed the scene of the crash, the front of a large truck embedded in the steel rims of the central barrier, a white car with its roof shorn off resting on the hard shoulder. Ambulances already leaving the scene, blue and red lights flashing, traffic slowing to ease through the cones, police officers guiding her passed, she tried to ignore the debris, the burned up rubber, shattered glass, the blood on the tarmac, telling herself not to take the incident as an omen. She must erase the dark superstitions – whistling in the theatre, uttering the name of that Scottish play, wearing peacock feathers on stage, visitors entering the dressing room left foot first, the number 13. And look, there she was, just as she was having these thoughts, passing Junction 13 for London (West), Hounslow and Staines. Unlucky for some. Not for her, but for those poor people in the car with no roof, the lorry driver. Of course, how could she be so self-centred, so… what was the word?… solipsistic. She drummed away on the steering wheel, turned up the radio, hummed away to herself, tried to calm her agitated mind.

It had been years since she had done any theatre, she had become so used to the film world with the luxury of only having to learn blocks of lines at a time, the possibilities of countless takes, the absence of a live audience, and yet in just over twenty-four hours she was going to step back on stage. All by herself. Alone in the spotlight. A two-hour performance. Vulnerable. Exposed. Naked. Yes, that was how she was beginning to feel. Now that she had stripped herself of her ego, her relationship with Jack, her lovely house in North London, and the remnants of her film stardom. Naked. And all being filmed for a documentary.

For yes, everything was going to be properly digitally recorded. As from earlier this morning, when she had been sitting alone in the theatre dressing room and there had been a knock on the door. Without turning away from her mirror, she had called out to whoever it was to enter. She saw in the reflection of the open doorway, a well-built young man standing there.

'And you are?' she asked.

'Andy,' he said. 'Remember me?'

She turned round to look at him. 'You do seem familiar.'

'One of the crew that filmed your play in the London pub.'

'Oh God, yes. The Australians. Don't tell me you still haven't been paid?'

'That's all been sorted. We've been sent to film this one too.'

'Who sent you?'

'Sal.'

'Sal bloody Yerksaw. Sorry, but I don't have money to pay for a film crew.'

'Here.' The young man passed over his mobile. There was an email highlighted on the screen, part of which directed Andy to show Laura the message:

Hey Laura – I'm sending you down the guys to film your opening night if you'll have them. Don't worry, I've paid them up front. And you get to own the rights to everything they record. Happy to do the edit on my dime if you still trust me. It would be a shame not to get Georgie by Georgie *down for posterity. After all, I'm still a fan. And I owe you. Least I can do. Sal.*

She let her foot slip on the accelerator, had to break hard to avoid hitting the car in front. What was she doing? What had she been thinking of when she decided to do this play? And now she was going to be filmed live for a documentary as well. Sal bloody Yerksaw. She always had found it difficult not to like the man. Life would have been so much easier if she had taken Edy's offer, she would be off in California by now, rehearsing for *The Boston Tea Party*, earning some decent money, soaking up the sun instead of this heavy English rain bouncing off the M25 like a strafe of bullets. She could have been acting alongside Jack. Or just being with Jack. Lying in bed with Jack. Instead of sitting in her Mini with this stop-start jerking along the motorway, all 250 seats sold out for tomorrow's opening night. Press in attendance with their iPhones charged, ready to text in to base the slightest fault or failure. *Georgie by Georgie*. What had she been thinking?

She arrived at Quentin's with a headache, although thankfully the rain had stopped. She had come back to the house to somehow connect with Georgie, breathe in inspiration from her spirit. She ate a simple lunch with Quentin in the kitchen, the conversation was light, the talk away from the theatre altogether, Quentin seemed to understand her mood, she was grateful to him for that. She was also grateful that after lunch he said he would leave her alone, that he was going upstairs for a nap. She poured herself a glass of wine, wrapped up warm, went out into the garden, walked down the lawn, the grass still wet from the rain, cut blades sticking to her shoes, she didn't mind. She remembered coming out to this house for the first time with Sal, thinking how quintessentially English the view was, with the rolling fields, the village with its church spire in the distance, and now all she could think was how quintessentially Georgie it all was.

She found the apple tree. She sat down on a nearby bench, closed her eyes, tried to imagine Georgie there on her little ladder, reaching for the fruit she had decided to pick. Had she stretched too much, toppled off her ladder? Or had there been a heart attack, a blood clot to the brain? She wondered what the death certificate had said, she had never asked Quentin. He had only told her that he had found her dead on the ground. As she sat there, she pictured Georgie going down to the cottage in Sussex to visit her ailing mother just after the war, how they had gone out to pick apples together just as they had done when Georgie was a child. But this time it was her mother who had remained on the ground with her pinny open, ready for the apples that Georgie stretched to pluck. The mother became the child, the child became the mother. Would it always be thus?

She sipped her wine, a slightly cidery taste like the apples in her imagination, she thought about the conversation with her own mother that very morning.

'You've moved to Brighton,' her mother had said, ever disdainful of any location beyond the M25 unless it was a port – air or preferably sea – designed to take her out of the country. 'What will I tell everyone?'

'That I've moved to Brighton.'

'But you've always lived in London.'

'It's time for a change then.'

'But why? Why?'

'London is too crowded, too expensive these days.'

'Is there something I should know?'

'What do you mean?'

'Are you ill? Do you need the sea air? Some bronchial complaint?'

'I'm fine.'

'You could come stay with me.'

Laura let the offer hang somewhere in the telephone line between them, both of them knowing that while upbringing dictated such a proposal should be made, reality dictated it should be politely refused. 'That's kind of you to say,' Laura said. 'But I can manage.'

'You know I'd lend you money if I had it.'

'I know you would.' Although her mother's financial circumstances were always a bit of a mystery to her. Not enough to pay for her husband's nursing care but plenty to keep the London property and to fund her various cruises. Laura had thought for many years that when her mother said 'I'm going on a cruise', what she really meant was 'I'm having an affair' now that her husband had no idea who she was. A choice Laura would not have blamed her for, if ever she had been confided in. 'Have you been to see Daddy recently?' she asked.

'I go when I can. Although I often wonder why I bother.'

'They say the voice of a loved one is comforting.'

'I'm not so sure I am a loved one. It's better for you to be the one to visit.'

Laura wasn't so sure she was such a loved one either. Perhaps the sound of the sea outside the care home was enough comfort for him. She changed the subject. 'Are you coming down to see the play?'

'To Brighton?'

'Yes, Brighton.'

'Why this little play then? What has happened to your career?'

'I'm going back to the theatre, that's all. Lots of actors do that.'

'I suppose so.'

'Are you coming then?'

'Of course, I'll come.'

'I'll reserve a seat for you. Just the one?'

'What do you mean?'

'Would you like to bring someone?'

'Who would I bring?'

'I don't know. A friend? One of your cruise buddies? Someone to keep you company.'

'It'll just be me. Your mother.'

She must have fallen asleep, tired from the drive, the wine making her drowsy, she didn't know for how long. Quentin coming out to join her, the weight of him beside her on the wood causing her to jolt awake.

'Sorry,' he said.

They sat quietly for a while after that until she asked. 'Was this Georgie's bench? Or did you put it here afterwards?'

'I actually put it here on her bequest. A condition of the will.'

'That's funny. I want to do the same thing. For me, it's a bench in Highgate Wood.'

'The two of you have so much in common. She really would have liked you. I'm sure of it.'

Again they drifted into silence, Laura pulling her jacket in tight against the cold, Quentin looking slightly ridiculous in a grey woollen hat with a red pompom. 'Here you are,' he said. 'On the verge.'

'Of what?'

'Of greatness. Of doing your own thing.'

'On the verge of a nervous breakdown is more like it.'

'You'll be fine. I'm convinced of it.'

'I've just agreed to Sal filming the whole damn play.'

'Back on the scene, is he?'

'He felt he owed me.'

'Seems fair. I always thought he'd come good in the end.'

'The jury is still out on that.' She laughed, it felt for the first time in ages since she had done so. 'It's been a long journey, Quentin.'

'For both of us.'

'I suppose it has.' She looked over at him. With his tiny eyes, hard to know who it was that lay behind them, but yes, it had been a long journey for him too.

'Has it changed your opinion of Georgie?' he asked.

'Finding out she had a daughter was a huge shock.'

'It was hard for a woman in those days.'

'Oh, I don't blame her for what she did. I don't blame her at all. Unmarried, pregnant, her dreams of being a movie star shattered. She was at her lowest ebb.'

'It certainly adds a little more drama to your play.'

'I actually discovered something else in her papers I wasn't expecting.'

'Oh, do tell.'

'I think I'd rather wait for tomorrow night.'

Chapter Sixty

Handwritten notes by Georgie Hepburn, written on guest stationery of The Savoy hotel, Strand, London. Date: 16th May 1982

The hotel is very still yet there is always that constant hum. Whether from generators, elevator shafts, air conditioners or giant refrigerators, I do not know. It is a comforting sound, like a mother's early morning vacuuming while the child lies in bed in a half-sleep. I'm so tired, so very tired, but I cannot sleep myself. That interview at the Beeb still lingers, putting me in a reflective mood. I have left the curtains open to the night. I can see a few stars, the hotel courtyard, rooms opposite mostly with lights extinguished, drapes closed. London is out there somewhere too with its wet pavements and black cabs, with its men and women of the wee small hours, their various secret and sequinned lives to lead. A newspaper headline on the dressing table tells me that the Price Commission has been abolished, another that Elton John is to perform live in the Soviet Union. At an earlier stage in my life, such events would have been of interest to me. Now they belong to the consciousness of other generations.

I used to play this game with myself. I would be alone in my bedroom at the cottage in Five Elms Down or perhaps in the beach-house in Malibu or in a hotel room as I am now and the world is ending in some undefined apocalyptic disaster going on outside my window. I am lying on my bed listening to the explosions, the screams and the sirens outside, flashes of light on the pane, this general feeling of panic and hysteria when suddenly there is a knock on the door. I would turn my head, lift myself from my bed and slowly walk towards the door. I would reach out for the handle and then I would stop. Who would I want to be there when I opened it?

When I was a young girl, the answer was always my father. He would come in to me as a comforting shadow, bathed in an aroma of pipe smoke, his whiskers would tickle my forehead as he kissed me goodnight. I am sure my mother would have been there with him or had come in earlier but it is always my father I remember. Even after he was killed – more so after he had been killed – I would want him to be behind that door, in his flying suit and goggles, his face stained from fumes and dirt, his helmet in one hand, the cord of the parachute that had floated him to safety in the other. Even when Max came along, it was always my father I wanted to see behind that door.

Rollo changed all that. He changed it when he was alive, he changed it after he disappeared. When I look back now on the span of my life, I realise that we hadn't even spent all that much time together, yet it is always him that I want to see behind that door. If I could distil my life down to one moment of happiness, one photograph on an index card of memory, it would be sitting behind Rollo in our tiny Gypsy Moth as he grappled with that awkward camera of his, singing that stupid song about *Flying Down to Rio*, trying to get there on time. And why should my choice alight on that moment? Of course, I was in love with him. But there were other factors too. The element of adventure, of danger, of freedom that heightened my senses. There was the energy and vigour of my younger self contained in that moment as well. And the aesthetics of a vast azure vault, the late morning sunshine glinting off the tops of the clouds, the land and ocean peeking through below. To be above everything yet so totally immersed in love and beauty and excitement. Yes, it is Rollo I still want to see behind that door. And because he never really died, but merely disappeared into thin air, I think that one day he truly might be there.

I am going to try to sleep now. I have a magic pill the doctor gave me which helps when my mind is spinning like this. Quentin is due to meet me for breakfast in the morning, drive me back to Oxfordshire. He dotes on me so that sometimes I suspect he knows my secret. That I am really his grandmother and not some batty old cousin. I should speak to him about organising my papers, about whether to do something with those indulgent extracts of memoir I've been writing over the years. Perhaps I should arrange to have them published now that I have taken my first step into the public domain with my interview at the Beeb. Or should I set them on fire the same way as I did to Doug's memorabilia? Perhaps I should think about making a will. Everything to Susan, of course, a few charitable bequests, the RAF Benevolent Fund, a bench in the orchard, the negatives of all my nature photos to Quentin. Later on if I am not too tired, I might sit with him in the garden, listen as he tells me about how the world continues to amuse and interest him even as it spins away from me.

I think again about Susan asking me to go over to America with my exhibition. Well, that is not going to happen. I am too weary these days to traipse all over the United States talking endlessly about my work. I just want to potter around in the garden. Not to grow giant vegetables and spectacular flowers like my mother for the village fête. I have no need to compete on such a level. I merely want to be with nature as I'm sure we all do towards the end of our lives. To be one with the seasons, to witness the cycle of birth, bud, bloom and death. I have flown over the earth, I will spend my last days working on it and then my ashes will finally be scattered across it. Until then, I find myself returning to the orchard, waiting for the fruit to ripen so that I can get up there on my ladder, look up to the sky through the branches and reach for my reward.

Chapter Sixty-One

Georgie by Georgie

It had come to this, Laura thought. No make-up artist, no obsessive director, no frantic producer, no harassed production assistant, no screenwriter, no continuity girl, no gaffer, no grip. Just her, alone in her dressing room. Somewhere out in the auditorium there would be her sound-and-lighting guy, the Australian film crew. And the audience, of course. A packed house.

Her mother would be there, seated beside Quentin, the two of them thick as thieves already even though they had just met. Victoria had come down from London, bearing flowers and chocolates and a new man in her life, Alfred was his name. Who was called Alfred these days? They had both laughed at that although Victoria didn't care as Alfred was five years younger than she and very good looking. Marcus Green had turned up too. Marcus who had delayed and diluted her tax liability as much as he could but in the end she had sold the Highgate property to release her equity, to fund the play, to invest in herself. For if nothing else she had learned from Georgie, it was to do that. The thought led her to recall a conversation she once had with Jack over at his place in the States. They had been talking about happiness as lovers often do.

'What do you think?' he asked. 'Better to be poor and happy than rich and miserable?'

'I'd prefer to be rich and miserable than poor and miserable.'

'Answer the question.'

'Rich and happy,' she replied.

He laughed at her stubbornness. 'That's the holy grail, isn't it?'

'Well, you seem to have found it,' she pointed out.

'Don't be too sure,' he said. 'And you?'

Well, now she was certainly a lot poorer but happier too. Jack had sent roses with the simple message – *Proud of you. Let's catch up when this is all over* – it was probably the most promise for a future together she could ever expect from him. Caroline had texted in her support as had Edy although how her former agent knew about the play was a mystery to her. There was a smattering of press hacks present as well, one local, two from the nationals, movie star returns to the boards in a provincial theatre, a story hard to resist. She had given some interviews already, was due on BBC Radio Sussex in the morning.

She looked at the clock. Two minutes to curtain, the black arrow of the second hand making a reluctant clunking sound completely out of synch with the rhythm of her heart. She patted some more powder on her cheeks, sponged it lightly to set it, breathed in deeply, then again. Calm down, calm down, calm down. She gazed at herself in the mirror. *Hi Georgie,* she said. *We've finally made it.* Clunk, clunk. One minute to showdown.

She was pleased with the set. Jack's producer friend had given her lots of good advice about that. The whole backdrop was plastered with black and white photographs of Georgie's work. There was a mock apple tree just to the left of centre, a small step-ladder underneath where she would sit and speak to the audience. Other props too, a make-up table and mirror to represent Georgie's acting days, an open cockpit, camera on a tripod, arc lamps. Various special effects – war-time bombing, London fog, ghosts from the past. But most of all, it was she who would be the centre of attention. She pushed her face close to the mirror, her breath steaming up her reflection. *It's time, Georgie. It's time.*

It was not far from her dressing room to the side of the stage, only a few paces really, but what a momentous transformation she had to make in each of those steps. She moved out into the short corridor, the film crew already crouched down and ready to record her every movement. She spoke a '1-2-3 testing, testing' into her microphone, got a thumbs up from the sound engineer. She sucked in a quick breath. A spotlight snapped on, she moved into its centre, let it follow her up to and across the stage. Her stomach was doing flip-flops, her legs shaking so much she thought she might collapse before she reached the step-ladder. She sat down on the top step, grateful to be able to grab the sides, to steady her trembling body. She fought to compose herself, breathed deep into her abdomen, then on her outbreath she cast out her voice to the theatre:

'Born in nineteen hundred, I am as old as the century itself, an only child who grew up in the tiny village of Five Elms Down in Sussex where nothing very much ever happened.'

She heard the tremor in her speech, the slight hesitancy, but slowly, she gained confidence as she folded into the part, let the words, the voice and gestures take over until she lost herself in Georgie, until she became Georgie. Until she possessed Georgie and Georgie possessed her.

There had been a standing ovation, several encores, she had lost count of how many, the emotion from the audience so strong it hit her like an actual physical wave rushing towards her. She felt like laughing and crying all at the same time. A young girl came on stage with a bouquet of flowers, it took her a few seconds to realise it was Victoria's daughter Pru. She bowed again, took the flowers, kissed Pru, went off stage in search of a towel. The audience settled back into their seats, began their chatter, searched for coats and bags, ready to leave, some for restaurants or home, others for the after-party. But the houselights didn't come back on, the illusion between actor and audience not yet shattered, just that single spotlight clicking on to highlight the step-ladder under the tree. She wandered back on stage, still caught up in the excitement of it all, dressed in black polo and slacks, no shoes, she sat on the top step. She inhaled deeply, and with the exhale hoped she was expelling the spirit of Georgie so she could relax back into herself. She waited. The audience quietened.

'Thank you so much for coming tonight,' she said. 'As many of you know, this play meant so much to me.'

She waited for the applause to climax then die.

'From the moment I was given the opportunity to play the part of Georgie Hepburn, I knew it was right for me. It was one of those personal epiphanies when time, place and person seemed to fit together perfectly. Some may call it destiny. Others may call it luck. All I can say is that I have been extremely fortunate to have been given this chance. I would like to make special mention of Quentin Holloway who is here tonight.' She extended her hand in his direction. 'For allowing me access to Georgie's papers. For his gracious support.'

More clapping. Again she waited.

'Quentin, as you have discovered this evening, was Georgie's grandson, a fact which he himself did not know until a few years ago when he came across Georgie's letter to Max Rosen among her papers. I am grateful to Quentin for allowing me to expose this secret so publicly in tonight's play. It adds a whole new dimension to the kind of person Georgie was. Even those we admire so much for their authenticity and integrity can carry with them their own secrets. Whether you feel that Georgie's secret undermines or enhances her integrity is up to you, the audience.'

She shifted on her perch, took out a sheet of paper from the pocket of her slacks.

'However, there is one more secret I would like to share with you this evening. While I was going through Georgie's archives, I came across a bundle of letters. They were all tied up in a pink ribbon, the type you might see binding together a bundle of legal documents. At first, I thought they might be love letters. When I undid the ribbon, I discovered that they were indeed a kind of love letter. They were fan letters, written to Georgie across the decades. To my great surprise, I discovered that one of them was from me.'

She paused as she heard the collective inhale of breath. She waited another couple of beats. This might have been an extremely personal moment for her, but she was still an actress at heart.

'I must have been about sixteen years old at the time, Georgie would have been in her later years. My mother – who is also here this evening – took me to see a certain exhibition. The letter speaks for itself.'

Dear Miss Hepburn

Last week, I visited your photographic exhibition at the National Portrait Gallery in London. To tell you the truth, I didn't want to go. My mother dragged me along and I am so glad she did.

I want to be an actress when I grow up and I read in the notes that accompanied the exhibition that you used to be an actress too. I was happy to discover that as it makes me feel we have a common bond. I don't want to be a photographer though. I have never owned a camera in my life and I have no desire to use one. However, your photographs moved me very much. I have thought about them often in the last few days and wondered why they had such an effect on me.

My mother told me that your photographs reminded her of her own mother – my grandmother – in the period after the war, and how she too felt she had been forgotten. Of course, I don't have a connection like that. I started off really liking the photographs of the Bedouin camp in the Sinai desert because they seemed so exotic. And then I couldn't help but be fascinated by all the glossy shots of those famous film stars Cary Grant and Audrey Hepburn. However, as I moved into the gallery with all those portraits of the old people in the retirement home I became quite emotional. I think it was because I felt your photographs helped me see right through to the heart of these people. It was as if they were not images flat on the paper but somehow solid – my mother tells me the phrase is 'three-dimensional'. I realised then that this is the quality I want to be able to strive for when I become an actress. To be able to show the audience not just the outside of the person but the inside as well.

I am not sure I have explained myself very well and I am not sure I understand it myself. I just wanted to tell you that your work – and the story of your life – has really inspired me.

Yours sincerely

Laura Scott (Miss)

Acknowledgements

I would like to thank Sian Webber for the gift of the kernel of an idea that eventually grew into this novel. Thanks also to my editor Iain Maloney at Freight for his excellent insights as well as to Sara Sarre at the Blue Pencil Agency for her invaluable feedback.

Finally, I am extremely grateful for the financial support given to me by Creative Scotland without which the writing of this novel would not have been possible.